AVALON

AVALON

MINDEE ARNETT

Balzer + Bray

An Imprint of HarperCollins*Publishers*

Balzer + Bray is an imprint of HarperCollins Publishers.

Avalon
Copyright © 2014 by Mindee Arnett
www.epicreads.com

Library of Congress Cataloging-in-Publication Data
Arnett, Mindee.
        Avalon / Mindee Arnett. — First edition.
                pages   cm
        Summary: "Seventeen-year-old Jeth Seagrave, the leader of a ragtag
team of teenage mercenaries, skirts the line between honor and the law in an
attempt to win freedom for his sister and himself in the form of their parents'
old spaceship, Avalon." — Provided by publisher.
        ISBN 978-0-06-223560-2
        [1. Mercenary troops—Fiction.   2. Space ships—Fiction.   3. Brothers
and sisters—Fiction.   4. Life on other planets—Fiction.   5. Freedom—
Fiction.   6. Science fiction.]   I. Title.
PZ7.A7343Av   2014   2013005155
[Fic]—dc23   CIP
                                                                    AC

Typography by Ray Shappell
14 15 16 17 18   PC/RRDH   10 9 8 7 6 5 4 3 2 1
❖

First paperback edition, 2015

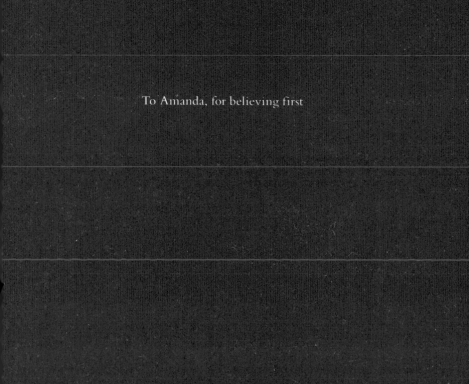

To Amanda, for believing first

AVALON

CHAPTER 01

STEALING A SPACESHIP SHOULDN'T BE THIS EASY.

Jeth Seagrave peered around the corner and counted the number of sentries standing at the docking bay terminal. There were two of them, both sporting the tan uniforms of local guards, with matching bored expressions.

He slipped back before being spotted. Around him, Kordan Spaceport's massive concourse, filled with restaurants, shops, and hotels, was mostly empty of people. Even in space, there was such a thing as nighttime.

Jeth brushed back auburn hair from his forehead and gazed down at his companion, who stood leaning against the wall, one leg propped up, her head tilted back, and hands on her hips. Celeste smiled up at Jeth, her lips parting in a sensual gesture, an inviting smile. An outside observer would think she had only one thing on her mind. No one would guess these two, both just seventeen, were actually casing the place.

Beside Celeste a large window looked out into open space, providing partial views of some of the ships moored at the docks beyond the terminal entrance. One of those ships was the *Montrose*, the cargo vessel they were here to steal.

Celeste and Jeth were members of a gang of thieves known in criminal circles as the Malleus Shades, named in honor of their employer, the infamous crime lord Hammer Dafoe, and indicative of their uncanny ability to come and go like ghosts in ancient stories.

"How many?" Celeste whispered, still smiling. Black hair framed her face, stopping short of her shoulders. Dark red lipstick exaggerated the paleness of her skin. The contrast accentuated her natural beauty, evident despite the digital prosthetics she wore. The prosthetics obscured Celeste's features just enough to make her unrecognizable, even to the most sophisticated face-recognition programs. Jeth wore similar ones.

Bracing a hand against the wall, Jeth leaned down as if going in for a kiss. Celeste was tall, but he still had half a head on her. Combined with the width of his muscular shoulders, he made her seem small. "Two," he said against her ear. "Both locals. No ITA."

Celeste sighed, the sound of it containing a definite smirk. "Too easy."

Jeth nodded as he pretended to nuzzle her neck. Local security was always easier to deal with than the ITA.

The lack of ITA presence didn't surprise him. The Interstellar Transport Authority rarely bothered posting agents at dinky backwater spaceports like Kordan, with its low tax revenue. The ITA cared more about the bigger, wealthier spaceports, the kind that could afford to employ more than two guards to man the entrances in off-peak hours, where

Not choosing CoC - Higher costs Students determine based on price

40% of Students turn

Not Going - College - HE enrollment has declined from 20M from 20M to 20M 18-19 m

Up to 40% of low income students don't make it to First..

Taking Longer can't afford load

12 credits (15) 4 year grad rate is 41 percent US News

even in the middle of the night the shops and businesses teemed with travelers.

The ITA didn't actually govern the planets and spaceports that made up the United Planetary Confederation, but given the amount of power they wielded, they might as well have. They controlled all aspects of space travel, including the manufacture of the metatechnology that made it possible. For the most part, no one went anywhere in the universe without the ITA's approval—and without paying their price to fly.

Even though he knew he should be glad about how easy this job was turning out to be, Jeth couldn't help but feel a stab of disappointment. Easy meant boring. He preferred more of a challenge.

Jeth glanced at his watch, which he'd made sure to set to Kordan time. Five minutes to go. He lowered his hand, trying to ignore his growing restlessness. He felt an urge to do something wild and stupid, just to make things more interesting. Like maybe walk through the security terminal around the corner right now and set off the spaceport alarms. *That* might put a little fun into this snoozefest.

But no. He couldn't do that. *Wouldn't.* There was too much at stake.

He looked back at Celeste and saw a knowing glint in her eye. Her sensual smile had turned mischievous. She was thinking the same thing he was, evidently. This was one of the reasons they worked so well together. Also one of the reasons they'd had so many close calls in the past.

Celeste raised her hand to her neck, pushing back her hair

as she casually placed an index finger on the communicator patch hidden behind her ear.

Understanding what she intended to do, Jeth shook his head. Somewhere, not far from here, Lizzie was supposed to be hacking into the security system to disable the alarms at the nearby terminal, allowing them access to the *Montrose*. Celeste wanted to see if she was done early.

"Only take a second," Celeste said.

"No." There was always the chance the communication could be intercepted. And even if Lizzie had finished ahead of schedule, deviating from the timeline was not an option. He and the other four Shades had carefully planned and coordinated their movements. They'd studied the flight plans for hours, making sure there were no departures or arrivals scheduled at the terminal during the time they would make their move. They'd double-checked that the *Montrose*'s small crew had all booked rooms in one of the nearby hotels for the night.

"Oh, come on," Celeste whispered, wrinkling her nose.

Jeth shook his head again, even as that restless feeling prodded him once more to give in. He might've been willing to risk it if someone besides Lizzie had been running tech on this job.

A defiant look came over Celeste's face, her finger hovering over the communicator. "Liz isn't a baby."

Jeth shook his head a third time.

Celeste dropped her hand to her side. "You are such a killjoy."

Turning on the charm, Jeth winked at her. "That's why

I'm the boss, sweetheart." *Besides,* he thought, *it's not worth risking the money.* The job might be easy, but the pay was still good. From the outside, the *Montrose* appeared to be a common cargo ship, but on the inside it contained a brand-new metadrive, a device that would allow a ship to make a metaspace jump independent of the ITA-manned gates. A metadrive couldn't take you as far in a single jump as a gate, but the anonymity it afforded outweighed those drawbacks. That kind of freedom made the drives especially valuable to Hammer's customers, who were the type of people unlikely to pass the background check required to secure a licensed metadrive from the ITA.

Jeth leaned toward Celeste again. They needed to keep up the farce that they were two teenagers who'd come to this remote corner of the spaceport to get the kind of privacy they couldn't get at home. She turned her face toward his, playing along. It was convenient how easily adults ignored a romantic interlude between a pair of teenagers. You could hide all kinds of suspicious behavior behind the appearance of recklessness. That attitude had helped Jeth and his crew become one of the most successful gangs of thieves in the galaxy.

Jeth checked his watch twice more. When it was finally time to go, he scanned the concourse for activity. It remained lifeless, the only movement from the flashing neon sign in the window of a bar across the way.

He turned back to Celeste and nodded. Grinning, she pulled out a sleeper pill from the front pocket of the snug black pants she wore. She placed the small pill in her mouth, pushing it as far back on her tongue as she could without swallowing it. Then, taking a deep breath, she wrapped her hands around Jeth's head and yanked his mouth down to hers, kissing him. She was careful not to exhale. The pill itself was harmless, but the fumes it produced as it dissolved would knock a person out for hours.

Holding his breath as well, Jeth stumbled backward as Celeste pushed him around the corner with her body, playing the part of eager lover. Now in view of the two sentries, he grabbed her by the hips, kissing her back. Their performance was completely believable. This was just a part of the job, a con to get them in position.

"Hey, you two!" one of the sentries called. "You're going to set off the alarm."

Jeth kept his eyes closed and his body engaged in the make-out session, but he focused his attention on the sound of approaching footsteps. They now stood within a meter of the alarm sensor, but Jeth didn't worry. Lizzie would've signaled if she hadn't gotten the job done in time. He refused to consider the possibility that she might've been caught. Such thoughts only led to mistakes.

"What are you doing down here?" the man said.

Jeth pretended not to hear as he pulled Celeste even closer.

"All right, come on." The sentry prodded Jeth in the shoulder with the barrel of his stunner.

Jeth held the kiss a moment longer, then pushed Celeste away from him. She swayed on her feet as if drunk.

"You kids can't be down here." The sentry's eyes shifted from Jeth to Celeste and back again. He had a narrow, pointed face, like a rat's, and his tan uniform hung loose on his slight frame.

Jeth glanced at the other sentry, still standing at the security station a good twenty meters away and watching them warily.

Maybe this won't be so boring after all.

Jeth's body tensed in anticipation, as if his muscles were threaded with strings pulled taut by the idea of danger. If the other sentry called for help, this was all over.

Remembering the part he had to play, Jeth forced his gaze back to Rat Face. He flashed a grin, wiping away the wetness on his lips. "Oh, sorry. We were . . . uh . . . just . . . you know."

The man shook his head, annoyed. "Not here you're not. This corridor is for docking customers only. Find another place for this."

Celeste giggled and stepped toward Jeth, making to kiss him again.

"Whoa." Jeth grabbed her hands before she could seize his head. Then with practiced ease, he pushed her sideways toward the sentry. Celeste stumbled into him, and the man caught her one-handed, righting her.

"Is she drugged?" Rat Face's eyes narrowed on Jeth's face. "Did you *give* her something?"

Jeth shrugged, flashing the man a rakish wink. "Whatever works, right?"

Celeste giggled again and grabbed Rat Face by the

shoulders before he could respond. Then she kissed him, spreading her mouth wide and finally exhaling the dangerous fumes from the sleeper pill. The sentry was so taken by surprise, he made no effort to pull away. They never did. Celeste was fast and far too attractive to resist.

Rat Face's eyes rolled back as the drug took effect. Pretending to catch him, Jeth grabbed the man by the elbow and simultaneously yanked the stunner from his hand.

Before Rat Face had finished falling, Jeth strode through the terminal entrance, taking aim at the other sentry. The grinning, cocky teenager from a moment before vanished, replaced by someone with command beyond his years and possessed of a singular purpose. No alarm sounded as he passed. Lizzie had gotten the job done.

Jeth closed the distance between him and the other sentry, who raised his own stunner. Blood pounded in Jeth's ears, adrenaline pumping through his veins, but he resisted the urge to panic or speed up. He knew not to fire early or let his aim wander from the target with unnecessary motion. Instead he took a deep, almost lazy breath, letting a calm sweep over him.

Like so many before him, the sentry didn't know what to do about this teenage boy with the cold, calculating gaze charging him, whether to fire or hit the alarm. He stood there, frozen in indecision.

The moment Jeth was in range, he exhaled and pulled the trigger. The flash of the electric bolt lit up the gray walls, turning them blue as it soared toward the sentry and struck him in the chest. The man stumbled backward, then slumped to the ground.

Grim satisfaction, mingled with relief, came over Jeth, and an involuntary smile crossed his lips. Celeste rushed past him, withdrawing a syringe from her pocket as she went. She stopped beside the fallen sentry, knelt, and then plunged the needle into his arm.

Scanning the entrances for more sentries, Jeth headed toward her, the stunner already charged for another shot.

"It's done," Celeste said, standing up. It would be hours before either man regained consciousness. She slid the now-empty syringe into her pocket, being careful not to leave evidence behind.

Jeth came to a halt in front of her. "Right. Good job."

"Did you expect anything else?" Celeste said as she retrieved the stunner lying a short distance away.

The loud slap-slap-slap of footsteps sounded behind Jeth. He spun around, his finger tightening on the trigger. Then he relaxed as he saw Lizzie approaching.

She grinned at him, the expression making her look more like a ten-year-old than her actual thirteen. Her auburn hair hung in adolescent curls around her freckled face. "You guys sure are noisy."

Resisting the urge to scold outright, Jeth smirked. "Look who's talking, stomping around like that. You're lucky I didn't shoot you." Lizzie was the newest and least experienced member of the Malleus Shades. She was also Jeth's baby sister.

Lizzie rolled her eyes. "Like I have anything to worry about with *your* aim."

Celeste snorted.

Jeth glanced at the sentry he'd taken down with the stunner, trying to judge how long the shot had been. A good eighteen meters at least, helluva range for a stunner. "You're absolutely right. No worries at all."

A snide smile curled one side of Celeste's lips. "Cocky much?"

"With good reason."

"You're bound to make a lucky shot every once in a while," said Lizzie, brushing past him. "Law of averages." She stepped over the fallen sentry to reach the security station control panel. As she placed her hands on the touch screen, the amused expression on her face turned serious. Her eyes, a pale shade of green, the same color as Jeth's, fixed unblinkingly on the screen. She didn't look like a child right now; more like a surgeon in the midst of a complex operation. Then she began to work her magic, her fingers flying over the screen as she overrode the locks on Docking Station 42, where the *Montrose* was moored.

Jeth watched, in awe of Lizzie's abilities, which she'd undoubtedly inherited from their mother. She could talk to computers in ways he would never understand. That talent was the reason she'd started working jobs with the crew a few months ago, replacing their prior ops tech. Michael had been a solid tech, but Lizzie could run circles around him. When Michael got too old to pass as seventeen, Hammer insisted Lizzie join the crew, despite her age and Jeth's protests. Jeth would've preferred that she do something more normal and a lot less dangerous, but Hammer's word was law, at least to the Shades.

Ignoring the usual resentment such thoughts provoked, Jeth returned his focus to the terminal. Easy or not, more sentries could come along any second, not to mention passengers from the other ships. He took up position across from Celeste, who already kept watch.

A few moments later, Lizzie announced, "It's done. Go get 'em, Jethro."

Jeth shot her a withering look. Lizzie was the only one of his crew he let use his full name. Sibling right of annoyance. The rest of them liked to call him "Boss," the name a semi-affectionate joke and only slightly more tolerable.

Jeth turned and headed up the docking bay tunnel and onto one of the moving walkways designed for those customers whose ships were docked farther down. He walked along the conveyor belt, a cool breeze from the acceleration ruffling his hair. Lizzie and Celeste followed behind him.

The numbers on the bulkhead doors counted up as they passed, lit up yellow for active docks with moored ships beyond them, red for empty ones. The tunnel seemed to stretch endlessly onward.

When Jeth spied bulkhead 42, he stepped off the walkway and approached it. Lizzie came up beside him. Jeth took in the expression on her face, her lips lifting into an eager smile and her eyes twinkling. He knew that look. Elizabeth Marie

Seagrave was hooked on the job—the thrill of the steal, that rush at the possibility of getting caught, the flush of success at getting away with it.

A tiny spark of guilt threatened to ignite inside him at the knowledge that he'd played a part in turning his baby sister into a criminal, but he squelched it at once. What they were and what they did was necessary for survival. There wasn't any room for morality. His folks were proof of that. They had never broken a law in their lives, and yet they'd ended up imprisoned and then executed by the ITA, the very regime they'd so faithfully served and obeyed.

"Move back," he said, waving at Lizzie. He pressed a button on the control panel beside the bulkhead door, and it slid open with a mechanical groan. It seemed the maintenance in this place was as much in need of attention as the security.

The rear door of the ship itself opened a second later, and Jeth stepped inside onto a narrow walkway high above the *Montrose*'s massive cargo bay. The pungent stench of fermentation assaulted his nose. Below, hundreds of barrels of beer, wine, and other alcohols stamped with the Wellforth Corporation logo filled the cargo bay from the floor to the network of walkways crossing the ceiling.

Lizzie whistled from behind Jeth. "Bet this is worth a fortune."

"Oh yeah," said Celeste, closing the door behind them. "That's why we waited those few extra days until it was loaded before stealing the ship. Hammer's all about maximizing his profit."

Jeth snickered. "Assuming he decides to sell all this and not keep it for himself. The real profit is the metadrive."

Lizzie leaned over the nearest edge. "I don't get it. Why would Wellforth go to all that trouble securing a metadrive for a ship like this just to transport alcohol? I figured they'd use it for something illegal." She sniffed, then grimaced at the stench. "But that's definitely alcohol."

"Not everybody wants a metadrive for illegal activities," said Celeste. "Just the people who buy them off Hammer."

Jeth shook his head as he headed across the walkway to the nearest door. "Not true. At least not in this case. Hammer told me this ship is on its way to Rosmoor. And that *is* illegal."

"Oh," Lizzie said, following after him. Then, a moment later, "Why's it illegal again?"

Jeth sighed. Without looking back, he said, "Because the ITA placed an embargo on Rosmoor a couple of years ago. Confederation-aligned vessels like this one aren't allowed to trade with them."

Rosmoor was one of the few Independent planets. Although Confederated planets were self-governed, they had to adhere to regulations on issues like human rights and war treaties as well as pay taxes to the ITA in return for lower rates when using metagates or purchasing metadrives. Being Independent didn't automatically make a planet an enemy, but Rosmoor had clearly pissed off the ITA somehow. With the embargo, Rosmoor was just barely surviving today, at the mercy of the few other Independent planets willing to trade with it or those Confederation merchants willing to risk illegal shipments of price-gouged goods.

"Still, they could've picked a ship with more flair," said Celeste, trailing behind.

"Too right," Jeth muttered. The *Montrose* looked to have the speed and maneuverability of a beached whale. Usually, one of the best parts of stealing a spaceship was getting to pilot something new and flashy. But not this clunky, bloated thing. *Just think about the money,* Jeth reminded himself. *That's what matters.*

They were almost done, although the hardest part lay before them. They had to unmoor the *Montrose* and fly it away from the station without drawing the attention of passing patrols. A difficult task with a ship this large and cumbersome. A welcome thrill of excitement shot down Jeth's spine.

Once in the living quarters, he turned right onto a flight of stairs that ended at the entrance to the bridge. The lights brightened automatically as he stepped inside, giving him full view of the cockpit at the front and the row of control panels lining the walls.

Lizzie stepped past him, heading for the nav station on the right. "I'll have us ready to launch in a minute."

Jeth nodded, his gaze fixed on the front windows that looked out onto open space. That restless feeling burst anew inside him. For one insane moment, he considered just jumping right then and there into open space, making a run for it instead of handing the ship over to Hammer. Jeth wanted to fly away into that vast stretch of unknown, to see how far he could go, what new places he could find. There were plenty of them still out there, he was sure. His parents had been space surveyors for the ITA, and he'd inherited their wanderlust. It was like a constant vibration inside him that refused to be stilled. He wanted to live a life where no one told him what to do and where adventure and new discoveries waited around every turn.

But all the stupidity of such an idea occurred to him at once: This wasn't an explorer ship. Not enough food and water capacity and way too noticeable. All it had going for it was the new metadrive.

No, when he sailed away into that black unknown, it would be on his own ship, *Avalon*, the same one his parents had flown for so many years. *Just as soon as I have enough money to buy her back from Hammer.* He was almost there. A couple more jobs like this one, and he'd finally have her back.

Brightened by the prospect, Jeth tucked the stunner into his belt as Celeste made her way to the pilot's chair. She and Jeth took turns flying the ships they hijacked. She was definitely getting the short end on this one.

Jeth was about to take the copilot's chair when the door to the ready room across from the nav station slid open and a man stepped out.

The first thing Jeth noticed was the .45-caliber Mirage handgun he was carrying, the barrel pointed at Jeth. The man wore gray fatigue pants and a fitted black jacket. His outfit was completely inconspicuous, all except for the shiny silver badge with a star and eagle emblem hung at his belt. The badge of an ITA Special Agent.

Jeth blew out a breath at the sight of it.

And here comes interesting.

CHAPTER

"WELL," THE MAN SAID. "IT'S NICE TO MEET YOU AT LAST,
Jethro Seagrave."

Jeth blinked first in surprise and then in outright fear. He
glanced at Lizzie. "Didn't you scan the ship to see if anybody
was on board?"

Lizzie's mouth fell open in a horrified grimace. "You
didn't tell me to!"

No, he hadn't. Someone experienced would've intuitively
known to do it. *If we get out of this, I'm going to kill her.*

Jeth faced the stranger again, trying to appear calm, like
he wasn't terrified to find an ITA agent waiting for him on
board the ship he was trying to steal.

A slight man with a fit, wiry physique, the agent had a
vague, forgettable appearance, the kind that would make
him hard to pick out in a crowd. Jeth couldn't place his age,
but flecks of white peppered his black hair, and age lines
rimmed his dark eyes and thin mouth.

"How do you know my name?" Jeth said.

"I knew your parents. You're the spitting image of your
father. At least you would be, minus those prosthetics you're
wearing."

A funny, tightening feeling gripped Jeth's chest, and he forced a deep inhale. Across from him, Lizzie was staring at the man like he was some kind of ghost come back to haunt them. She might be four years younger than Jeth, but she'd been old enough to remember their mom and dad and to bear the scars of their absence.

"I'm Marcus Renford."

The name didn't mean anything to Jeth. Lots of people had known his parents. They'd been somewhat famous for their deep-space explorations and discoveries that were often sensationalized to the general public by the ITA. "Never heard of you. But if you're going to arrest us, get on with it already." *And leave my parents out of it,* he silently added. Fear still made his heart race, but anger over the subject began to temper it.

Unconcerned, Renford motioned at Celeste. "Why don't you step up there next to Jethro?"

Jeth eyed the Mirage in Renford's hand. He flexed his fingers, trying to figure out how long it would take him to draw the stunner from his own belt. *Too long,* he decided, assuming this guy was of a mind to shoot him. He glanced at Celeste as she stepped up beside him, hoping she could make a move. But she'd stowed her stunner as well.

"You too, little miss," Renford said, turning the Mirage on Lizzie. "And I must say that *you* are the image of your mother. It's remarkable."

Jeth bit his tongue, fighting the instinct to shield his

sister. Lizzie stood up from the nav station and joined him and Celeste.

"It's a shame, however," Renford said, "that Robert and Marian's children turned out to be criminals."

Jeth smiled, masking his anger with sarcasm. "Well, one could argue that we're just following in their footsteps."

Renford sighed and shook his head. The reaction didn't surprise Jeth. There were a lot of old people around who still admired his parents even though they'd been executed for treason. Just what his parents were supposed to have done, Jeth didn't know. The ITA had classified the entire incident. What Jeth did know was that he wasn't about to fall into the same trap of trusting the ITA.

"No matter," said Renford. "I'm not here to arrest you."

Hiding his shock at this news, Jeth said, "What do you want, then? In case you hadn't noticed, we were kinda in the middle of something here."

Renford snorted. "Indeed. But I couldn't wait for a better opportunity."

"But how'd you know to wait for us in *here*?" said Celeste, sounding spooked.

"I overheard Hammer talking about this job."

Jeth frowned. Nobody just overheard Hammer. He was too smart, and his security was airtight. Officially, Hammer was the governor of Peltraz Spaceport, where Jeth and his crew lived. In reality, he was an interstellar crime lord and the man behind everything to do with the Malleus Shades. Although, as the leader of the crew, Jeth had chosen its members, Hammer had determined the candidates.

But how could this guy know about the Shades, about this job?

Only one explanation occurred to Jeth, and it made his pulse skip a beat. Renford might be an Echo. One of the ITA's special operatives. Most people didn't believe Echoes existed, but Jeth's mom had told him once that they were very real and capable of extraordinary feats. Including uncovering secret information about a man as powerful and well insulated as Hammer.

Jeth wanted to pursue his theory but held back. If this man was an Echo, he wasn't likely to admit it. "If you're not here to arrest us, what do you *want*?"

"I've come to discuss your next job." Renford paused, eyeing all of them skeptically. "You've got to admire Hammer for his cleverness in using teenagers to steal for him. No wonder people fail to see you coming."

Celeste made a noise of disgust and put her hands on her hips. "That's right. But we *only* do jobs through Hammer."

Renford cocked an eyebrow. "Only? But surely young mercenaries such as yourselves would be interested in exploring other, *better* offers."

Jeth stared at the man for the span of several heartbeats, unsure how to answer. None of this made sense. "You want to hire us to steal something?"

"Yes," said Renford at once. Then he paused, the silence a preamble. "From Hammer."

Lizzie drew a startled breath, and Celeste visibly stiffened.

Jeth managed not to react, although he couldn't blame the others. Hammer might murder the lot of them for even listening to such a notion, let alone entertaining it. This was betrayal with a capital B. And people just didn't do that sort of thing to Hammer. Not unless they hoped for a slow, horrible death.

Still, Hammer wasn't here at present, and Jeth couldn't exactly tell the guy with the gun to piss off. "Steal what?"

Renford's easy smile pricked Jeth's nerves. *The arrogant asshole believes he's won already.* Jeth smiled back, content to leave him to his delusions for the time being.

"A ship, naturally. That is what you do, after all."

Jeth slid his tongue along his teeth, feeling the urge to bite something. "Naturally. But which one?"

"Ah, that's the catch. Hammer doesn't have the ship yet. He intends to send you to get it for him as soon as you return from this job. But I'm here to convince you to bring the ship to me instead."

Celeste tapped the toe of her boot, the sound punctuating her displeasure. "Why don't you just take the ship yourselves? You *are* the ITA." Her gaze dropped to the man's badge for a second. "Isn't that what you do? Confiscate things?"

Jeth managed not to snicker. Celeste had a good point, but he didn't think it wise to openly provoke this man. Especially with his little sister in the danger zone.

The smugness receded from Renford's expression. "I'm afraid it's not so simple. The ship is lost. You're meant to find it, not steal it."

Jeth frowned, his confusion returning. They were thieves, not salvagers. "Why us? We don't do that sort of thing, and like she said"—he inclined his head toward Celeste—"you're the ITA. Why not send your own people to find it?"

Renford adjusted his grip on the gun, the black hole of its mouth leering at Jeth. "Because the ship went missing inside the Belgrave Quadrant."

Immediate understanding clicked inside Jeth, followed at once by a swell of dread. The Belgrave. *That's where it happened.* Whatever it was that had led his parents down the path toward inexplicable treason and death had started in that strange area of space. It was known across the galaxy as the Devil's Boneyard. Lots of ships had disappeared inside it, never to be seen again. Equipment tended to malfunction within its borders, particularly navigational systems. The ITA had declared it completely off-limits; even flying through it was illegal. Some people said the place was haunted or cursed.

Jeth didn't know what to believe. All he could say for sure was that his parents had spent more time in the Belgrave than anyone else. It was one of their primary areas of exploration. Over the years they'd made unique configuration changes to *Avalon*'s systems in order to make her resistant to the Belgrave's strange energy fluxes. *Avalon* was the only ship that could navigate the area with any hope of success.

Jeth unclenched his jaw, working past his surprise. "And you need *Avalon* to find it. That's why you're here talking to a bunch of criminals."

Renford nodded.

Lizzie cleared her throat, the sound mocking. "So why not confiscate *that* ship?"

Jeth glared at her, wishing she would keep her mouth shut. Didn't she know what kind of damage a gun like that could do?

The first hint of annoyance flashed in Renford's eyes. "There's no time for such things, little girl. Despite your belief that the ITA merely takes at whim, such actions must be justified, documented, and approved by the Confederation Board. But I wouldn't expect *you* to understand the complexity of government."

Lizzie looked ready to argue, but Renford ignored her, addressing Jeth once again. "Hammer plans to send you to find it as soon as you finish here." He motioned toward the *Montrose*'s bridge. "The ITA has learned that two days ago one of his men intercepted a distress beacon from the missing ship's flight recorder."

A dozen questions occurred to Jeth. He settled on the first one. "Why does Hammer want the ship?"

"Why does Hammer want anything?"

Profit, Jeth thought, although he had a feeling this was about more than metadrives. They were valuable, sure, but Jeth didn't think Hammer would risk sending the Shades into the Belgrave only for that. Besides, why had his men been close enough to the Belgrave to intercept the beacon? Jeth supposed it was possible they'd been just flying by and caught it by chance, but given Renford's interest in the ship, he doubted it. Too coincidental. Most likely, Hammer had been monitoring the area on purpose. Which meant that something *extremely* valuable must be on that missing ship.

So valuable I might earn enough to finally buy Avalon *if I find it for Hammer.*

The idea sent an automatic grin to Jeth's lips, but he suppressed it before it could surface. He had to get out of this mess first. And if they didn't make a break for it soon, they were never getting out of here. Someone might notice those unconscious sentries any moment. It was time to press.

He folded his arms across his chest, the position placing his hand within centimeters of the stunner's hilt. "This has been real interesting, but I'm afraid we'll have to pass."

Renford shifted his weight from one foot to the other. "But you haven't heard what I'm willing to pay yet."

Jeth rolled his eyes. "Yeah, and what's that?"

Renford reached a hand into his inside pocket and withdrew a thumb-sized object that Jeth recognized as a personal calling card. The card worked like a homing device, one that would allow them to contact Renford no matter where he might be in the galaxy. Renford held it out to him. "Bring the ship directly to me, and in return, I will give you *Avalon.*"

A noise of surprise threatened to escape Jeth's throat, and he clamped his mouth shut. This man knew far too much. A trickle of cold sweat slid between Jeth's shoulder blades and down his spine.

"I know you're working to buy the ship back from Hammer," said Renford. "I can expedite your ownership."

Still, Jeth said nothing, his breath shallow. He didn't want to believe this guy, but the promise of finally achieving what he'd been working toward for so long made his nerve endings tingle with hope. Even if they couldn't confiscate the ship immediately, the ITA would likely be capable of wresting it from Hammer's grasp without too much trouble.

They executed my parents.

"No thanks." Jeth forced the words through gritted teeth. "I've no reason to trust the ITA." He didn't care what his parents might've done. They didn't deserve to die like that, and he wasn't about to either.

Renford scoffed. "Oh, and I suppose you have reason to trust Hammer? Come on now, Jeth. You can't really believe he'll let you have your ship, no matter how many jobs you pull off. Seems to me your little gang of thieves is too valuable for him to give you that kind of freedom. You might stop working for him, which would cut into his bottom line. That doesn't sound like the Hammer I know. He never gives up his toys."

Jeth opened his mouth to argue, his temper like a whiplash. He was not a toy.

Renford cut him off. "And there's something else. If you bring me the lost ship, I promise to tell you what really happened to your parents."

A shot of adrenaline surged through Jeth so hard, his vision blurred. Temptation opened up before him like a hidden trail in a dense forest.

He started to respond, then froze as noise erupted all around them.

The spaceport's alarms were going off. Someone had found the stunned sentries.

CHAPTER

SURPRISE CROSSED RENFORD'S FACE, AND HE LOWERED the Mirage a fraction. It was all the window Jeth needed. He drew his stunner and fired.

Two simultaneous blasts—one from Jeth and one from Celeste—struck Renford, throwing him backward. Before Renford hit the ground, a bullet exploded from the Mirage. Jeth felt it soar past him.

"Lizzie!" Celeste screamed.

Jeth's heart launched into his throat. As he turned, a vision of Lizzie lying dead on the ground, blood spurting from a crater-size hole in her body, flashed in his imagination.

"I'm all right," Lizzie said. She was still standing, the bullet imbedded in a container behind her. She held up her arm. "It just grazed me."

"Let me see." Jeth grabbed her hand and yanked her arm straight. Terror at what might have happened made his fingers tremble.

"Ouch. Take it easy, will you?"

Jeth could barely hear her over the sound of the alarm, still blaring. "Turn that off!" he shouted at Celeste, who was already at the nav station, working on it. The noise stopped a moment later, leaving behind a terrible ringing in Jeth's ears.

Ignoring it, he grabbed the tear in Lizzie's shirtsleeve and ripped it off, exposing the wound. He wiped away the blood, nausea twisting his stomach. But the wound was superficial. He wanted to hug her but didn't. She would never stand for it, and Celeste would never let him live down such an emotional display.

"You'll be fine," he said, letting go of her. He'd managed to sound calm, reassuring even, but inside, his fear still throbbed like an infection. A centimeter closer and the bullet might've blown off her arm. Might've killed her.

Jeth forced the thought away, unable to face such a possibility. Not now, with disaster crashing down on them.

They needed to get out of here, but they had to get Renford off the ship first. They couldn't risk the distrust it might provoke if Hammer found out that he had been there. What Hammer didn't know wouldn't hurt him.

Keeping your options open, aren't you?

Jeth let the rogue thought come and go without consideration as he turned toward where Renford had fallen. He blinked once, twice, his mouth dropping open.

Renford wasn't there.

"That's impossible," said Celeste, panic in her voice. "Where the hell is he? We hit him with *two* stunners."

An Echo. A shiver went through Jeth like a current. He shook his head, focusing, then faced Lizzie. "Get us unmoored. Celeste and I will search for him. There's no telling what he might do now."

"Hurry up," said Lizzie, returning to the nav station. "Before they figure out which ship we're on."

Jeth and Celeste left the bridge, racing down the stairs. Jeth turned left toward the living quarters and the only exit through the cargo bay, while Celeste made a right toward the engineering deck. He thought he heard footsteps in the distance, but he couldn't tell over the ferocious pounding of blood in his ears.

The cargo bay was empty as far as he could tell, and he raced to the rear access door to check if Renford had made it outside. He pulled it open and peered out.

"You there!"

Jeth glanced sideways and saw a sentry taking aim with a stunner. The shot zoomed out a second later, whizzing by his head close enough to warm his face.

He lurched backward. *Enough with the close calls already.* Had he really thought this job was going to be boring? Jeth shut the door and pressed the communicator patch behind his ear as he ran back across the walkway. "Get us loose, Lizzie. They've found us. Celeste, get to the bridge."

"Already on my way," Celeste answered a second later.

Jeth almost crashed into her as he reached the living quarters, but she raced ahead of him. When they hit the bridge, she dove into the pilot's chair, taking hold of the control column. A second later, the ship pitched forward with a loud scrape of metal on metal. The *Montrose* wasn't quite loose from the docking bay locks, but the ship was powerful enough to break free.

Jeth sat down in the copilot's chair, adrenaline bringing his thoughts into sharp focus. He scanned the control panel, quickly locating the comm switch. He adjusted the frequency, then said into the mike, "You reading me, Joyrider?"

A couple seconds passed before Will Shady's loud, gruff voice said back, "Got you, Boss. You heading out?"

"Oh yeah, with a firestorm on our ass. Get ready."

"Yee-haw," said Shady.

Ahead of them, the Kordan Spaceport's patrol ships were already starting to swarm. Their narrow, upright shape reminded Jeth of piranhas he'd seen in First-Earth textbooks, except instead of teeth filling their front ends, they had guns. Lots of them.

The *Montrose* had no offensive weapons, but it came equipped with the most powerful field shielding available. Jeth located the shield button and activated it in time to deflect the first stream of gunfire. The patrols were aiming for the rear of the *Montrose*, trying to knock out the main engines. Jeth pulled up the shield system status screen, keeping his eyes fixed on the integrity readouts and wishing he could shoot at something instead.

Please don't fail, please don't fail, he thought. The shield needed to last long enough for them to make a metaspace jump. He pulled up the nav system and saw Lizzie had already entered the coordinates into the metadrive. As soon as they reached the minimum safe distance from all surrounding objects, the red light would turn green and they would be off.

29

Celeste flew them onward, going for maximum speed. Two patrols dove toward them, and she banked hard to the left. Jeth gripped the arms of his chair, panic expanding in his chest. She'd pushed it too far. Any moment now they would start spinning out of control. But somehow Celeste held on to it, her muscles clenched so tightly, the veins in her hands and forearms popped out.

With an effort, Jeth pried his fingers off the chair.

"They're telling us to stop," Lizzie announced.

Jeth looked over his shoulder to see she'd slipped on a communicator headset.

"Just thought you should know," she said, winking. "Can I tell them to piss off?"

"Oh sure," Jeth said, not nearly as amused by the situation as she was. "Just be polite about it."

Lizzie grinned and said into the comm, "This is the *Montrose*. The captain says piss off. Politely."

Celeste giggled even as she managed to dodge another spray of gunfire.

"Glad you two are having so much fun," Jeth said, turning his attention to the radar screen. They wouldn't be, if they had been the ones who would have to explain all this to Hammer afterward. *Assuming there is an afterward.* As leader, Jeth was the one to deal with Hammer directly. But with the way their luck was going, he wouldn't be surprised if the patrols blew them out of the sky instead of bothering to capture and arrest them.

Jeth counted five Kordan patrols, a higher number than

he'd expected. As he watched, two more yellow dots appeared on the screen as if from nowhere—Shady and Flynn, the other two members of the Malleus Shades. Each piloted an X-86 Scout equipped with an illegal prototype stealth drive. The small, four-man ships belonged to Hammer, but Jeth and his crew used them on most every job. Once out of stealth drive, the ships were visible to the Kordan Patrol, who quickly turned their attention to the new threat.

Barrage after barrage of gunfire flashed beyond the *Montrose*'s window. Unlike the *Montrose*, the Scouts came armed, and while neither Shady nor Flynn was as skilled at the helm as Celeste, they were both excellent shots. Especially Shady, who enjoyed nothing so much as shooting at moving targets.

"Take it easy, Joyrider," Jeth said over the comm. "Don't blow up anything. Just ground them." *And don't get blown up yourself,* he thought as he watched Shady swerve out of the path of an incoming patrol.

"Aw, come on, Boss," Shady came back a second later. "Where's the fun in that?"

Before Jeth could respond, Shady had doubled back on the patrol ship and taken out its starboard engine. Jeth exhaled in relief. Shady might be trigger-happy, but he wasn't stupid. Not usually, anyway.

Meanwhile, Celeste had piloted them far from the spaceport. Jeth checked the integrity of the *Montrose*'s shield. It was weak but still holding. The ready light on the nav system remained red.

"Come on," Jeth said. "Give up, already." He couldn't

remember any job where they'd been pursued this long. There wasn't much point, really. Most ships were insured against theft. Especially ones owned by corporations like Wellforth.

Finally, Jeth saw the dots on the radar screen begin to fall back.

"Looks like they're bugging out," Flynn's voice said over the comm a moment later.

"Right," said Jeth. "Let's get out of here. Jump as soon as you're clear."

Both Flynn and Shady echoed a confirmation of his order.

Jeth pulled a pair of dark goggles from a nook on the dash in front of him and slipped them on while Celeste did the same beside him.

"Here we go." Jeth engaged the metadrive. A moment later, a brilliant light like a raw, living energy enveloped the *Montrose*. It burned so brightly Jeth had to shut his eyes too, despite the tinted goggles. Still, he could see the light through the skin of his eyelids as if his eyes remained open. Weightlessness came over his body. Not like being in zero gravity, but as if he had no body at all, his existence blinking out. He didn't move, didn't breathe. His heart no longer beat and his mind no longer thought.

A fraction of a second later, they came through the other side, traveling thousands of light-years in an instant.

Jeth shook the odd, I-died-for-a-second feeling from his body and pulled off the goggles. A moment later a bright light flashed in front of him, and the two Scouts appeared. They'd made it.

Lizzie let out a whoop behind him, and a huge grin lit up Celeste's face. Jeth put his hands behind his head and leaned back in his chair, savoring the thrill of victory.

It didn't last nearly long enough. Warning messages and system errors began flashing across the various screens on the console in front of him. The ship was still spaceworthy, but there had been damage. Some of the gunfire must've penetrated the shields. Hammer would be furious.

Knowing there was nothing he could do about it now, Jeth tried to push the worry away. But his mind refused to be still. At once, his thoughts turned to Marcus Renford. What was on this lost ship that made it so important? And could Renford actually know the truth about Jeth's parents?

Jeth shook his head. That train of thought would lead him nowhere. There were too many questions, too many complications. It didn't matter why his parents had died. They would still be dead even with the knowing. He liked his life simple, straightforward. Do the job, get the money, move on to the next. Looking back wasn't an option.

What about Avalon? *Renford could give her to you,* his mind persisted. *Do you really think Hammer will let you go?* he heard Renford say again.

"Celeste, run an internal scan," he said. "We need to figure out if Renford is still on board."

"I doubt it, but I'll check," she said.

Nodding, Jeth walked over to Lizzie and examined her arm once more. It really wasn't bad at all. The bleeding had already stopped. "Let's get this cleaned up. I'm sure the sick bay is stocked."

Lizzie looked on the verge of protesting but changed her mind. She turned and strode off the bridge.

Jeth followed after her but paused when he caught sight of something small and black lying on the floor. He stooped and picked it up. Renford's calling card.

Then, for no reason he was willing to contemplate, he stowed the card in the pocket of his flight jacket and followed his sister off the bridge.

CHAPTER 04

"WHAT THE HELL DID YOU DO TO THAT SHIP?"

Jeth hid a wince as he stared at the man on the video screen. They were only now within docking range of the *Ferdinand*, the enormous ship that served as one of Hammer's chop shops, and already one of the operators had noticed the damage to the *Montrose*. *Must be worse than I thought.*

A lot worse, as Jeth found out once they finished docking.

On the outside, the *Ferdinand* appeared to be an ordinary Tetra Freighter, the kind used to transport goods across the galaxy from one star system to the next. And for the most part, the *Ferdinand* did just that. Only the goods weren't fresh off the assembly line or harvested out of the fields of some agricultural planet, but were disassembled pieces of stolen spaceships.

The moment Celeste landed the *Montrose* on the flight deck of the *Ferdinand*'s converted cargo bay, a swarm of chop techs surrounded them, ready to tear the *Montrose* apart.

Jeth stood up from the copilot's chair, hearing the distant thump and grind of machinery. By the time he reached the living quarters, more technicians were already inside. He recognized one of them as the chief operator, a man he knew only as Bentley.

"Run into a bit of trouble, did you?" asked Bentley, hooking his thumbs through his belt loops.

"A little," said Jeth. *It could have been worse,* he thought. At least Celeste had been right, that Renford had gotten off the ship at Kordan.

Bentley grunted but didn't ask for an explanation, which was fine by Jeth. He was still working out what story to tell Hammer, and he'd asked Lizzie and Celeste not to mention anything about Renford to Shady or Flynn until they were home and safe from any potential eavesdroppers.

"Well, go on then," said Bentley. "The kitchens are still open if you want to eat before heading home."

"Great," said Lizzie from behind Jeth. "I'm starving."

Bentley offered her a rare smile but didn't comment.

"Did somebody mention food?" a familiar voice asked.

Jeth glanced past Bentley to see that Flynn and Shady had arrived, both of them eager to take a look at the spaceship they'd helped boost.

Bentley eyed the newcomers, his gaze coming to rest on Flynn, who'd spoken. "Boy, you sure do look like you could use an extra meal."

Flynn grinned. The expression emphasized the narrowness of his face, making his pointed chin even pointier. Flynn Emerson might've been thin and slight, but he had the appetite of someone three times his size. His role in the Malleus Shades was that of engineer, responsible for the fixing and building of their ships, weapons—anything mechanical, really. It was lucky he was so good at it, given the cost of keeping him fed.

"Don't let him fool you," said the much taller and more physically imposing Will Shady. He had a face like a lion's, with a broad nose and a wide, droopy mouth. His shaggy mane of blond hair exaggerated the resemblance. A smattering of crude tattoos lined his neck and hands. He smacked Flynn's bony shoulder. "Never skipped a meal in his life."

"Nope," Celeste confirmed. "The world would come to an end first."

A dubious look crossed Bentley's face, but before he could comment—if he would've commented—another technician came charging up the corridor and said, "Got some bad news, sir."

Jeth held his breath, bracing for whatever new disaster was coming. Maybe they'd been wrong about Renford.

"It's the metadrive," the technician said.

Bentley didn't reply but turned and headed down the corridor toward the engineering deck.

Waving for the others to stay put, Jeth followed after Bentley, wanting to see the damage for himself. He didn't understand how the metadrive could've been affected by the firefight at Kordan. They hadn't sustained any major hits, and the metaspace jump had gone just fine.

Once in the engineering room, Bentley headed for the metadrive compartment. The compartment's window stood open, with the metadrive itself visible through the glass. Not much bigger than a human head, the drive's frame looked like any other piece of machinery, metal with thick black coils and other wires spreading out from it. But the power source at its center was a cluster of odd, colorful material that reminded Jeth of the coral decorating the inside of Hammer's extensive aquarium back on Peltraz. It was bright orange, except along the edges, where the porous material had started to fade to the color of bone.

"I thought this was supposed to be brand-new," Bentley said to no one in particular.

Jeth exhaled. "Hammer's intel said Wellforth just bought it off the ITA a couple of weeks ago."

Bentley grunted. "Sons of bitches. Why do they got to keep turning out these shit drives?"

Such outrage coming from the usually placid Bentley would've struck Jeth as funny under different circumstances. But at the moment he was too preoccupied with his own anger. New or not, this metadrive was a piece of junk, the odd discoloration an indicator that it would soon stop working entirely. No one outside the ITA knew how metatech was made or even what the material inside the drive was comprised of, but everyone knew the universal signs of metatech on the verge of crapping out.

Jeth swore under his breath, his hatred of the ITA absolute. No matter how hard he tried, they kept screwing up his life. The damage to the *Montrose* was bad enough, and with the metadrive on the fritz, this job had turned out to be a total bust. He didn't understand what the hell was going wrong with the metatech lately. Bitterness burned the back of Jeth's throat, and he swallowed it down. At this rate, he would never make enough to buy back *Avalon*.

But he couldn't think about that now. Couldn't risk losing his cool in front of these technicians or his crew. So with a straight face and a churning gut, he headed back to the others.

"Let's go," he said.

They all knew him well enough not to argue.

By the time they made it home, it was midnight, Peltraz time. They landed the Scouts in their customary docking bays and then headed into the station. Even though everybody looked beat to Jeth's eyes, he knew none of them would turn in just yet. They needed to let off the usual post-job steam.

"Well," Flynn said, rubbing his eyes, "I'm gonna grab a sandwich at Five Fry's if anybody wants to come."

Celeste rolled her eyes. "The rest of us have *normal*-size stomachs."

He shrugged. "More's the pity for you." He turned and strode off on his skinny legs.

Shady nudged Celeste in the arm. "Feel like some one-on-one? Sector Four is open late."

Celeste shook her head. "I'm heading to Twelve."

"Oh. Right." A smirk crossed Shady's face. Celeste had recently decided on a new boyfriend—the only distraction she preferred over spending a couple of hours killing computer-simulated aliens in the game room.

Celeste winked. "See you later."

As she walked off, Jeth heard Lizzie sigh beside him. He glanced down at her, an anxious feeling in his gut. "What?"

"Oh nothing." Lizzie twirled a piece of hair around her finger, a lingering childhood habit.

"What's a matter, Liz?" Shady wagged his bushy blond eyebrows. "Wishing you had a boyfriend to run off to, too?"

Lizzie went scarlet, and Jeth had to bite his tongue to keep from exploding at Shady. Why did he have to speculate? The last thing Jeth needed right now was adding *that* particular worry to his already full plate.

"No, of course not," Lizzie said, a little too defensively. "I just hoped Celeste would go shopping with me. It's not as much fun by myself."

Shady backed up, hands raised. "Don't look at me. I'm off to the games." He turned and hurried away, as if fearing that Lizzie would con him if he lingered long enough. Jeth didn't doubt it. The crew were a bunch of softies when it came to Liz.

She sighed again, casting Jeth a sideways look. "Don't suppose you want to go?"

"Sorry, Liz. I've got stuff to do."

"Okay." For a moment, her crestfallen look was almost enough to make him change his mind, but she brightened a moment later. "Maybe Cliff's working tonight at the Garden and Menagerie. He might let me inside after hours."

Jeth smiled, hoping she was right. The Garden and Menagerie was the safest thing she could be doing at Peltraz this late at night, short of being at home. He didn't even consider forcing a curfew on her. She was getting too old for that. *Old enough to get shot on a job.* He exhaled. *What a night.*

"Be careful."

"Yes sir, Boss," she said, grinning.

Jeth watched her walk off, and then he turned and headed for home. To *Avalon*.

The ship was docked in one of the long-term bays in Sector 15. Only "docked" was too kind a word. She was imprisoned, and had been since Jeth's uncle Milton had lost her in a card game in one of Hammer's casinos seven years ago. It had happened not long after Jeth's parents had died. Milton, who had been a doctor in the ITA for most of his life, defected in protest, taking custody of Jeth and Lizzie. The three of them left their home planet, Therin, aboard *Avalon*, in search of a suitable Independent planet to call home. Peltraz spaceport was just supposed to be a stop on the way, but once Milton lost the ship, they were stuck.

Jeth had hated Hammer ever since. Working for him now was just acid in an open wound.

But at least Hammer had allowed them to keep living on the ship even after he took possession. *Avalon* was made for long-term inhabitation. And later, once the idea of forming a teenage gang of thieves had come to him, Hammer decided to let all of the crew live on the ship. "To ensure a familial loyalty among the group," he had claimed. But Jeth knew it was really just for the cheap accommodations.

He didn't mind though. It made the ship home for all of them.

Jeth took the long way, down one of the scenic pedestrian walkways high above the spaceport's city center. Lined with glass on both sides, the walkway was built so you could look down at the sprawl of businesses or out into space and Peltraz's renowned star field. Peltraz was a massive spaceport, easily the size of any of the major cities on the nearby planets and home to more than 300,000 people. There were hundreds of places Jeth had never seen in the city-state, entire neighborhoods he'd never even heard of.

Jeth wasn't interested in the tourist views from up here. He just wanted a good look at his ship. Seeing *Avalon* from the outside always made him feel better. When he was kid, the sight of the ship meant his parents were home from whatever weeks- or months-long journey they'd been on. He rarely got to watch their departure, but he was always there for their return. Except for that last time, of course.

Even so, the sight still comforted him, which he needed right now. His dread about the inevitable meeting with Hammer over the fiasco at Kordan had been building inside him for hours. He would pay for the damage to the ship, one way or another. How much and with what currency, whether money or blood or both, he couldn't guess. Hammer never seemed to react the same way twice. Once he'd even let Jeth off scot-free, but he doubted he would get so lucky this time. Not with the bum metadrive to boot.

When he reached the familiar point where the walkway began to curve inward, he stopped and faced the outside glass, dropping his gaze to the outlying docks. From here he could see *Avalon*. She was a Black Devil spacecraft, old enough to be considered a classic, but still as tough as they came. With her streamlined body, she looked more weapon than ship, something fierce and predatory. She was the best, most versatile spaceship around, fast and powerful, yet still capable of deep-space exploration. And with her own metadrive, she could take him anywhere he wanted and be completely off the ITA's radar. *And she's mine.*

Almost.

Jeth leaned his forehead against the glass and exhaled, his breath fogging the surface. He had to have her. She was his only way out of this life. His desire to be free was so strong, it was almost a physical pain. He hated living here, hated being under Hammer's heel, one of his tools. One of his *toys*, like Renford had said.

For the last few years Jeth's plan had been to buy *Avalon* back from Hammer, gallivant around the universe for a while, and then finally settle down on Enoch, an Independent planet all the way in the farthest corner of the galaxy. Enoch was self-sufficient and wealthy enough to have a space exploration program he could work for—one day.

Jeth stayed there, staring at his ship, until fatigue made his eyelids begin to droop. After the third yawn, he turned and headed toward the nearest elevator. He rode it down to Sector 15 and started walking, navigating the complicated path to *Avalon*'s dock without conscious thought.

The longer he walked, the dimmer the light became and the less touristy the scenery. Sector 15 was the seedy part of town. The long-term docks on Peltraz spaceport were mostly inhabited by people who couldn't afford the tax to fly their ships out of there or pay for housing in one of the nicer sectors. The farther in you went, the more well-to-do Peltraz became. Hammer lived in a massive estate at the dead center of the port.

As he rounded a corner into the darkest corridor yet, Jeth froze. Movement somewhere to the left caught his eye. He clenched his fingers, wishing he had a gun, but civilian fire-arms were prohibited on Confederation-aligned stations, one of the few overarching regulations the ITA enforced. Only Hammer's soldiers were allowed to carry weapons, and they served as law enforcement for the entire spaceport. The ITA agents stationed at Peltraz oversaw only the comings and goings at the public docks, leaving everything else under Hammer's complete authority. So long as Hammer kept Peltraz in good standing with the ITA, his rule was guaranteed.

Still, that didn't mean that whoever was lingering in the shadows ahead of him wasn't carrying a gun illegally. Jeth looked around, hoping to see someone else nearby. No such luck.

He considered doubling back and taking another route, but he was so close to home. *And I'm not a coward,* he reminded himself. He faced danger all the time. He could handle who-ever was lurking down here.

Steeling himself, Jeth marched on, but he kept his gaze fixed on the place where he'd seen movement. Nothing was going to take him by surprise.

As he approached, he heard someone moan. He stopped and squinted, his eyes adjusting to the dimness. A man was sitting on a bench recessed into the wall. Jeth must've passed the bench a thousand times before, but this was the first he'd ever seen someone occupying it.

"Hey, are you okay?" Jeth asked.

He regretted the question at once. This man was far from okay. Even in the dim light he could see that. The man looked like nothing but bones held together in a bag of human flesh. Jeth had never seen someone so emaciated before in real life. He'd seen a couple of photos of severe starvation in history textbooks, but the images were little more than vapor compared to the real, visceral presence of such suffering. The sight made Jeth's knees tremble and his muscles contract from a terrible mixture of shock and pity.

The man stirred on the bench, his eyes opening to narrow slits. "I'm hungry," he said, each syllable strained from the effort it took him to speak. Even in the dim light, Jeth could easily count the bones in the man's chest, exposed by the shirt barely clinging to his frail shoulders. Blue veins were visible in his forehead beneath his ashen skin.

Jeth took an involuntary step back, suddenly aware of how much the man smelled. Like piss and shit and death. Every instinct Jeth possessed screamed at him to run away. But he managed to stay put, body tensed from the effort.

"Hungry," the man repeated. "Please." Only a few teeth remained in his mouth, those black with decay. The man's body was eating itself in an attempt to find the nourishment it needed to stay alive.

"I don't have any food." Pity choked Jeth's voice, tinged with inescapable revulsion. The only thing in his pockets was Renford's calling card. There would be food on board *Avalon*, though.

Then Jeth noticed the mark on the man's forehead, two thin black lines in the shape of an X. The mark was so faded, Jeth at first thought it was simply more veins showing through. Now he understood. That mark had been placed there by Hammer's order.

It was a fate reserved for the worst of offenses—betrayal. This man must've been one of the Malleus Brethren, the elite of Hammer's soldiers. Jeth knew it because the lower order of soldiers, the Malleus Guard, were incapable of betrayal. The Guard were little more than slaves, all traces of identity and self-will erased by the brain implants they wore. Membership in the Guard was involuntary, a punishment Hammer reserved for offenders.

The men who filled the ranks of the Brethren, however, were handpicked by the crime lord himself and entrusted with his secrets and personal faith. To betray that faith meant death. But not an easy, graceful one. The X on the man's forehead served as a warning. He was an untouchable. To offer him charity or help of any kind would be to risk becoming an untouchable, too, as if the man's crime against Hammer were an infectious disease.

Cruel. And very effective.

The man sat up, his limbs shaking from the exertion. "Please," he said again.

Bile burned the back of Jeth's throat. Why hadn't he gone around? How could he just walk away now? *You have to,* a voice hissed in his mind. *If Hammer finds out you helped him, this is what will happen to you. And Lizzie. And the others.*

Jeth closed his eyes, wavering with indecision. He knew what he ought to do, but terror held him in a paralyzing grip. As long as he and the others were at Peltraz, they were completely at Hammer's mercy. He controlled everything, monitored everyone. Even away from the spaceport, they had reason not to defy Hammer. The man's reach was long and deadly.

Don't be a coward. Nobody will see. No one will find out.

"Please," the man croaked.

Jeth opened his eyes, but he didn't respond. It was better that the man not know that he had planned to help him. Then there was no risk of him telling somebody. Still, guilt squeezed the breath from Jeth's chest as he turned and hurried away, the man's pathetic cries following after him like an accusation.

By the time he turned the corner toward *Avalon*'s dock, he was almost running.

He slid to a stop at once, his heart clenching inside his rib cage. Three men wearing long black coats trimmed in indigo silk stood outside the entrance to *Avalon*. The Malleus Brethren. Dread pounded in Jeth's temples. They were waiting for him. Bentley had sent the damage report to Hammer already.

And now it was time to pay.

CHAPTER
05

JETH RECOGNIZED THE NEAREST MAN AS SERGEI CASTILE, Hammer's general. Like most of Hammer's soldiers, Sergei was massive, with arms the size of support beams and a body nothing but muscle and sinew. His short-cropped haircut didn't suit his broad face. It left the black brain implant attached to the back of his skull clearly visible, its tentacles curled around the sides of his thick neck like a rubbery vise. Unlike the identity-erasing implants forced upon the Guards, the Brethren's implants enhanced their physical and mental abilities, turning them into super-soldiers. They were not a force to be messed with.

Screwing up his nerve, Jeth approached. He swept his gaze over the other two soldiers, taking in their implants, too. The sight of them always creeped him out. Having that thing imbedded in your skull had to *hurt*, for one thing. For another, there were times he could swear he saw the tentacles moving, as if the implant were some kind of giant parasite that fed off brain matter. Rumor had it the implants gave the wearers a form of swarm intelligence, enabling them to act as a single unit and to communicate with each other and with Hammer without speaking. True or not, Jeth didn't want to know.

"Hammer wants to see you," Sergei said, his voice a low grumble.

"No kidding," Jeth said, unable to stop himself. He felt reduced to a jumble of nerves, his brain temporarily inoperative.

Sergei glared at him in a way that suggested how much he would like to break Jeth's fingers. The other two soldiers fixed malevolent gazes on him. Surprisingly, Jeth took comfort in their response. At least the Brethren were mostly normal to be around, unlike the Guard, with their vacant, eerie expressions that made them seem less than human.

Not bothering to comment, Sergei turned and headed down the hallway in the opposite direction from where Jeth had come. Jeth fell into step behind him, letting out the breath he'd been holding. He was glad they were going this way. He didn't want to know what the Brethren would do if they discovered the man on the bench. Openly mock him perhaps. Or initiate a semipublic beating.

They walked along in silence and then entered an elevator. Jeth stood in the rear of it, the safety bar pressing against his back. The Brethren stood semicircled around him, ignoring him completely.

The elevator doors opened moments later onto the expressway deck, and they climbed into a shuttle. Fifteen minutes later they reached Hammer's private estate. Leaving the other two Brethren behind, Sergei and Jeth entered through a side entrance, out of sight from any late-night tourists.

The upper level of the estate sat like a castle in the middle of the city, surrounded by extensive gardens full of statues, fountains, and real live flowers and other plants, all carefully grown and maintained by an entire army of gardeners. Even among interstellar crime lords, the place was beyond decadent. As far as Jeth knew, Hammer was the only crime lord based out of a spaceport; most of them preferring dwellings planetside. The obscene display here was just an attempt to one-up the competition.

They entered the estate, navigating hallways as lavish as the garden outside. Jeth had been here often enough that he found it easy not to gawk at the floor-to-ceiling paintings and row upon row of ancient First-Earth vases stuffed full of fresh flowers. Plush, indigo-colored carpet covered the floor.

Sergei led him past two Malleus Guards standing watch outside a large sitting room. Jeth didn't have to see the clear implants on the backs of the men's heads to know they were Guard. The vacant, frozen expressions on their faces, like upright corpses, were enough.

"We wait," Sergei said as he and Jeth stepped inside.

Shrugging, Jeth sat down in one of the chairs. In moments, the steady *tick-tick-tick* of the antique grandfather clock in the corner began to grate on his nerves. He focused on other sounds and slowly became aware of raised voices beyond the door opposite him. He couldn't make out any words, but the tone was hostile.

A short while later, the door slid open and a man emerged, a glower on his face. He too wore a black implant, marking him a member of the Brethren. But unlike Sergei and most of the other Brethren Jeth knew, this man was smaller of build, less daunting. The moment he spotted Sergei and Jeth, his scowl vanished, replaced by an easy grin. Jeth did a double take. He'd never seen any Brethren grin before. Ever.

The man winked at Sergei. "Good to see you, Serge."

"Dax," Sergei said, not returning the friendliness.

Jeth's eyes went wide as he realized who the man was— Daxton Price. Jeth had never met him before, but everyone associated with Hammer's operation knew him by reputation. Dax worked as a tracker for Hammer, and the stories about him were nothing short of legendary. They said he could find anyone anywhere in the known universe no matter how cold the trail, and that he could shoot straight down the barrel of an opponent's gun before the person had time to take aim.

Dax turned his gaze to Jeth. He had black hair and caramel-colored eyes, with a long, straight nose and broad chin. "And you must be Jeth Seagrave, the latest test baby. Heard a lot about you."

Jeth frowned, unsure how to respond. On the one hand, having a guy like Dax know who he was felt like a compliment. On the other hand, he didn't like the phrase "test baby" or the derisive undertone he sensed. He didn't exactly understand the term either, although he figured Dax was referring to Hammer's infamous aptitude tests. All the kids who lived and attended school at Peltraz were required to take them. Hammer's way of keeping inventory of potential resources. Though Hammer had zeroed in on Jeth long before any test results.

"Same here," Jeth said at last.

Dax pointed his thumb over his shoulder at the door. "If you're going in there, Golden Boy, I would step careful. The big man's in a fiery mood tonight."

"Right," Jeth said, his stomach giving a nasty lurch. "Thanks."

Dax winked again and then swept past them, leaving the room without another word.

"Go on." Sergei motioned toward the door.

Jeth gritted his teeth, then forced himself to relax. He needed to appear calm, like he didn't have a reason in the world to be afraid of Hammer. Hammer was a ruthless tyrant, but he didn't tolerate groveling or cowardice. He detested any sign of weakness. If Jeth went in there looking guilty, Hammer would devour him whole.

Jeth stepped inside, closing the door behind him. A large dining table made from some dark wood filled most of the room. The floors were hardwood as well. They were so highly polished, Jeth could see his blurred reflection in the soft glow of faux torches hung at intervals around the walls.

Hammer sat at the head of the table, but he didn't look up at Jeth's entrance. He kept his attention focused on a plate overflowing with what looked like a slab of real steak. The smell of it filled the room, making Jeth's stomach rumble. Real meat was a delicacy at spaceports. Most of the stores and restaurants couldn't afford the extra import costs and relied instead on synthesized imitations. The imitations weren't bad, but nothing beat the real thing. He closed his eyes, reveling in the scent and the memories it invoked from when he was a kid, living planetside and having meat whenever he wanted.

Yet Jeth's appetite vanished as quickly as it had come as he remembered the starving man and the way the bones in his chest had stuck out like a mountain range beneath his skin, and how he had pleaded for food. The longer Jeth stood there waiting to be acknowledged, the more volatile his hatred for Hammer became.

Having no desire to watch Hammer eat, Jeth locked his gaze on the foot of the table, but it was impossible to ignore the squishing sounds issuing from Hammer's mouth as he chewed.

When Hammer finally finished eating, he set his utensils aside and said, "So I hear the *Montrose* job didn't go as smoothly as planned."

Jeth blinked in surprise at Hammer's casual tone. He couldn't believe it. He wasn't in trouble. Hammer's reactions might be unpredictable, but Jeth could read his moods well enough. This was not an angry Hammer, not the ruthless tyrant ready to condemn a man to slow death by starvation. This was Hammer the politician. The only time he was ever diplomatic was when he wanted something without having to use force.

But what does he want from me? Right away, Jeth's thoughts turned to the lost ship. Was recovering it important enough to stay Hammer's wrath at how badly things had gone at Kordan? Hammer was cruel but not stupid. He knew when to use the carrot and when the stick. Such instincts were one of the reasons he was so successful.

"Yeah, I guess you could say that," Jeth said. He looked at Hammer directly for the first time. He had a bulldog face with black, piggy eyes and perpetually red cheeks. His bald head gleamed nearly as brightly as the polished floor. Like his soldiers, Hammer wore an implant. Only his was dark red, the color of old blood.

Hammer let out a dramatic sigh. "Your theatrical exit drew the attention of the ITA, the *Montrose*'s shielding system was unsalvageable, not to mention the metadrive, and you brought back both Scouts with damage that will cost me thousands of unis to repair."

"Hey, now," Jeth said, testing the waters. "The metadrive wasn't my fault."

Hammer scowled, the expression making his piggy eyes even smaller. "That's beside the point."

Jeth didn't respond. Hammer might not be truly angry, but that could change in a second if Jeth pushed him too far.

"Now," Hammer said, "why don't you tell me what went wrong at Kordan?"

Jeth shrugged. Lying to Hammer was risky, but telling him about Renford would be downright stupid. Unless he wanted to spend the next couple of months having his every activity monitored and probed for possible betrayal. "It was just bad timing with some reserve sentries. But we got away all right, and with the ship salvageable. Mostly. So, job done. Now, what's the next one?"

Hammer leaned back in his chair, the wood groaning in protest. His belly was so large, he had to sit back from the table to make room for it. Too many midnight feasts. "You're awfully cocky for someone so young, you know that?"

Jeth flashed a mirthless grin. "I've earned it, wouldn't you say?"

Hammer snorted, his feigned anger vanishing with the sound. "You do okay, I suppose. But I tolerate your cockiness because I like you, Jeth. Like you could be my own son."

Horror at the idea sent a scowl rising to Jeth's face, and he quickly tamped it down before Hammer spotted it. Jeth's real father might've died a prisoner, and he might've lived a short life, clinging to naive ideas like the betterment and well-being of all mankind, but he'd been *good*. A father worth having.

And nothing at all like Hammer. *Please,* the starving man had said. *I'm hungry.* If Hammer were Jeth's father, he'd have committed patricide long before now. And only a son would be able to get close enough to him to do it.

"It just so happens that I do have your next job lined up," Hammer said, not noticing Jeth's reaction. "Something . . . different."

Jeth arched an eyebrow, feigning ignorance. "Yeah? What's that?"

"It's a salvage mission. Need you to use *Avalon* to retrieve a lost ship." He paused. "From the Belgrave Quadrant."

Jeth frowned, doing his best imitation of surprise. Fortunately, he didn't have to fake his trepidation over the notion of flying into the Devil's Boneyard. That emotion was genuine.

"Now, I know the Belgrave has a certain reputation, but

considering how much you kids like a thrill, I imagine you'll be up for it."

You don't know them very well, Jeth thought. They all liked a good challenge, but the Belgrave was on a whole new level. It was one thing to face danger in familiar territory, but something else to face it in the complete unknown.

"And even if there is some hesitation," Hammer continued, "I think the two hundred-K payment ought to smooth things over."

Jeth gaped, his surprise genuine this time. That was a lot of money, way more than they'd ever made on any job. It was enough to put him within spitting distance of buying back *Avalon. That's one helluva carrot.*

The idea of trying to bargain suddenly occurred to him. He'd never dared such a thing before. There wasn't much point when Hammer held all the power. With a single word he could cut them all off like he had the beggar. The only way out of such a death sentence was if some relative or friend outside Peltraz was willing to come and take you away from the spaceport, assuming Hammer would allow them to land and take off again. But Jeth's and Lizzie's only relative was Milton, and he lived on *Avalon* with them. The other members of the Malleus Shades were orphans, wards of the state already. Wards of Hammer Dafoe.

And the money wasn't just for him, but for the others, too. He had no right to bargain with it. Yet . . .

I'm so close.

Jeth inhaled deeply, ignoring his squirming insides. "What

if I were to say you give the crew twelve K apiece and keep the rest?"

Hammer frowned, not in anger exactly, but definitely not thrilled. "In exchange for what?"

"Avalon."

Hammer laughed, his entire belly wriggling. "Very funny, Jeth. Never knew you were such a jokester."

Do you really believe he'll let you have your ship? Jeth heard Renford say. He supposed it was time to find out.

"I'm not joking. My cut of that money puts me pretty close to buying her back, by my count anyway. And if you're already going through the trouble of letting *Avalon* out of her cage, why not make it simple and let her go for good? Once I've brought back the missing ship, of course. You know I'm good for it."

57

Hammer's gaze hardened. "Ah, but that's the catch, isn't it? It's *Avalon* I need, not you. Who's to say I don't get someone else to take her out? Someone who'd be happy with the pay I'm offering?"

Jeth balled his fingers into fists as he fought to keep his cool. Hammer had to be bluffing. The Malleus Shades might not be salvagers, but they had an unbeatable track record, and nobody else was familiar with *Avalon*. "Like who? The Dark Sol Gang out of the Antares System? I hear they're pretty good, but could you really trust them like you trust me?"

Hammer considered the point. Jeth held his breath, leery of Hammer's response and what it might reveal about his real intentions. *Will he let me go?* It would mean the end of the

Malleus Shades. There was no way Jeth would leave Peltraz without the rest of the crew—assuming they wanted to leave with him.

When Hammer finally answered, his tone was too genial. "Like I said before, I do like you, Jeth. So, let's make it ten K apiece for your crew, and we've got a deal."

Jeth's heart plunged like a boulder down his chest into his stomach. Hammer's answer was all wrong. He'd given in too easily. Jeth could tell when he was being placated. For whatever reason, Hammer wanted Jeth happy and committed to the job.

Emboldened by a sense of futility, Jeth decided to keep playing Hammer's game. "Ten K it is, but I want the money and *Avalon*'s title in my name up front."

Hammer laughed. "No way. You'll have no incentive to complete the job if I give you all that."

"It's like you said, the Belgrave's got a reputation. The crew will be a little happier with that kind of reassurance. I mean, who's to say if we fly in there that we'll ever fly out again?"

Hammer sneered. "Those rumors are grossly exaggerated, as you well know."

"Maybe, but the ITA shut down all the trade routes through it for some reason or other." They'd done it not long after Jeth's parents returned from their last expedition. Milton had told him that, for a time afterward, the ITA had sent dozens of explorer ships into the Belgrave. Whether or not they found what they were looking for Jeth didn't know, but they'd kept the routes closed ever since.

"That's just because the ITA wants to force travelers to use an extra gate to go around it rather than save money by flying through it," said Hammer. "Really, I thought you had the measure of them by now."

Jeth smacked his lips. He did have the measure of them. *Greed*. Same as everybody else.

Hammer sighed at Jeth's lack of response. "Fine. I'll give you *half* the money up front."

"What about the papers?" Jeth said, deliberately pressing now.

"I'll give you a copy of the transfer papers, but I'm not signing until after you come back."

Jeth exhaled, shifting his weight from one foot to the other. It was better than nothing. Signatures could be forged. And it was a sign of good faith, for whatever that might be worth. He supposed there was still a chance that Hammer would honor the arrangement, that he was just being paranoid because of what Renford had said. "Okay, it's a deal. Now, what are the details on the lost ship?"

Hammer leaned forward, his manner all business now. "She's called the *Donerail*. I'll have the specifics on her loaded into *Avalon*'s databanks in the morning. Your job is simple. Find the ship and haul her in. I'll give you two weeks to search for her. If you haven't found her by then, you need to come out of the Belgrave and check in with me."

"Okay," Jeth said. "But why do you want the ship? Surely not for the metadrive. There's no guarantee it's even working, right?"

"No, it's not the metadrive this time." Hammer drummed his fingers against the table, as if debating how much to tell him. "The ship's carrying a . . . weapon. Something new and valuable, of course."

Of course. Jeth sighed, a little disappointed. New or not, weapons were nothing special. All they did was kill and destroy. That song and dance was as ancient as human beings.

"The weapon's dangerous, too," Hammer added. "And it could be unstable. I've got to insist that nobody boards the ship."

Jeth frowned. Exploring the ship might've been the only fun part of this job. Then again, the weapon could be viral or radioactive.

"I mean it, Jeth," said Hammer. "If you do board her, then our little agreement about *Avalon* goes null and void, as well as the money. Understand?"

"Yes," Jeth said, agreement a given. He'd rather face an ITA firing squad than death from radiation poisoning.

"Besides, there's no reason you should have to board," Hammer continued. "The *Donerail* disappeared two months ago, well beyond her food and water capacity. Any passengers would be long gone by now. The ship's a Marlin."

Jeth nodded. Marlins were a transport class, short-range ships, the fastest of their kind and surprisingly well armed and well shielded for nonmilitary vessels. This made them the ship of choice for corporations that had expensive goods to transport as well as for pirates and smugglers. Jeth supposed if someone had a secret weapon they needed to move quickly, a Marlin made sense.

He wanted to ask more, but he worried Hammer would wonder about his interest beyond the basics, which usually sufficed for him. He would have to do some research on the net when he got home instead. He'd get Lizzie to help. She had a knack for tracking down information.

"How soon do you want us to leave?" Jeth asked.

"Right away. I'll have *Avalon* stocked and fueled by tomorrow morning."

"All right, we'll fly out not long after."

"Good. I'll expect to hear from you in two weeks. Now, I'm sure you can let yourself out the way you came."

Jeth retreated from the room, walking slowly, though he felt like running. His mind churned with doubts and questions. What would the crew think if they found out how much money they could've made? Why had Hammer agreed to his terms so quickly? What was his endgame? Nothing good, Jeth was certain.

But the idea of flying *Avalon* for the first time in years made those worries seem like pale shadows in strong light. Maybe, just maybe, if he played it right, he might soon get to fly her forever.

CHAPTER

SILENCE GREETED JETH AS HE STEPPED ONTO *AVALON*. He wasn't surprised to see that none of the others had made it back yet. He went to the galley and quickly gathered some food, stowing it in a small satchel. Then he returned to the recessed bench.

The beggar was gone. Jeth wondered if the Brethren had discovered him after all. He doubted the man had been strong enough to leave on his own.

Jeth returned to *Avalon*, his heart heavy with regret. Not that he could've done anything differently to help the man, but the truth offered poor consolation.

Soon, he thought. *Soon I will be someone else, living a different life from this one.* He paused in front of the door into *Avalon* and placed his hand against the cool, smooth metal of the ship's hull. His journey into that new life would start tomorrow. No matter what Hammer planned.

With his determination solidifying inside him, Jeth stepped aboard *Avalon*.

Dim lights lining the corridor floor punctuated the darkness as Jeth passed the row of crew cabins on the way to his own. When he saw that the door to Milton's cabin was open,

Jeth stopped and looked inside. It was never a good sign to see the door open. Most nights, his uncle locked himself in as a way to guarantee that no one would bother him until he was ready to be up. He was so serious about this, he would fasten an actual metal lock on the door's handle when he turned in.

But tonight Milton was lying in an awkward heap on the bed. Jeth reckoned he had probably passed out, given all the empty bottles lying around. Milton's drinking always worsened whenever Jeth and the others were away on a job. Milton might be his guardian legally, but in reality it was more the other way around. Ever since Jeth's mother had died, Milton had stopped caring about everything except drinking, and for a time, when he could still afford it, gambling. Jeth's mom had been Milton's younger sister, a good twenty years having separated them. Still, every time Jeth looked at him, he couldn't help but remember the uncle from before, the man who wasn't broken, but who laughed often and handed out sweets and who always had time to play with his niece and nephew.

Sighing, Jeth stepped into the room and rearranged Milton's limbs into a more comfortable position. He needed his uncle sober and in as good a mood as possible tomorrow morning when he broached the subject of the Belgrave job. Milton's presence would make the crew happier. They respected him in a way they probably had never respected their own parents. Milton never told them what to do or tried to get them to behave in any particular way. But Jeth knew his uncle could easily opt to stay on Peltraz, checking into a comfortable hotel while they were away.

When he finished, Jeth tossed a sheet over Milton and closed the door. Then he went to his cabin, where he spent the rest of the night in fitful sleep, his unconscious mind alive with dreams about what the future would hold.

As Jeth emerged from his room the next morning and made his way down to the galley, he heard the sounds of chatter and plates clanging. He grinned at his luck. It seemed everybody was home and in a good mood. It would make getting them to swallow the news about the Belgrave job easier. He suspected at least some of them might not have made it to bed yet. Quickening his pace, Jeth trotted down the steps from the passenger deck to the common area below.

Something yellow and furry scurried into his path. He lurched sideways to avoid it, but the furry thing hissed as Jeth stepped on its tail. He lost his balance and skidded down the last few steps on his bottom, taking the creature with him as he flung out an arm to brace himself. It dug its claws into his hand as they came to a stop, and then it scurried up the stairs and disappeared around the corner.

"Lizzie!" Jeth yelled, picking himself up. He glanced down at his stinging right hand and the three shallow— though still blood-speckled—claw marks running down from his knuckles.

The noise in the galley ceased, and Lizzie's face appeared in the doorway. "Problem, Jethro?"

"Yes, there's a problem," he said, striding into the common room. "Why the hell is there some animal running loose on my ship?"

Lizzie grinned. "You met Viggo already?"

Dear God, she's already named it. "*Who* is Viggo?"

Her grin broadened, and she began twirling the end of her brassy-brown hair around a finger. "Just a kitty I picked up last night off One-Eyed Johnson."

Jeth closed his eyes and took a deep breath. He was going to kill her. "You went to One-Eye's last night? Wait, don't answer that." He took another breath and focused on the worst of her offenses. "You brought home a cat?"

"No, I brought home a kitty." She strolled through the galley door and walked over, stopping right in front of Jeth. She stared up at him, her green eyes wide and her enthusiasm electrifying. "A really cute, fuzzy, adorable kitty, who'll bring us lots of laughs and fun and love and will really brighten up the place."

Jeth's lips twitched as he held back a smile. Lizzie knew how to play the adorable card. "Oh sure, fun and lovable." He waved his injured hand in front of her face. "I thought I told you no pets."

Completely unconcerned about the scratches, she feigned surprise. "Did you? I sure don't remember you saying that."

"Uh-huh. Well, now I'm saying that if you brought a cat on board, you need to keep the mangy thing confined to your cabin."

A pout spread across Lizzie's face. "Viggo is *not* mangy."

"He looks it."

She grinned. "Well, so do you most times, but we don't keep *you* confined in your cabin."

"Is that so?"

"Yep. You need a haircut."

Jeth brushed his fingers through his hair, which was a darker shade of auburn than Lizzie's. It was a little long, perhaps, but definitely not mangy. "Huh, well, maybe so, but my point is, try to keep that thing from killing me, okay?"

"Yes, Boss." Lizzie saluted him and clicked her heels together. "Will do, Boss."

"No respect," Jeth mumbled as he walked past her and into the galley. The rest of the crew sat crammed around the table in the small room, and they looked up at him with varying degrees of amusement on their faces. All except for Milton, who was bleary-eyed and cradling a cup of coffee beneath his lips, breathing in the steam. Milton's once-brown hair was mostly gray, and his short-trimmed beard and mustache were white in places. His lingering hangover emphasized the cavernous wrinkles covering his face.

Walking over to the sink, Jeth said, "What're you all smiling about?"

Flynn snickered. "Heard you had an encounter with a vicious man-eating kitten out in the hallway."

Jeth looked at him, widening his eyes. "Have you seen that thing? It's all hairy and it's got claws and stuff." He held up his hand as evidence. Like Lizzie, the crew didn't seem impressed.

Shady, half choking on a bit of food, pounded his chest and said, "Damn straight. That thing's ferocious. Are you okay, Boss? Need the doc to take a look at those battle wounds?"

Milton blinked, then lowered his cup. "Yes," he said, his gravelly voice deadpan. "We could head to sick bay right now for an examination."

Relieved to find Milton in a good enough mood to joke, Jeth grunted. "I doubt I can afford your rates."

Milton gave a noncommittal shrug.

Once he finished rinsing the scratches, Jeth crossed to the counter and scooped helpings of imitation bacon and eggs onto a plate, trying not to think about the beggar from yesterday. Flynn must be in a good mood, to have cooked for everybody. Jeth's mind began to buzz. Everything seemed to be falling into place.

He carried the plate back to the table and sat next to Lizzie, who'd come in behind him and had resumed eating.

"So, did everyone have a good night?" Jeth asked.

A clang echoed around the room as Shady dropped his fork onto his plate. "Uh-oh."

Jeth glanced at him. "What?"

Shady's eyes narrowed. "You're going to drop something heavy on us, aren't you, Boss?"

"Oh, yeah he is," Celeste said from the other side of the table. The short ponytail she wore this morning swished back and forth as she bobbed her head.

Jeth frowned. "What are you talking about?"

"Come on, Jethro," Lizzie said. "Everybody knows the

only time you ask questions like that is when you're setting us up for bad news."

"Yep," said Shady, "Like the time you told us we had to get vaccinated for the Feria job. My ass still hurts from those shots."

"Please spare us references to your ass," said Celeste.

"That wasn't my fault," said Jeth, trying to look indignant. "That was Hammer."

"Or," said Flynn, "like the time you said we had to climb down the sewage duct to snatch that giant ruby on Grakkus."

"Now hang on a minute. That wasn't everybody," said Jeth.

"You're right," said Flynn. "It was just *me*."

"It's not my fault you're so agile." Jeth eyed him askance. Flynn had an unnatural ability for getting into hard-to-reach places like the inside of a ship's engine. It came in handy more often than you'd think.

Flynn scoffed. "So is Lizzie, but you'd never have made *her* climb down that funky-smelling thing."

"That's because I'm a girl, and he likes me better," said Lizzie.

"Jury's still out on that," Jeth said, motioning to his scratched hand.

At the far end of the table, Milton cleared his throat. That was all it took for the crew to fall silent. "What's the job?" Milton asked, before taking a sip of his coffee.

Jeth considered sugarcoating his answer, but there really wasn't a way to do it. "We're going into the Belgrave."

"What?" said Flynn, his indignant tone becoming serious. "But ships that go in there never come out again."

"Not *every* ship," said Lizzie.

"Yeah, but those that do talk about malfunctioning equipment and strange stuff happening to the people on board," said Celeste. The amount of fear in her voice increased Jeth's own worries. Celeste was usually the most fearless person he knew.

"She's right," said Flynn. "That place is a dead zone: unreliable comms, poor nav. And there's supposedly antimatter pits too. They even say parts of it are haunted."

Lizzie laughed. "Now you're being dumb. That stuff don't exist."

"*Doesn't* exist," Jeth said.

"Whatever."

Jeth clenched his jaw. Lizzie hadn't seen the inside of a classroom since Hammer had recruited her for the gang, and it bothered him when she spoke improperly. Someone so smart shouldn't sound so ignorant.

"Please tell me you're not serious about going into the Belgrave," Celeste said in an unnaturally quiet voice.

Jeth forced his gaze to her, feeling the first threads of panic tugging at him. They were reacting worse than he'd anticipated. "Yes, I am. The take is killer on this one, and all we have to do is find some ship, the *Donerail*, and haul it back. We're even required *not* to board it. Simple, really." *Besides,* he silently added, *it's not like we even have a choice about it.* He didn't think the others had as firm a grasp as he did on how thoroughly under Hammer's control they were. The crew was more removed from the reality of it. Jeth preferred it that way. It was better for morale.

"How much?" asked Shady.

Jeth let out a breath. "You all get ten K apiece," he said. "Half of it up front this time."

Shady whistled. "That means your cut is forty, right? Not bad for a salvage job."

Jeth glanced down, unable to look him in the eye. Their cut could've been a lot higher. He shouldn't have bargained it away without asking them first, even if he had been surprised by Hammer's response.

"No, the job's not bad," Jeth said. "But I'm not exactly getting any money on this one."

"Then what *are* you getting?" asked Celeste.

"Once we bring back the *Donerail*, Hammer's agreed to give me *Avalon*."

Nobody said anything for several moments, mulling over the news. Lizzie looked the most contemplative of all. She knew better than the others what it meant for Jeth to have *Avalon* back. She too thought of *Avalon* as a part of the family. True, they'd never lived on her until after their parents died, but *Avalon* still represented an important part of who they were.

Shady broke the silence first with a loud belch. "So what does that mean for the rest of us? Are you gonna kick us out?"

Three worried gazes locked on Jeth's face—all but Milton and Lizzie, who already knew they had a permanent home on *Avalon*, no matter what.

"Of course not," Jeth said. "You can stay or go as you want, same as always."

"Will we keep working for Hammer?" said Lizzie. "I suppose we'll get more money for each job if you're no longer paying off *Avalon*."

"I'm not sure what'll happen," said Jeth. He'd never dared tell any of them his plan to settle on Enoch, afraid of jinxing it. "We've got to finish the job first."

"Aren't we forgetting something here?" Flynn said, sounding on the verge of hysteria. "How the heck are we supposed to find something in the middle of the Belgrave? Horror stories aside, it *is* a dead zone, which means we might get lost with no way of calling for help. We might die. We might even run out of *food*."

"Equipment malfunction won't be an issue," said Jeth.

"How do you know?"

"Because we're taking *Avalon* for this job. That's one of the reasons Hammer wants us for it. Her nav systems were specifically modded to handle the energy fluctuations in the Belgrave. She'll guarantee we find the ship *and* our way out again."

"How can you be so sure?" asked Celeste in a voice not much more than a whisper.

"Because my parents used her for all their expeditions."

Celeste exhaled. "What about that ITA guy, Marcus Renford? How does he fit into this?"

"Who?" asked Flynn.

Celeste and Lizzie looked at Jeth, who nodded after a slight hesitation. Lizzie launched into a quick recap of what had happened with Renford aboard the *Montrose*, including how she'd been grazed by that bullet. A disturbing note of pride colored her voice as she spoke.

When she finished, Shady said, "Well, it sounds to me like this Renford dude doesn't play into things at all. Not if Hammer's giving us the ship *and* a fat payday." He glanced at Jeth, a sheepish expression crossing his face. "No offense, Boss, but finding out what happened to your parents doesn't seem worth much if it means running afoul of Hammer."

Jeth pinched his lips together. Shady was right, but Jeth had a hard time saying so when he caught the forlorn look in Lizzie's eyes. Valuable or not, the truth still meant something to her. Jeth risked a glance at Milton. It meant something to him as well, although his expression remained inscrutable.

It means something to you, too, a voice said in Jeth's mind. As usual, he ignored it.

"No offense taken," Jeth said at last. "And you're right. Renford's offer, whatever my parents did or didn't do, none of it matters as much as getting this job done. Now, Hammer wants us on the move as soon as possible. So take the morning to buy any personal supplies you're running low on. We fly out this afternoon."

Everyone nodded. A couple of minutes later, the conversation returned to normal and eating resumed. When the meal ended, Jeth volunteered to clean the dishes. It wasn't his turn, but he was still feeling guilty about bargaining away some of their money and figured any kind of penance would help ease his conscience.

The crew slowly departed until only Milton remained. Jeth watched warily as Milton withdrew a pipe from his coat pocket and began packing it with greenish-brown leaves. The sweet, herbal smell of the smoke filled the galley in seconds, tickling Jeth's nose.

"So," Milton said as Jeth started gathering plates. "You don't really believe a man like Hammer is going to just let you have *Avalon* so easily, do you?"

Jeth sighed. Leave it to Milton to say what he already feared. "Not really. Mom and Dad didn't raise me to be stupid."

Milton flinched like he always did whenever Jeth mentioned his parents. "No, they didn't. But if you know that Hammer has other intentions, what are you going to do about it?"

"Don't know yet. But Hammer did say he'd give me a copy of the title and transfer papers. That's something, at least, isn't it?" Jeth couldn't help the sudden flare of resentment that heated his body. It was hard talking about this to the man who'd lost *Avalon* in the first place. He loved his uncle, but that didn't mean he didn't hate him sometimes, too.

"Maybe." Milton took a long drag on his pipe. "Let's assume for a second that you succeed in getting *Avalon*. Where will you go?"

Jeth ran a hand through his hair, struggling with his temper. "Not sure. Figure I'll find out when I get there."

Milton sighed as he turned his gaze toward the single window in the galley that looked out into open space. "Were you tempted by Renford's offer?"

Jeth swallowed, his throat tight. "No. The ITA are even more dangerous than Hammer."

"Yes, they are." Milton sucked on his pipe and then blew out a long puff of smoke. "And no matter how much we might want to know what happened to your parents, the truth is too dangerous. Whatever they found out there, the ITA killed them for it, make no mistake. They will kill you, too. And me. And Lizzie. And anyone else who gets too close to the truth."

Jeth turned away from his uncle, focusing his attention on the dishes. He didn't need the situation put into perspective. He could do that well enough on his own.

A scrape of chair legs echoed behind him. Then Milton stepped beside Jeth, close enough that their arms touched. In a low, tremulous voice, Milton said, "Don't do this job, Jethro. Let's just take the ship and go and never look back. It won't be easy, but we can escape, somehow, disappear."

It wasn't what Jeth had expected to hear from his uncle. He looked over at Milton, keenly aware that he was taller than him now by at least half a head. He wondered how long it had been so. Strange how life just happened sometimes, sneaking up on you like a thief in the dark. "Why do you say this, now?"

Milton took a long drag on his pipe and an even longer exhale. "There's something . . . *off* about all of it. The ITA's interest, that agent singling you out. And it's the Belgrave, an unlucky place for this ship and this family."

Jeth blinked rapidly as an unexpected swell of emotion made his eyes prickle with tears. He couldn't think about that. Couldn't let his parents' death get in the way now. It had been getting in the way all his life. But not anymore.

With an effort, Jeth forced the pain and fear back into that deep, secret place inside him. "What happened to them won't happen to me. I've been paying for their mistakes my whole life. I'm not going to make the same ones."

Milton made a sound between a grunt and a moan of despair. "Spoken like a boy instead of the man you ought to be by now."

The words hit Jeth like a slap. *What do you know about it?* he wanted to say. *I've never been a boy, thanks to you. Thanks to your gambling and drinking.*

"You're not going to make me change my mind," Jeth said.

"Yes, I know." Milton made to leave, but stopped in the doorway. "I just hope you're right."

"Does this mean you're coming?" Jeth held his breath, waiting for the answer.

"Yes," Milton said after a long pause. Then he left without another word.

Jeth let out his breath, relief flooding him. Despite the friction between them, Milton's presence made him feel safer, almost like having a real parent around.

Not that a parent would be able to save him. Jeth swallowed. He hoped he was right, too.

CHAPTER 07

WHEN JETH LEFT THE GALLEY SOMETIME LATER, HE RAN into Celeste, coming through the door at the same time.

"Ouch," she said. "You stepped on my foot."

"Well, you shouldn't ambush me."

"You ambushed me." She punched him in the shoulder.

Jeth grunted. It didn't hurt—much—but it wasn't exactly a love tap. "What do you want?"

"I . . . I . . . can't go into the Belgrave," she said in a rush.

Jeth blinked, not surprised she felt this way, only that she'd admitted it. For Celeste, admitting to fear would be like Flynn going on a hunger strike.

"I've been trying really hard to deal with the idea of going in there, but I'm not sure I can."

"Well, you've got to, so get it together."

She scowled at him. "You don't have to be such an ass, you know."

Were those tears in her eyes? Being a little afraid was one thing, but this seemed like a lot more than that. "What's wrong with you?" he asked.

Celeste choked on an angry breath, and some of the tears pooling behind her eyes leaked out, leaving glistening streaks over her pale skin. She punched him in the arm again. "It's where my mom died. It's why I ended up here."

Oh. Now he really did feel like an ass. This was a complication he hadn't been expecting. Not that it was his fault. There'd been an unspoken rule among all the members of the Malleus Shades from the very beginning—no talking about dead parents.

Feeling awkward and having no idea how to handle an emotional girl, Jeth said in what he hoped was a sincere voice, "I'm sorry. I didn't know."

Celeste let out a sob. The reaction was so unexpected that Jeth stared at her a full five seconds, wondering if this was the same person he'd known the last three years. If someone had told him yesterday that Celeste would be crying in front of him now, he would've laughed them off the ship.

Now he found himself stepping forward and hugging her. "It's okay," he said, patting her back. "What happened?"

She took another shaky breath and then the words began to spill out from her, as if the pressure to tell the story had been building for a very long time and finally reached its breaking point. "Our ship got lost. We were moving from Magren, my birth planet, to Peltraz for my mom's new job. The cheapest route was through the Belgrave. This was just before the ITA shut down the routes. I was nine. Don't really remember most of it. Except one night, after we'd been lost for two weeks, my mom just disappeared."

Jeth frowned, grateful that Celeste's position in his arms kept her from seeing it. He didn't know what to think. "What do you mean she *disappeared*?"

"Just that. We went to sleep in our cabin, and when I woke the next morning she was gone. The crew searched the ship, but there was no sign of her."

Jeth didn't say anything, unsure what to believe. Just like Flynn, he'd heard a lot of crazy tales about the Belgrave. Inexplicable equipment malfunction, communication breakdowns, supplies going bad, even ships vanishing and presumed lost. But this one was by far the craziest. How could a person go missing off a starship in the middle of space? Unless she'd been pushed out an airlock. Although he would never say such a thing aloud, Jeth couldn't help but wonder if her mother had simply abandoned her. A poor, single woman, trying to raise a child out here? Wouldn't be the first time.

"Sssshhh," he said, rubbing her back. "We're going to be fine. My parents surveyed the Belgrave for years and never once got lost in there. Or misplaced a crew member."

The joke fell a little flat, but he felt Celeste draw a breath against his chest, recovering. That was good. He needed her on her game for this trip. Even though he wasn't wild about going into the Belgrave, his trepidation had nothing to do with ghosts or some unexplained phenomenon.

Celeste took a step back from him, wiping her eyes.

"Feeling better?"

"A little. I guess I just needed to get it off my chest."

"I get it." Jeth patted her arm, the awkwardness returning. It was funny, considering how physically intimate the two of them often were while working jobs. Then again, in his experience, that kind of thing was a lot easier than opening yourself up.

As Celeste started to go, Jeth stopped her with a touch to the arm. "If you've got time, I've got a job for you."

Celeste put a hand on her hip. "What?"

"Hammer told me the lost ship is carrying some kind of new weapon. If that's true, there might be some chatter about it on the net. I'd like you to poke around, maybe see if we can figure out why exactly the ITA is so interested."

Celeste looked down, examining her fingernails. "All right if I ask Lizzie to look into it? I, uh, need to make a quick trip to Sector Twelve."

Jeth stifled a grin. A visit with the boyfriend would be an even better distraction. "Just don't be late coming back."

The next few hours crawled by as Jeth waited for Hammer's final instructions to come in, along with the copies of *Avalon*'s title and transfer papers. He spent the time searching the net with Lizzie. To Jeth's disappointment, they didn't find anything. No mention of the *Donerail*, a missing ship, or even Renford. There wasn't a single rumor about a secret weapon, even on the conspiracy sites.

Hammer's instructions and the details on the *Donerail* finally arrived, but the transfer papers were nowhere in sight. Dismayed, Jeth was about to do something rash and try to get Hammer on the comm when the entry door to *Avalon* buzzed. He ran down to the cargo bay to answer it.

Daxton Price stood in the doorway.

"Uh," Jeth stuttered.

Dax grinned and held out an envelope. "Hammer wanted me to give you this before we left."

Jeth accepted the envelope without even realizing what he was doing. His mind was still several seconds in the past, trying to come to grips with the reality that Daxton Price was standing in front of him.

"You awake there, Golden Boy?"

Jeth blinked away the confusion. "What is it?"

Dax folded his arms, shrugging. "No idea. But I'll be ready to go in twenty minutes. You're to meet me with *Avalon* just outside the short-term docks in Sector Two. I'm going to escort you through the gate, which will get us there a lot faster than the metadrives. Once there I'll run interference on any passing patrols around the Belgrave until you get inside it."

Jeth nodded. Hammer's instructions had said as much, although they hadn't identified the pilot of the other ship. "Why has Hammer got you doing this?"

Dax chuckled. "Didn't ask. When the big guy says 'jump,' I head for the nearest ring of fire."

Jeth wasn't sure whether to smile or frown and ended up doing something in between, looking ridiculous in the process, no doubt. It was clear Dax was joking, and Jeth couldn't make sense of it. The Malleus Brethren never spoke ill of Hammer. They *chose* to enter his service and have that thing inserted into their brains.

"Well, see you in a few," Dax said, and then he strode off,

the black implant on the back of his head reminding Jeth again of a giant spider.

He shook off the disorientation and headed inside. It occurred to him that Hammer's decision to send Dax was yet another indication of how important this job was to him. Whatever this weapon was, he must want it pretty bad. The idea tickled Jeth's mind with possibilities. Obsession could be a powerful pressure point. If only he had a way to apply that pressure. But he didn't see how. It wasn't like he could steal the weapon and hide it. Not if being near it was potentially fatal. There wasn't much point in finally getting his ship back if he was dead.

Stowing away such thoughts for now, Jeth opened the envelope and examined its contents as he walked along.

"Son of a bitch," he said when he realized what he was holding. Hammer had sent him a *print* copy of *Avalon*'s title and transfer papers. On actual *paper*. Jeth's hands curled into fists. He should've seen the ploy coming. A print copy would be harder to counterfeit than the official electronic one.

Still, Jeth couldn't deny the hope he felt at seeing his name there beside the "owner" heading. He hurried to his cabin and stowed the papers in a hidden compartment beneath his bed.

Fifteen minutes later, after he'd wrangled the crew back onto *Avalon*, Jeth darted up the stairs to the bridge, excitement exploding in his chest. He was going to pilot *his* ship. Jeth placed his hands on the control column to keep them from trembling as he waited for the locks that had held *Avalon* captive for so long to finally come undone. A loud, grating creak of metal echoed a moment later.

He waited, unmoving, for a full minute after the sound faded.

"Um, Jeth?" Lizzie said from the copilot's chair. "Are we going anywhere today, or are we just gonna hang out here?"

In answer, Jeth eased the controls forward, keeping the pace slow despite his desire to push it hard. He met up with Dax, who was piloting the *Citation*, one of Hammer's Vipers. Vipers were cruiser class ships, flashy and expensive, but this one didn't stand a chance of keeping up with *Avalon*.

"We'll meet you at the Cerulean Metagate," Jeth said over the comm line to Dax's ship. "*Avalon* hasn't been out in a while. I want to stretch her wings."

"Have at it," Dax replied. "But wait for me before queuing up."

"Right," Jeth said, and he disconnected the link. He maintained a steady pace until he was clear of the spaceport's restricted zone, the area clearly marked on *Avalon*'s nav system. Then he let her go, pushing her as hard and fast as she would go.

"Hey, whoa," Flynn's voice called from the engine room on the ship's main comm line. "Take it easy up there. The old girl ain't exactly in shape, you know."

Jeth pressed the mute button. He didn't care if Flynn was right or not. He didn't care about consequences. A wild recklessness had come over him. *Avalon* felt like something alive, a massive bird of prey. She had so much power and force, yet smooth, graceful control. Jeth had flown dozens of ships in the last few years, and none of them had come close to making him feel like this—as if the entire universe awaited his command. The planets and stars would flee before their path or risk being blown apart in their wake. He could fly her forever.

They came into range of the Cerulean Metagate some time later, and Jeth was finally forced to slow down as the nav system flashed a warning that he was entering a zoned area. Speed limits were regulated around the gates due to all the ships traveling in and out. At the moment, the place was so congested, Jeth couldn't have sped even if he'd wanted to. Twenty ships were waiting in line to use the gate ahead of them.

"What the crap?" said Lizzie. "Why's it so backed up?"

Jeth turned the ship to port, flying aimlessly as they waited for Dax to arrive. "The ITA closed down the Lateritus Gate for repairs a couple of weeks ago."

Lizzie made a face. "Another one? They still haven't reopened the Aurelius Gate. What the heck is taking so long?"

"Don't know." Jeth pulled up the nav system, prepping it for connection with the metagate's Master Control. "But don't complain too loudly. Shortage is good for our business."

"Yeah, so long as it doesn't turn into a *none available anywhere* situation. Just *imagine* the lines then."

"Good point," Jeth said, picturing the *Montrose*'s metadrive. "All right, here's Dax."

Dax piloted the *Citation* in behind *Avalon*, and they headed to the line.

"What's the holdup, Boss?" Shady said, entering the bridge a few minutes later. "Errr, or should I call you 'Captain' now, seeing how this is your ship and not Hammer's?"

Jeth ignored the question and waved out the front window. "Traffic."

"What else is new?" Shady sat down at the comm station to the left of the cockpit.

Lizzie sighed. "At least they're pretty to look at."

"What are?" Shady propped his feet up on the comm station's instrument panel. His big boots made a loud bang as he set them down.

Jeth winced. "You break something, and Flynn will kick your ass."

"Heh," Shady said, flipping his shaggy hair behind his shoulders, "like to see the little weasel try. So what's the pretty thing we're looking at?"

"The stars," Lizzie said in her most sarcastic tone. "The metagate, you moron." She paused. "It's the strangest thing to see colors like that in the middle of space."

Jeth nodded, fixing his gaze on the nearest edge of the gate, still several thousand kilometers away. The thing was so large that you could see only one section of it when you were this close, but Jeth knew its shape was mostly conical, like a giant malformed doorway in space. Similar to the *Montrose*'s metadrive, the gate was mostly comprised of that rough colored material, with a metal frame surrounding the outer edge and inlaid with wires and conductors and other tech. This one was colored in varying shades of blue, and it glowed bright enough to illuminate all the blackness around it in an aurora display.

"Why do you suppose they come in different colors?" Lizzie asked.

Nobody replied. It was the kind of question people voiced out of habit. The most anybody knew about metatech was that the material that came to make up gates and drives had been invented by ancient First-Earth scientists more than five hundred years ago.

The dazzling light hurt Jeth's eyes, and he looked away.

"Finally," Lizzie said some time later as the nav system beeped, indicating an incoming request from the Cerulean Metagate's Master Control. Jeth opened it, the message the usual payment prompt. He did a double take at the amount.

Lizzie whistled. "Damn, that's high."

Shady stood and walked over, taking in the fee as Jeth started to key in Hammer's account number. "Ouch," Shady said. "Sure that's not the rate they charge Independents?"

"I'm sure," Jeth said, finishing.

Shady scratched his head. "Why are we bothering with the gate at all? We should've just used the metadrive."

"It was supposed to save us time."

Shady grunted as he returned to his seat.

Jeth switched on the main comm line. "We're getting ready to head through the gate, people." He picked up the safety goggles from the dashboard and slipped them over his head as Lizzie and Shady did the same. Then he piloted them into the large, yawning mouth of the gate until the Master Control took over, propelling them through it.

The familiar dead—not dead feeling came over him, the state seeming to both last forever and no time at all, as if the seconds it took them to travel though metaspace were seconds stolen from a different timeline, a different existence.

They came through the other side a moment later, emerging into a vast expanse of empty space, with nothing but the Belgrave awaiting in the distance.

CHAPTER

NOT LONG AFTER THEY FINISHED THE JUMP, AVALON'S comm beeped with an incoming call from the *Citation*, which must have just completed its jump. Jeth switched on the video screen to find Dax once again grinning at him.

"There are no ships on the radar right now, so we might be in luck, but give me a ten-minute head start to make sure. If I run into any ITA patrols, I'll get their attention and lead them away from your path. Still, get in there as quick as you can. You should be undetectable once you pass through the border."

"Yeah, okay," said Jeth.

Dax killed the link between the two ships and then piloted the *Citation* away from them. Ten minutes later, Jeth followed. It would've simplified things if they could've made a metaspace jump directly into the Belgrave, but that was impossible due to the unusual energy signature that marked the Belgrave's border. A ship could jump within the quadrant but not into it.

Keeping an eye on the radar and proximity scans, Jeth set *Avalon* to autopilot. They arrived at the border without any sign of Dax or the ITA. A good omen, Jeth decided.

"We're at the border," he announced over the main comm.

Moments later, everybody congregated on the bridge for the crossing.

"It doesn't look any different," Celeste said from the copilot's chair, which she had commandeered from Lizzie. Celeste seemed calm enough, but she sat unusually rigid for someone normally as languid as a cat.

Behind them at the nav station, Lizzie snorted. "What'd you expect? A big neon skull and bones?"

"Yeah, I know what you mean," said Shady. "I thought it would look all weird and scary, but it's just more space."

"That's because that's all it is," Jeth said. "Just another little bit of space." It was more pep talk than denial. An odd mixture of excitement and dread churned in Jeth's belly, all of it infused with the wanderlust vibrating harder than ever inside him.

As they passed through the energy field, all the lights on the ship dimmed. A moment later, a burst of white noise crackled out of the comm speakers, making everybody jump. For a second Jeth thought he heard voices among the static.

Nobody said anything as the noise died away. Somehow the silence was even more unnerving, all the normal ship sounds louder and weirdly ominous.

Shady was the first to work up the courage to speak, but when he did, his voice was subdued. "So . . . what the hell was that?"

Nobody answered, not even Jeth.

After a moment Shady spoke again in a more normal

voice. "Where do we head now, Captain?"

Jeth cringed a little, not thrilled with the new nickname. "Boss" was bad enough.

Lizzie answered for him. "The *Donerail*'s last known position was alpha-two-six-one, also known as the Specter Sea."

"Of course it is," said Flynn, his voice higher-pitched than usual. "Because that's exactly what you want to a name a place everybody is afraid of. I mean, why couldn't they have called it the Sea of Puppies or maybe the Sea of Fluffy Kittens?"

"Don't be such a wuss," said Lizzie.

"How do we know that's where the ship was last?" asked Shady.

"We don't," said Jeth. "It's just an estimated location. One of Hammer's ships was outside the Belgrave when they recorded the distress beacon, but with the dead zone screwing up the signal, they couldn't triangulate exactly."

"But why was the *Donerail* in the Belgrave in the first place?" asked Milton.

Jeth shrugged, wishing they'd found *something* about this job on the net.

Sitting up from his slumped position, Shady said, "The doc's got a good point. Why would the *Donerail* go into this place? I mean, nobody goes in here except for criminals and nut jobs."

"You mean like us?" said Flynn.

"Look," Jeth said, "it doesn't matter why they came in here. All that matters is that we find the ship and bring her out. Lizzie, get us prepared for a jump to those coordinates."

She saluted him. "Yes, Captain."

Five minutes later, *Avalon*'s metadrive successfully delivered them to the *Donerail*'s last known position, but to no one's surprise, it was empty.

Jeth spent the next hour going over how to run *Avalon*'s Explorer program. Part nav comp, part radar, the program had been designed years ago by Jeth's mother. She had calibrated it specifically to handle the Belgrave's energy fluctuations. Fortunately, the program mostly ran itself. All the crew had to do was keep an eye on the readouts and they'd be able to stay on course and search for the *Donerail*. Everyone got the hang of it pretty quickly, including Shady. Jeth considered this a small miracle, given his lack of interest in anything that didn't involve a trigger followed by an explosion.

Of all the crew, Shady was the only one who'd done time in a juvenile detention center. His high score on Hammer's aptitude test, combined with Jeth's intuition that he would be a good match for the crew, was the only reason he wasn't still in juvie.

Once he finished the demo on the Explorer program, Jeth went over the search strategy of using the shuttles to fly preprogrammed sweeps over the surrounding area. Then Jeth and Shady took the first shift and each boarded one of the two shuttles that Jeth's parents had affectionately named *Sparky* and *Flash*.

"Make sure you spend as much time checking the readouts as you do playing video games," Jeth said to Shady through the comm link. Flynn had suggested installing the gaming units in the shuttles a year ago, after multiple fights among the crew about needing more game time on the main unit installed in *Avalon*'s common room.

"Oh, I will, Captain," Shady said in a tone that suggested the opposite.

Jeth sighed and hoped for the best. At least the *Donerail* was too big for Shady not to notice her. He hoped. Jeth switched on autopilot, and *Sparky* soared away from *Avalon*.

Less than thirty minutes later another burst of white noise echoed from the comm speakers. Jeth gave a little yelp of fright, almost falling out of his chair. It was one thing for stuff like that to happen on board *Avalon*, with everybody else around him to lessen the impact, but out here he was completely alone and more prone to panic.

Hands shaking, Jeth reached for the game controller and switched it on, turning up the volume. Anything to make him forget that noise. He was glad he had, as it kept happening at random intervals.

By the end of the four-hour shift, Jeth had almost gotten used to it. Shady reported experiencing the same thing on his shuttle, while the others said it was occurring on *Avalon*, too.

"We can live with it," Jeth said, trying to reassure everybody, including himself. "It's just the weird energy fluxes in this place. No big deal."

Turned out he was right. By the third day, they'd mostly gotten used to it. The only other strange phenomenon was that they had to keep readjusting the nav equipment's calibration settings.

"It's weird," Lizzie said to Jeth after the sixth time she had to do this. "Almost as if there's some kind of massive gravity field out there that keeps pulling us toward it."

Jeth shrugged. "Maybe it's a black hole."

Lizzie didn't offer an opinion. She'd been acting strangely the last two days, oddly withdrawn. She'd turned in early every night and slept in late every morning. Such antisocial behavior was anti-Lizzie, but Jeth chalked it up to the strain of being in the Belgrave and the constant reminder of what had happened to their parents.

On their fifth day in the Belgrave, one of the cooling units broke. It took Flynn half a day to fix it.

By the sixth day, Jeth was starting to worry about their lack of progress. Two weeks wasn't a lot of time, and they hadn't found so much as a drifting heat shield, and those fell off ships all the time in normal areas of space. No, for all the Belgrave Quadrant's reputation of being a spacecraft boneyard, it was turning out to be more of a wasteland, devoid of anything except more space.

Jeth crawled out of bed early on the seventh day, exhausted from a restless night. He'd tossed and turned for hours, his mind obsessing about what would happen if they failed to find the *Donerail*. Would Hammer let him continue to search beyond two weeks? Or would the deal for *Avalon* go bust and life return to normal? Jeth didn't think he could handle more normal. Not after coming so close to the life he wanted rather than the one he was stuck with.

These thoughts continued to cycle through his mind

as he walked onto the bridge. To his surprise, Lizze was there, lying on the floor with her head and shoulders hidden beneath the life support station.

"What are you doing, Liz?"

There was a loud bang, followed by the sound of Lizzie groaning. She scooted out from underneath the station and scowled up at him, one hand rubbing her forehead. "Crap, Jeth. You made me jump and hit my head."

Jeth pressed his lips together, trying not to laugh. It wasn't funny, really, and yet it still was. "What are you doing under there?"

Lizzie rolled her eyes, but before she could answer Jeth heard a meow.

He gritted his teeth. "Please don't tell me there's a cat stuck inside the life support control panel. You know, the thing that makes sure the air we're breathing doesn't turn poisonous and kill us in our sleep?"

"He's not stuck, just playing hard to get. I think." She scooted back under the station—probably to avoid Jeth's glower.

A couple of seconds later, and after much scratching, meowing, and cursing, Lizzie reemerged with a struggling Viggo in her arms. She set the cat down and he raced off. No doubt to cause havoc somewhere else.

Jeth sighed as he sat on the nearest chair, then stared down at his sister. "So why are you up so early?" He didn't think she was on the bridge merely to rescue the stupid cat.

"Oh, I, um . . ." Lizzie bit her lip and got to her feet. "I couldn't sleep. I was wandering the ship and heard Viggo crawling around up here."

Jeth huffed, refraining from saying anything more about the cat, not when he sensed that his sister was distraught over something. "I couldn't sleep much either."

Lizzie nodded, shoving both hands into her front pockets.

Jeth could tell she had something on her mind, and so he waited, leaning back in the chair. He knew not to press.

"There's, uh, something I've been wanting to tell you. . . ."

When she didn't go on, Jeth said, "What is it, Liz?"

"I found something in my cabin a few days ago. It's—"

She broke off as *Avalon*'s proximity alarm started to blare. Jeth jumped out of his seat, his heart heading into overdrive. He turned to the front window and froze at the sight of a spaceship only a few meters off, so close it nearly swallowed the entire view.

"What the hell?" He dashed toward the pilot's chair, switched off the ship's anchoring system, and then pulled back on the control column. The ship lurched hard enough that Lizzie stumbled, half falling into the comm station chair. She turned off the proximity alarm as Jeth steered them a safe distance away.

By now, the rest of the crew was piling into the bridge, all of them in various stages of disarray.

"Whoa, where did that come from?" said Shady. He had one boot on and the other hanging from his hand.

Wonderment filled Lizzie's voice. "It just appeared. One second, empty space." She snapped her fingers. "Next second, that."

Jeth frowned. It did seem like the ship had just appeared,

but then again, neither of them had been paying attention to the front window. Still, the ship had been right on top of them before *Avalon*'s proximity alarm had gone off. *Maybe the sensor is faulty,* Jeth told himself.

"Is she the one we're looking for?" asked Shady.

"I don't know," Jeth said. It looked like other Marlins he'd seen, but he didn't know for sure. "Let's find out."

"Already on it," Celeste said from the copilot's chair.

Flynn approached the window and pointed out. "Look at that hole."

Jeth turned his attention the direction Flynn indicated. A large hole marred the ship's lower bow. It wasn't the kind of hole you'd expect on a ship that's been in a firefight or suffered a collision. It wasn't a ragged, chaotic shape but perfectly symmetrical, like it had been carved with a giant hole punch. The sight of it sent ripples of dread skidding over Jeth's skin. What had made it? He crossed his arms to keep from shivering.

"It's the *Donerail*," said Celeste, her voice tense. Jeth turned his gaze toward her, bracing for whatever she was about to say next.

"And according to the scan, there are three life signs on board."

Nobody spoke. Nobody breathed. The ship had been missing for two months, Hammer had said. Well beyond her food and water capacity. She was adrift, dark, and forlorn.

But not dead.

"HOW'S ANYBODY STILL ALIVE ON THAT THING AFTER ALL this time?" said Shady.

"Got to be some mistake in the scan," said Flynn, his pointed face pinched with worry.

"No, it's not," said Lizzie. Her fingers moved over the control panel in front of her as she examined the results. "The ship still has twelve percent power. Looks like nav and comms are offline, but life support is at seven percent. The gravity drive is fully functioning and cabin pressure is normal."

Jeth exhaled at this news. Normal cabin pressure meant that whenever that hole had been made, the *Donerail* had had enough power to lock down the bulkheads surrounding the affected area and maintain hull integrity. If any of the crew or passengers had been near that area when the hole was made they would've been blown out to space, but the people elsewhere would've been fine.

"With reads that consistent, the scan must be accurate," Lizzie concluded.

Three people still alive. Jeth cleared his throat. "Hammer's intel must've been wrong."

"So, what do we do next?" said Milton.

Lizzie gaped at him. "What do you mean? We go over there and rescue them, of course."

"It's not that simple, Liz," Jeth said, running his hands through his hair.

"How do you figure?" She waved at the front window. "They've got to be starving. And with life support that low, the air will be more than a little toxic. Not to mention wicked cold."

"But Hammer insisted we're not to board," said Shady. "Job stipulation."

Lizzie scowled at him. "Hammer didn't think there would be survivors. The rules have gone out the window. Besides, people's lives are more important than some stupid paycheck."

"It's not just the paycheck," Jeth said. *It's Avalon.*

"Right," Shady continued. "It's our asses too, if we ignore what Hammer said."

"The complication," Milton said, "is the weapon that ship is supposed to have on it. Isn't that right, Jeth?"

Jeth nodded and sat up straighter. "Lizzie, run a scan for radiation levels and any possible biohazards." If the scan came back with the results he expected, then those three people over there were dead already. Time just hadn't caught up with them yet.

Lizzie sniffed but did as he asked.

Only the scan came back negative. For everything.

Jeth read the results four times, his mind refusing to believe it.

"The scan might be faulty," said Flynn. "This is the Belgrave."

"It's not faulty." Lizzie stood up, turning a fiery gaze on Jeth. "We have to go over there and rescue them."

Shady crossed his arms. "How many times do we have to say it, little girl? Hammer told us not to board."

"Hammer doesn't have to know," said Lizzie.

Shady made a sound like a growl. "He will, though. He's got his ways. Like the time he found out I took that tiara on the Feria job."

Celeste snorted. "That's only because you went around wearing the stupid thing afterward."

Jeth was tempted to point out that hiding a stolen tiara was a lot less complicated than hiding three strangers, assuming they brought them aboard *Avalon*.

Lizzie turned an expectant gaze on him. "Come on, Jeth."

Jeth sighed. His sister—savior of strays and the stranded. He knew he should feel the same, but dread kept getting in the way. And it wasn't just because of the risk of breaking the deal with Hammer or the possibility that the scan was wrong about the radiation and toxin levels.

No, he dreaded going over there because there had to have been a lot more than three people on the *Donerail* when it went missing. What had the survivors done with the dead bodies? Were they just lying about? He doubted the hole had taken care of most of them. Maybe those survivors had gotten desperate during all that time adrift and done something else with the bodies.

Shuddering, Jeth forced the thought away before his stomach rebelled.

"Well, Captain?" said Shady. "What do we do?"

Jeth took a deep breath, wishing he didn't have to make the decision. He wanted to be selfish and cowardly and just leave those people where they were. It would be so easy to hitch the *Donerail* to *Avalon* and tow it out. The *Donerail*'s passengers had survived this long. They might make it a little longer.

But no, he couldn't do that. He refused to take the coward's route. This was just the starving man all over again. Only this time, Jeth wouldn't be too late to act.

"We check it out. Just me and Shady. Everybody else stays here."

Both Celeste and Lizzie objected to the arrangement. Flynn looked relieved and Shady nervous.

Jeth shook his head at the girls. "There's no point arguing. If there are people over there, they might be dangerous. And if there aren't, well, two of us are more likely to get away with exploring the ship without leaving behind any evidence than four."

Celeste folded her arms across her chest. "Since when are you two the graceful, careful ones around here?"

"We can be graceful," Jeth said, glancing at Shady and trying not to picture how stupid he'd looked wearing that sparkling, diamond-encrusted tiara around like some kind of ugly fairy-tale princess. "Besides, we've definitely got better aim."

"Yeah, and we're braver," said Shady, even though he'd never looked more terrified.

Lizzie opened her mouth to protest, but Jeth cut her off with an upraised hand. "No time to argue. I'm pulling rank." He turned to Shady and said, "Get your guns and meet me at the airlock."

Shady exhaled, looking marginally better at the idea of guns. "You got it, Captain."

Jeth turned back to the girls. "Celeste, go ahead and line us up for hauling. Lizzie, you go with her in case she needs help overriding the airlock. Shady and I will hook up the towlines first and then go in."

Celeste and Lizzie nodded, and Jeth left the bridge. He entered his cabin, opened the hidden cabinet beneath his bunk, and pulled out his Triton 9. Its silver plating glistened in the soft light overhead. Everything he knew about shooting he'd learned from his father, but the Triton was the first gun he'd purchased for himself.

Jeth slid the Triton into a holster hung from the end of his bed, then grabbed two extra clips and shoved one into each front pocket. He slung the holster over his shoulder and headed down to the cargo bay.

Shady was already there, pulling on a space suit. Flynn was helping him, while Milton stood nearby, watching.

As Jeth started suiting up, Milton came over and helped him with the fastenings. "Be careful over there," he said. "Keep your helmet on. If *Avalon*'s scans were wrong after all, the suit should protect you."

"Okay," Jeth said, suddenly finding it hard to breathe. He didn't care for Milton's use of the word *should*. He took a deep inhale, slid on the helmet, and double-checked the seal.

Then Jeth buckled his gun holster around his hips and stomped over to Shady, the space suit heavy and awkward. "Can you hear me?" he asked, testing the helmet's proximity mike.

"Gotcha," Shady replied, his voice echoing inside Jeth's helmet.

Jeth nodded as he pressed one of the switches on the side of the helmet, opening the link to *Avalon*'s main comm line. "You getting us, Celeste?"

"Yep," Celeste said from the bridge. "It looks like all three survivors are in the same place, rear and starboard. The cargo bay, according to this Marlin schematic. Assuming it's accurate, the nearest hatch from the tow ports should be right behind the two crow guns up top. It'll lead you to the passenger deck."

"Right. Thanks."

Jeth and Shady entered the airlock together and Milton sealed the door behind them. Jeth approached the hatch leading to the outside, deactivated the gravity drive, and slid the hatch open, his body now weightless in the zero G. He grasped the safety rail outside the door and peered over the edge, allowing himself one thrilling, terrifying look at the nothingness of space surrounding them. Then he focused on the *Donerail* in the distance. The hole in its bow looked even more ominous from here.

Jeth glanced at Shady. "You ready?" Shady answered with a thumbs-up.

Here we go, Jeth thought. Following the rail, he pulled himself outside the ship to where one of the two towline mechanisms sat inside a compartment just beyond the door. He opened the compartment, grasped the small propulsion unit that made up the head of the towline, and yanked it out. Then he pointed the unit toward the *Donerail* and switched it on. The engine jerked him forward, pulling him over to the other ship in seconds.

Jeth grabbed onto the railing that ran along the front of the *Donerail* a couple of meters below the bridge window and switched the engine off. Then he moved left, following the rail as it led him to the *Donerail*'s starboard tow port. To his right, Shady was doing the same with the other towline.

As soon as Jeth attached the towline's unit into the port, he heard Celeste's voice. "Okay, *Avalon*'s establishing a connection to the *Donerail*'s network now. . . . All right, connection's a go. Lizzie should be able to override the locks on the hatch. Just give us a minute."

While Lizzie worked, Jeth and Shady met back in the middle and then climbed their way up and over the bridge to the crow guns and the hatch just beyond them. When Celeste gave them the go-ahead a few moments later, Jeth pulled the hatch open and slipped inside. Shady followed after him, sealing the door shut behind them. Gravity activated inside the hatch automatically.

Jeth stooped and pulled up on the handle of the door to the corridor below. The light on his helmet barely penetrated the inky blackness, and even through the space suit, he could tell how cold it was down there, almost as cold as it had been outside the ship.

Looks like a big black mouth.

Pushing the image away, Jeth dropped through the hatch, trying to land as softly as possible, without much success. Shady's descent was even louder. Jeth winced and pulled the Triton from the holster around his hips. He looked around, his eyes adjusting to the dimness of the emergency lighting that had come on the moment it had detected movement.

In a second his pulse doubled, until his heart felt like a fist pounding against his breastbone. Something was wrong. Something terrible had happened here. Parts of the corridor were missing. Not blown away or damaged but *missing*, holes carved in the walls as neatly as the one in the ship's front. Some of the holes were small, hardly big enough for Lizzie's cat to fit through, while others were large enough for Jeth and Shady to pass through side by side.

The nearest of the bigger holes was a few meters down and to the right. It was cut at an angle through the corridor wall into a passenger cabin and also downward into what was probably the common room or maybe sick bay. Jeth stared at the exposed cross section into the ship's innards, taking in the shorn ends of wires and ductwork. Everything had been sliced off so precisely that the edges looked smooth and sharp enough to cut skin. An odd, fuzzy sensation filled his head, as if the receiver in his brain were out of tune, unable to process the images his eyes were sending to it.

"What the hell happened here?" Shady asked.

Jeth jumped at the loud sound of his voice, amplified by the mike. He shot a glare at Shady. "Keep quiet. We don't want anybody to know we're here until we're ready."

"Oh. Right."

Jeth shook his head, trying to get his heart rate back into the normal range. Orienting himself toward the rear of the ship, he moved on, steering clear of the hole in the floor. He wondered if the weapon Hammer was after had survived all this damage. *Or maybe it had caused it.*

A few of the cabin doors were still intact and closed, and as Jeth reached one of them, curiosity got the best of him, and he slid it open.

The door to the cabin might be fine, but the inside of the room contained more of the same destruction. A hole had been cut through the bed. Only the bed wasn't empty. Or at least it hadn't been whenever that hole had been made.

Something harsh and slithery seemed to crawl up Jeth's throat at the gruesome sight before him. The head, arms, and legs of a man still lay on what remained of the bed, but the torso was missing, cut away from the body with the same precision as the rest of the hole. No blood stained the mattress, as if whatever had done the cutting had cauterized the wounds as it sliced through.

Jeth turned away, choking back vomit and terror. Shady had started to follow him inside, but Jeth pushed him back. "Trust me, you don't want to see."

Shady looked ready to argue, but then he backed off.

Through the glass of his helmet, Jeth could see his face had gone pale.

They moved on down the corridor. Jeth led the way, but Shady followed close behind him. Jeth kept to the left, which seemed to have sustained less damage. There were holes on that side too, but most of them looked like they'd been made by ordinary bullets. That was good. Bullets, Jeth could handle. He welcomed them. Anything was better than mutilated bodies. All he wanted at the moment was to get out of there alive and in one piece, an expression that had taken on a new and ghoulish meaning.

A loud click sounded inside Jeth's helmet, followed by Celeste's voice. "Heads up, guys. Somebody's moving your way."

They both froze. Ahead of them the corridor ended in two sets of stairs, one on either side.

"I'll cover the left, you right," Jeth said, aiming the Triton.

A hand descended on his shoulder. Jeth cursed and spun toward Shady. *"What?"*

Shady's fingers on Jeth's shoulder clenched and unclenched as he pointed his gun toward something on the right side of the wall in front of them. "What could do that, Jeth? How'd something like that happen? It's not . . . it's—"

"Shut up." Jeth shook off Shady's hand, trying to make out whatever had rendered his friend speechless.

A bulge protruded out from the wall. It wasn't the wall itself bulging outward, but something lodged *into* the wall, grafted into it like some kind of weird art sculpture.

No, not something. *Someone.* That fuzzy sensation came over Jeth's brain once more as he realized that it was a human head. The person's face was turned sideways, exposing one opened eye, shining in the light from their helmets.

Slowly, more of the person came into focus. Above the head, one hand pointed out from on high, as if the crewman had gotten trapped inside the wall while reaching for something. The protrusion of a foot and knee marked the lower half of his body. Even though the guy was clearly dead, Jeth half expected the hands or feet to start moving or the eye to start blinking. He didn't think the man had been dead for very long. No signs of decay marked the exposed parts.

Shady grabbed his shoulder again. "Something's coming!"

Panic squeezed Jeth's heart for a moment, and then his brain reengaged. Whatever had happened here was horrible, but Jeth wasn't about to end up the same way. He focused his gaze toward the stairs once more, the Triton held tight in his hand.

A tiny figure appeared, standing only a little taller than the stair railing.

Jeth's mouth fell open as he saw it was a little girl, maybe five or six years old. Pale, almost colorless hair hung around her shoulders, framing her round-cheeked face. She wore a space suit, one four times too large for her, but no helmet. Someone had pinned up the excess material on the arms and legs of the suit for her. Dirt smears marred the suit in places, but the girl beneath looked to be healthy. She stared at them with large, dark eyes that seemed all pupil and too little white.

This can't be happening, Jeth thought. He'd been expecting some kind of monster to rival his worst nightmares. Not this. Not her. He ought to feel relieved, yet his fear remained firmly entrenched.

The girl's gaze shifted from Jeth to the gun in his hand. Terror spread across her face, her eyes widening, exposing the whites. Then she turned and bolted back down the stairs, moving remarkably fast considering the bulky suit.

"Wait," Jeth called, taking off after her. He hurried down the stairs, catching a brief glimpse of her as she rounded a corner. It was like chasing a shadow. He followed her down the corridor, then turned right onto another flight of stairs. He had to move slower than he wanted, to avoid more holes, the destruction continuing onward. But at least he didn't come across any more mutilated bodies.

At last Jeth spotted brighter lights in the distance. The next moment he came to a stop on a walkway overlooking the cargo bay. Two more figures stood among the haphazard rows of crates and containers below, the little girl between them. Both of the figures wore armored space suits and helmets, the dark visors hiding their faces. The one on the left looked as big as a mountain compared to the smaller figure on the right. Both carried guns.

The moment they spotted Jeth and Shady, they raised their weapons.

"Stop right there," the big one shouted, the words muffled

by the helmet but still discernible.

Jeth froze at once, but Shady took a step forward, aiming his gun. Whether he hadn't heard the man or was just ignoring him, Jeth couldn't tell. He reached for Shady, meaning to haul him back, but it was too late.

The two strangers below opened fire.

CHAPTER 10

JETH HIT THE FLOOR AS A STREAM OF BULLETS SWEPT PAST him. For a moment he couldn't think in the onrush of adrenaline.

Need to get out of here. He rolled sideways, off the walkway to the floor below, finding cover behind a storage crate. Shady landed beside him a second later. Then, each taking a side of the crate, they leaned around the edges and returned fire.

The Triton's kickback pounded Jeth's arm muscles with every shot, but he held his hand steady, kept his breath even, willing the calm and focus he needed to come over him.

"What's going on?" Celeste's alarmed voice echoed inside Jeth's helmet, breaking his concentration. "Is somebody shooting?"

"Hold on," Jeth said. He knew if he didn't answer she would keep pestering him. But he couldn't exactly give her a blow-by-blow account with bullets flying around him. They made loud, terrifying shrieks as they passed.

Then, without warning, the incoming bullets stopped. Jeth eased his hand on the trigger, motioning toward Shady to stop, too. Shady let off a couple more rounds, then ceased.

Jeth scanned the area beyond the crate for signs of the two

armored figures or the little girl. His eardrums throbbed in the silence. Sweat ran down his neck and back. But he was oddly calm. At least a gunfight was within the realm of normal, something his brain could easily process.

"What do we do now?" Shady said.

"Hell if I know."

A single gunshot erupted from behind a line of barrels across the way. *Crack-whish-bang.* The shot passed so close, Jeth felt it even through the thick padding of his space suit. Sudden outrage made his muscles clench. They'd come over here to help these people, and now they were trying to kill them.

He and Shady fired back once more, taking aim at the barrels near where the shot had come from.

The next moment, a loud, piercing wail filled the cargo bay. It was worse than any siren Jeth had ever heard. For a second he wondered if there was some ferocious animal on board, a massive beast powerful enough to have torn those holes in the walls.

Then he thought no more as pain shot through his skull from the sound. He lurched back behind the crate, almost dropping his gun as he instinctively covered his ears. Never mind that he couldn't reach them through the helmet. The noise was inside him somehow, a living, vicious thing, hellbent on ripping him apart.

To his right, Shady looked to be in the same level of agony.

Desperate for the noise to stop but powerless to make it happen, Jeth squeezed his eyes closed. He needed to get away from it. He lowered himself to the ground, determined to crawl since he didn't think he could stand.

On and on it went, getting louder. The dim lights in the cargo bay began to flicker as if they too were affected by the sound. The floor trembled, letting out a noise like warping metal. A buzz of electricity joined the chorus.

What's happening?

The two shooters appeared around the corner of one of the containers in front of Jeth, both struggling to walk. They were as affected by the noise as he and Shady were. Jeth knew he should take cover, but his body was beyond his control.

The strangers dropped their guns to the floor.

As if in response, the noise began to die down and the panic in the room ended.

When silence finally came, Jeth exhaled in relief. His brain felt squishy inside his skull. He eased himself up to a standing position and faced the two strangers. It had to be some kind of trap. The sweat on his neck and back felt like flakes of ice.

"Are they surrendering?" Shady said from behind Jeth.

"I guess."

"Can I shoot 'em?"

Tempting. . . . "Uh, no."

Jeth took a tentative step forward, aiming his Triton. The two didn't react but stood still, hands at their sides. Jeth glanced around, suspicious of booby traps. To his left he spotted a toolbox and a pile of maintenance materials. From those and their spacesuits, Jeth guessed the two shooters had been about to attempt some kind of repair to the outside of the ship when *Avalon* showed up.

He returned his gaze to the strangers. Bending his elbow, he pointed the gun toward the ceiling. "We're not looking for a fight," he shouted. "Nod if you can hear me."

Both did, and Jeth lowered his gun, pointing the barrel at the floor.

The shorter one raised his hands to his helmet and pulled it off. A mound of long blond hair spilled out. Not a guy. A girl. Jeth mentally kicked himself for not realizing it before. She looked about his age, her face pale and a little too thin. Even so, he was struck by how pretty she was, her features delicate like porcelain, yet her expression fierce, like marble.

He caught himself staring and was glad when Celeste's voice suddenly filled his ears. "What's going on, Jeth?"

"We're fine. We found the survivors."

"Who are they? Why was there shooting? There was shooting, right?"

"Not now, Celeste." Jeth pressed the button to terminate the link.

Across from him, the other shooter was pulling off his helmet. This one was a he, a guy with dark, spiky hair, as if he usually wore it shaved but had been growing it out. He looked young, too, not much older than Jeth.

Jeth examined the two of them, deciding that neither appeared diseased. That, combined with his faith in *Avalon*'s scanning equipment, was enough that he holstered the

Triton, then pulled off his helmet. The frigid air bit his face, the smell of it rank, like something long dead.

"You sure you want to be doing that, Boss?" Shady asked, his voice muffled inside the helmet.

Jeth waved him off. "Who are you?"

"Who are *you*?" the blonde replied, her eyes narrowed on his face. She might have put down her gun, but Jeth got the feeling that surrender wasn't in this girl's vocabulary.

"My name's Jeth Seagrave, and this is Will Shady."

"I go by Shady," Shady shouted, still refusing to remove his helmet. He also hadn't lowered his gun.

Jeth reached over and pushed the barrel downward. The last thing he needed was for Shady to shoot one of them by accident. If that happened, whatever had made that noise might start up again. What had it been?

And where was the little girl?

As if on cue, the girl slid out from behind a row of nearby barrels and raced over to the blonde, grasping her hand.

The blonde stepped in front of the girl as if to shield her. "Did you say Jeth *Seagrave*?"

Jeth frowned. "Yeah, that's right. What of it?"

She looked away from him, visibly nervous, as if she had made some kind of blunder. "Nothing. So who are you? Why are you here? You're not ITA, that much is clear."

"We're . . ." Jeth didn't know yet how much to share. *When in doubt, lie quick and keep the conversation moving.* "We were just passing by. And you are?"

She hesitated, then said, "Sierra Hightower, and this is Vince Mallory."

Jeth nodded, glad to finally get a question answered even as a dozen more popped up to take its place. He chose the easiest one next. "And who's she?" He inclined his head toward the little girl.

Sierra's expression hardened as if Jeth had made a threat toward the girl rather than asked a perfectly reasonable question.

"I'm Cora," the girl said, peering around Sierra's side.

"Hello, Cora." Jeth flashed an awkward smile at her. Talking to kids always made him feel inadequate, as if they spoke a language he didn't quite understand.

Cora hid her face in Sierra's side, demonstrating "a case of the shies," as Jeth's mom used to call bashful behavior. He remembered Lizzie had been prone to doing the same thing. He wondered if Sierra and Cora were related, but the only resemblance he could see was their light-colored hair.

"So, not to be rude or nothing," said Shady, shifting around nervously, "but what was making all that noise?"

Sierra looked away, her gaze roaming around the cargo bay even as she pulled Cora tighter against her side. "We don't know. It's been happening off and on for a while now."

"How—" Jeth began.

Sierra cut him off. "What are you doing on our ship?"

Jeth frowned at the command in her voice. That was a pretty reckless attitude considering the position she was in. Feisty. He kind of liked it. Of course, he would've felt a lot different if it had come from her big-muscled companion. The realization annoyed him, and he glared at her, remembering the unfriendly greeting moments before.

"We came to rescue you, but we weren't expecting to get shot at." He paused. "Why did you shoot at us?"

Sierra returned his glower. "Have you seen this place? What did you think we were going to do when you appear out of nowhere, carrying guns? And you didn't stop when we told you to."

Beside Sierra, Vince straightened up to his full height. The gesture spoke volumes to Jeth about the nature of their relationship. If anybody threatened Sierra, Vince would take care of it. Simple as that. Jeth wondered if they were together, like a couple. Surely they couldn't be related. They looked nothing alike, plus the different last names.

Jeth took a deep a breath. He supposed she had a point about the guns. Not to mention plenty of reasons to be on edge, stranded here. He glanced away from her, sweeping his gaze over the holes scattered around the cargo bay. He was glad to see none of them contained body parts. "So, what did all this exactly?"

Sierra bit her lower lip and shivered.

Vince cleared his throat. Then in a smooth, deep voice that made him seem much older than he looked, he said, "We don't know that either. We got lost in the Belgrave, and then a few days later those holes just started tearing their way through the ship. Then some of the crew started disappearing, too. Just vanishing."

Sierra nodded, her mouth drawn into a thin, frightened line. "It was complete chaos."

"Whoa," Shady said. "So the stories about the Belgrave *are* true."

"Let's not jump to conclusions," said Jeth, even as he remembered Celeste's story about her mother.

"What else could've done what we've seen?"

Ignoring Shady, Jeth said, "So how did you three manage to survive?"

"We got lucky," said Vince.

"Yes," added Sierra. "Some of the others would've survived, too, but in the panic they started firing and killing one another. We barricaded ourselves in one of the passenger cabins and rode it out."

Puzzled, Jeth examined the three of them as a group, wondering what connected them. "What are you all doing aboard a transport like this? You don't look old enough to be crew members."

Vince folded his arms. "You're one to talk about looking old enough."

Sierra cast Vince a warning look. "We were just hitching a ride."

Jeth raised an eyebrow. "Marlins aren't generally used to transport passengers."

Sierra pressed her lips together, looking as if she were struggling not to give him a tongue-lashing. Perversely, it made him want to smile. "This one is," she said. "Or at least it was, if the captain felt the price was right."

Aha, Jeth thought. *So this is a smuggler's ship.* That made sense. He wondered how anybody his age could afford to hire passage on a smuggler's ship, but he didn't think it important enough to ask at the moment, not with other questions pressing their way forward. What *did* matter was that as passengers on this ship, they might know a thing or two about the rest of its cargo.

"We heard a rumor about a ship like this that was transporting some kind of special weapon. Know anything about that?"

Sierra shook her head. "The *Donerail* was carrying lots of illegal goods, as far as we could tell, but the captain and crew kept a tight lid on that stuff and we didn't go poking around."

Cora sneezed, drawing everyone's attention. Jeth had half forgotten she was there.

"Listen," Sierra said, sounding annoyed once more. "I know you've got questions and so do we. But we've been stranded for almost two weeks. The metadrive is completely blown and we're out of fuel and food and almost out of water. Any chance we can get on with the rescuing you mentioned?"

Jeth winced, suddenly feeling guilty. He couldn't imagine what they must've gone through, and Cora was just a kid. He started to nod, then frowned as something occurred to him. "You say you've been here *two weeks*?"

"Yeah, that's right," said Vince.

"But this ship's been missing two months."

Sierra swallowed. "That's . . . that's impossible."

No more than a dead man trapped inside a wall, Jeth thought. A shiver skidded down his spine. "Maybe, but it's true."

She and Vince exchanged bewildered looks.

Jeth could tell it was news to them, that somehow they had been completely unaware of how long they'd been missing. Celeste's story didn't seem so farfetched anymore. He wondered how many other crazy stories about this place were true. *Seems we've got our own to tell now.*

Jeth shook off the thought and said, "Okay, we can finish talking later." He motioned toward Shady. "Let's get out of here."

CHAPTER 11

THEY MADE THEIR WAY BACK TO THE AIRLOCK AFTER LOCAT-
ing the helmet for Cora's space suit. As Sierra was fitting it
over the girl's head, Jeth signaled Celeste. "We're bringing
the survivors over. Give everybody a heads-up."

"What? Already?" Celeste answered back, her voice loud
enough to make Jeth wince. "Who are they? And how do
you know they're not diseased, or psychos who'll kill us in
our sleep?"

Jeth turned away from the others and walked down the
corridor a couple of steps to avoid being overheard. "They're
not diseased or psycho, Celeste. Two of them are our age or
a little older and the third's just a kid."

Silence answered him, the pause long enough that he figured Celeste was pacified.

Wrong.

"I still don't like it, Jeth. Hold up and let me ask Milton if
he thinks it's safe."

"*No,*" Jeth said, putting as much authority into the command as he could without shouting. "I'm in charge, not
Milton. And leaving them over here is not an option. Now
get ready to open the airlock."

Celeste was silent once more, but he could picture her sitting over there, fuming.

"Fine," she answered at last. "But if you're wrong about those people, then *I'll* be the one murdering you in your sleep."

Jeth jumped up and grabbed the edge of the hatch. "Assuming they don't get you first."

"Ha. Ha. Seriously, Jeth. Have you thought about how you're going to hide three new passengers when we get back to Peltraz?"

He gritted his teeth. "Not yet. But we'll figure something out. One challenge at a time, same as always."

"If you say so."

Jeth heard a click as Celeste terminated the connection.

He reached down through the hatch, offering a hand to Sierra, but she waved him back. He obeyed, frowning in surprise as she jumped, grabbed the edge, and then hoisted herself up with perfect ease.

Pretty, feisty, and strong. That was a whole lot to like.

Don't be stupid, the voice of reason broke in. *You don't need that kind of distraction.*

No, he didn't. Girl distractions were the worst kind. Downright dangerous, as his brief thing with Celeste when they'd first met had taught him. They'd gotten into an argument on a job and nearly been caught by a couple of spaceport guards. They ended their brief romance shortly after, and Jeth had sworn off girls ever since. He focused all his energy on *Avalon,* the only girl he really wanted or needed.

Once all five of them were crammed inside the airlock,

Jeth opened the hatch and climbed out. Then he and the others pulled themselves over to *Avalon* using the towlines. Vince did it with Cora strapped to his back for safety.

The rest of the crew was waiting for them when they stepped out of *Avalon*'s airlock into the cargo bay. Jeth had known they would be, but that didn't make him any less annoyed by it. There were still so many questions he wanted answered, but he couldn't ask any of them with everybody else hanging about. He'd already made Shady swear not to tell the others about the strange damage on the *Donerail*. *No reason to induce panic.*

As Jeth pulled off his space suit, he kept his attention on Sierra. Vince might be the more physically imposing of the two, but Sierra was clearly the leader. And even though he'd told Celeste they weren't psychos, Jeth didn't exactly trust them. He'd given their weapons to Shady for safekeeping.

Sierra removed her suit quickly and then scanned the cargo bay with an appraising gaze. For some reason this made Jeth nervous, and he glanced around, trying to imagine what she was thinking.

Nothing good, he decided, taking in the dark stains on the floor. Most of the walls looked as if they were regularly used for target practice. They weren't—the bullet holes had been there for ages, since before his parents died—but he couldn't expect her to know that. To top it all off, exposed wiring hung here and there, and the water pipes were so rusted, they looked like they might start leaking at any moment. The gray color of everything in the place, combined with the dim lighting, gave it a cavelike atmosphere.

She must think Avalon's *a dump.* Jeth resisted an insane urge to start defending his ship to this stranger. It wasn't like him to give a damn about what other people thought, but something about Sierra seemed to challenge this attitude. He decided it was the regal way she carried herself: not stuck-up, exactly, but as if she were a princess who'd recently been forced into poverty.

Lizzie punched him in the arm, drawing his attention away from Sierra. "Aren't you going to introduce every-body?"

"Oh, right." Jeth motioned toward the crew and rattled off their names. Sierra then did the same for her group.

"So what are you guys still doing alive over there?" Flynn said.

Jeth winced. There had to be a better way to phrase it.

"I believe those questions can wait for now," said Milton. "I'd like to get our guests up to sick bay for an examina-tion, make sure everything's all right." For the first time in forever, he sounded like a real doctor, someone responsible and trustworthy. Like the man Jeth had known as a kid. Jeth might have introduced Milton as a doctor, but he'd done it only out of habit.

Sierra put a protective arm around Cora, who was leaning into her, hiding her face once again. "That won't be neces-sary for Cora and me. We're fine, but Vince has a wound that might be infected."

Vince shot her an annoyed look that she ignored.

Milton smiled, the gesture making the dark bags beneath

his eyes bulge. "I'll look at him first, but I need to check all of you, regardless."

"Cora is afraid of needles," Sierra said, her voice insistent.

"No needles, I promise."

Sierra opened her mouth to respond, but Lizzie squatted down, putting herself at eye level with the little girl. "Hey there, Cora." Her voice was warm and friendly, almost childlike. Unlike Jeth, she knew how to talk to little kids. It was another talent she'd inherited from their mother. "Do you happen to like kitties?"

Cora peered around Sierra's side and bobbed her head.

"I thought that might be the case. Well, it just so happens I have a kitty. His name is Viggo. Would you like to meet him?"

Delight lit Cora's face. "Yes, please."

"Okay, then." Lizzie stood and grinned at Sierra. "I'll bring Viggo in while Milton examines her." She winked down at Cora. "Kitties make everything less scary."

Cora giggled and for the first time stepped away from Sierra, who looked ready to haul her back again any second. Jeth supposed he couldn't blame her for being protective, considering what they'd just lived through.

"See?" Lizzie said to Jeth. "Bringing a cat on board was a *great* idea."

Before Jeth could finish rolling his eyes at her, she turned and dashed out of the cargo bay, eager to fetch Viggo.

"Follow me," Milton said, his tone suggesting how less than thrilled he was about having a four-legged visitor to his sick bay.

Sierra, Cora, and Vince fell in behind Milton.

The rest of the crew made to do the same, but Jeth waved them off. "They don't need an audience. Flynn, why don't you see about some food? Celeste and Shady, get the spare cabins ready."

Jeth didn't wait for confirmation of the tasks, but turned and hurried after Milton before the others could protest.

When they reached the common room on the deck above, Jeth invited Sierra and Cora inside while Milton led Vince up the stairs to sick bay.

As she had in the cargo bay, Sierra surveyed the room with a penetrating gaze, taking in the mismatching sofas and armchairs scattered haphazardly around the large circular gaming table in the center of the room.

The decorations on the walls were a conglomeration of all the crew's tastes. A man dressed like an old-timey cowboy and carrying an ancient pistol glared at them from a poster with the title of Shady's favorite movie across the bottom— *Harry Rides Again*. The cheaply framed photos of a panda, a koala, and a pack of wolves had come from Lizzie, while Celeste had contributed the row of tribal masks. Flynn was responsible for the still-life prints, which were mostly of food.

Sierra's gaze fell on the only quality painting in the room, one that had been hanging there as long as Jeth could remember. It had been his mother's favorite—a fantastical landscape, full of massive trees shrouded in mist and punctuated by plants so colorful no one would mistake them for real, no matter how many planets there were in the universe.

"Do you like it?" Jeth said, unable to resist the question. Sierra seemed transfixed by the painting.

She nodded. "It's Empyria, right? The lost planet?"

"Yeah, that's right." Jeth tried to keep the surprise from his voice. The legend of Empyria wasn't exactly obscure, but he didn't know many people their age who knew it well enough to recognize a painting of it. The only reason he knew about Empyria was because his mother had been obsessed with the myth. She'd once confessed to Jeth that the legend was one of the reasons she joined the ITA and became a space explorer. She'd been enchanted by the idea of an ancient, lost planet, one just waiting to be rediscovered.

"It's also supposed to be the first planet," Jeth added, "the so-called origin of all life in the universe. Not that I believe that or anything."

"It's so pretty," Cora said, staring up at it.

Sierra smiled down at the girl and then turned and sat on one of the sofas. She patted the seat beside her, and Cora joined her a moment later. Jeth took the armchair opposite them. It was his favorite, the lumps perfectly formed for his body.

A few awkward seconds passed while he tried to decide which question to ask her first. There were so many. Sierra watched him with that same mistrustful expression. Cora was watching him too, but her expression was now more curious than fearful. She was twirling a finger through her hair just like Lizzie sometimes did. He found himself staring back. Cora was so unusual looking, with her white-blond hair and dark, dark eyes. Exotic, really.

"I like this ship," Cora said. "It's bright and warm." She rubbed her arms enthusiastically.

Jeth smiled. "She's fast, too."

Cora's eyes widened, exposing more of the whites and making her look closer to ordinary. "Oh, can I see? I want to go fast."

Jeth chuckled. "I'm sure we will soon."

A huge smile broke across Cora's face, but it wasn't directed at him. Lizzie had arrived, carrying a struggling Viggo in her arms. Cora leaped up and raced over to them. Seconds later, she had managed to wrap her arms around the yellow-furred cat.

Lizzie convinced Cora to set Viggo down in the most open area in the room, not far from the door into the galley. The position placed them far enough away that Jeth decided he could ask Sierra some of his questions without being overheard.

"You really had no idea the *Donerail*'s been missing so long?"

"No, not at all."

"But how's that possible?"

Sierra shrugged, not meeting his eyes. "You saw the damage. How's any of it possible?"

Jeth frowned. Her response seemed believable enough, but her words sounded hollow. He could tell she was hiding something. But before he could press her, Sierra asked, "So what do you plan on doing with us now?"

"What do you mean?'

She rolled her eyes. "There's no reason to act innocent.

I know you didn't rescue us out of the goodness of your heart. You were hired to find that ship. Probably because of that secret weapon you mentioned."

Jeth sat up straighter in his chair. It was true, but he didn't care for the way she described the situation, like he was just some unfeeling mercenary. Well, he *was* a mercenary when it came down to it, but he cared about some stuff. His crew for one thing, and definitely his sister. "How did you know we were hired?"

She smirked. "You didn't expect me to believe you were just wandering around the Belgrave for the hell of it, did you?"

"No, I suppose not."

Her expression suggested she wasn't surprised by this admission. "So who do you work for?"

He debated whether to tell her the truth, but saw no reason not to. "Hammer Dafoe, governor of Peltraz Spaceport."

Sierra arched one eyebrow. "You mean the crime lord?"

Jeth scowled. She was far too knowledgeable for her own good. Or for his own good, rather. And this conversation wasn't going at all like he planned. *He* was the one who was supposed to be asking the questions. "Yeah, that's right. What of it?"

"Are you going to hand us over to him then?"

"I—" Jeth broke off, suddenly aware of how defensive he was getting. He shut his mouth and breathed in deep through his nose, trying to regain his focus. Ever since he'd found these people, he'd felt as if the floor beneath his feet had been tipped sideways.

Loud giggles on the other side of the room distracted him for a moment. It was a musical sound, oddly harmonic and soothing.

Fixing his gaze on Sierra, he said, "You're right that we were hired to find your ship, but you're a complication I hadn't planned for. All the passengers were supposed to be dead."

She swallowed. "We really have been missing for a long time, haven't we?"

Jeth nodded. "Matter of fact, I was under strict orders not to board the ship at all, which means I've no idea what to do about you three now."

Sierra met his eyes, her expression thoughtful. "Are you saying you'd rather your employer *not* know we were on board?"

"Yeah, I suppose I am."

A bright smile crossed Sierra's face. If he'd thought her pretty before, she was stunning now. Jeth blinked, feeling his face grow warm.

"I'm glad to hear you say that," Sierra said.

Jeth tilted his head sideways, more of her story coming into focus—a passenger on a smuggler's ship, the kind of smuggler who didn't ask questions about who you were or where you were going so long as you could pay. "So, who are you running away from? Or what?"

It was Sierra's turn to look surprised by his knowledge. "I . . ." She hesitated, uncertain, then her expression hardened. "It's complicated, and frankly, none of your business."

Jeth grinned, amused once again by her feistiness. He leaned back, assuming his most charming manner. "Okay. Then I guess you'll understand why—"

Crack.

Jeth jumped up, his stomach doing a hard dip. He looked around. The loud noise seemed to have come from everywhere.

Crack-crack-crack.

Pinning the direction of the sound, he glanced up. Sierra dashed across the room and picked up Cora, as if to protect her from incoming danger.

"What was that?" Lizzie said.

"It's happening here," Sierra said, her panicked gaze locked on Jeth. "Just like on the *Donerail*."

All the air vaporized from inside Jeth's lungs. Light-headed, he turned and sprinted out the door and up the stairs to the passenger deck. Sierra had to be wrong. What had happened to that ship couldn't be happening here. Not on *Avalon*.

Jeth glanced down the row of crew cabins at Celeste and Shady emerging from two of the rooms. They stared at him with matching stunned expressions. Farther down the row, Milton and Vince stood in the doorway to sick bay.

"Did that noise come from up here?" Jeth called. He was careful not to look at Vince, afraid of the comprehension he might see on his face.

"No," said Celeste.

"Check the other rooms," Jeth said. Then, swallowing back fear, he continued up the stairs to the bridge.

He froze mere steps into the room as the cracking sounds echoed again, punctuated by a flash of light so bright, it blinded him for a second. When his vision cleared, he saw that four perfectly symmetrical holes had appeared across the front of the nav station control panel. Each was the size of his fist. Panic rose up in his throat at the sight of them. The nav station monitor was dark, the system offline.

This couldn't be happening. He charged over to the nav station and started pressing buttons. Then he slapped it with the palm of his hand, desperate for the screen to power on. Without a functioning navigational system they could wander around lost in the Belgrave forever, never finding their way out again.

Jeth heard footsteps behind him and several gasps of fright.

"It's just like the *Donerail*," Vince said, his voice a low, ominous rumble.

Jeth turned to look at him, his terror a wild animal thrashing around inside his chest.

"We need to get out of here," Vince said. "Before this ship is torn apart."

CHAPTER

12

Jeth had known it even before Flynn crawled beneath the nav station to take stock of the damage. He stood by, watching Flynn's feet twitch back and forth as he worked and bracing for the worst. Only a few short minutes had passed since the holes had appeared, but each passing second felt like hours.

"Crap oh crap oh crap," said Flynn as he crawled out from underneath the nav station. "We are so screwed. I mean, screwed-screwed. Like, get-into-the-lifeboats-'cause-this-ship-is-going-down screwed."

"Flynn," Jeth hissed, crossing his arms. "This isn't the high seas. This is the middle of *space*. We don't have any lifeboats, and we don't need panic. We need solutions."

Flynn stood up, glaring. "I'm not a miracle worker, Jeth. We're light-years from the closest outpost or relay, and without a nav computer we can't calculate a safe path for the metadrive to jump us. Which means we're stuck here. Forever."

Jeth scowled, trying to ignore all the worried faces watching him right now. The bridge was entirely too crowded with everybody congregated there. "Thanks for enlightening us with the obvious. I'm sure we all feel better now."

"Well, good," Flynn shouted. "Glad I could help!"

"Why's that boy yelling?" Cora said.

Sierra shushed her. The two of them had been the last to arrive, and they now stood nearest the door, next to Lizzie, who was still clinging to Viggo. She didn't look like she was going to be able to help, and, given Flynn's attitude, it didn't seem likely a solution was going to come from him either. *There might not be a solution.*

No, there had to be.

"What about the shuttles?" said Shady. "Can we use the nav systems on them instead?"

Flynn shook his head. "They're network systems. Won't function if the main one's down."

"Oh," Shady said, rubbing his chin.

"Tell me something useful," said Jeth.

Flynn took a deep breath. "The good news is that whatever made these holes missed the memory banks, so the Explorer program your mom designed is still intact. But I can't repair the main unit without parts. The stuff's not broken, it's *gone.*" He waved at the holes, a desperate look on his face. "How'd it even happen?"

"I'll tell you how," said Shady. "It's the Belgrave. This place really is haunted. Or cursed or something."

"Don't be ridiculous," said Lizzie.

"I'm not," said Shady. "You didn't see what happened to the *Donerail*. It's—"

"Shut up, Shady," said Jeth. "That doesn't matter right now."

"But it does," said Sierra, stepping further in. "If you want to keep this ship intact, we need to find a way out of here."

Flynn grunted. "Now who's enlightening us with the obvious?"

Jeth grimaced—Flynn had a point. Still, Sierra had been dealing with this for some time. Maybe she or Vince knew something helpful. "I take it you have an idea?"

"Yes. We should be able to find replacement parts on the *Donerail.*" Sensing a protest, she addressed Shady. "Last we checked, the nav unit itself isn't damaged, just some of the external wiring into it."

Flynn took another deep breath. "Well, okay then. Let's do that."

"You think you can?" said Jeth. *Please say yes, please say yes.*

Flynn nodded, looking considerably calmer.

Jeth exhaled as some of the pressure that had been squeezing his chest eased.

That was until Lizzie said, "But what if it happens again before we're done?"

A vision of *Avalon* riddled with holes flashed in Jeth's brain, making his stomach clench. The feeling only worsened when he pictured what those holes would do to the crew if they were in the wrong place the next time it happened.

"If it goes down like it did on the *Donerail,*" said Vince, "then we've got a little time. It started off slow at first, just a couple here and there, and then it got worse at increasing intervals."

"How long?"

"A day. Maybe."

"Oh that's just great," said Flynn. "There's no way I can get this done that fast. The recalibration will take most of a day all by itself."

Jeth closed his eyes. The pressure around his chest strengthened again, cutting off his ability to breathe. *Avalon* had been wounded. She was in danger. All of them were.

Lizzie stepped forward, biting her lip. "We've been in the Belgrave almost a week and nothing like this happened until we got to this area of space. So if we jump out of this area, we should be safe again, right?"

Jeth looked at her, hoping that some brilliant idea was sprouting in her genius brain.

"Well, obviously," said Flynn, sneering. "That's why we've got to fix the nav computer."

Making a mental note to strangle Flynn later, Jeth kept his gaze locked on Lizzie. "What are you thinking?"

"If we can hardwire the portable maintenance computer into the metadrive control unit, I might be able jump us manually."

"That's insane," said Celeste. "Without navigation we'll be jumping blind. We could end up too close to a star or crash into the Belgrave's energy field or a hundred other things."

"That's just it," said Lizzie. "It won't be a blind jump. I think I can plot one."

"How?" asked Jeth.

Lizzie began to fidget, twirling a finger through her hair and shifting her weight from foot to foot. "I've got some detailed charts on the Belgrave. They're not complete, but I think it's enough that I can calculate a safe course."

"Where did you get these charts?" said Milton, voicing the question before Jeth could.

Lizzie glanced at him. "On a data crystal I found a couple of days ago." She shifted her gaze back to Jeth. "That's what I was going to tell you about this morning. I think it was Mom's. At least it's got a lot of her video journals and stuff on it, too. She must've hidden it in this little compartment inside the air vent in my room. Viggo got up there while we were in the Belgrave, and when I went to get him out, I found it."

A weakness struck Jeth's knees, and he wished he could sit down. Lizzie had found a lost relic from their parents' past? She might as well have found a ghost. The ITA had confiscated all their personal items when they'd been arrested "Why didn't you tell me when you found it?"

She shook her head.

After a moment Jeth nodded, intuitively understanding that she hadn't wanted to tell him. She wanted to explore the data alone for the same reasons he would've wanted to—the desire to experience this hidden piece of their parents' forgotten lives without having to share. No wonder she'd been spending those long hours in her cabin.

But what else was on the crystal? Why had their mother hidden it? With an effort, Jeth forced the questions away. There would be time for that later—he prayed.

He turned his attention to Sierra and Vince, once again hoping their experience on the *Donerail* might help. "Our mother was an ITA surveyor in the Belgrave. If she put these charts on this crystal, they're accurate. What do you think? Should we risk staying here or should we jump?"

Vince answered at once with no hesitation. "If you can't repair the nav by tonight, then jump."

"And I can help her set the coordinates," added Sierra. "I'm familiar with meta technology."

Jeth eyebrows shot up. Someone familiar with metatech? A teenager no less? But he didn't question her. No time to waste. Plus, he trusted Lizzie not to let anyone else trip her up. "All right. Let's do it then."

"Okay," said Lizzie. "I'll go get the data crystal. Be right back." She turned and left the bridge.

"And I guess I'll get the maintenance computer and start hooking it up to the metadrive system," Flynn said. He cast Sierra a somewhat dubious glance. "Do you want to help me?"

"Yes." She looked down at Cora. "I need you to stay with Vince for now. Okay?"

"Okay," Cora said.

"I still need to examine her," Milton said. "Just a routine check to make sure everything's all right. Besides, it'll give us something to do while we stay out of the way."

Sierra looked ready to argue, but Vince said, "She'll be fine. I'll make sure." Vince turned his gaze to Jeth. "But somebody should check the rest of the ship. It's possible there's more damage than what's up here."

Jeth swallowed. "Yeah, okay. Celeste and Shady and I can do that."

Vince nodded as he scooped up Cora. Then the two of them followed Milton off the bridge.

Sierra took a step toward Jeth, drawing his attention. "You might want to use one of the shuttles to check *Avalon*'s exterior, just in case. There could be damage to some of the shielding that's too minor to trigger any warnings. It couldn't hurt to check."

Jeth exhaled, then turned to Celeste and Shady. "I'll do a sweep of the ship with *Flash* and then check the engineering deck. Shady, you take the cargo deck, and Celeste, you check the common deck and *Sparky*. Once you two finish, tackle the passenger deck together. All right?"

"All right," Celeste said, then marched out the door with Shady following after her.

Jeth trailed behind them, afraid of what he might find. Once outside the bridge, he took the stairs up to the engineering deck. He scanned the machinery and the various equipment racks as he walked down the long bay toward the shuttle entrance. Nothing looked amiss, but he would have to check more closely once he finished the sweep.

He stopped beneath the ladder to the shuttle and pulled it down. Once inside *Flash*, he scanned around, relieved to see no obvious damage here either. And when he powered the shuttle on, everything booted up correctly except for the nav system display, which showed a "no signal" error across the screen. But that was okay. He didn't need the nav for this.

Jeth piloted *Flash* out of the dock and began his scan. He did four sweeps, just to be sure, but he found nothing amiss, not so much as a new scratch. He knew his ship well enough to be certain.

Relieved, Jeth docked the shuttle and stepped back down the ladder onto the engineering deck. He checked the time, pleased to find that he'd burned up forty minutes already. He was tempted to go down to the bridge to check on Lizzie's progress, but he resisted. He doubted she could be done yet, and he still needed to check all the equipment and machinery up here.

A loud shriek from behind him made him jump. He spun around, certain the holes were about to start again. He spotted Cora dashing up the stairs toward him, hot on Viggo's tail. The cat's paws, ill adapted for the hard floor of the engineering deck, slipped out from underneath him, forcing him to take an extra four strides for every normal-sized step forward, but still he managed to escape her, disappearing underneath one of the racks.

Jeth sighed. *And this is why cats have no business on starships.*

Cora slid to a stop, and the crestfallen look that came over her face was so miserable, Jeth almost laughed.

"Cora," Vince called as he marched up the stairs. "You can't just go running around by yourself."

"It's all right," Jeth said. He squatted before the little girl, taking pity on her. "If you want to catch a cat, you've got to use the right tools."

Cora looked up at him with her big dark eyes. "What kind of tools?"

"This kind." Jeth stood and walked to the maintenance cabinet near the stairs, where he knew Flynn kept old pieces of wiring that he thought might be usable for some future repair job. Jeth selected a suitable-sized piece and walked back to Cora. Kneeling, he slid one end of the wire underneath the rack where the cat had disappeared and started to wiggle it back and forth. In seconds, a furry yellow paw poked out, trying to snag the wire.

Jeth worked it back and forth, slowly coaxing the cat out while a delighted Cora watched.

The moment Viggo was fully out from underneath the rack, Cora grabbed him and hauled him into her arms. The cat struggled, but the little girl was too much for him, and after a moment he gave in to the inevitable and let Cora stroke his head and neck.

"Have you found anything?" Vince asked, now that Cora was distracted.

Jeth shook his head. "Nothing on the exterior, but I just got started in here."

"I'll help you look." Vince headed for the starboard side and began examining the first equipment rack.

Jeth took the rack opposite and did the same. They searched all the way down while Cora played with the cat. He was relieved when they reached the end of the deck without finding any holes. Only the metadrive compartment remained, but from the outside it looked as undisturbed as everything else.

Just as Jeth was about to pull open the door, a burst of white noise erupted around them. The screech was louder than any that had happened before, and it made Jeth's hair stand on end. Behind him, Cora cried out. He turned to see Viggo racing down the stairs away from them and Cora clutching her arm. At the sight of blood seeping out from the ragged scratch across the top of her hand, she started to cry.

Vince stooped and picked her up. "Shush. It's okay, Cora," he murmured, stroking her hair. He was so big, she seemed to disappear inside his arms. "It was just an accident. Doctor Milton will make it all better in a moment."

"Are you sure?" Cora said between sobs.

"I'm sure." Vince glanced at Jeth.

He waved them on. "I'll finish up here."

"Okay," Vince said, and he carried Cora toward the stairs.

Crack.

Jeth instinctively ducked at the sound that echoed as loudly as cannon fire. At the head of the steps, Vince did the same, wrapping his body completely around Cora as a human shield. Bright light filled the room, and Jeth shut his eyes, only to hear the loud shriek of metal splitting.

He opened them again. A smattering of fist-sized holes marked the wall near the stairs, exposing the ship's insides. Vince and Cora stood less than a meter away from them.

Jeth raced over. "Are you two all right?"

Vince nodded as he struggled to calm Cora.

Jeth turned toward the holes, examining them with his

heart in his throat. They weren't deep, and the area behind them appeared mostly empty. He didn't think anything critical had been damaged. At least not here.

"Take her to sick bay," Jeth said to Vince, and then he raced down the stairs toward the bridge, terrified at what he might find when he got there.

CHAPTER 13

"I NEED MORE TIME," LIZZIE SAID AS SHE STOOPED toward the maintenance computer's screen.

"We don't have more time." Jeth paced back and forth across the bridge. Once he'd determined no new damage had occurred, his impatience to get out of there had quadrupled.

"I *know.*" The glare she shot him was hot enough to incinerate. "But this isn't something you rush. One mistake and we all die."

Jeth stopped pacing, all the muscles in his body tense from the effort to be still. He knew pressuring her was counterproductive, but he was having a hard time keeping calm with his ship falling apart around him.

"You keyed that wrong," said Sierra from where she stood beside Lizzie. She pointed at the screen. "The last four should be eight, zero, one, five."

"Oh. Right." Lizzie made the correction.

Unable to stand inactivity a moment longer, Jeth said, "I'll go check on the others."

Sierra glanced up at him, her expression cool. "Sounds like a good idea. We'll be done soon. I promise."

Jeth didn't reply as he exited the bridge. He was determined to stay away until they were done. He wasn't stupid. He understood the danger of performing a manual jump. Navigating space wasn't like driving a land vehicle. It was like jumping blindfolded off the top of a building and trying to catch hold of a passing jet. At least that was how Jeth imagined it in terms of difficulty. One single decimal point of miscalculation and the jump could be off by hundreds of light-years, launching them out of metaspace into anywhere.

Or nowhere at all.

Shuddering, Jeth headed back up to engineering. Flynn stood near the top of the stairs, already making repairs to the new set of holes. He looked up at Jeth's approach.

"Anything important damaged?" asked Jeth.

Flynn grimaced. "Nothing I can't repair, but only because I'm brilliant and I stocked up on supplies before we left Peltraz." He pulled a piece of candy out of his pocket, unwrapped it, and popped it into him mouth.

Jeth considered asking him if by "supplies" he really meant chocolate, but he refrained. "Well, good thinking."

Flynn seemed surprised by the compliment, but it was momentary as he returned his attention to the task at hand. Jeth left him to it, heading down the stairs to the passenger deck. He heard voices from the common deck below, including Shady's, and figured he and Celeste must've finished their second damage sweep of the lower decks. He was about to head down to check for an update when he saw that Milton was still in sick bay.

The austere room was the only place aboard *Avalon* that Jeth ever found uninviting. Milton kept the place immaculately clean and organized, a complete one-eighty from the clutter of empty bottles in his cabin.

Milton looked up from where he stood in front of his main worktable. Some kind of medical instrument whose name and purpose Jeth didn't know sat on the table. A soft whirring sound issued from it.

"What are you doing?" Jeth said.

"Nothing important. Just some boring doctorish stuff." Milton pressed a button on the machine and the whirring stopped.

Jeth shook off his curiosity. Milton doing *anything* doctor related was better than his usual activities of boozing and pipe smoking. "Anything get damaged in here?"

"No. Everything's fine. You should check with the others."

"Did our passengers check out all right?"

Milton smiled. "Yes, at least Vince and Cora. I'm sure Sierra will pass inspection, too. They've been very lucky."

Depends on how you look at it, Jeth thought, considering everything that had gone wrong since he'd brought them on board. The desire to run back to the bridge and check on Lizzie's progress gripped him again. Ignoring it, Jeth said, "Yeah, very lucky." He inclined his head toward the doorway. "I'm gonna check in with Celeste and Shady."

Jeth headed down to the common deck, flinching at every sound he heard. He'd never before realized how noisy a starship could be. Even the low, constant hum of *Avalon*'s engines seemed ominous at the moment.

He arrived in the common area to find Celeste, Shady, and Vince standing in the middle of the room and looking down at one of the armchairs—his favorite one. Jeth spotted the holes in it right away.

Son of a bitch.

Lucky, indeed.

"Is that the extent of the damage?" Jeth asked, motioning toward the chair. It wasn't entirely ruined, but he doubted it would be very comfortable to recline in anymore with the series of holes running up its back.

"Yes," Celeste said. "Unless there's some in the cabins. We haven't checked them yet."

Jeth grunted. "I guess one damaged armchair is good news."

Cora, who had been sitting on the sofa when Jeth arrived, stood up and walked over to him. "See my bandage?" She held up her arm. Milton had placed a small white bandage over where the cat had clawed her.

"Um, yeah. It's great, Cora."

She beamed at him.

Feeling awkward, although mildly pleased by the kid's delight, Jeth cleared his throat. But whatever he'd intended to say got lost, as Lizzie's voice echoed out from the comm speakers. "We're ready."

Without a word, Jeth turned and bolted up the stairs. Lizzie was already sitting in the copilot chair with Sierra at the nav.

Jeth sat down in the pilot chair and looked toward his sister. "Are you sure you're done?"

She nodded, her expression a little too fearful for comfort.

Jeth glanced at Sierra in a silent question.

"The calculations are as accurate as humanly possible."

Jeth grimaced. Whatever that meant. He turned back to the front and switched on the main comm. "We're jumping now, people. Get ready." Then, not bothering with goggles, he leaned forward and placed his finger against the button that would the engage the jump. Butterflies flitted through his stomach. "I guess if this doesn't work none of us will be around to complain about it, right?"

"Not funny, Jeth," Lizzie said.

He exhaled and pushed the button.

The familiar weightlessness came over him, same as always. But then it changed, and everything felt wrong. The weightlessness wasn't definite like it should be, but tenuous, as if he were being held in a spiderweb that might break any moment. Even worse, he was so *aware* of being in that state. Never before had he been conscious of his thoughts while in that suspended, living-death moment.

It lasted too long. Normally, traveling through metaspace was like being swallowed by a giant animal that found you distasteful at once and spit you out again. Not this time, though. The animal held on, as if it never intended to let go.

What seemed like hours later, they finally came through on the other side of the jump. Jeth stood up, stooped over, and dry heaved a couple of times. His insides felt as if they'd been run through a meat grinder. Lizzie was dry heaving, too. Jeth looked over at Sierra and saw her face had turned an alarming shade of green.

"Was that more Belgrave crap?" he asked, pressing his palms against his temples to still the pounding in his skull.

Sierra shook her head, unable to speak, it seemed.

He turned and checked the system readouts, making sure the *Donerail* had made it through the jump. Then he turned back to Lizzie, who looked better recovered. "Any idea where we are?"

"No, not yet." She placed her shaking hands on the control panel. "I'll run an area scan."

Jeth patted her back. "We're still, alive, Liz. That's good enough."

She ignored him, her concentration completely focused on the screen as she started running the scan. Knowing it would take a few minutes, Jeth called down to the common room to check on Celeste and the others.

"Nobody puked," Shady told him, which Jeth guessed meant they were fine.

Next Jeth checked in with Milton in sick bay and then with Flynn in the engine room. Everybody had come through the jump okay, and they were all still here. No unexplained vanishings.

Finally, Lizzie said, "I don't believe it." A huge grin split her face.

"What?" Jeth and Sierra said in unison.

"We're not far from the Belgrave border. I don't know where we'll come out exactly, but we made it!"

Jeth squeezed her shoulder. "I knew you could do it."

Lizzie smirked up at him. "Of course. That's 'cause I'm the best."

"Well, every now and again, I suppose."

Flynn's voice came over the intercom. "Um, Jeth. Can you come up to the engineering room a sec? We got a little problem."

Dread did a tap dance on Jeth's chest, stomping out his relief at once. He flipped on the comm switch. "What is it?"

"I need to show you."

Please don't let it be any more holes. Jeth swept his gaze over Lizzie and Sierra. "Stay here. I'll be back."

He exited the bridge, taking the stairs up to the engineering deck two at a time. He spotted Flynn standing beside the metadrive compartment. There wasn't any new damage in the room that he could see.

"What is it?" Jeth said, worry making him breathless.

Flynn's gaze shifted to the metadrive compartment, then back to Jeth. "Um, I'm no expert or anything, but I'm pretty sure the metadrive is shot."

Jeth didn't respond. He couldn't. This wasn't happening. It wasn't possible. Not on *Avalon*.

"I figured after that jump there might be something wrong," Flynn went on. "It's never felt like that before. And—"

"Just show me."

Tight-lipped, Flynn slid open the door into the compartment.

Jeth's body went numb. Normally, the power source of *Avalon*'s metadrive was a swirl of purples in every shade. But not anymore. The porous material had faded to ash around the edges near the frame, with myriad pale streaks running through its center like a web. It was just like what he'd seen on the *Montrose*, but worse. Much worse.

"I don't think we'll be making any more jumps anytime soon," Flynn said, quite unnecessarily.

Jeth wanted to punch him, if only to have an outlet for his anger and the despair fueling it. He ran his hands through his hair instead.

"Any idea where we are?" said Flynn.

Jeth exhaled. "Close to the border out of this damned place."

"But that's great." Flynn clapped once in emphasis. "We just fly over the border and call Hammer to come get us."

Jeth didn't say anything. It was definitely the obvious solution, but not one he wanted to take. Not yet. He still had a couple of days before the deadline. If he called Hammer now, there was no way to hide the three extra people on board. Hammer would void their deal about *Avalon*, and if they were lucky, that was all he'd do. Then again, Jeth still doubted Hammer planned to honor the deal anyway. So what did it matter?

You could call Renford.

Yes, he could. But was that the better option? He didn't trust the ITA. Renford might've been lying; he might arrest them instead. He knew they were thieves, after all. Even if Renford did follow through with getting *Avalon* for him, there was no guarantee he would protect them from Hammer afterward. And Hammer would certainly seek revenge after a betrayal like that. If he caught them, he might decide to turn Jeth and the other boys into members of his Guard, implants inserted into their brains, all identity erased. And there was no telling what he would do with the girls.

That was a lot to risk. Maybe too much. Jeth didn't know what to do. He needed time to think.

Flynn cleared his throat. "So, what's the plan now, Boss?"

"Nothing. It's been a stressful enough day already, so for now let's keep this between us."

"Sure, okay."

Jeth couldn't tell if it was relief or concern he heard in Flynn's voice. He decided it didn't matter. He turned and left the engineering room, fighting back the rising despair that threatened to overwhelm him.

He kept it at bay long enough to convince the others that nothing was wrong and that whatever repairs and plans they needed to make could wait until they'd had a good night sleep. He made sure that Sierra, Vince, and Cora got something to eat and a chance to clean up. Then, once they were settled into their cabins, he retreated to his quarters.

The moment he was alone, the dam of emotions broke inside him. It was so horribly, impossibly unfair. Seven years *Avalon* had been imprisoned at Hammer's spaceport. Seven years Jeth had dreamed and planned and hoped for his freedom. And now, just when he was on the verge of succeeding, this happened.

Even if he had money, there weren't any metadrives he could buy. For every metadrive the Shades managed to steal, Hammer had ten customers in line to buy it, customers who bid up the price well beyond what Jeth could afford to pay.

Hell, he couldn't even buy a different ship. The money he earned toward *Avalon* went directly to Hammer, kept in trust. *I'll be stuck working for him forever.* The bitter thought burned its way through Jeth's body like acid in his veins.

He stretched across the bed, burying his face in the pillows. For so long he'd thought *Avalon* was the answer, the ultimate solution. He was wrong. She was just a ship, an object that could break and fail him as easily as his parents had failed him. As Milton had.

For the first time in his life the idea that freedom might not exist at all threatened to overwhelm him. Was the promise of freedom just something the desperate and oppressed clung to because they didn't have anything else? Had it always been just a dream, a fantasy built up in the mind of a boy forced to grow up too soon?

Jeth didn't know. And as the hours ticked by, he tried to convince himself that he didn't care.

CHAPTER 14

JETH STARED THROUGH THE FRONT WINDOWS OF THE BRIDGE, not really looking at the sea of black punctuated by bits of light. It was early but he was wide-awake, his mind a tempest of thoughts, all of them the wrong ones. He should have been thinking about what to do, whether to call Hammer or Renford.

Instead he was thinking about the last time he'd seen his parents. The memory was far hazier than he could've imagined. It didn't seem all that long ago, and yet the memory felt ancient. He couldn't recall the exact sound of their voices. The ITA had confiscated all their old video journals. Their faces were easy; he had lots of photos, but the voices were hard, almost impossible to remember.

Instead of his father's deep baritone telling Jeth they would be back in a couple of months and that he should look after his sister and focus on his studies, he kept hearing Milton's gravel-lined voice. Instead of his mother's throaty laugh as she kissed Lizzie's head, tickling her to keep her from crying, he heard Celeste's full-bellied one.

Jeth might not be able to remember his parents as well as he wanted, but he had no trouble remembering himself and how unconcerned he'd been about saying good-bye that day. He'd been impatient to see his friends, waiting for him at Metis Academy, the ITA-run boarding school on Therin where he lived during the long periods of time when his parents were out exploring. If he'd known it was the last time he was going to see his parents, he would've paid more attention. He would've hugged his mother longer and not protested when she kissed him on the cheek.

He would've begged them not to go.

For a moment his longing for them was so strong, he almost forgot where he was—in the Belgrave Quadrant with a world full of trouble waiting just over the border.

Jeth closed his eyes and rubbed his temples, wishing he could scrub away the memories. Especially the ones that came afterward, when his parents returned from that last trip. All the news stories and the whispers from the other kids at school—*Arrested for treason. Sealed trial. Execution.* He never got to see them. Not even to say good-bye.

Why was he thinking about this now? Why did his parents' death seem so near after years of distance?

Down deep inside him, he knew the answer. For the first time in long time he wished for a parent to make the hard choices for him. But he refused to admit it. Instead, Jeth told himself it was just because they were in the Belgrave and because of the data crystal Lizzie had discovered. He'd briefly considered asking to see it last night, but with the shock of *Avalon*'s metadrive failing, he hadn't had the will to face anything else painful. Besides, examining its contents wouldn't help him make a decision about what to do next.

Hammer. Renford. Hammer. Renford. Which one? Neither? Have to choose.

"Good morning."

Jeth lurched up from his chair and spun around, completely caught off guard. Sierra stood behind him. He had no idea how she'd managed to get so close without him hearing. A head taller, he frowned down at her. The last thing he wanted was company. Especially hers. She was one-third the cause of his trouble.

"What are you doing up here?" he snapped.

A look of surprise crossed Sierra's face followed by a glower. "Excuse me. I didn't realize the bridge was *off-limits*." She turned around so fast, her ponytail swatted him in the face.

Jeth scowled after her, resisting an urge to give her hair a good hard tug.

At once guilt pricked his insides. She didn't deserve the brunt of his bad mood. "Wait a second."

She froze, then turned to face him, crossing her arms in front of her. "What?"

To his surprise, her annoyed expression made him want to laugh. It reminded him a bit of Viggo when Jeth had accidentally stepped on the cat's tail—pissed off but incredibly cute in a fearsome, fuzzy sort of way.

Oh, she's more than cute. Jeth ignored the thought as he forced his eyes to stay on her face and not wander to any other parts of her he might find distracting. Not that her face wasn't a distraction all by itself. She looked better after a night's sleep, bright-eyed and less pale.

He rubbed his cheek where her hair had lashed him. "I didn't mean to snap. You just startled me, is all. How'd you manage to do that, anyway?"

A smirk curled her lips. "You mean walk about without making all kinds of noise? Easy—I'm a girl."

Jeth snorted. "Right. Well, even so, you shouldn't sneak up on a person like that."

"Why? Are you afraid of me?" she said, a tease in her voice.

He grinned. "You did try to kill me the first time we met."

"Yes, but I imagine a professional thief like you gets that a lot."

Jeth's good humor flipped back to bad. "How do you know about that?"

The smile slid from Sierra's face. "Um, Shady mentioned it," she said at last. "He said you're known as the Malleus Shades. It's . . . catchy. *Malleus*, the Latin word for hammer."

I'm going to kill him. Jeth took a deep inhale. "So, what do you want? 'Cause I know you didn't come up here this early to discuss my line of work."

Sierra's expression turned serious. "I came to talk to you about what's happening to *Avalon's* metadrive."

Jeth gritted his teeth. "What do you know about it? Have you been wandering around my ship in the middle of the night?"

"No—"

"Lemme guess, Flynn told you."

She shook her head. "No one told me. They didn't have to. I know the symptoms of drive failure, and it's exactly what we felt in that last jump."

"Really. So how does somebody like you know so much about metatech?"

"Because I'm ITA."

"What are you talking about?"

"I'm an ITA agent."

Jeth scoffed. "That's impossible. What are you, sixteen?"

Sierra put her hands on her hips. "Seventeen, not that it matters. I joined the ITA at fifteen, spent a year and a half as a probationary agent, and received full field status a few months ago."

Jeth crossed his arms. "You'll understand if I find that hard to believe. I know a thing or two about the ITA. You can't even submit an application until you're seventeen." He knew this well, because when he was a kid it was all he'd ever wanted: to be old enough to join the ITA and to become a space explorer alongside his parents.

"I didn't *apply*. I was recruited."

The idea made him cringe. It was a concept he associated with Hammer, the way he was always seeking out new talent, new blood. "Why would the ITA want to recruit a kid?"

"Because I'm gifted, but if you don't believe me . . ." She reached into her pocket and withdrew an item he had no trouble recognizing—the badge of an ITA agent, with the star and eagle emblem.

Jeth stared at it, incredulous. Sierra certainly wasn't dumb, but would the ITA actually go so far as to recruit her? It broke every ITA rule and regulation that he knew of. And yet the concept wasn't farfetched at all—that is, if he replaced "ITA" with "Hammer."

Jeth held out his hand, and she gave him the badge. He examined it carefully. It certainly seemed genuine. Then his mind made a new connection. "You're on the run from *them*, aren't you? The ITA?"

"Correct," Sierra said, her voice clipped.

Jeth thought about Renford, trying to remember everything about their brief meeting. He'd mentioned only the ship, saying nothing about survivors. Jeth had assumed that, like Hammer, the ITA was only after the weapon on board and didn't believe there would be survivors—that the ship had been missing two months and not two weeks like Sierra insisted. And yet Sierra being an ITA protégé couldn't be coincidence, could it?

He considered telling her about Renford but held back, worried that she would clam up and refuse to tell him more. "Why are you on the run?" he asked, trying to sound casual as he handed her back the badge. If he could get her talking, get her to trust him, she might reveal more on her own.

Sierra stared at him for several long seconds, considering her answer carefully. She slid the badge into her pocket. "Once you join the ITA, you can't quit. They don't tell you that beforehand, and I found it out the hard way. But I didn't like being *owned*. I didn't know it would be like that, with them dictating your every move, every decision. I wanted to be free to live my life on my own terms."

Something moved inside Jeth's chest, a feeling like butterflies. Only it had nothing to do with nerves but rather like calling to like. Her words might've been stolen right out of his own mind, his heart. He cleared his throat. "Yeah, I understand that."

She sighed. "I imagined you would. I know the story about your parents."

Jeth blinked. He hadn't been thinking about his parents at all, but he wasn't surprised she knew the story, given her background. That must be why she had recognized his last name when he introduced himself. And what she said made sense. Their lives had been fully bought—and expended—by the ITA's will.

Shaking off uncomfortable connections, he asked, "What about Vince? Is he ITA, too?"

"He was an elite combat soldier."

"And now he's a deserter."

Sierra flinched. "Yes, but not because he's a coward. We both learned some awful truths about the ITA. Things neither of us could stomach. Stuff so horrible you couldn't imagine."

Jeth slid his fingers into the belt loops of his pants, more curious about what she knew than he cared to admit. "Oh, I can imagine a lot. But no worries here. Anybody who's ever told the ITA to piss off is welcome on my ship."

Some of the tension in Sierra's body eased a little. "Good

to know. So I guess this means you can understand why I'm so concerned about what you decide to do next."

Jeth gritted his teeth, knowing exactly what she was getting at even though he hadn't agreed to anything yesterday. "You don't want me to call Hammer to come fetch us." Of course she didn't. If Hammer found out they were wanted by the ITA, he would turn them in and collect the bounty. The ITA did not take desertion lightly.

Jeth turned and sat down, falling into the chair as he ran his fingers through his hair. He wanted to yank it out, if only it would relieve the pressure inside his skull. Maybe the pain would inspire him to some solution to the problem. But in his heart he knew he had to call Hammer. It was the only choice. How could he call Renford now, knowing Sierra and Vince were ITA fugitives?

Jeth looked up at her. "I don't want to call him either, but I'm out of options."

"No, you're not. I've another option. One that will solve both our problems."

"Yeah, and what's that?"

"Your sister told me about your deal with Hammer for this ship." Sierra motioned to the bridge. "I know how much it means to you, but a ship without a metadrive is practically worthless to anyone who wants to come and go as they please."

Jeth exhaled, his fury with Lizzie a dead weight against his chest. How dare she share such secrets with these strangers? *She was under a lot of pressure with the manual jump,* his conscience reminded him. And no doubt she'd blathered out of nerves. But that didn't excuse it. She'd exposed a powerful pressure point for Sierra to use against him. "What does that matter?" he said.

"Because I have a way for you to get a replacement metadrive."

Jeth snorted. He'd been wrong about her. She wasn't smart. She was crazy. "Oh sure, because those are just lying about for the taking."

"You can get anything if you've got the right bargaining chip."

"Like what?"

"Like the weapon Hammer is after."

Jeth narrowed his gaze. "You said you didn't know anything about a weapon."

Sierra folded her arms. "I lied."

"Well then, now I'm ready to believe everything you say."

She tapped her foot. "I didn't know if I could trust you, and ignorance is safety."

"Not to mention an ace in the hole, right?"

"Right." She drew a breath and let the air out through her teeth. "Also, I didn't realize what you were talking about at first. What he's after isn't a weapon in the traditional sense. It's not an explosive or viral or anything like that."

"Oh yeah? Then what the hell is it?"

"The most dangerous weapon there is: information. And I happen to know exactly how much it's worth."

"How much?"

Her lips parted in a smile. "It's *priceless*."

Jeth slowly exhaled, not daring to believe. Information, she said. A dangerous weapon. He did a mental review of the conversation with Hammer, remembering the way he'd stumbled ever so slightly when he'd first mentioned the weapon. Had he lied? *Of course he did. He's Hammer.*

But Jeth wasn't biting. Not yet. "Okay, tell me more. Why do you think this information is the weapon that Hammer's after?"

"Because it was the only thing of real value on the *Donerail*. There were a couple of crates of guns and ammunition, but I imagine Hammer has plenty of those types of conventional weapons already."

Jeth thought about it, conceding the point. "All right. Then what exactly is this information?"

"The code name the ITA uses for it is the Aether Project."

Jeth ear's prickled with recognition. He'd heard that title somewhere before, a long time ago. His mom and dad had mentioned it a couple of times between themselves in whispered conversations he wasn't meant to overhear.

"What it contains is everything there is to know about metatech," Sierra continued. "Where it comes from, how it's manufactured. Everything. The entire project is on a data cell that I have hidden on the *Donerail* for safekeeping."

Jeth's head spun with questions and doubts. If she was telling the truth, kings, dictators, and other world leaders would give anything to possess it. For centuries, the ITA had held the monopoly on space travel, charging whatever they wanted for the use of metatech. Breaking that monopoly would indeed be priceless. And keeping it in place would mean a lot to Hammer. Without the monopoly, his metatech black market would crumble. And it obviously explained the ITA's interest in retrieving the ship.

Still, Jeth wasn't about to take her word on it without proof. "You say that you've got this data cell hidden on the *Donerail*. But how did you come to possess something so valuable in the first place?"

Sierra grimaced. "Not easily."

Jeth couldn't help the grin that spread across his face. "Are you implying that *you* stole it?"

She stood up straighter, that affronted kitten look on her face again. "And why is that so hard to believe?"

"Well, as you pointed out, I happen to know a thing or two about thieving, and I imagine stealing that kind of information would take a lifetime of experience and a planet's worth of funding. Where was this project kept, anyway?"

"On First-Earth."

Jeth laughed. "So you're telling me you managed to escape from the heaviest ITA-traveled bit of space in the universe with that kind of booty in tow—and not get caught?"

"We had a lot of help."

"Yeah, from who?"

"The captain of the *Donerail* for one. But that's not the point, anyway."

No, he supposed it wasn't. The point was whether or not she was full of it. If not, this might be the answer to all his problems. But it was too soon to get his hopes up.

Jeth leaned forward, pinning her with his gaze. If she was lying, he would catch her on it. "Okay, next question. How does a probationary agent in the ITA gain access to the project in the first place?"

Sierra scoffed. "I already told you that I made *full* agent. Not that you have room to talk about being young."

"This isn't about me. It's about you convincing me that this isn't some kind of hoax. I've never met anybody who knows a thing about meta technology. Even my parents didn't know, and they were pretty high up in the ITA at one point."

The scornful look vanished from her face. She let out a breath. "I suppose it's a little hard to believe from your perspective. So I'll tell you what I can of my story, okay?"

Jeth sat back, arms folded. "I'm all ears."

Sierra took a deep breath. "Like I said, I'm only seventeen, but I've been an agent for two years now. I have an extremely high IQ and a certain aptitude for biology and genetics. These skills made me valuable to the Aether Project scientists, and they offered me an internship. Eventually, I was given more and more access to the project, which was how I ended up with a chance to take the data."

Jeth slid his tongue against his teeth, thinking it over. She didn't appear to be lying, and he had no trouble believing the IQ bit, although he didn't understand what biology and genetics had to do with metatech. No, it was the thieving he didn't believe. "Why?"

"Why what?" Exasperation colored Sierra's voice.

"Why did you steal it?"

A flush blossomed in her cheeks, and she said through gritted teeth, "The same reason anybody steals something. For the money."

"True enough," Jeth said, thinking about his own employment situation. Yet he didn't believe that motivation in her. She struck him as a girl who'd grown up in a moneyed household, what with her smarts and proper speech and what might be considered aristocratic good looks. "But you don't exactly seem like the type desperate enough for cash to pull off something so tough."

"You're wrong," she snapped back. "I already told you that I wanted out of the ITA and so did Vince. We needed something valuable enough to buy our protection. The Aether Project is it. Once the information is out there, the

ITA will be too concerned with trying to hold on to their power to worry about us anymore. And then there was Cora to think about, too."

"Cora?" Jeth had completely forgotten about her. How did she fit into all of this?

"Yes, Cora. She was in a bad situation. Her father was one of the scientists on the project. A horrible, abusive man. I had to get her out of there."

"I'm sorry to hear that," Jeth said, horrified by the idea of someone abusing Cora. No wonder the girl clung to Sierra. A swell of sympathy made his throat burn. "What about her mother?"

"She . . . I never met her mother."

Jeth frowned. What was she hiding? Then a more

troubling thought occurred to him. "But why you? I mean, why would you do it? Is she a relative? A sister? Or are *you* her mother?"

"Of course I'm not her mother," Sierra said. "She's six, almost seven. Physiologically impossible."

"Right." He should have known that. "So, sister then?"

"No."

"Then what is it?" Tension spread through Jeth's body as he waited for an answer. He needed it to be a good one, an explanation he could embrace and believe. Otherwise he would have to dismiss all this as one horrible, cruel lie.

"It's . . . it's because she's me." Sierra bit her lip. "I mean, she reminds me of me, and my situation growing up."

The atmosphere seemed to thicken, as if her words were made of some kind of dense gas that drove the oxygen from the air. He didn't know what to say. This girl was a stranger and the topic so personal. He felt guilty for forcing the confession out of her.

After a moment, Sierra went on. "I'm adopted, Jeth. Vince and I both were, actually, by the same man."

"You're brother and sister?"

"Not by blood, but in every other way, yes."

"Then why the two last names?"

"Our guardian insisted on it. For reasons that were all his own. He . . . he isn't *sane*, I don't think. He was an ITA soldier, and he raised us to be like him, tough and brave and fighters. His methods were harsh."

As she was speaking, Jeth noticed the unconscious way

she was rubbing the fingers of one hand over the knuckles of the other in a nervous habit. To his shock, he realized her fingers were deformed. It wasn't severe, but the knuckles were larger and knottier than they should've been, and several of the digits were crooked. Almost as if they'd been . . . *broken*. Repeatedly, by the look of it. No wonder Vince was so protective of her. Jeth found himself wanting to comfort her, but he didn't know how.

"My attachment to Cora just sort of happened," Sierra went on. "Her father was my superior. We worked long hours, sometimes through the night. At first I was occasionally required to watch her for an hour or two. Then later I volunteered to spend time with her. She grows on you."

"Yeah, I can see that," Jeth said. He'd only known the girl for a day and already the idea of someone *hurting* her made him want to break things. Like her dad's face.

Jeth swallowed, believing her story at last. "So what kind of deal are you offering?"

Relief appeared in Sierra's expression. "I want you to guarantee that you won't call Hammer until after Cora, Vince, and I are off this ship and far away from here. In return, I will get you a new metadrive."

"Okay. How?"

"Before the *Donerail* got lost, we were on our way to Olympia Seven to meet with the buyer we'd lined up. He's a very wealthy man who operates completely off the grid. He's got an entire arsenal of metadrives at his disposal. He's made a habit of collecting backups, even failed drives, for years now. And I know he wants the Aether Project badly enough that he won't even blink at giving up one of them. All you have to do is fly *Avalon* out of the Belgrave long enough to make the call and then we come back in and wait for him to arrive."

Jeth leaned back in the chair. "That's an interesting deal, but it seems to me that the Aether Project is worth a helluva lot more than a single metadrive."

Sierra scowled. "Are you angling for a cut?"

"Of course. It's what I do, sweetheart."

The look on her face suggested she would like to gouge out his eyes. He didn't find it nearly so amusing this time. In fact, he felt like just accepting her offer outright, her words from earlier echoing inside him—freedom, like calling to like.

But he couldn't just accept, not with so much on the line. He'd been living this life too long, knew too well that you couldn't let opportunity for gain pass you by, not even to do the right thing. The right thing got you nowhere. Got you dead. And Sierra needed his help too desperately. She was stuck on his ship with no chance of escape or rescue, at the mercy of whatever he decided to do next.

"The alternative," Jeth said, "is that I cross the border and call Hammer. Then let *him* decide how much of a cut the crew and I deserve." That would be the wisest thing to do, really, the safest. As much as he hated Hammer, the idea of betraying him scared Jeth to the core. The back of his neck prickled at the thought of one of those brain implants.

"Really?" Sierra arched an eyebrow. "But I thought

Hammer will void the deal once he finds out you boarded the *Donerail*. Which he will surely know with three strangers on your ship."

Yeah, but at least I'll get to live a little longer. Then again, if they pulled off this exchange, Hammer would never have to know about the betrayal. That was a risk Jeth was willing to take if it meant keeping his ship flying. He stretched out his arms, feigning boredom. "That's possible. Then again, he might be grateful that I managed to hand him something so valuable."

"Only a fool would think Hammer would spend a single uni more than he has to."

The words stung, but Jeth didn't let his reaction show. She was right. But Jeth knew a thing or two about bargaining— you never took the first offer.

After a few tense moments, Sierra drew a quick breath. "Fine. I'll give you ten percent. But that's it."

Jeth tented his fingers beneath his chin as he stared her down.

Sierra put both hands on her hips. "Come on, Jeth. I'm the best chance you have of keeping this ship viable. Even if Hammer sells *Avalon* to you, she'll be worthless without a metadrive. That is, unless you think Hammer will be generous enough to just give you one himself."

Jeth suppressed a scowl, hearing the certainty in her voice that Hammer would do no such thing. "All right. Fifteen percent and it's a deal." Fifteen percent of a whole bunch would still be a whole bunch. And besides, another idea had taken shape in his mind—a backup plan, insurance. Sierra's replacement metadrive would solve the mechanical problem with his ship, but it did nothing about the ownership issue. Jeth needed a way to guarantee Hammer would give him *Avalon*. And the Aether Project was just the leverage to do it. He just needed to make a copy.

If Sierra's plan went down the way he foresaw it, Jeth would turn the *Donerail* over to Hammer with every appearance that the job had gone smoothly—that they'd just found the ship and brought it out, simple as that. Once Hammer got done searching the *Donerail*, he would realize the Aether Project wasn't there. All he would have was a worthless, derelict ship. But he would have no reason to blame Jeth. Afterward, when Jeth pressed Hammer to honor their deal with *Avalon*, if the big guy refused or balked in any way, Jeth would play his ace—offering him up the Aether Project in exchange for the ship and his freedom. It was risky, but he knew it could work if he took the necessary precautions. The information was too valuable for Hammer not to bargain. And all Jeth had to do to pull it off was make a copy of the data cell. Then Sierra could sell the first one to her contact with no one being the wiser.

"So, what do you say?" Jeth said.

Sierra sighed. "I guess I can live with fifteen percent."

"Good. So you've got the data cell hidden?" asked Jeth, trying to sound casual.

Sierra frowned. "Yes, somewhere only I can find it."

Of course it was. She wasn't stupid. You didn't keep

something so valuable in your pocket where it might get damaged or lost or discovered. For a brief moment he considered just asking if he could make a copy, but he abandoned the idea at once. The more copies that existed of the data, the less valuable it would become, and she struck him as the honest type, for the most part. Besides, he had a feeling she wouldn't be keen on handing that kind of information over to a man as power-hungry and ruthless as Hammer. Under normal circumstances, Jeth wouldn't either, but this was his best chance of getting his ship.

"Well, I'm going to have to see it. I need some proof that all this is for real," Jeth said in his most diplomatic and reasonable voice.

Her eyes narrowed on his face. "Why would I lie about it?"

He resisted the urge to squirm. "All sorts of reasons." Not that he could think of any right now. He decided not to press. "Okay, I understand." If she wouldn't show him the data, he would have to find it on his own. Lizzie might have some tool or gadget to help him. He just needed time.

Jeth searched his mind for a reason to stall, the answer coming easily. "But we have to do this seamlessly. No signs that you three were ever here. That means we've got to repair the nav system so we can send your buyer specific coordinates on where to meet us. Otherwise, we would have to wait around while he triangulates our position through the communication link. That'll take time, and every second we're outside the Belgrave we risk getting picked up by the ITA."

Sierra rubbed her knuckles. "Yes, you're right. The less we're outside, the better."

"Yep." And doing those repairs meant time aboard the *Donerail* and a chance to search for the hidden data cell. They had a couple of days to spare before their two-week deadline for contacting Hammer. Even if he had to rummage through every nook and cranny, Jeth would find it. Sierra might even give away the location through some unconscious gesture. He would just have to pay attention.

"So, does this mean we have a deal?" Sierra said.

Jeth assumed his most charming smile. "It's a deal."

CHAPTER 15

JETH WAITED UNTIL AFTER EVERYONE HAD EATEN BREAK-fast before telling the crew the plan to get a new metadrive. He told them most of it, anyway. Even though Sierra, Vince, and Cora had retreated to their cabins to give the crew time to discuss in private, Jeth kept the part about using the Aether Project as leverage against Hammer to himself. The others didn't need to know that part. At least not yet.

"So is everybody okay with what we're going to do?" Jeth asked.

"I don't know," said Flynn. "This involves keeping a lot of secrets from Hammer. And some of us don't have the best track record with that." Flynn cast Shady a significant look.

Shady waved him off. "I know how to keep secrets when it really matters. Besides, if we do this right, Hammer won't have a reason to even question us. And that makes keeping quiet a cinch."

"He's not wrong," said Celeste. "Plus this might be our only chance to keep *Avalon* flying. It's not likely Hammer will just give us a metadrive out of the goodness of his heart."

"Right, and a ship like this without one is as good as junk," said Shady.

"Shady," Jeth said.

"No offense, Captain." Shady flashed a sheepish smile. "But you know what I mean."

Yes, he did. He had to get a new metadrive. If Hammer decided to renege on their deal, Jeth was pretty sure he would send *Avalon* to the scrapyard rather than install one of his metadrives. *Only if he plans on sending my dead body entombed inside her.*

He had to get a copy of that data cell.

"Well, I think the plan's perfect," said Lizzie. "Everybody wins."

Jeth heard Milton make a doubtful noise, but he didn't look at his uncle. Sure, there were risks involved with this plan. A lot of them. But the chance for gain far outweighed them.

"We all agreed, then?" asked Jeth. When nobody said anything, he went on. "Right, first things first. We need to scavenge for the parts to fix the nav station."

"Yeah, about that . . . ," said Flynn, an anxious expression on his pointed face.

Jeth stifled a groan. "What now?"

"I was looking at the damage and, honestly, it might be easier to just swap out *Avalon*'s nav station with the *Donerail*'s."

Jeth blinked, at first horrified by the idea of such an endeavor, but then realized that this was exactly the chance he needed. "And how long will that take?"

Flynn rolled his shoulders. "A day or two, probably."

"Um," said Celeste. "Won't it be kind of obvious we boarded the *Donerail* if we do something so major?"

Lizzie shook her head. "Not if we reinstall the broken one on the *Donerail*."

"She's right," said Flynn. "Those units are standard on ships like this. The only thing that makes *Avalon*'s special is the Explorer program, but I can swap out the memory banks easy. Hammer won't realize we switched the units unless he goes looking for it."

Jeth hid a grin. This was getting better and better. A day or two would surely be enough time to find the data cell and copy it. Now he just needed a chance to talk to Lizzie alone.

That chance didn't come until several hours later. Lizzie spent most of the day on the bridge, trying to reroute some of *Avalon*'s power to the *Donerail*.

"We need to be able to land one of *Avalon*'s shuttles inside the *Donerail*'s cargo bay," Lizzie said when Jeth asked why she was doing this. "The nav systems won't fit through a hatch. Besides, I'm rerouting power to life support too. I can't work in a bulky space suit, and I don't want to freeze to death."

Seeing her point, Jeth sat down to wait without arguing.

Sierra and Cora spent the morning on the bridge as well. Sierra was helping Flynn with the tedious job of extracting the nav station. Cora was there because of Lizzie—and Jeth, it seemed. Once Cora grew bored with chasing Viggo around, she climbed into Jeth's lap and asked, "Will you read me a story?"

"Um . . ." Jeth went red. Should he push her off? Somehow

that didn't seem like the best response, so he put an arm around her back, and she leaned into him as easily as if he were her dad instead of a complete stranger.

Lizzie stopped what she was doing and came over, an amused expression on her face. "What would you like him to read?" she asked.

Cora tilted her head, thinking it over for a couple of seconds. "'Cinderella.'"

"Okay, give me a second to find it." Lizzie bent toward the screen nearest to where Jeth sat and entered a search for the story in *Avalon*'s digital library.

Jeth groaned inwardly. Great, a fairy tale about a princess. And he had to read it in front of this audience? He'd rather have a tooth pulled. But he doubted he could beg off without hurting the little girl's feelings, and he didn't want to do that. Especially not now that he knew her story.

And so he spent the next thirty minutes reading the ancient tale aloud. It was awkward at first, his voice ill adjusted to the activity, but it got easier as he went along. Cora asked him questions, and he found her emotional responses to the story's events amusing. He'd never realized just how dramatic the story really was until he witnessed her reactions, the way she gasped when the stepsisters were being mean or how she cheered at the fairy godmother's arrival.

When he finished, Cora clapped her hands, then threw her arms around his neck. He hugged her back, the gesture natural instead of awkward for once. He caught Sierra looking at him, her expression one of approval.

"Thanks for doing that," Sierra said from where she sat crouched on the floor beside the nav station.

Jeth cleared his throat. "No problem."

Flynn crawled out from underneath the nav station. "You did a good job, Boss. You voiced the fairy godmother perfectly. Sounded just like I always imagined she would." Flynn batted his eyelashes.

Jeth glared, but before he could say something back, Lizzie shouted, "Done!"

Jeth gave Cora an encouraging push, and she slid off his lap, her attention once more centering on Viggo, who was rolling a screw across the floor with his paws.

Jeth stood up from the comm station chair and stretched. "About time. So we good to dock now?"

"Uh-huh. I'll head over and start working on detaching the *Donerail*'s nav," said Lizzie.

"And I'm coming with you," said Jeth.

Sierra fixed her gaze on him. "So am I."

Of course you are. Jeth did an inward eye roll. He wondered if she suspected his motives for wanting to go over there. He had a feeling she was one of those people who were super smart *and* clever. Shame. Super smart and gullible would've worked out a lot better for him.

"It's not necessary," he said. "Lizzie and I can manage."

Sierra shot him a skeptical look. "Maybe so, but I'm more familiar with the ship and will probably be of more help."

"She's got a point, Jeth," Lizzie said, grinning. "You're better at breaking things than fixing them."

Jeth glared at her. *Not helping,* he tried to say with his eyes, but Lizzie failed to notice.

Flynn raised his hand. "I second that motion. It's important to do the thing right and with no breakage."

"Thanks for the vote of confidence," Jeth muttered.

"You're the one who divvied up the work assignments," said Flynn, his tone scathing.

Jeth ignored the comment. Flynn was just irritated that Jeth had insisted Lizzie handle the job of unhooking the *Donerail*'s nav system. He'd wanted to do it himself. Jeth had his reasons though. Lizzie knew enough about wiring and hardware to manage it, and of the two of them, she was less likely to be rattled by the body stuck in the wall. Or at least he could count on her to keep quiet about it and not upset the rest of the crew.

"I'll ask Vince to come up and take over for me," Sierra said to Flynn. "He's not doing anything important right now anyway."

No, he wasn't. Last time Jeth checked, he, Shady, and Celeste were playing Robot Revenge 7 on the gaming console in the common room. *Must be nice sometimes not to be in charge.*

"Better him than Shady," Flynn said, then disappeared underneath the station again.

Jeth flashed an appreciative grin at Sierra. She had a knack for smoothing things over.

Sierra smiled back, once again stunning him with the way it transformed her face from pretty to beautiful.

"Come on, Cora," Sierra said, holding out her hand. "Let's go find Vince."

"Meet us down in the common room," Lizzie said. "I'm going to throw on some warmer clothes before we go."

Relieved the time had finally come, Jeth waited a moment after the others had left before heading down to the passenger deck himself. He double-checked no one was watching and then slipped into Lizzie's cabin.

"Hey!" she shouted, as she struggled to pull down a heavy shirt over the rest of her clothes. "How about knocking next time?"

Jeth shrugged. "Why? Not like you might have a boy in here." He frowned, realizing the joke wasn't as funny as he'd intended. If she ever did have a boy in here, Jeth would have to kill him.

Lizzie stuck out her tongue. "No, but I might've been naked. Ever think of that?"

Jeth scrunched up his nose. There were some topics you should never discuss with your older brother.

"So what do you want, anyways?" Lizzie said, hurrying on.

He stepped closer to her, lowering his voice. "This data cell that Sierra's got hidden, how difficult do you think it would be to make a copy?"

"Well, it depends. If it's encrypted, it could take me an hour just to access the data. If it's not, shouldn't be more than a couple minutes."

"So we have the equipment on board to do it?"

"Sure." Lizzie walked over to the desk in the corner and

opened a drawer. She pulled out a small rectangular object that Jeth vaguely recognized. She handed it to him. "That cell there should be big enough to hold all the data, and *Avalon*'s got a couple programs for running a copy."

Jeth shook his head, amazed by Lizzie's resourcefulness.

"So, whatcha planning?"

"I want to make a copy of the Aether Project."

She gave him a withering look. "Put that one together for myself, thanks. But why?"

"To use as leverage."

She frowned. "On who?"

"Hammer. You heard what that guy Renford said. Hammer might not go through with selling me *Avalon*. Not if he thinks we're too important to him."

A knowing expression crossed Lizzie's face, and she nodded. So she had thought about it, too. Jeth wasn't surprised. She might be an optimist at heart, but she'd grown up the same way he had, in a world with few illusions of safety or a certain future.

"I take it you want to make this copy without Sierra knowing about it?"

Jeth ran a hand through his hair, not meeting his sister's eyes. "Don't see any way around it."

"Yeah, you're probably right." She sighed. "Still, I hate deceiving her. She and Vince seem really nice. And Cora's a sweetie."

"Yeah, she is," Jeth said, guilt making him antsy. It had to be done, though. He had to do what was best for him and his crew. Taking care of them was his job. His *life*. "Anyway, do you have any tools or equipment that might help me figure out where Sierra's got it hidden?"

Lizzie snorted. "You're kidding, right?"

"What?"

"It's a data cell, Jeth. You know, just like that one. All it does is hold data. It doesn't emit any kind of signal or pulse."

Jeth huffed, disappointed. This was going to be a lot harder than he thought.

"No worries," Lizzie said, winking. "We'll just have to steal the data cell once she shows it to us. She's going to have to sooner or later. Fortunately, we are the best gang of thieves in the galaxy. Should be easy, right?"

"Right." Jeth's heartbeat quickened, his grip on the empty data cell tightening. *One last con.* That was all. Then he would finally be free.

CHAPTER 16

TEN MINUTES LATER, JETH PARKED *SPARKY* INSIDE THE *Donerail*'s narrow shuttle compartment, and he, Lizzie, and Sierra stepped out into the cargo bay.

Lizzie whistled, surveying the damage. "You weren't kidding."

"Not at all," Sierra said, leading the way across the room to the ladder.

"And you've no idea what caused this?" Lizzie said as she followed after her.

"Nope. Happened here just like it did on *Avalon*."

"Yeah, only worse."

They headed out of the cargo bay and down the passenger deck. Fortunately, Lizzie didn't say anything as they passed the body stuck in the wall. Jeth had warned her about it beforehand, but he guessed her lack of comment was because it genuinely frightened her. The only time Lizzie ever got quiet was when she was scared. But, as predicted, she didn't freak out.

When they arrived on the bridge, Lizzie let out a sigh. For the most part, the place looked normal, albeit in disarray, with holes scattered through most of the chairs and several of the control panels torn in half, but no random body parts.

"The nav's over there." Sierra pointed.

Lizzie crossed the bridge and squatted in front of the nav station. Jeth followed her over, setting down the massive toolbox he'd brought with them. Lizzie selected a couple of tools and then slid under the panel.

"Is there room for both of us?" Sierra said.

"Sure, have at it," Lizzie said, her voice muffled.

Sierra fetched her own set of tools and then slid under the panel beside Lizzie.

"I'll just keep watch," Jeth said, deciding sarcasm was the appropriate response to his sudden feeling of inadequacy.

"Knew we brought you along for something," Lizzie shouted.

Jeth grunted as he settled himself in one of the less-damaged chairs. He briefly considered doing a search for the data cell, but Sierra was bound to notice. Besides, he decided Lizzie might have the right of it. He should wait and steal it once Sierra revealed its location. There'd be time. He'd make sure of it.

"Crap," Lizzie said several minutes later. She scooted out from under the station and grimaced up at Jeth. Grease marks covered her forehead and chin. "I gotta go back to *Avalon*."

"Why?" he asked as a considerably cleaner Sierra scooted out from underneath as well.

"There's an older fifteen-x plasinum-coated fiber optic cable that I need to disconnect, but I don't have the right tool for it."

Jeth rolled his eyes.

Lizzie scowled at him. "Don't even. If you think you're so much better, try doing this yourself. I've got about a hundred bolts to unscrew still."

Jeth rolled his eyes a second time. "That's not so hard. Even I can do that."

"Good." Lizzie thrust the wrench she'd been holding at him. "You do that while I get the fifteen-x."

"You sure you want to go by yourself?" Jeth said as she hurried past him.

Lizzie froze, no doubt thinking about the horror show waiting in the passenger deck. She glanced over her shoulder at him, a determined look on her face. "I'm sure."

"I could go get it for you."

She shook her head. "It'll take you forever to find."

Jeth couldn't argue with that logic.

Once Lizzie was gone, he shrugged once at Sierra and then crawled under the station. She joined him a moment later. Awareness of how close she was—her arm and leg touching his—shot through Jeth's body. He ignored it as best he could as he set to work.

"So," Sierra said after a while, "how did you and the others end up working for Hammer?"

Jeth cast a sidelong glance at her, less than thrilled about the question, although he understood her interest well enough. "Nothing special, really. He got the idea that a crew of teenagers would be ideal for stealing spaceships from unsuspecting folks. The rest just happened."

"Did he just pick you at random?"

"Nope." Jeth slid the wrench over a bolt and started loosening it. "He determined a list of candidates based on these aptitude tests that all the kids at Peltraz are required to take. Everybody on the list was exceptional in one way or another. Like with Flynn, the tests predicted how good a mechanic he could be. Then once I picked him for the crew, Hammer sent him through a specialized training class."

Sierra grinned. "I see, although I'm surprised his tests didn't indicate he should be a chef."

Jeth chuckled. "They probably did, but I think Hammer thought the mechanic stuff would be more valuable."

"Good thing. I'm amazed he stays so skinny."

"Yeah, we keep asking Milton to check him for worms, but he hasn't found any yet."

Sierra snorted as she finished removing one of the bolts and moved onto the next. "Then I guess Lizzie's talent is her computer skills. But what about Shady?" A note of skepticism colored her voice. Jeth wasn't surprised. Only a rare few would ever spot Shady's talent without help.

"He's good with firearms and explosives. That, and he's brave enough to do anything, no matter how stupid."

Sierra laughed. "I suppose that's a vital skill in a thief."

"Yep." For some reason, her amusement at this bothered him. He didn't want her to dismiss them all as just thieves. They were more than that. He was more than that.

Are you sure?

Something like shame roiled in his stomach as he remembered the next bit of thieving he planned to do.

"What about Celeste?" said Sierra. "What's her area of expertise?"

"She's kind of the exception to the rule."

"How so?"

"I convinced Hammer to make her part of the crew after I caught her trying to pick my pocket. I was already working for Hammer by then, but we hadn't finished putting the crew together yet. I got to pick the members from the list of candidates he compiled—that's how it worked. But in the meantime, Hammer had me stealing personal comm units from people at the gambling halls on Peltraz. I'd pick one up, run it through a cloning device, and then return it before anybody realized it was missing."

"What for? It's not like those things are valuable."

"They are to a man like Hammer. He uses them to spy on high rollers. Once he has a unit cloned, he can tap incoming and outgoing calls on the ship. You'd be surprised the kind of dirt you can get on people just through casual conversation." Jeth stopped speaking, embarrassed by the way he'd sounded, like he was in awe of Hammer's criminal ingenuity. He supposed he was, in a way, but he didn't want Sierra to know that.

"Anyway," Jeth continued, "Celeste tried to steal one of the units I'd just stolen. She got so mad when I caught her in the act, she punched me in the face."

"That's a heck of a first impression," said Sierra.

"That's Celeste." Jeth often suspected that punch was half the reason he'd chosen her. You had to respect a girl who could hit like that. "Anyway, I shoved her back, and we ended up causing such a scene, we both got hauled off by security. Hammer was pissed, because the comm unit belonged to the son of some big-shot politician he was hoping to put the squeeze on. But when Celeste and I started fighting, the guy saw what was happening and took the unit back before I could clone it."

"What'd Hammer do then?"

"Nothing to me, but when he found out Celeste was an orphan and ward of the station, he decided to, ah, put her into a different line of work."

"What kind?"

Jeth grimaced. "Oh you know, one that involves young girls and rich older men. Celeste always has been a looker." Jeth had been furious about it. Even now the idea made him want to hit something.

He felt Sierra give a little shudder next to him, and thoughts of what had almost happened to Celeste vanished from his mind at the reminder of Sierra's close proximity. She smelled good, flowery and entirely female. He turned his head and realized she was looking at him.

She glanced away at once and started twisting the wrench again. "That's horrible."

Jeth stared at her misshapen hands grasping the tool. She held it awkwardly, as if the position hurt. "Are you sure you're all right doing this?" He had a sudden urge to take the wrench from her. He didn't want her to be in pain. In his mind's eye he saw himself running his fingers over hers.

Sierra glanced at him again, surprise on her face. "I'm . . . I'm fine. Really."

Jeth nodded and returned his attention to his work. What was wrong with him? He shouldn't let her distract him so much. She wasn't a lost, helpless kitten in need of protection or sympathy or whatever this thing was she made him feel.

"So how did Celeste end up on the crew?" Sierra asked.

Jeth clenched his teeth as he struggled with a particularly stubborn screw. "I managed to convince Hammer that she would be useful at distracting marks. We've been together ever since."

"You mean together, together?"

Jeth's grip on the screw slipped and he almost hit himself in the forehead. "No, nothing like that. At least not for a while."

"I see."

They fell into silence for a couple of moments. Jeth searched his mind for something to say, but everything sounded stupid or too personal. He felt an insane urge to tell her about his dream of settling down on Enoch, but he didn't dare. Why would she even care?

Finally, Sierra broke the silence for him. "So did Hammer recruit you through an aptitude test, too?"

He exhaled, relieved to be talking again. "No. I wasn't quite eleven when I started working for him. I don't think I remember how it all started, but I first met him after Milton lost *Avalon* to him in a card game. When I found out about it, I snuck into the casino and tried to attack Hammer with this pathetic little pocketknife. I thought I could force him into giving us back the ship. Yeah, it worked about as well as you can imagine. But I started doing odd jobs for him not long after. He must've been impressed by my bravery or attitude or maybe my sheer stupidity."

"It's not stupid to fight for what's yours," Sierra said quietly.

Something moved in his chest again. *What's yours. Like the right to live your own life, the way you want to live it.*

"And she's a great ship," Sierra went on. "An entire world unto herself."

Jeth's breath caught at the compliment, a pleasant shiver going through his body. He cleared his throat. "Are you finished with that other wrench?"

"Yeah." Sierra reached down beside herself, picked up the wrench, and turned back to him. "Well, I suppose Ham— Uh!"

Jeth rolled toward her. "What is it?"

He saw the answer at once. A big drop of system coolant had fallen on her face, right beneath one eye. "Crap, let me get it. Keep your eyes closed."

Sierra dropped her hand from her face and held still. Jeth reached for her, but he couldn't quite manage it in the tight space.

"We've got to do this out there. Can you scoot out?"

"Yes."

Jeth slid out from underneath the station and then helped her do the same. He pulled her into a sitting position. Then he cupped her face in his hands to hold her steady as he wiped away the coolant with his thumb, being careful not to push it into her eye.

Sierra smiled. "That tickles."

A flush of heat enveloped Jeth, and he shivered again. Somehow he managed to make his tone playful as he said, "Shhhh, don't tell me that. Or I might have to tickle you on purpose."

Her lips parted. "You wouldn't dare. I'm a highly trained ITA agent. I can hurt you with nothing but my big toe."

Jeth chuckled, the sound huskier than normal. "Okay. I think we got it."

Sierra opened her eyes, and Jeth realized he was still holding her face. He ought to be embarrassed by the intimacy of it, and yet he wasn't. Her mouth was still open, her eyes locked on his, and her expression unwary. She made no move to pull away from him. He once again realized how pretty she was. Beautiful, really.

He felt a wild urge to lean forward and kiss her. He fought it back.

But then she leaned forward and kissed him.

He was so surprised that his whole body went rigid for a moment. In the next, instinct took over, and he pressed into the kiss. Tingly heat, so intense it almost hurt, burst over his lips. An onrush of sensation spread over him, obliterating all thoughts. His mouth parted, and he inhaled, breathing her in as he savored the feel and taste of her.

Then someone coughed from behind him, breaking the spell.

"Am I interrupting something?" Lizzie said, close to giggling.

Jeth pulled back, dropping his hands from Sierra's face.

He stood up. "No. I was just helping her get some coolant out of her eye."

Lizzie chortled. "Sure you were. Did she have some in her mouth, too?"

Jeth scowled. "Did you get the tool?"

"Uh-huh." Lizzie waved it at him. "You want to do the work for me? I mean, you two seem to be doing such a good job."

"Very funny, Liz," Jeth said.

Her grin broadened. "Well, if not, you could go for a romantic stroll through the ship. Just the two of you. Alone. In the dark."

Sometimes Jeth despised having a little sister.

He risked a glance at Sierra, who'd gotten to her feet. To his surprise, she was grinning, too, her cheeks flushed and lips wet. He wanted to kiss her again.

With an effort, he pulled his gaze away. *Don't be an idiot,* a voice whispered in his mind. *That's a bad idea and you know it.*

Yes, he did. No distractions. Especially not on board his ship and with a girl that he had every intention of betraying— even if it wasn't likely she would ever find out.

No, he needed to stay focused on the task at hand. Copy the project, get the metadrive, and move on. There would be a time for this sort of thing, but now wasn't it.

CHAPTER 17

JETH SPENT THE NEXT DAY AND A HALF DOING HIS BEST TO avoid Sierra. It was hard, and not just because the living quarters were so tight with this many people aboard. No, trouble was, he wanted to see her. A lot.

Instead he made sure there was always someone else present whenever they were together. It wasn't too difficult, given the attachment between her and Cora. And there was nothing like having a kid present to stave off romantic inclinations.

Not that Jeth resented Cora's hanging around. Just the opposite. He was actually starting to enjoy it. He'd never realized how much kids laughed. And at the simplest things, like funny faces and corny jokes. Being around her made him feel light, oddly removed from himself and his troubles.

It was this lightness perhaps that finally gave him the courage to ask Lizzie for their mother's data crystal that night.

"Oh," she said, eyes widening. "I don't have it. Milton took it yesterday."

"Huh." The news didn't surprise Jeth. He should've guessed it for himself. Milton had just as much interest in it as they did, and unlike Jeth, he wouldn't fear facing the pain that opening those memories would bring back. Milton had never moved on, never buried it deep inside. No, he buried it deep in a bottle, only to have it rise up again and again, waiting to be drowned by more booze.

Jeth went to Milton's cabin after saying good night to Lizzie, but Milton wasn't there. At the end of the corridor, the door into sick bay stood closed. Jeth knocked on it, leery of just charging in.

Rather than call for him to enter, Milton opened the door a crack and peered out. "What is it?"

Jeth shot him a penetrating look. What was his uncle up to? Surely there was nothing doctor related for him to be doing. "Lizzie said you have the data crystal she found."

An odd, guarded expression enveloped Milton's face. "Yes, that's right."

"Well, I'd like to take a look at it."

Milton shook his head. "I'm not done with it yet."

Jeth opened his mouth to argue but closed it once more at the sight of Milton's watery gaze. He swallowed, realizing yet again that he wasn't ready to face it. He might never be ready. And if Milton was offering him an excuse to delay, Jeth would take it.

"Okay. Just let me know when you are."

Milton nodded, then closed the door without another word. Jeth retreated to his room, pushing all thoughts of his parents as far from his mind as possible.

Late the next evening, Flynn pronounced the job done.

"Done, done?" Jeth said. He, Lizzie, and Flynn were alone

on the bridge. "Like, we can fly out of here now?"

Flynn raised his hands over his head, fingers laced. Several loud pops echoed around the room and he sighed. "No, not yet. I just initialized the system recalibration. Should be done come morning." He patted his stomach. "I'm starving. And it's my turn to cook."

Jeth and Lizzie exchanged a grin, both of them knowing they were in for a feast tonight. The last few days had been tough on Flynn, and cooking was his favorite way to unwind—or the eating that followed it was. It worked out great for everybody, except perhaps for the unfortunate souls stuck with dish duty afterward.

Ready by the morning, Jeth thought, doing a mental calculation. That left them four days before their deadline with Hammer. Such a short time frame would make things tight for the meetup and exchange with Sierra's contact, but still within the realm of doable.

Jeth entered the common room an hour later to find the atmosphere electrified, excitement a palpable, buzzing feel surrounding them. Word that they would be crossing the border had infected everyone with anticipation.

Jeth's excitement swung closer to nervousness. He still hadn't decided how to go about stealing the data cell from Sierra without her noticing. He had several scenarios in mind, but none of them was the perfect plan he hoped for. He supposed he'd have to settle on one tonight. He'd need time to go over it with Lizzie and anybody else he might require to pull it off. He intended to keep the job on a need-to-know basis.

Loud, fast music blasted out from the speakers in the common room. Lizzie was dancing to it, side by side with Cora, who was throwing her arms wildly in the air like she was a helicopter trying to take flight. It looked painful, but judging by the huge smile on her face, Jeth could tell she was having fun. And she was laughing, of course, that light, musical sound that seemed to fill him up, making him light, too.

Celeste, Shady, and Vince were once again at the gaming table. Jeth spied Sierra through the doorway into the galley, helping Flynn with the cooking. He sat down, wondering where Milton was. Probably in sick bay. Jeth had barely seen him lately.

"Just a few more minutes," Sierra announced from the doorway, shouting to be heard over the music.

Cora stopped midtwirl and raced over to her. She grabbed Sierra by the hand and hauled her to the makeshift dance floor. "Dance, dance, dance," Cora shouted.

An exasperated look crossed Sierra's face, but she gave in to the girl, raising her hands above her head and twirling around in a circle. Her long hair, which she had let down from her customary ponytail, swung out around her like a golden cape.

Jeth's heart seemed to somersault inside his rib cage, and he sucked in a breath. He should never have let that kiss happen. The memory of it only intensified his guilt over what he planned to do. Not to mention the torment of unfulfilled desire.

"Ahem," a voice said from above him.

Jeth looked up, his face going red as he saw Vince staring down at him with his arms folded across his chest in a manner that emphasized his large muscles.

"See something you like?" Vince said.

Jeth didn't answer. If he said no, Vince would know he was lying. If he said, yes . . . well . . . Jeth wasn't interested in finding out what big brother might make of such a declaration.

Vince sat down beside Jeth, close enough that he had to resist the impulse to scoot over.

"I'd be careful if I were you," said Vince.

Jeth rolled his eyes. "Are you about to give me the if-you-hurt-her-I'll-break-your-face speech?"

"Nope. She's perfectly capable of breaking your face on her own."

Jeth snorted, although a part of him didn't entirely doubt this statement. He'd certainly seen for himself how silently the girl could move. She should've been a career assassin instead of scientist. She could kill him in his sleep if she wanted to.

"My sister has a hard time trusting people," Vince said. "Especially with everything that's happened recently." His voice grew quiet. "I was shocked when she admitted how much she'd let you in on how we grew up. I think that might be the first time she's ever told anyone."

Jeth swallowed, uncomfortable with this news. He didn't want to read too much into it. Something like hope fluttered in his chest, a pair of delicate wings. Across from them, Sierra stopped dancing. She looked over at them, a mixture of curiosity and concern on her face.

Forcing as much aloofness into his voice as he could, Jeth said, "Are you saying that she trusts me?"

Vince turned his head, pinning Jeth with his gaze. "No. I'm saying she's *thinking* about trusting you, and I suggest you don't screw it up. If you give her a reason not to, you'll regret it forever. I promise."

The fluttering feeling evaporated in Jeth's chest, replaced by a tremor of guilt. Did Vince know he planned on copying the Aether Project? Was this some kind of veiled warning? Jeth wasn't exactly afraid of Vince, but he had a good healthy respect for his size, not to mention his background as an elite combat soldier. Jeth stared back at Vince, trying to look calm and innocent.

No, he decided, a moment later. Vince didn't know. How could he? No one knew about his intentions except for Lizzie. And besides, it was such a little thing, really. By the time Sierra's buyer found out there was more than one copy of the project around, she would be long gone. No harm done.

Fortunately, Jeth was rescued from having to dwell on the subject any longer when Flynn shouted from the galley, "Soup's on."

"We're having soup?" asked Cora as everyone filed in and sat down.

Jeth laughed, giving her blond head a pat. "It's just an

expression. Although from the looks of this table, everything's on the menu."

Milton arrived a few minutes late, muttering a thin, awkward apology that no one paid attention to. Jeth felt a moment's pity for his uncle. He supposed it wasn't easy being the only old guy surrounded by a bunch of teenagers.

In minutes, the group had descended into their typical rowdiness, Sierra, Vince, and Cora blending among them as if they'd been there forever. Most of the jokes and stories they shared were old, but the presence of new ears made them fresh again.

"Oh, do you remember when Shady shot himself with a stunner?" Lizzie said as dinner was winding down.

"Did not," said Shady, mouth agape.

Lizzie poked him in the chest. "Yes, you did. It was my second job. How did that happen again?"

"I remember," said Flynn. "Shady was showing off for that woman with the big boobs, one of Chopper's mistresses." Flynn stood, pushing back his chair. Then he raised his hand like he had a gun. "He was going like this, and then he tried to twirl the stunner on his finger, but he did it wrong and BAM!" Flynn stumbled backward, crossing his eyes and sticking out his tongue. Then he fell down, landing with a loud thump.

Cora burst into shrieks of laughter. Most of the jokes had gone over her head, but not this one. Physical comedy she understood completely.

"Do it again!" Cora said. "Please, please, please."

Flynn stood up, wiping his mouth with the back of his hand. He moved to reenact the story, but froze at the sound of a loud *crack*.

Liquid splashed Jeth's arms, and he leaped back from the table. "What the hell?" He glanced around. Everybody else had stood up, too. The next second he realized why—all the drinking glasses on the table had vanished. Nothing else. No holes—just one second, glasses full of water or juice or wine, and the next, nothing but free-flowing liquid.

"Whoa," Shady said after a long moment, his eyes wide. "More Belgrave stuff?"

"It would appear so," Milton said as he picked up a towel and dabbed at the red wine stains on his shirt.

Jeth glanced around the room, looking for more damage. He'd thought they were safe here, so close to the border, from whatever strange phenomenon had caused the damage to the *Donerail*. But it seemed he was wrong. *Haunted*. They'd been talking about it all along, the things people said about the Belgrave, but it was the first time the thought actually crossed his mind. Jeth didn't know anymore if it could be true or not, but something was out there, all right. Something that had either grown more powerful in the days since they'd first crossed the border into the Quadrant—or that had followed them back.

Jeth shivered once, then glanced at everybody in turn. "Everyone okay?"

"Just wet," said Celeste, fear undermining her casual tone.

Jeth's gaze landed on Cora. She wasn't laughing anymore but looked terrified. Ignoring his own fear, Jeth forced a smile. "It's okay, Cora. We'll be out of here before you know it."

From the expressions on all the faces staring at him, he knew it couldn't happen soon enough.

CHAPTER

18

SO MUCH FOR A PARTY. ALL THE GOOD VIBES AND celebratory spirit had vanished from the room.

"Shouldn't we leave the Belgrave now?" Lizzie said, looking first at Jeth and then at Sierra. "Aren't we in danger of more weird stuff happening if we stay?"

"By weird, I think you mean dangerous," said Flynn.

Sierra turned her gaze to Vince, and the two shared a silent exchange.

Finally Vince said, "I'm not sure this is the same as what happened before. Seems more like a parlor trick than the full-on magic show we got deeper inside the Belgrave."

Jeth considered the idea. Disappearing glass did seem a little less ominous than the holes. But still—it might be somebody's hands or head that vanished next.

"Seems risky enough to me," said Shady.

Sierra pursed her lips. "Yes, but if the nav isn't ready, we'll risk even more if we move outside the Belgrave."

Jeth ran his hands through his hair. He was tired of these between-a-rock-and-a-hard-place scenarios they kept getting into. But Sierra was right; they couldn't risk getting picked up outside the Belgrave. He faced her. "What if we move closer to the border or just somewhere farther down from here?" He glanced at Flynn. "The recalibration only has a few hours left, right?"

"Sure, as long as nothing goes wrong with it," said Flynn.

Jeth ignored the implication and fixed his gaze on Sierra and Vince. "What do you think?"

"Moving certainly won't hurt any," said Vince.

"Okay," Jeth said, not as reassured as he would've liked. "I'll move us down a ways, and we'll try to wait it out until morning. But if anything else weird happens, we'll reevaluate our options. All right?"

Everyone agreed, and while the others started to clean up, Jeth left for the bridge. As soon as he sat down, he heard footsteps behind him. He turned, surprised to find it was Milton. Jeth frowned at the unopened bottle of whiskey tucked beneath his arm.

"When you're done, come down to sick bay," Milton said, his smoke-broken voice oddly low, as if he feared being overheard. "But wait until everyone has gone to bed, and come alone."

"What's up?" Jeth said.

"I need to show you something."

A strange prickly sensation slipped over Jeth's arms and the back of his neck. He didn't know what Milton would show him, but he knew it wouldn't be anything good. In his experience, good things rarely needed to be kept secret. "Okay."

Milton patted his shoulder, then turned to leave, opening the bottle of whiskey as he went.

Jeth returned his attention to the front window, taking

hold of the control column. As always, *Avalon* came to life in his hands, her engines a soft rumble, like a gigantic metal cat set to purring. Jeth didn't know if moving the ship would help at all, but he sure didn't mind the excuse to fly her.

He piloted *Avalon* as close to the border as he dared and then he flew her alongside it, following the energy border on the readout like a trail through space. He didn't stop for nearly an hour. Not until he heard someone come onto the bridge behind him.

He smiled automatically as he spotted Sierra and Cora.

"She wanted to kiss you good night," Sierra said, letting go of Cora's hand as the girl came forward, opening her arms for an embrace.

Embarrassed, but not ashamed, Jeth pulled her onto his lap and planted a kiss on her forehead. She giggled, then turned his head so she could kiss his cheek.

"Good night, sweet girl," Jeth whispered.

"Good night." Cora slid down and then walked back to Sierra.

"See you in the morning," Sierra said. The two of them left.

Only four days until they're gone, Jeth realized. *I'm going to miss them.* He ignored the thought and the tight squeeze in his chest.

He flew on for another twenty minutes before deciding he'd taken them far enough. Nothing amiss had happened since dinner, and he was feeling better about their chances. Besides, as much as he dreaded what Milton had to show him, he was eager to find out what it was, too. He anchored *Avalon* once more and then stood up and stretched before heading down to the passenger deck. He could tell at a glance that everyone had turned in.

He walked silently past the closed cabin doors to sick bay. The moment he stepped inside, a familiar voice filled his ears. The sound cut into him like a dull knife, realization slow and painful.

Mom.

He hadn't heard her voice in ages, yet he had no trouble recognizing it. How could he ever have thought he'd forgotten? For a moment, he just stood there, frozen in place as all his other senses slid away.

"I've tried and tried to get a message to Charles, but he hasn't answered," his mother was saying. "He was our only hope, but I don't think he's going to help me now, even though he said he would." She sounded broken somehow, a woman standing on the edge.

Jeth walked farther into the room, his eyes moving automatically to the source of her voice. It came from the video screen on the wall above the operating table. Milton sat on a stool in front of it, his head bent back, the whiskey bottle half empty in his hands.

"But there's no one else I can turn to," his mother went on. "Not now. We've come too far. He's not the person I thought he was."

Jeth stared at his mother, hardly believing it was her. She looked just like he remembered. Except there was something different about her, too. She looked impossibly young, her skin smooth and eyes bright. She seemed to exude an aura of vibrancy completely at odds with her broken, panicked tone. And yet gray hairs he couldn't recall threaded through the auburn like silver streamers.

"Who's Charles?" Jeth said.

Milton gave a little jump, then looked over his shoulder. "I don't know. Someone in the ITA, someone she trusted and thought could help her out of whatever situation she was in." He turned around and paused the video. "She was always too trusting," Milton muttered. "Always seeing what she wanted to in people. Just the good, rarely the bad."

Sounds like Lizzie, Jeth thought, stepping closer. His eyes remained fixed on the image of his mother. He didn't think he could look away even if he wanted to. "This is from the data crystal Lizzie found?"

"Yes." Milton took a long drink from the whiskey bottle, then wiped his mouth with the back of his hand. "I knew it would hurt, seeing it, but I never guessed how much."

Jeth didn't say anything. He understood exactly. He had known how the content would make him feel. The way he did now—empty inside except for an angry, pain-pulsed hole where his heart used to be.

And terribly, utterly alone.

Milton set the bottle on the table and picked up the video remote. "I wish I did know who this Charles was. Marian . . ." Milton paused, a hitch in his voice, as if speaking her name caused him physical pain. "In the next entry, she says that he betrayed her. Told the ITA their location."

The floor seemed to drop out from Jeth's feet. "What? What happened?"

Milton shook his head. "I don't know. Looks like she and your dad knew the ITA were after them and tried to hide. She recorded a lot of this then, but she doesn't say what's happening. She doesn't say much of anything. Half of it's gibberish. Like she was suffering from some form of dementia."

"How do you mean?"

In answer, Milton pressed a button on the remote. Marian's face disappeared from the monitor, replaced by the main screen that listed the contents of the data crystal. Jeth saw the problem at once. His mother had always been extremely organized and logical about everything. She was fond of alphabetizing jars of food and folding towels with such precision they might've been on display in a store. But the contents on the crystal were a mess. Random letters and numbers comprised the file names, none of them comprehensible. It was the sort of thing that would've driven his mother mad.

"What is all that stuff?" Jeth said.

"Mostly the Belgrave star charts she and your dad mapped out. The rest are video journals and sensor readouts that are still in computer code. Looks like she did a straight data dump from the system to the crystal for most of them without bothering to run a translate analysis."

"Why would she do that?"

"Who can say, given the state she was in?" Milton made a fist and slammed it on the table. "Why didn't she come to me instead of this Charles? She might still be alive."

Jeth gaped. Milton rarely lost his temper. Anger required too much effort. You had to care to get worked up, but Milton only cared about the next drink and living as undisturbed a life as possible.

That's not true and you know it.

Jeth sighed, conceding the point. He knew the drinking and apathy were just an act, nothing but a defense mechanism. Trouble was Milton cared *too* much. Anybody could see that. Jeth took in his uncle's appearance, dismayed at the ruination on his face from old age and alcohol abuse. Purpled flesh covered his cheeks and nose. Red hash marks speckled the whites of his eyes.

"I'm sorry for shouting," Milton said.

"It's all right."

"No, it's not. Nothing about this is all right." Milton stood, swaying a bit.

Jeth stepped forward and grabbed his arm to steady him.

Milton jerked away. "I'm fine."

Sure you are, you stubborn old man.

Jeth moved aside as Milton walked past him. His uncle stopped at one of the supply cabinets and opened a drawer, pulling out another data crystal. Then he came back to the control unit and switched out Jeth's mother's crystal with the new one.

"I called you up here to show you this." Milton opened one of the files, and an image appeared on the screen, some kind of medical readout comprised of bars with thin blue lines etched sideways across them in a random pattern.

Jeth stared at it, his mind blank. "What is it?"

"DNA test results."

"Okay?"

"So is this." Milton pulled up another file that appeared right below the first. This one showed a similar pattern of bars and blue lines, except there were more of them— hundreds more.

"The top one is my DNA," Milton said. "The bottom is Cora's."

Jeth blinked a couple of times, still not understanding. Although he supposed this was one of the reasons why Milton had shut himself up in here the last two days. He wondered how he'd gotten a sample of her blood, but then he remembered the scratch on the back of Cora's hand. "Why the difference?"

"No idea," Milton said, his frustration palpable. "All I can tell you is what it means on a biological level."

Jeth waited for him to go on, breath held.

"She's not human."

Shock drove all thoughts from Jeth's brain as he stared at the bottom image, his mouth slackening. In his mind's eye, he pictured Cora as he'd first seen her—something wild and exotic, and with her eyes too large and dark.

Milton cleared his throat. "I should clarify. She's not *entirely* human. Some of this is human DNA, but the rest of it isn't."

"Animal?"

"Not any animal I know of."

"Then what is it?"

". . . Nothing I've ever seen."

Jeth closed his mouth to keep from asking the next question that occurred to him. It was stupid, impossible. In the entire universe, there was no such thing as aliens. Humans had colonized all the inhabitable worlds and had never found anything else. Not one sign of life in hundreds of surveyed planets.

He pictured Cora again, this time as he'd last seen her, with a sleepy smile on her face as she kissed him good night. Was there something wrong with her beneath all the normal little-girl things? Something dangerous? For the first time in days he remembered that horrible, animalistic scream he'd heard on the *Donerail* and the way it had gotten inside him, like a predator intent on consuming him from the inside. Sierra and Vince had been just as affected by that sound as he and Shady were. But Cora . . . there'd been no sign of her.

Jeth shuddered, pushing the idea away. Things were complicated enough. "Why did you want me to see this?"

Milton scratched the thick stubble on his chin. "Because if there's more to Cora than meets the eye, then there might be more to their entire situation. Stuff they're not telling us."

Icy fingers seemed to stroke Jeth's neck. "You think Sierra and Vince know what she is?"

"It's certainly possible. They did rescue her from an ITA scientist. And it wouldn't be the first time the ITA experimented on children. An organization so powerful and autonomous has little reason to worry about moral consequences." Milton shuddered, and Jeth had a feeling that he was speaking from experience. He'd been an ITA doctor for a very long time. Jeth wondered if that wasn't the reason why his mother had called Charles for help instead of him.

Jeth rubbed his temples, suddenly aware of how late it was. "Why show me this? I mean, what does it matter what Cora is? She seems harmless."

Does she? Are you sure?

Milton shook his head. "That's just it. She might not be harmless. She might be a ticking bomb ready to go off at any moment. I've seen it happen before with some of the ITA's test subjects. And," Milton said, his tone growing more ominous, "if we assume Cora was part of an ITA experiment, how do we know that *she* isn't what Sierra and Vince stole, instead of this so-called Aether Project? What if that was just a lie to hide the truth from us?"

"They didn't steal her. They rescued her from a bad situation."

Milton raised his hands. "I'm not saying they have bad intentions toward Cora."

"Clearly not," Jeth said.

"But they would lie to protect her if they had to. Even to us."

Jeth considered the idea, trying to look past his personal feelings. He supposed it was possible. And it did seem more likely that Sierra would've gotten to know Cora through their roles as scientist and subject rather than as occasional babysitter. But did that mean the Aether Project data cell didn't exist? He didn't want to believe it, and yet here was a thread of doubt, a possibility that Sierra and Vince might be lying, might be keeping a dark, frightening secret.

Jeth met Milton's gaze. "What do you think I should do about it?"

Milton rubbed his forehead. "Find out the truth about what's really going on. There'll be hell to pay if Hammer finds out about any of this. You know that as well as I do. I don't blame you for believing them. I like them too, but we shouldn't ignore this." He motioned toward the screen. "And I don't want you to make the same mistake your mother did in trusting the wrong person. People can't be trusted, Jeth. Not without earning it."

Jeth supposed he had a point. He had no proof at all that the Aether Project data cell really existed. And he didn't know any of them well enough to be aware of what their true motivations might be.

Doubt rose up inside Jeth like a fog, blurring everything. He locked his eyes on Milton. "I'll confront them about Cora tomorrow. And I'll insist Sierra show us proof she's telling the truth about the data cell."

"What if she refuses?"

Jeth thought about it a long time, playing out all the possible scenarios. The only thing he knew for certain was that if he couldn't get a copy of the Aether Project, then he had no leverage against Hammer to ensure he'd get what he wanted most of all—*Avalon*. And he couldn't let his ship get turned into scrap metal. He just couldn't. That left him with only one alternative. An awful one, but still a means to an end.

"If I don't get the answers I want tomorrow, then I'll have to call Renford instead. He's—" Jeth paused. "Did you hear that?"

Milton frowned. "Hear what?"

Jeth walked to the door and peered outside. At first he thought he'd imagined the sound, but then he saw something small and yellow scurrying down the corridor. He turned around again. "Stupid cat."

"Don't let Lizzie hear you calling it that," Milton said. "But are you sure Renford is the solution? If Cora is an ITA test subject, you'll just be handing her back over to them."

Jeth swallowed. *Please let them be telling the truth,* he thought, the words like a prayer. He definitely didn't want to hand them over to the ITA. Then he realized he might not have to. If Sierra and Vince failed to show him the data cell, he could throw them in the brig, and then fly out of the Belgrave directly to the nearest planet or spaceport. Surely there had to be something within *Avalon*'s direct flight range. Once there, he could unload the three of them and then call Renford.

Jeth considered running this alternative past Milton, but he held back at the glossy look in his uncle's eyes. He sighed. "All I know is, if Cora is valuable, then she's better off with the ITA than with Hammer."

"That's like saying a mouse is better off with the trap than the cat."

"I *know*," Jeth whispered, struggling to hold back his temper. He didn't like those options either. The universe was a terrible, fucked-up place, but he didn't make it that way.

He just had to live with it. "But I don't have to make that decision yet. I'm prepared to give Sierra and Vince the benefit of the doubt."

"Yes, me too," Milton said, although the listlessness in his voice suggested he hadn't much hope of it.

Jeth's hands curled into fists at his sides. He wished there were someone else in the universe he could call for help. But there wasn't. *Alone, completely alone.*

Milton covered his mouth as he started to yawn. He reached over to the video unit and ejected the data crystal. Then he picked up the bottle of whiskey, a tremor in his hands. "I'm turning in. But I want to be there when you question them about Cora."

"All right," Jeth said, realizing Milton was far more intoxicated than he seemed. He wondered how much of this conversation his uncle would remember in the morning.

Milton walked past him, then paused in the doorway. "For what it's worth," he said, not turning around, "I'm sorry for all the mistakes I made after your parents died. I never meant for you and your sister to end up like this."

Jeth didn't say anything. He'd heard this speech before, and while he believed Milton, the apology didn't hold enough weight to matter.

But then Milton surprised him. He looked over his shoulder, and with tears in his eyes, said, "I hope you know I love you, Jeth. You and Lizzie both. You can always come to me with anything. There's nothing I wouldn't do for you. Just like there was nothing I wouldn't have done for your mother."

Jeth swallowed. "We love you, too." The words were automatic, spoken without any consideration of whether he meant them or not. Only, deep down, he knew he did. Milton wasn't perfect, but he was family. Jeth might not hold with a lot of what his parents stood for, but he did that one—nothing mattered more than family.

Milton walked out of the sick bay and down the hall to his cabin. There was a faint click as he locked himself in.

Not long afterward, Jeth slipped out of his cabin and headed down the stairs to the nearest shuttle. He knew it was a long shot, but he had to find the Aether Project. He wanted answers. He didn't want to wait and confront Sierra about it. He'd rather have proof now that she'd told him the truth. Everything depended on it.

He spent hours searching. He started in the *Donerail's* cargo bay and worked his way up, through the galley and common area and finally to the passenger deck. He searched every room, rummaging in drawers and scanning the walls and crevices for hidden compartments.

In the end he found nothing. Jeth tried to tell himself this was only because Lizzie had been right. The thing was too small to find on a ship so large. And except for possibly hiding the truth about Cora, Sierra and Vince had given him no reason not to trust them. Just the opposite. They'd *helped* him from the start. He drew some small comfort from this truth.

And yet, as he walked up the stairs from the shuttle to his cabin, he dreaded the morning.

CHAPTER 19

JETH WOKE THE NEXT DAY, UNCERTAIN IF HE'D ACTUALLY slept at all. Terrible images of corpses stuck in walls and of a little girl with too-black eyes and a killer scream had plagued his mind all night.

Even though it was early, Lizzie and Flynn were already up, running a final diagnostic on the nav system, both of them anxious to be on their way. Celeste, Vince, Milton, and Sierra were still in their cabins, but Shady and Cora were in the common room. Shady was lying on a sofa, watching one of his favorite shows on a handheld video screen with a pair of earbuds in.

Cora sat at the gaming table, playing with an art program that allowed her to draw pictures on the table's touch-screen surface with her fingers.

"Hello, Cora," Jeth said, walking over to her.

She smiled up at him. She looked so normal, nothing at all like the creature in his nightmares. She seemed so *human*. Maybe the test had been wrong. Maybe the Belgrave had distorted the results somehow. *Stranger things have happened.*

Everything from the night before seemed less intense now that it was morning. Jeth wondered if Milton was just being paranoid. He'd been very drunk, not to mention his emotional jag from watching the video journals.

Jeth shifted his gaze toward Cora's drawings. He'd expected hearts and rainbows, maybe a unicorn or two. Instead he saw a crude outline of a spaceship he easily recognized as the *Donerail*.

Cora was drawing little circles on it.

"What are you doing?" Jeth said, unsettled by the slow, methodical motion of her hand as she trailed her fingers around and around.

"Drawing," Cora said with no hint of sarcasm.

Jeth let out a breath, wondering if maybe Cora had seen whatever had done the damage to the *Donerail*. He knew children were supposed to be more perceptive about certain things. Or maybe her strange DNA gave her special sight or something. "Are those circles supposed to be the holes on the other ship?"

She nodded.

"Did you see what made those holes?"

She pressed her lips together.

"Cora," Jeth said, assuming his best parental voice, the kind his father had always used when he thought Jeth was hiding something, "did you see what made those holes?"

"What's going on?" a voice said from behind Jeth.

He straightened from his hunched position and turned to see Sierra watching him, her expression wary. "Cora was just explaining her drawing to me."

"I see."

Jeth frowned at the tone of her voice. True, he didn't know her very well, but he'd lived with girls all his life. And he had no trouble recognizing the universal sound of an unhappy female. She was pissed at him about something. Just what, he couldn't say. In his experience, girls rarely needed a rational reason. "Something wrong?"

"No. I mean . . . *yes.*" She turned and walked across the room, motioning for him to follow.

He did so, mentally bracing himself for a scolding.

"Look," Sierra whispered the moment he was in earshot. "I know that Cora really likes you and everything, but that doesn't give you the right to start asking her questions about what happened on the *Donerail.* That experience was too traumatic to ask a child to relive it."

Jeth opened his mouth to argue, then closed it. He supposed she was right. He tried to imagine how he would've felt when he was Cora's age, seeing that man stuck in the wall. *I'd probably be scarred for life.* "I'm sorry."

Momentary surprise crossed Sierra's face. "It's okay. I should've mentioned it earlier."

Jeth nodded, realizing now was the perfect opportunity to ask her what Cora really was. He racked his brains for the best way to phrase the question, but nothing came to him. They all sounded so awful. *So what is Cora, anyway? Or Is Cora some kind of genetic experiment? Or Is Cora an alien?*

He could barely *think* the questions with any kind of seriousness, let alone say them. Because no matter what Milton's test results might indicate, what Jeth saw was a little girl, bright and maybe a tad unusual, but still sweet and funny and about as normal as everybody else on this ship.

"Are you all right?" asked Sierra, frowning.

Jeth ran a hand through his hair, his fingers snagging in the long strands. He seriously needed a haircut. "I'm fine. Why?"

"It looks like you slept in your clothes."

He glanced down. "Uh . . . that's because I did." It had been so late by the time he got back from the *Donerail*, he hadn't bothered with undressing. He shrugged. "It happens."

"Oh-kay," Sierra said, her voice skeptical. "So, we'll be leaving soon?"

"Yep, Flynn should be just about done with the diagnostics."

"Right. Then I suppose it's time for me to get the data cell off the *Donerail*."

It took Jeth a moment to realize what she'd said. When he did, relief flooded him, making him giddy. She'd been telling the truth after all. At least about the data cell. That was good enough for him. He didn't have to confront her about anything. He briefly wondered why she was revealing it now when he'd expected her to wait until the very last moment, but then he remembered what Vince had told him: *She's starting to trust you.*

He grinned, fighting back the sudden urge to kiss her. "Great," he said. "Want me to come with you?"

She nodded.

His grin widened. "Just give me a sec to fetch my coat."

"Meet me at the shuttle."

○ ○ ○

Several minutes later, he and Sierra entered *Sparky*. This was the first time he'd been completely alone with her since they'd kissed. He tried his best not to think about that but failed miserably. He was too happy, too relieved, to ignore his attraction to her. He was hyperaware of her every move, the way she crossed and uncrossed her legs or folded her hands in her lap or rested them on the sides of her chair.

He could tell she was tense, too, and he could only guess it was for the same reason. He wanted to kick himself for avoiding her these last few days. What harm would a little kissing do? The thought should have scared him, and yet it didn't. Instead, it only bolstered his confidence. Everything was going to work out all right for once. He was certain of it.

"So," he said as he set down *Sparky* inside the *Donerail*'s shuttle bay, "I've been thinking about what happened the other day."

Sierra stiffened in her chair, not looking at him. "What do you mean?"

"About you kissing me." He couldn't keep the grin from his voice as he said it. There was no denying *she* had kissed *him*. He found the knowledge good for his ego.

"What about it?"

Jeth frowned, disconcerted by the rigidity of her tone. "So, why did you?"

Sierra stood up and opened the shuttle door. "Seemed like a good idea at the time."

Jeth stared after her, his certainty deflating, but only for a moment. He'd been stupid to remind her she had done the kissing. Celeste always claimed most girls would rather be pursued than do the pursuing. *Okay,* he thought. *I'm game for that.*

Sierra led him to the passenger deck and stopped before one of the closed cabin doors. Jeth remembered searching it the night before and thinking that a girl had been living in there. He supposed it must've been her room.

She stepped in and Jeth followed. Then, before she had a chance to do anything else, he reached out and took hold of her hand, turning her toward him.

Some emotion he couldn't quite name crossed Sierra's face, but she didn't retreat. That was all the encouragement he needed.

He placed his hands on her shoulders and said, "Does it seem like a good idea now?" Then he bent down and kissed her. She braced against him for a second, but then opened her mouth, stepping closer as her body became languid. This kiss lasted longer than the other. There was no noise except for the sound of their breathing. No one to interrupt them. Jeth wrapped his arms around her, pressing her body to his.

Finally, Sierra pulled away. He let her go, his breath coming hard and his mind fuzzy from the overload of physical sensation. All the times he'd kissed Celeste, never once had he felt like this. *You shouldn't be doing this,* the voice of reason whispered in his mind.

Jeth knew he should listen, but he just couldn't seem to do it with Sierra so near.

"We should be going," she said.

Jeth nodded, ignoring the hurt that she could dismiss him so easily when he couldn't do the same to her.

Sierra turned toward the wall. "The data cell is just in here."

"Okay." He watched as she pushed against the flat surface. A moment later, a hidden panel slid open. No wonder he hadn't found the thing. More relief flooded him, and he fought back the urge to spin her around and start kissing her again.

"You know, I—" He froze as an odd, familiar noise echoed in the room. *Wha-wang*. It was the sound of a stunner charging.

Sierra turned toward him, pointing the barrel at his chest. The gun took less than five seconds to go from cold to full charge.

Jeth froze, as startled by the fierce look in her eyes as by the weapon.

"I'm never going back to Renford," Sierra said, fury in her voice.

The sound of Renford's name seemed to reverberate inside Jeth's skull like a bullet. How did she know about Renford? Jeth hadn't mentioned him once until last night with Milton. But then he remembered the noise outside sick bay. Maybe it hadn't been the cat.

Jeth opened his mouth to respond, but it was too late.

Sierra pulled the trigger.

The electric bolt shot out from the gun and hit him point-blank in the chest. Pain radiated outward, covering his entire body with searing, crackling heat.

Then Jeth felt nothing at all as the world blinked out of existence.

CHAPTER 20

THE FIRST PRO JOB THE MALLEUS SHADES HAD EVER worked ended in disaster.

There'd been only four of them on the crew then—Jeth, Celeste, Flynn, and Shady. Lizzie was still a few years away from catching Hammer's notice, and they hadn't yet found a suitable teenage candidate for tech ops. Instead, a man named Trent Danforth had been running tech for them. Well, Danforth ran everything, actually. Hammer didn't think Jeth was ready to lead yet, insisting the four of them were too young and inexperienced to be flying around the galaxy on their own.

Jeth hadn't liked Danforth much—an instinct that proved true a year or so later when Jeth discovered Danforth making side deals behind Hammer's back that cut into Jeth's profits. But right from the beginning, the best Jeth could say about the man was that he wasn't one of the Malleus Brethren or Guard. No, he was more a garden-variety criminal: amoral, crass, and with hygiene bad enough it even bothered a bunch of teenage boys. Jeth had a hard time listening to instructions from a man who smelled like three-week-old garbage. He just couldn't respect someone like that, no matter if Hammer had put him in charge.

It was perhaps this very lack of respect that had caused the disaster when they went in to steal a painting from a private collector on Gallant Prime, the nearest planet to Peltraz spaceport. Danforth had wanted Jeth to wait before entering the vault where the painting was stored when it wasn't on display, but Jeth was certain it was okay to go in. He'd done all the checks, run all the scans. Shady was with him, his impatience to get on with the job feeding into Jeth's.

And so the two of them went in. Screw Danforth and his paranoia about secondary alarm systems. Jeth knew what he was doing. He was a natural at this. *Besides,* he thought, taking in the sight of the painting they'd come to steal, *who would bother adding extra protection for that ugly thing?* The woman in the painting looked more like a man, despite her long black hair and plump chest. Her smile seemed more like a smirk pointed right at him.

As Jeth took a step toward the painting, an alarm began to sound. *Shit, shit, shit.* So much for instincts. Even worse, this meant Danforth had been right. Damn him. Scowling at the woman, Jeth ripped the painting off the stand and bolted for the door after Shady.

Three guards armed with stunners were waiting outside. Jeth stared at them, wondering how they could've gotten there so fast. They stared back, shouting at him to hold still. Jeth didn't believe they would actually shoot him. He was just a kid. He'd once been a *good* kid, from a well-known and respected family.

He made a run for it. All three men shot at him at the same time, three stunner blasts striking various parts of his body and knocking him unconscious for hours. During that time strange, painful dreams had kept him company.

There weren't any dreams this time.

Jeth woke to the feel of someone prodding him hard in the shoulder.

"Come on, Jeth. Get up!"

Celeste.

What's she doing here? Where is here? What happened?

Jeth opened his eyes. His thoughts remained incoherent until he tried to move. Then agony shot through his body as if someone had doused his nerves with acid. He knew the aftereffects of a stunner well enough, and the memory of what had happened struck him full force.

Sierra shot me.

That bitch.

"Good, you're alive," Celeste said. Jeth looked at her, but she'd already stood and headed for the door. "Jeth's awake!" she shouted.

He pushed himself up, trying not to groan. His pride had taken enough of a beating already. He looked around, realizing he was still on the *Donerail*. "What's happening?"

Celeste turned back to him. "We've been double-crossed."

"Double-crossed?"

"You know: tricked, duped, betrayed, made to look like idiots. Take your pick."

Jeth scowled as he lurched to his feet. "Tell me what *happened*."

"We're over here on the *Donerail* while Vince and Sierra are over there on *Avalon*. They forced us over here at gunpoint."

"What?" Jeth pushed past Celeste, breaking into a run. He spotted Flynn coming toward him. That made two of his crew members where they shouldn't be. Jeth kept going, making his way to the *Donerail's* bridge. The moment he arrived, he spotted *Avalon* through the main windows, and the hammering in his chest slowed a little. His ship was still here. As always, he found comfort in the sight of her.

Lizzie was at the central control station, her fingers flying over the buttons.

Forcing his attention on her, Jeth said, "What's going on?"

She didn't look up. "They just disconnected the towlines."

"What?" Jeth's heart began to pound again.

"They're leaving."

But they weren't just leaving. They were stealing his ship. Waves of outrage and dread erupted inside him.

"I'm trying to hack into *Avalon's* nav system, but nothing works on this stupid ship."

Of course it didn't. The *Donerail* was a wreck. Which was why they wanted *Avalon*. Even with a busted metadrive, Jeth's ship was better than this one.

He watched in horror as *Avalon* began to soar away from them. "They're heading for the border." He turned to Lizzie. "We've got to stop them."

"Working on it," Lizzie said, moving to another screen.

"Okay, I've diverted what power is left on this heap to the remaining engines. It's not pretty, but we might be able to follow."

Jeth dashed to the pilot's chair, instinct taking over. He grabbed the control column and felt the sluggish response. Still, it was better than nothing.

"What do we do?" Celeste asked from behind him.

Jeth glanced over his shoulder. She and Flynn were standing side by side and looking at him like lost children. He ignored them, fighting back the helplessness that made him want to scream and kick something. They'd never be able to keep up with *Avalon* on this ship.

"Are the guns working, Liz?" Celeste asked a moment later.

"Far as I know. The crow guns, for sure."

Out of the corner of his eye, Jeth saw Celeste stride toward the ladder leading up into the crow guns. She yanked it down and started climbing.

"What are you doing?" Lizzie said.

"I'm going to slow them down."

"You can't. Milton might get hurt."

"What?" Jeth said, glancing back at Lizzie.

Her voice shook as she answered him. "He's still over there."

Jeth turned to the window. What would they want with Milton? Then the answer came to him—they wouldn't want him. Milton was probably still passed out in his room, the door chained shut from the inside. It had been impossible for Sierra and Vince to get to him, not without taking the time to saw through the door.

"What about Shady?" Jeth asked, pushing even harder on the *Donerail*'s controls. It seemed as if the ship was slowing down rather than going faster.

"Down in the cargo bay," Celeste said. "He put up a good fight, but Vince took him down with a stunner. Then he threatened to do the same to the rest of us if we didn't do what he said."

Jeth had no trouble picturing it. Shady was a helluva good fighter, but he was rough, relying more on brute strength and courage. Vince, on the other hand, was easily as big and strong, but he possessed all the training and experience of an elite combat soldier, too. Shady hadn't stood much of a chance.

But at least he put up a fight, unlike me. Shame seared Jeth's insides.

"Get up to the crow," Jeth said to Celeste. "We've got to stop them."

And with that, he switched on the targeting system and centered the crosshairs of the pilot guns over *Avalon*'s portside thrusters. He exhaled, preparing to do the impossible and fire on his ship.

He pulled the trigger, a spray of gunfire bursting out from the *Donerail*, but the bullets fell short of the mark. "What the hell?"

"It must be interference from the border. They're crossing through now," Lizzie said. Then she gasped. "Oh God."

"What now?" said Flynn.

"They're engaging the metadrive."

"They *can't*," Jeth said. "The metadrive is failing. The jump won't work." Or it might work, but not all the way. They might enter metaspace but never come out of it again, lost forever. Dead. Jeth pushed and pushed against the controls, his hands and forearms aching from the effort. If he could just get into firing range, he might be able to stop them.

A brilliant, pulsating light flashed in front of Jeth's eyes, making them burn and half blinding him. He blinked the tears away a moment later and looked out at the empty scene before him.

Avalon was gone.

CHAPTER

21

JETH STARED FOR A LONG TIME AT THAT EMPTY PATCH OF space where his ship had been. *She's gone.* His *Avalon.*

And Milton.

He couldn't believe it. Refused to believe it. This was just a dream, a horrible nightmare. Two of the most important things in his life had just vanished into the nothingness of metaspace.

He wanted to hit something, except his entire body had gone numb with shock. *I won't go back to Renford,* Sierra had said. He closed his eyes, realizing his mistake. He should've made sure he and Milton were alone last night. He should've been more careful and less trusting. Milton must've been right about Cora. Calling Renford meant returning her to the ITA, and that was something Sierra would never let happen.

Jeth shook his head, refusing to justify Sierra's actions. He didn't care. Sierra had stolen his ship. He would kill her.

"Jeth?" Lizzie said from behind him.

He didn't respond. He didn't know how to without losing it.

"Um, Boss?" Flynn said. "You all right?"

Jeth closed his eyes, willing the numbness to retreat from his mind. He had to think about the others. He needed to be strong. His ability to lead under stress was one of the reasons Hammer had put him in charge of this crew in the first place.

Drawing a deep breath, he opened his eyes and nodded.

"What do we do now?" asked Flynn.

And there it was, the question Jeth knew had been coming.

When he didn't answer, Lizzie said, "I don't get it. Why would they steal *Avalon*?"

"Because they wanted all the money for themselves *and* a great ship," said Celeste.

"But they seemed . . . nice," said Lizzie. "I really thought Sierra liked you, Jeth."

"Shut up, Lizzie." Jeth closed his eyes and rubbed the bridge of his nose. He was so angry that sweat coated his skin despite the frigid air.

"I'm sorry." Lizzie cleared her throat. "But we'll get Milton and *Avalon* back. We just got to figure out where they went. Can't be too many options, assuming they really are headed for Olympia Seven and that they made as big a jump as *Avalon*'s metadrive can handle."

"You mean as long as the jump even worked," said Flynn.

Jeth opened his eyes in time to see Lizzie shoot Flynn a glare. "You're not *helping*."

"Oh, right. Need to be helpful." Flynn clapped his hands. "Let's see. We're stuck in the Belgrave on a ship with no real power, no metadrive, and probably only a day or two of oxygen left with this many people on board. Not to mention all the freaky dead bodies. So what can I do that's helpful? I know. I can kill myself now and get it over with."

"You can start by not being such a jerk," Celeste said, hands on hips.

"Well, pardon me for seeing the reality of things," said Flynn.

"You're just focused on the negative. As usual," said Lizzie.

"Oh right, because there's so much positive going on around here. Did you forget that the nav system we just installed doesn't work? And it's anybody's guess about the comms."

An all-out screaming match erupted. Jeth recognized it for what it was—channeled panic. Unlike him, they were frightened instead of angry.

"That's enough," Jeth said. He stood and everyone fell silent. "Celeste, you go check on Shady, make sure he's all right. Flynn, Lizzie, see if you can repair the comm system so we can call for help." Jeth glared at each of them in turn, daring someone to protest.

Nobody did.

"I'm going to the passenger deck to check something. When I get back, we'll figure out our next move."

Jeth strode off the bridge and made his way back to the cabin where Sierra had shot him. He stepped in and pulled the door closed behind him, not wanting to be seen. Then he ransacked the room, finding an outlet for his anger in the act. Even though he'd searched the room once before, he did it again, desperate to find anything that might help them out of this situation. He yanked out all the drawers on the dresser. He upended the mattress. He reached inside the hidden wall panel, scraping the bottom with his fingers. He even pulled off the air vent to see if she'd hidden anything up there.

Nothing. Nothing. Nothing.

Yanking his hair, Jeth let out a scream. It was pointless. Stupid. There was nothing to help him up here. His only option now was to call Hammer and submit to whatever punishment he saw fit to give. What had he been hoping for anyway? That she'd left behind a copy of the Aether Project? Or a calling card for their contact on Olympia Seven?

Calling card. If only . . .

Not daring to breathe, Jeth looked down and saw he was wearing his flight jacket. He'd put it on before he and Sierra had come over here. This was his favorite jacket, the one he wore on almost every job. The one he'd worn on the *Montrose* job, when he'd met Marcus Renford.

Jeth slipped a hand into the right side pocket. For a moment, he found nothing in there but fuzz and worn fabric brushing his knuckles. Then he felt it, something small and hard: Renford's calling card.

Jeth pulled it out and stared at it, hardly believing his luck. This would let him contact Renford directly. Jeth closed his hand around it, weighing his options once again. *Hammer or Renford.* Renford was ITA, the most powerful organization in the universe—surely they could track down *Avalon*. And there was no telling what Hammer might do when he found out how badly Jeth had failed. It was possible he might forgive him, but Jeth doubted it—not if the Aether Project was real. The prize was too big. And Jeth had a feeling Hammer would be able to piece together what had happened here, or force the truth out of him.

But calling Renford meant betraying Sierra, Vince, and Cora. The ITA would know they were still alive. Could he do that?

The answer came all too quickly—yes. They had betrayed him first. They'd stolen *Avalon*.

Firming his resolve, Jeth returned to the bridge where the others had gathered, including Shady, who was sitting on the floor with his back and head resting against the nav station, his arms thrust out in front of him, elbows on knees, eyes closed. A massive black, puffy bruise covered the left side of his face, the eye nearly swollen shut.

"What've we got?" Jeth said, scanning their expressions. None of them looked willing to speak. He zeroed his gaze on Flynn.

Flynn fidgeted a moment, then gave in. "The good news is the comm system was easy to fix. Just a couple of loose wires I was able to finagle. It should be coming online soon. We just need to cross over the border to transmit. The bad news is we've got two days max on life support. So we better get ahold of somebody willing to come rescue us fast."

"Well, it seems the good outweighs the bad for once," said Jeth.

Shady looked up, squinting at Jeth with his good eye. "So, we call Hammer then?"

"Yep," said Flynn. "Going to be a great conversation, too. He'll be thrilled when he finds out we disobeyed his order not to board the *Donerail*, brought the survivors onto *Avalon*, made plans to betray him, and then got our ship stolen in the process."

Lizzie rolled her eyes. "Like we're going to tell him all that."

"Oh, he'll know on his own," said Celeste. "Hammer's not dumb."

"No, he's not," said Jeth. "And no matter what story we spin for him, he's going to make us pay for this." *Not that we haven't paid enough already,* Jeth thought. *With Avalon gone.* A terrible sense of loss made the muscles in his chest contract. He drew a ragged breath.

Lizzie frowned. "But who else can we contact who'll help us?"

Jeth reached inside his pocket and withdrew the calling card. "Marcus Renford."

"Are you talking about the guy the three of you attacked on Kordan?" said Shady.

"Uh-huh," said Lizzie. "He sure is."

"Well, don't you think he might not be too happy with you after that?"

"It's not like we hurt him," said Celeste, no doubt remembering the way Renford had vanished off the ship, despite the two stunners he'd taken to the chest.

"Right," said Jeth. "And it doesn't change the fact that he wanted us to bring him the *Donerail*. So we bring it to him. Or have him come get it, rather."

"You think he still wants it?" asked Flynn, looking around.

"Of course, he doesn't," said Celeste. "He wants the

Aether Project, or whatever it is that Vince and Sierra just escaped with."

"Maybe," said Jeth. *Or he wants them.* "But either way, he might help us in order to get the information we can give him about where they went. I mean, he doesn't even know they're alive."

Shady grunted. "That doesn't sound like much of a plan. We don't have any real leverage on the guy."

Jeth sighed. "I know, but it's the best one we've got for getting *Avalon* back. If it doesn't work, we'll call Hammer. Unless any of you have a better idea."

As he expected, no one did.

x

A short while later, Jeth piloted them over the border, then inserted the calling card into the comm reader.

With nothing else to do while they waited for Renford to answer, Lizzie huddled down next to Celeste on the floor beside the comm station, the two of them sharing a blanket and body heat. Flynn sat across from them on a pile of pillows he'd gathered from the cabins. Shady hadn't moved at all.

"So how long do we wait before we give up?" asked Shady an hour later.

"Long enough," Jeth snapped, unable to hide his impatience.

Flynn patted his stomach. "Would've been nice if they'd left us some food."

"Go take a nap," said Celeste. "You'll burn fewer calories and be less hungry."

Flynn rubbed his arms. "Sure, like I won't burn them trying to stay warm inside this icicle."

"I hope they'll remember to feed Viggo," said Lizzie. "They probably will, right? I mean, they're not completely heartless. They could've killed us instead of herding us over here."

"Oh, sure," said Shady. "They're real *saints*."

Jeth gritted his teeth. If Renford didn't answer soon, he was going to shoot somebody—*Yeah, right, using a gun you don't have*. Everything he owned was on *Avalon*. He'd built his whole life around that ship, only to have a couple of strangers snatch it away.

"It's true," Lizzie protested. "They could've taken the ship when we first brought them on board."

"Oh, no they couldn't," said Celeste. "They had to earn our trust first. Ain't that right, *Captain*?"

"Yeah," said Shady, turning his one-eyed gaze on Jeth. "How'd Sierra manage to get the jump on you so easy, anyhow?"

Jeth felt a blush threaten to color his face, and he turned toward the comm station. *Screw it*. He'd just contact Hammer and be done with it. It was better than all this waiting around, wallowing in frustration and guilt. He'd been an idiot. If he'd been less preoccupied with kissing Sierra and more concerned about getting the truth out of her, none of this would've happened.

Just as he was about to press the kill switch, the call button started blinking. Someone was finally answering.

Marcus Renford's face appeared onscreen a moment later.

He looked exactly the same as Jeth remembered: thin, with black hair turning to steel.

"Jethro Seagrave," Renford said, a false smile rising to his lips. "Nice to see you again. Although I'm a bit surprised, to be honest, considering how our last interlude ended."

Jeth didn't bother playing nice. He was too cold, too angry, and too desperate for games. "We found the *Donerail*."

"I can see that. Judging from your incoming source protocol, I'd say you're calling *from* the *Donerail*." Renford paused. "But how is it you're still breathing on a ship that long gone?"

"Maybe because it wasn't as long gone as you thought. And maybe not everybody on board was dead either."

"What?"

"That's right. There were three survivors."

Renford's eyes narrowed, the expression making his face suddenly snakelike. *"Who?"*

Jeth shook his head, knowing full well those names were the source of his leverage. "First things first. We need your help. We're stranded just outside the Belgrave. The nav's down, so not sure where."

Renford leaned back from the screen. "But where is *Avalon*?"

"Stolen, by those same survivors. Who I'll be happy to identify once you pick us up."

"I see. But why call me? You made it clear you only work for Hammer."

Jeth gritted his teeth. "I'm reconsidering the situation. I'd like to take you up on your offer. The *Donerail* for *Avalon*."

"But you just said *Avalon* was stolen."

Hearing the truth spoken aloud stung, but Jeth ignored it. "So she was, but I know who took her, and I've got a pretty good idea what their next move is. And I'm willing to help you find them. I'll do whatever it takes."

"Really?" Renford arched an eyebrow. "That's an interesting proposition. Tell me, is the rest of your crew still with you?"

Jeth frowned, wondering why it mattered. "Yeah, they are. What of it?"

Renford made a show of examining his fingernails, not answering. "So, you're offering to tell me everything you know about the *Donerail* survivors *and* to track them down in exchange for your ship?"

"Yes, and we want some reassurance that the ITA will protect us from any retaliation Hammer might attempt."

Renford looked up. "There's no way I can guarantee your complete safety. Hammer is a powerful man. His criminal network has a far reach."

Jeth swallowed. He knew this well enough. "All I'm asking is you repair any damage to my ship and give us some cash and supplies to help us stay hidden from Hammer. At least for a while." *Surely there was somewhere in the galaxy where Hammer couldn't get at them.*

"All right. I think I can do that. But on one condition."

Jeth took a deep breath, trying to keep the exasperation from his voice. "What?"

Renford leaned toward the screen. "I will send a ship to come get you right now, but you must give me the names of the survivors first."

"How do I know you'll still come get us once I've told you?"

"Simple. I've given you my word. And I'm not Hammer Dafoe. Besides, you said you had more information to share. I'm interested in all of it."

Jeth considered his options. They were just names. He didn't have to say anything about the Aether Project or that *Avalon*'s metadrive was failing or about Sierra's contact on Olympia Seven.

I'll never go back to Renford, he heard Sierra say once more. *Are you really going to betray her? Betray them?*

Jeth steeled himself against the doubt. They'd stolen his ship. They would get what they deserved.

What about Cora? What does she deserve?

Jeth closed his eyes, doubt making his head swim.

"What's your answer?" Renford pressed.

Just names. Nothing more. *And I don't have a choice. Not now.*

"Jethro?" said Renford.

Jeth looked at him and said, "Sierra Hightower, Vince Mallory, and a little girl named Cora."

An intense, nameless emotion crossed Renford's face. Surprise? Alarm? "Thank you, Jeth. This is most helpful. Leave the comm line open so I can triangulate your position. As soon as I've got it, I'll send my nearest ship to fetch you."

Jeth sighed, relieved it was over. "How long?"

"An hour, at most."

He nodded, and Renford ended the connection.

"Well, *that* went well," Shady said. "So we're really going to trust this guy?"

Lizzie shook her head. "We should've just called Hammer. Renford gives me the creeps."

Jeth didn't reply, although silently he agreed with Lizzie, at least about the creepy part.

Should've gone with the devil you know, a voice whispered in his mind.

Jeth ignored it. Renford was the best choice. The only choice, now. Hammer wouldn't give a damn about Milton. Or *Avalon.* And Jeth hadn't forgotten about Renford's offer to tell him the truth about his parents.

But in the end, choice didn't matter.

When a ship finally arrived a half hour later, it wasn't an ITA ship at all.

It was one of Hammer's.

22

THE FIRST PUNCH STRUCK HIM IN THE GUT, JUST BELOW the rib cage. The second landed higher. Jeth felt the rib snap in a bright burst of pain that radiated outward like a bomb. He tried to hunch over to lessen the agony, but firm hands on his arms held him upright and in place.

Sergei Castile grinned at Jeth, pleasure making his broad face glow.

"Isn't this a little beneath you?" Jeth said between shallow pants. "I didn't think Hammer would use his general for something as mundane as a beating."

The two Malleus Guards holding Jeth in place tightened their grip on his arms, fingers biting into his naked flesh. They'd stripped him down to just his pants the moment they'd forced him into this cell, just minutes after their arrival at Peltraz. To Jeth's shock, he recognized one of the Guards as Trent Danforth, the smelly, oily man who had once run tech ops for the Shades. Jeth hadn't seen him in a long time, not since he'd been caught betraying Hammer. Danforth was horribly changed—twice as big as he used to be and with all traces of his former personality gone. He was nothing but a shell wearing Danforth's face.

Sergei's fist collided with Jeth's jaw. Starbursts shot across his vision.

"I volunteered especially for you," Sergei said.

Jeth spat blood. "Glad to know I rank so high."

Sergei adjusted the glove on his right hand, pulling the protective inner layer snug over his knuckles. The outer layer consisted of a material as hard and dense as metal.

Jeth eyed the glove, trying not to flinch. "Does it make you feel like a big man, beating up on someone who can't fight back? Or maybe you just get off on it."

Sergei's answer landed against Jeth's cheek and nose. Blood spurted from both nostrils and tears stung his eyes. A kick to the stomach followed next, obliterating any desire Jeth had to continue taunting.

Sergei rained down blow after blow, his fists as merciless as mallets and the Guards' grip on his arms as unyielding as steel. Jeth tried to turn his thoughts inward to block out the pain. He refused to cry or beg or ask the questions burning in his mind. *Where is my sister? What are you doing to my friends?* More than once he lost consciousness, only to be revived again when the Guards dumped ice water over his head.

Delirious, Jeth wasn't aware of when it finally ended.

He awoke sometime later, lying on the hard floor of the cell, his body damp from the puddle of bloodstained water beneath him. He forced his swollen eyes open and saw a pair of black boots so polished, they glistened even in the dim overhead light of the cell. Only one man Jeth knew wore boots so clean and expensive. He craned his neck and saw Hammer Dafoe standing over him, hands on hips, his expression made of stone.

Jeth lowered his head, content to lie there as waves of agony rolled through him. He'd known trouble was coming when Hammer's ship arrived for them instead of Renford's, but he'd never imagined pain like this. The mind was incapable. *It'll pass soon,* Jeth told himself. It had to. Either that or he would die, and even then it would still be over.

"Get him up," Hammer said.

Jeth squeezed his eyes closed as rough hands grabbed his arms and hauled him up. Bare feet slipping in the muck, Jeth groaned from the effort of trying to gain his footing and support his own body weight.

Hammer grunted disdainfully. Jeth wanted to scream at him, but that would require expanding his lungs, and there was nothing he wanted to do less at the moment.

"Set him down over there," Hammer said. "Doesn't look like he's man enough to stand on his own."

The Guard dropped him onto a concrete bench in the back of the cell hard enough that his teeth clanked together. With a massive effort, Jeth managed to stay in an upright position, his back propped against the wall.

"Leave us alone," Hammer said, and the Guards left without a word.

Jeth leaned his head back and gave Hammer the fiercest glare he could muster, a difficult feat with the swelling around both his eyes. "Where's my crew?"

"Not far from here."

Jeth swallowed. "If you hurt—" He broke off, unable even to voice the possibility of such a thing and wary of more pain. "Where's Lizzie?" He knew the question was pointless, but his worry for her consumed rational thought. He'd already lost *Avalon* and Milton. He couldn't lose her, too.

"Your sister is fine. For the moment. And I must say, I was surprised to see how attractive a young woman she's become. It's been a while since I've *really* looked at her."

Hot anger surged through Jeth at Hammer's insinuation. It burned the hurt right out of him, and Jeth leaped up, prepared to rip the man's throat out with his bare hands. It was foolish, stupid, but desperation spurred him on. Hammer's punch landed first, and in Jeth's weakened state, he crumpled beneath it. He hit the ground hard enough that all the air whooshed out of his lungs. He gasped, each breath a knife in his side.

Hammer yanked Jeth up and dropped him on the bench. "Try that again and I will have my men break your kneecaps. Understand?"

Jeth nodded, trying to think clearly through the haze of pain.

"Now, why don't you tell me the truth about what happened in the Belgrave?"

Jeth struggled to remember the story that he and the others had agreed on in those few short minutes they'd had before Hammer's men had brought them on board the starship. It seemed forever ago. No one had asked them a single thing during the entire trip back to Peltraz.

"And don't bother repeating that cock and bull about being innocent victims just trying to help the survivors," said Hammer. "I know it's not true. Too many things don't add up. My men tell me that not long before we picked you up, you made a call to an unidentified contact using an encrypted calling card." Hammer reached into his front pocket and withdrew Renford's calling card. "This one. Now who could you have called? And why? Even more peculiar, why would the thieves who stole your ship bother sending a message saying where I could find you?"

Jeth blinked. "A message?"

"Oh, yes," Hammer said. "It came from *Avalon*. Why would they go to such trouble?"

No idea. Jeth ran his tongue over his teeth, testing them for looseness. "Maybe it was Milton. He was still on the ship when they took it."

"Perhaps," Hammer said, returning the card to his pocket. "But I think it's time to tell me the real story. Unless you want me to have Sergei extract it from your crew instead."

Jeth closed his eyes as an image of Lizzie receiving the same kind of beating at Sergei's hands made him shudder. He didn't have any fight left in him, nor any strength left to spin a new story. "All right," he said.

Then he told Hammer the truth about what happened, about finding the survivors, the metadrive failing, and Sierra's offer of a solution. He even told him about Renford approaching them during the *Montrose* job.

Outrage seemed to sparkle in Hammer's tiny black eyes as he listened. "Agent Renford of the ITA? Marcus Renford?"

Jeth nodded, wondering vaguely at Hammer's recognition. "That's who the calling card belongs to."

"Ah," said Hammer. "Well, go on."

"That's it," Jeth said. "I told you everything."

Hammer inclined his head. "What about the Aether Project? Did you ever actually see it?"

"No."

"I see."

Jeth braced for whatever retribution Hammer would deliver now. He wouldn't be surprised if the man killed him with his bare hands.

Yet amazingly, Hammer kept his temper in check, pretending to be wounded instead. "What I don't understand is why you would betray me in the first place."

Jeth drew a defeated breath. "I wanted my ship."

"But I already promised you your ship when you completed the job."

"You lied."

Hammer gaped, as if Jeth had spoken in gibberish.

Jeth went on. "We both know you never intended to give me the ship and let me go. The crew is too valuable. So I figured I needed something to trade that you wanted more than us."

"Ah," Hammer said. "The Aether Project."

Jeth nodded.

A cold smile lifted Hammer's lips for a moment. "Yes,

something as valuable as that might've made the bargain work. Can you imagine it? All the secrets of metatech, everything the ITA has hoarded for hundreds of years." Hammer shook his head. "Pity you didn't manage to pull it off."

"So the Aether Project *was* the weapon you were after?"

"Yes. It's the weapon I'm *still* after."

The knowledge of how close he'd come to succeeding burned inside Jeth. He gritted his teeth, then stopped as he felt one of them move ominously.

Hammer folded his arms. "Still, you're resourceful, Jeth. Smart and good in a pinch. Remarkable for someone so young."

Unfazed by the change in topic, Jeth said, "Let me guess, I remind you of you, right?" Bitterness emboldened him as he remembered how Hammer had once said he was like a son.

Hammer smirked. "Not at all. At your age, I was prone to attacking first and thinking later. I only managed to get as far as I did then because I was so damn good at fighting. And I've never been afraid of doing what needed to be done."

Jeth didn't doubt it. He shivered. Nothing Hammer had said or done so far had frightened him as much as that statement.

Hammer turned around and walked to the door. *That's it? He's leaving?* But Hammer stepped to the right of the door and placed his hand on a metal panel on the wall. A second later a compartment opened above the panel, revealing two objects Jeth couldn't make out from where he sat.

Hammer picked both up, hiding them in his hands, and returned to Jeth. "Do you want to know what the key to my success has been?"

"Not really." Jeth knew he shouldn't be flip, but he couldn't help it. The hopelessness of the situation gnashed at him with razor-sharp teeth. A part of him wanted it to be over. All of it. He was so tired, so beaten down, loss like a giant gaping hole inside him. *If it weren't for Lizzie . . .*

"Loyalty," Hammer went on. "That's the key. It's what's made you so successful as well, you know. The loyalty of your crew. How they're willing to follow you anywhere. It's the mark of a good leader and one of the reasons I picked you."

Jeth didn't say anything. He didn't trust his voice to speak.

"Yes, loyalty. You have to command it in your people if you want to lead. Betrayal can bring down an entire empire. It's something I can't tolerate. Like a cancer, it must be cut out before it spreads."

Jeth swallowed. Here it was. The punishment that would make Sergei's thrashing feel like a pleasant massage. *Does dying hurt?* he wondered. *What will happen to Lizzie when I'm gone?*

Hammer said, "But disloyalty isn't a problem in my organization, because this device eradicates such behavior." Hammer turned his left hand over, revealing one of the objects. It looked like a large clear-colored spider with flaccid, rubbery legs—a brain implant of the Malleus Guard.

"You've seen these before, but do you know how they work?" Hammer flipped the thing over, revealing a long, thick needle. "Once this is inserted, it can never be removed. It controls electrical impulses in the brain. I can command it to block sensations of fear or pain. Or to take away your desire to think for yourself, turn you into something mindless, a drone who only follows commands. In other words, it can take away your free will."

Jeth stared at the thing. It looked more like a spider than ever, one that fed on souls instead of blood. *And Hammer commands it.* Jeth examined Hammer's appearance, realizing for the first time that he wasn't wearing his red implant.

"I use this particular device on the Guard because they are unworthy to be Brethren," said Hammer. "They might have committed a crime against me or they might lack the necessary intelligence, or their psychological profile suggests they are prone to cowardice. Or, more likely, betrayal."

Like me, Jeth thought, catching the subtext in Hammer's words. A cold sensation slid over his skin, seeming to absorb inward, chilling his heart. He pictured Danforth, remembering how he once had been and how he was now. The comparison made him shudder.

Hammer turned over his right hand, revealing another spider-like object, this one black. "This device is for the people whose loyalty I wish to keep willingly and not by force. It can be safely removed, and while it does enhance key cognitive abilities, it does not remove the ability or desire for self will. On the contrary, I *want* my Brethren to think and act on their own. There are too many situations that require reasoning and ingenuity, as I'm sure you can imagine."

Oh, Jeth could imagine it all right. It was the difference between sentience and machinery. Between life and a pale mockery of it.

"Oh, I almost forgot to mention," Hammer said, his tone

perversely casual. "This one"—he held up the clear-colored device—"can also shut down brain functionality entirely at a single command, or at the detection of a foolish attempt to remove it."

Jeth smacked his lips, which had swollen to the size of his index fingers. "You mean it can kill you from the inside."

Hammer bared his teeth. They were small in his fat face, white and sharp. "Precisely. Now, let's get down to it. One of these is destined for you. It's been in your future from the moment your uncle sat down at that gaming table and gambled first your ship and then your life away."

The world seemed to lurch sideways as the full meaning of Hammer's words struck Jeth. "He gambled *me*?"

"Oh, not so literally. He'd already lost *Avalon* and was desperate to get the ship back, but he had no collateral for the game. Instead I offered him a deal. If he won, he got *Avalon* back. If he lost, he would stay and become a permanent resident of Peltraz and do freelance doctoring when I needed it. At the time, I didn't realize what a valuable asset his young wards would turn out to be. Not that it took long."

No, it hadn't. Jeth had started working for Hammer mere months after Milton lost *Avalon*. It had never occurred to him to wonder why Milton hadn't just found some other way out of Peltraz, taking Jeth and Lizzie somewhere planet-side. A place where Jeth wouldn't have drawn the interest of a crime lord and where Lizzie could've gone to school and been a normal kid.

"So, you see," Hammer continued, "I decided years ago

that you would become a member of my personal security force. I've been molding you for it ever since."

Jeth glowered. "You haven't molded me into *anything.* I'm nothing like you."

Hammer gave him a patient look. "Then why don't you ask yourself why you're so good at being *bad*?"

Jeth managed a scowl despite the injuries on his face. "Fine, if you're so certain about me, why didn't you just implant the damn thing already and be done with it? I know you don't have a problem forcing people into your service."

"Not at all, although I prefer willing members instead of conscripted ones. The Guard have their uses, of course, but they could hardly be considered sufficient manpower for the kind of interplanetary organization I run. That's why I have the Brethren. And only the willing ever join the Brethren." He pulled out his personal comm and checked it briefly. "Now, there's one little hitch. You were born on Therin, which is a Confederated planet."

"So what?"

"These implants were designed by the ITA. They're legal, Jeth, and I'm not the only one to use them. There are many governments across the galaxy that do. The black ones are normally for soldiers, the clear ones for prisoners—or slaves. The ITA carefully monitors each device, and they cannot be activated on anyone registered with the Confederation who is under eighteen. Like you." Hammer paused. "Except you *will* be eighteen very soon."

Just a few days. Jeth closed his eyes, willing himself to be unconscious again, willing himself to somehow enter metaspace without a drive or gate and be gone from here. Gone so far that no one could ever reach him again. But it was a child's fantasy.

Jeth summoned what remained of his courage and said in an even voice, "What exactly are you threatening?"

"Oh, it's not a threat, merely a statement of fact."

Hammer returned the two implants to the compartment on the wall. Then he faced Jeth again and slipped a hand inside the front of his jacket, withdrawing a small, rectangular case. Hammer opened it, revealing the red brain implant he normally wore. Except for its color, the thing looked no different from the other two implants. He pulled it out, flipped it over in his hand, and then raised the sharp point to the back of his head. Then, with a sickeningly wet sound, Hammer pushed the thing into his skull. The flaccid red tentacles surged to life, stretching up and outward, wrapping themselves around the base of Hammer's head and neck.

Jeth flinched and looked away, his stomach churning.

"In a moment," Hammer said, "I will summon Sergei to take you to a private medical facility where my physicians will insert into your brain and spine the architecture necessary to support an implant. It's a relatively simple procedure, all things considered, and when you wake up you won't have much more than a headache. Then, when you turn eighteen in a little over a week from now, you will receive one of the implants I showed you. All of this will happen, whether you like it or not. *Which* implant you receive, however—now, that will be up to you."

Hammer took a deep breath and then leaned toward Jeth,

his expression menacing. "Betray me again, continue to defy me, or make any attempt to escape my service, and you will receive the clear one, the one for the Guard. I will have it inserted in you and, when the rest of your crew comes of age, in them as well. Shady and Flynn will become members of the Guard along with you, while Celeste and your sister will be placed in one of my brothels." A slow, icy smile formed on Hammer's face. "And the beautiful thing about this arrangement is that you won't even care."

If Jeth had had anything left in his stomach, he might have vomited. As it was, he could only sit there, frozen in place by terror and dread. And that suffocating hopeless feeling.

"If, in the time you have left, however," Hammer continued, "you can find some way to earn my trust, to convince me that your loyalty is certain and that you will never again attempt to betray me, I will give you the second implant. Things will stay just as they are now. You and your crew will continue to do jobs as appropriate, and you will slowly rise through my ranks of Brethren, perhaps even becoming a general yourself someday. You will never want for work or food or purpose."

Jeth didn't doubt it. But there was something so much more important that he would long for with every fiber of his being for as long as he lived.

Freedom.

It wasn't a choice at all. One way or another, this was a life sentence.

CHAPTER

THEY TOOK TO HIM A ROOM MADE OF METAL. METAL FLOORS and walls and ceilings. They cut his hair close to his scalp, then forced him to lie on his stomach atop a cold metal table with his face pressed against a padded hole. They strapped his arms and legs down, but it wasn't necessary. Mere seconds after the injection the doctor gave him—the needle a sharp prick against his neck followed by a rush of cold that spread through him like nitrogen in his veins— a paralysis gripped his body. He lay there with his gaze fixed on the floor, his mind aware that the doctors were doing something to his head and neck, but his body incapable of feeling it.

He heard the soft whir of some machine kicking on. It sounded like a drill. One that would dig into his skull, carving out a sheath to house the implant.

Guard or Brethren.

There was no question which he would choose. But how would he ever be able to convince Hammer to make him the latter? He had no aces left, no bargaining chip. Nothing at all.

The whirring grew louder. The doctors pressed in close to him. Another needle pricked his neck. This time the

medicine took him under, too deep even for dreams—
or nightmares.

They didn't give him time to recover after the procedure.
The second he was awake, Hammer's men hauled him up
while the doctors watched silently. Jeth swayed on his feet,
too dizzy to stand. The skin on the back of his skull burned
like he'd been branded with a hot iron, but the rest of his
head felt cold from where they'd cut his hair. The Guards
caught him before he fell. Then they carried him out of the
operating room and into a shuttle.

They took him to an apartment suite on the west side of
the city, the area where most of the Guard lived. Realizing
it, Jeth wondered if this meant that Hammer had already
made up his mind. *Of course he has. What could you possibly do
to convince him of your loyalty? Nothing. Not even grovel.*

As he stepped through the apartment door, Jeth noticed
the lock was on the outside. He didn't bother asking the
Brethren why they'd brought him here. With *Avalon* gone,
he had nowhere else to go.

But at least Lizzie and the others were waiting for him when
he walked down the hallway and stepped into the common
area. He kept a hand on the wall to steady himself. Lizzie
took one look at his bruised and bloodied face and burst into
tears. She threw her arms around him, and he yelped in pain.

"Oh, I'm sorry."

"Way to go, Liz," Celeste said. "Do you think Hammer's
men only work over faces? They beat him everywhere."

Celeste grabbed Jeth's shirt and hauled it up, revealing a dense patch of bruises beneath. Lizzie gasped. The sound cut off abruptly, as if she'd lost the ability to breathe.

Jeth hissed as Celeste's knuckles grazed him. He felt as if his entire body had been rubbed with sandpaper.

"Don't be such a baby," Celeste said, but Jeth heard the concern in her voice. She pulled his shirt all the way off.

"Damn," Shady said. "How're you still standing?"

"Because he's Jeth," said Flynn, a note of affection in his voice, along with a tremor.

Lizzie ran her hand over Jeth's shorn hair. "Why did they cut it?" He flinched away, terrified she would discover the answer. "Why did they do any of this?"

"We tried to pull one over on Hammer," said Shady. "What did you think he was going to do when he found out?"

"But we didn't tell him about that." Lizzie scanned each face. "None of us told him the true story."

"I don't think it mattered," said Flynn.

Celeste sighed. "Come on. Let's get these cleaned up. I can't believe they didn't take you to the hospital."

Oh, but they did, Jeth thought, and he resisted the urge to reach behind his head and feel the hole he knew must be back there, one large enough to sheath the stem of an implant. He prayed his friends would be too concerned with his face and bruised body to notice it.

Shady grunted. "Sure would be nice to have a doctor around to fix him up."

"Be quiet," Lizzie spat. She wasn't crying anymore, but

Jeth could tell she was teetering on the edge of it. He knew she held back because of how much it bothered him. He wanted to tell her it was all right, but he couldn't find the heart. Nothing was all right. It never would be again.

Celeste led him to one of the bedrooms, the others following behind. She pushed him down on the bed. He didn't protest, even as a sharp stab of pain shot through his skull when the back of his head touched the mattress. He wanted to lie on his stomach, but at least this way no one would see the implant architecture.

Celeste opened a drawer beside the bed, pulled out an electronic tablet, and started typing. "Head down to One-Eyed Johnson's and pick up these supplies." She handed the tablet to Flynn. "Shady, go with him."

"Do you know what you're doing?" said Flynn.

"It's the only option we got. I've helped Milton a couple of times."

Flynn nodded, then disappeared through the door, Shady trailing after him.

"Liz, get a warm washcloth." Celeste bent and pulled off Jeth's shoes.

Jeth closed his eyes, too tired and hurt to be embarrassed by the attention. He heard Lizzie return a moment later, and she started to wipe his face with a damp cloth. It hurt, but not unbearably.

"Um, guys?" Flynn said.

"Why are you still here?" Celeste snapped.

"We're locked in."

Lizzie's hand went still on Jeth's face. "What?"

"Yeah," said Shady. "The security system says we're on lockdown until further notice."

"What the hell does that mean?" said Celeste.

Jeth took as deep a breath as his battered ribs would allow. "That we're not going anywhere. Not for a long time." *Trapped, trapped, trapped.* The words pounded a relentless tattoo inside his head. He squeezed his eyes shut tighter. He thought he would've preferred actual chains to this kind of imprisonment.

Celeste let loose a long string of swear words.

"What are we supposed to do? Just let him lie here, bleeding all over the place?" said Lizzie.

"I'm fine." Jeth forced his eyes open.

Lizzie scowled at him. "No, you're not."

"I am. There's nothing serious."

"You can't know that."

"Don't argue with me, Liz. Not this time." A tremor threatened Jeth's voice, and he almost lost the tight grip on his emotions. "I just want to be left alone." He met her gaze, his eyes pleading. "All I want to do is sleep."

"At least let us finish cleaning your cuts," Lizzie said.

"No. I'll be fine. I promise." The lie throbbed inside him.

Bright tears shone in Lizzie's eyes as she frowned down at him. "What happened? What did Hammer *do* to you?"

Jeth turned away, unable to bear her anguished expression any longer. He knew she wasn't talking about the beating. She could tell there was something far deeper wrong with him, that he was broken in some fundamental way. "Let me be. Please."

Lizzie's voice came out a sob. "Okay."

Jeth shut his eyes as the others cleared the room, leaving him alone at last. When he heard the door close, he finally let go of the horror he'd been holding back inside, the overwhelming despair from knowledge of a future he had no hope of escaping. All his dreams about owning *Avalon* again and flying away were dying inside him.

He started to cry then, letting the emotion leak out. He had to get rid of it, because he knew come morning he would have to embrace a new life, one without dreams or hope. He had to find a way to earn Hammer's trust and to become one of the Brethren. He had to. For them. For Lizzie and Celeste and Flynn and Shady.

His family.

He had to save them from the fate that waited for him. He was all they had.

Hours later, Jeth crawled out of the bed, his body stiff and wounds still throbbing. He barely felt it. Somehow, through the night, he'd managed to cut himself off from feeling anything. Or at least from caring. He emerged from the bedroom, seeking a hot shower and then maybe some food. As the warm, soothing water poured over him, he raised a hand to the back of his skull and touched the hole for the first time. The skin throbbed from the slight pressure of his finger. He realized at once the thing wouldn't be very visible. It was almost funny how small it was.

And yet how huge.

When he finished, Jeth returned to his room and rummaged through the closet, where he found some new clothes waiting for him. He slipped on a pair of pants and a shirt and finally a hooded jacket. He hoped the hood, lying thick and fat against his neck, would hide the implant architecture.

Summoning as much courage as he could, Jeth emerged and headed for the living room. Shady and Flynn were sitting on the sofa in front of a view screen, watching a show. Lizzie sat in an armchair, reading. Celeste was in the kitchen, sitting at the table and drinking a cup of something steaming.

"How're you feeling?" Lizzie asked, setting aside the reader.

"Fine," Jeth said as he marched past her, heading to the computer terminal on the far wall. He sat down and pulled up the access screen to the savings account Hammer had given him. He had only view access, but it was a way to keep track of how much money he'd earned toward *Avalon*. Jeth made a habit of checking it regularly, and even though he'd resigned himself to the fact that *Avalon* would never be his and that none of this mattered, he entered his login name and password.

ACCESS DENIED

The large red words were like a punch to the chest. He sucked in a breath. He'd known it was coming, that deep down the money had never truly been his, but it still hurt.

He had nothing now, not even the pretense of something to hope for.

Despair pressing down on him, Jeth closed the screen and punched up the link to his personal messages. He did it out of habit, nothing more. The only person who ever sent him messages was Brian Carvell, one of his old school friends. But those had grown fewer and farther between as time went on. They had so little in common anymore. Brian was off to college soon, thinking about his future and a career in intergalactic law. Jeth was going nowhere.

The flashing icon of an unread message blinked at him as the screen opened. Jeth stared at it in surprise. The sender was listed as unknown. He clicked on it. The message was short, cryptic:

24-756-11-543. Come now. Hurry. —M.

Jeth reread it a dozen times, not daring to believe it was real. And yet he knew it was. He'd even known it was coming, deep down. That they had come through the other side of the metajump safely, and that, as long as he was still alive, Milton would find a way to contact him sooner or later. Although Jeth hated Sierra and Vince, neither had struck him as a killer.

Jeth's mind instinctively began to scheme for a way to get out of this apartment and steal a ship. Those numbers were undoubtedly coordinates, and he would fly there and reclaim *Avalon*. He could do it. He and his crew were the best around. They could find a way, especially here on their home turf, which they knew so well.

Except . . . what did it matter? What would he do once he had *Avalon*? Could they outrun Hammer forever? Would Hammer forget about them eventually?

No. Jeth understood now. Hammer did not accept losing. Sooner or later Jeth and his crew would be caught. *Flynn and Shady will be Guard. Celeste and Lizzie will go to the brothels.*

Jeth couldn't let it happen. He wouldn't.

And so, here was the answer to saving them. This information could be his ticket back into Hammer's good graces. Jeth's next steps formed in his mind as clearly as directions on a map. He would offer this information to Hammer as a sign of a good faith. And he would volunteer to find *Avalon* and to steal the Aether Project. Convincing Hammer of his desire to succeed would be easy. All he had to do was picture the look of surprise on Sierra's face when he took the data cell from her. If he could, he would leave her stranded somewhere, hopeless, just as she'd left him. Hammer hadn't given Jeth any indication that he was interested in Cora or any of the survivors, just the information.

And when I return, I'll swear to join the Brethren. But only so long as he lets the others go.

It might be enough. Just maybe.

But they'll never leave you behind, a harsh voice spoke in Jeth's mind.

They will. Jeth glanced around at Lizzie, Celeste, Flynn, and Shady. *They have to.*

CHAPTER

IT TOOK LITTLE EFFORT TO CONVINCE HAMMER OF THE plan. It was as if he'd been expecting something like this all along. *I knew you'd come around,* his eyes said. *I knew you'd choose to obey me.*

But it wasn't a choice. This was coercion, no matter the circumstance.

And it wasn't without consequence either. Hammer insisted Jeth spend a couple of hours in a regeneration chamber, a highly expensive treatment capable of healing a variety of basic injuries, including broken ribs.

"If I'm sending you on a job," Hammer said, "then you'd best be in top form."

Trouble was, the healing process hurt even more than the beating that had put him in such a state. Jeth knew Hammer most often used the regenerator as a torture device. He would have his enemies' bones broken, then heal them, only to break them again. After his session ended, Jeth understood just how effective the method could be.

Still, less than three days after arriving at Peltraz, Jeth and his crew left again, this time accompanied by Sergei and Daxton Price, their new babysitters. At least Dax's skill would come in handy if they had to track down Sierra and Vince. Jeth thought it likely they wouldn't stay on *Avalon*, not with the ship's failed metadrive.

They flew out from Peltraz on the *Citation*, the same C-94 Viper that Dax had used to escort them to the Belgrave Quadrant. The ship was registered to Roland Trudanth, a dummy name Hammer used when his own might draw too much attention. The *Citation* had been customized in one of Hammer's chop shops to include a stealth drive and an entire arsenal of weapons, all carefully concealed and, needless to say, completely illegal on a ship of that class.

"Are you sure of those coordinates?" Dax asked from the pilot's chair. Sergei sat copilot beside him.

Jeth glanced up from the nav station screen where he had just finished charting their flight path to an Independent planet known as Benfold Minor. "Yeah, I'm pretty sure. Lizzie double-checked that Benfold was within jumping distance from where we got picked up outside the Belgrave."

"All right. Moenia City it is," Dax said, leaning back in the pilot's chair. He had a cocky manner about him, far different from what Jeth was used to from the Brethren. Most of them were completely serious, with the personality of mud, a phenomenon he now understood completely. He'd been doing his best not to stare at Dax's and Sergei's implants, but it was difficult as random bursts of pain kept shooting over the back of his skull and down his neck from the architecture.

At least the hood disguise had been doing its job. None of

the others had noticed so far, although he thought he'd seen Dax cast a couple of knowing and sympathetic looks his way.

"We can get there in three jumps," Dax said. "Not too bad. Shouldn't take more than a couple of hours, allowing time for the drive to cycle up in between."

Jeth didn't comment. He gently rested his aching head against the back of the chair, settling in for the trip. He briefly considered joining Lizzie, Celeste, Flynn, and Shady down on the common deck but decided against it. Being up here would be boring, but he didn't want to spend a lot of time with the crew right now. Their presence only underlined the reality of the future he faced.

The journey to Benfold Minor went smoothly, each metaspace jump normal and effortless. The *Citation*'s metadrive was in good shape, it seemed.

"Okay, Jeth," Dax said as they began their approach, "as soon as the Moenia spaceport opens a line with us, run the trace program I showed you so we can figure out where *Avalon* is docked."

Jeth nodded, silently hoping that *Avalon was* still docked. If any of Sierra's story about having a contact with a metadrive was true, it was possible they'd gotten *Avalon* fixed and were gone by now. Olympia Seven wasn't too far from here by the metagate route.

A short while later, Jeth joined his crew in the common room, along with Dax and Sergei. Jeth felt better than he had in days. *Avalon* was there, docked less than a kilometer away. They hadn't been able to get a life-signs read on the ship due to the type of security system in the spaceport, but so far he was hopeful Milton was still there.

Dax opened a hidden panel on the wall next to the view screen and started pulling out firearms, which he handed to Jeth and the others. Jeth took his without hesitation. Independent planets could be rough. Moenia, unlike a Confederation-aligned spaceport, didn't have any restrictions on civilian firearms.

Dax flashed a look at Lizzie, whom he'd given a small but absurdly powerful M.U.L.E. 32. "Do you know how to work that, little miss?"

Lizzie rolled her eyes as she ejected the clip, checked the ammunition, reinserted it, and racked the slide.

Dax grinned. "I guess you'll do fine."

Jeth almost smiled, too. He didn't find Dax as intimidating as most of the Brethren. Mostly because he seemed so normal and decent. Jeth wondered why a guy like him would've joined the Brethren. Hammer said he only took those willing, after all. For some reason, Jeth gave Dax more credit than that.

Dax faced the others. "Everybody under age, which means all of you besides Serge, pick out a shoulder holster and get it adjusted. Make sure you keep your jackets on and don't draw any attention to the fact that you're carrying. Minors aren't allowed sidearms here. Got it?"

"We're not dumb," Shady said, grabbing a holster out of the compartment.

Sergei shot him a glare. "Watch your mouth."

Dax patted Sergei on the shoulder. "Take it easy now. Hammer has me running this show, and I don't mind the kid's mouth."

Sergei grunted in a way that told Jeth two things. First, that what Dax said was true—he was running the show. And second, that Sergei wasn't happy about the arrangement.

"So, what's the plan?" said Flynn.

"Recon first." Dax walked over to the conference table and pulled up a three-dimensional map of Moenia City spaceport. "We're here, and *Avalon* is docked there." The places flashed on the screen as Dax touched them. "We'll fan out and observe for a while, see who's coming on and off. Then we'll make our move."

"Why not just go in there and take them?" Shady asked, holding his gun aloft.

"Because Hammer doesn't want to draw any attention to our presence," said Dax. "Being a part of his organization is a death sentence on this planet." Dax reached up and pulled out his implant with a wet, sucking sound that made Jeth's stomach roil. "And they mean it. All the cops here carry weapons designed to disrupt the implant technology." Across from him, Sergei removed his implant, too, both stowing them in their pockets.

Looking even more likable minus the implant, Dax swept them all with a hard gaze. "So none of you better even look sideways at someone without a go-ahead from me. Yeah?"

A mutinous expression crossed Shady's face, and his skin darkened to red. Jeth held his breath, waiting for Shady to do something stupid. He had a real problem with adult authority figures.

But then Shady nodded once and glanced away, muttering under his breath.

"Okay." Dax clapped his hands, grinning. "Let me figure out where I want each of you and then we'll get going."

They left the *Citation* at intervals, everyone heading in a different direction, except for Lizzie and Jeth, who Dax had said should stick together. Dax might've been convinced Lizzie could handle a gun, but thirteen was a little young to run around a roughneck spaceport alone.

Jeth headed out of the docking bay and into the east wing of the spaceport. He wove his way through the throng of people walking here and there, heading for the shops and restaurants in the atrium or to some other wing.

Moenia City spaceport was an open, airy place, the feel exaggerated by the large glass windows letting in late-afternoon sunshine. It had been a long time since Jeth had been planetside, and it took him a few minutes to adjust to the slight but still noticeable difference in gravity. The artificial gravity used in space sometimes felt just like that—artificial; its hold on you not as certain as the pull of a planet's gravity, like a collar you could slip and then float away if you tried hard enough.

Jeth wished he could go outside and breathe in the natural air, free from the constant recycling and chemical treatment of the air in space, but there wouldn't be time for that. As a compromise, Jeth stopped in front of a nearby window for a few moments and watched Benfold Minor's two suns slipping beneath the horizon, leaving behind pale swirls of pink, purple, and gold in their slow decent.

He wondered whether he could bear working for Hammer for the rest of his life if it was somewhere like this, a place where beautiful things happened every day, if only for a short stretch of time. Or maybe he could be a tracker like Dax. He knew that Dax spent a lot of time away from Peltraz. If Jeth didn't have to see Hammer very often, he could at least pretend he was free.

Sighing, Jeth turned away from the window. He scanned the crowd as he moved on, hoping to spot Sierra. He'd imagined a hundred horrible things he would do to exact his revenge when he saw her. If she hadn't double-crossed him, he might've escaped such a bleak future.

Ahead of him, Lizzie had pulled off to one side near a sign for Docking Bay D. *Avalon* was moored somewhere down that corridor, at Dock 11. Unlike at a Confederation-aligned spaceport, the public was allowed into the bays, even if they didn't belong to one of the ships docked there. But Dax had ordered Lizzie and Jeth to stay outside the bay and watch for their targets.

Lizzie sat down against a wall across from the entrance to the bay, folded her knees against her chest, and pretended to read. Jeth spotted an open bench not far from her and sat down. Dozens of people passed by, but none of them turned down the corridor to Docking Bay D. His impatience rose with each passing second.

When more than an hour went by with no sign of Vince or Sierra and no word from the others, Jeth finally gave into his restlessness. He glanced at Lizzie. She'd long given up the pretense of reading and was leaning against the wall, hands jammed into the front pockets of her pants. He stood and walked over to her.

"What do you think?" she asked, turning to face him as he stepped up next to her, leaning one shoulder against the wall.

"I don't know," Jeth said. "Dax told us to wait for his signal."

Lizzie snorted. "Since when do you—" She broke off, her gaze fixed on something behind him.

Jeth glanced over his shoulder. His heartbeat doubled as he caught a glimpse of Sierra on the opposite side of the wing, heading this way amid the continous flow of travelers. He turned back to Lizzie, moving closer to her for extra cover, although he felt certain Sierra wouldn't spot them in the crowd.

Out of the corner of his eye, he watched Sierra passing them. She walked side by side with an elderly man in fancy clothes, some kind of blue tunic trimmed in gold. They turned down the corridor to Docking Bay D. Four men followed close behind them, marching in even points around a large gray container they were pulling along on a cart. All four wore firearms strapped to their sides. Judging from their matching green and gold uniforms, Jeth guessed they were some kind of special security detail. But what were they doing?

He was about to follow after them when Lizzie grabbed his arm, squeezing hard.

"Ouch." He hissed, then froze at the look in her eye. He waited, not daring to move, and soon saw Vince walking past them after the others.

"Did they see us?" Jeth whispered.

Lizzie shook her head.

Jeth raised his finger to the communicator patch behind his ear. "This is Longshot. We've spotted them."

Dax's voice came back a second later. "Where?"

"Coming down the east wing entrance. Should be at the ship any minute. Do you want us to follow?"

"Stay put. Goliath and I will move in."

Jeth stifled a groan. He hated being told to stay out of it, especially with an ape like Sergei stepping in. It wasn't right. He should be the one to capture them. He wanted to see the look on Sierra's face when she realized her attempt to steal his ship had failed.

"What are we gonna do?" Lizzie asked once Jeth switched off the comm.

"Dax ordered us to stay here."

"And since when do we do what we we're told?"

Since Hammer threatened to turn you into a prostitute and me into a mindless drone. "Since now."

"The hell we are." Lizzie spun around and marched toward the bay entrance. Jeth chased after her but slowed down at once when he realized the attention they were drawing.

"Don't do this, Liz," Jeth said, falling in beside her. "You don't know what kind of trouble you might step into."

"What I know is that our uncle is probably trapped up there. Not to mention my *cat*."

Frustration and amusement collided in Jeth. He didn't know whether to laugh or haul her to a stop and give her a good smack. In the end, he decided to go with her. He wanted to be there as much as she did. And it wasn't like he was disobeying Hammer directly.

Unlike the docking bays at Peltraz, this one contained observation alcoves in between the docks, giving passersby partial views of the moored ships. Jeth pulled Lizzie into the first one, needing to put more distance between themselves and the group ahead of them. They waited a few moments and then moved on.

As they passed Dock 7, Jeth stepped inside another alcove and looked out. All the air escaped his lungs as he realized there wasn't a ship moored at Dock 9. Instead he was looking at *Avalon*, some fifty meters away. It had been years since he'd seen her land-docked. She looked so strange and out of place, her faded black color a little pathetic in the twilight. Still, relief filled him at the sight of her. She was here, whole and intact.

"What do we do now?" Lizzie whispered.

"Not sure yet." Jeth peeked around the edge of the alcove in time to see Vince disappear inside *Avalon*'s rear access door.

A hand grabbed Jeth from behind, clutching his shoulder with a grip far too powerful to be Lizzie's. He spun around, reaching for the gun strapped to his back. But he froze as he saw it was Dax.

"Thought I told you to stay put." Dax stepped into the alcove, dragging Jeth with him. "I would've left you behind if I knew you weren't going to listen. What are you thinking?"

Jeth scowled. "Just trying to enjoy making my own choices while I still can."

A knowing look crossed Dax face. "Yeah, okay, Golden Boy."

"What are you talking about?" asked Lizzie.

"Nothing," Jeth and Dax answered in unison.

Dax glanced around the corner. "What are we looking at?"

"Sierra and Vince just went in, along with some old guy and four armed guards pulling a crate."

Dax nodded. "Let's assume the guards will drop off the cargo and come out again." He raised his hand to the communicator patch behind his ear and opened all channels. "This is Ringleader. All units check in."

One by one the others came back, identifying their current positions.

"Head toward the mark," Dax said. "But don't engage. Rally at the east entrance with me and the west entrance with Goliath."

Irritated by the idea of more waiting, Jeth turned toward the window and tried to content himself with staring at his ship.

Flynn joined them a few minutes later. "The others here yet?"

Dax shook his head. Then he pressed his finger to the communicator patch again. "Goliath, you in place?"

No response.

Dax reached into his coat pocket and pulled out his black brain implant. With practiced ease, he slid the stem into the back of his skull. Jeth flinched at the sight.

Dax's eyes went oddly out of focus for a moment, as if his consciousness had slipped his body. Then he blinked, his expression returning to normal. "Damn it."

"Sergei didn't respond?" said Jeth, feeling the first pangs of worry.

"No. He must not have his implant in."

Flynn stared at Dax, his eyes wide. "You mean you really can talk mind-to-mind with those things?"

Dax grunted. "Something like that." He gave it a couple of minutes, then tried the communicator patch once more. "You reading this, Goliath? Come back."

Again no response.

Jeth pressed a finger to his communicator patch. "You out there, Tailspin?"

Celeste didn't answer.

"Tailspin? Joyrider? Come back, somebody." Something was wrong. Jeth knew it. Celeste would never leave him hanging.

Finally, he heard the click of an incoming communication, and the frantic sound of Celeste's voice filled his ear. "Tailspin here, we're in trouble. It's—"

The communication cut off, but just before it did, Jeth heard a tiny hiss-pop noise, like the kind made by a gun shot with a silencer. He went still, frozen by shock and uncertainty.

"Was that gunfire?" asked Flynn.

"Why would someone fire on them?" said Lizzie.

Dax didn't answer as he peered around the corner again. Then he faced Jeth. "Think you can get *Avalon*'s door open?"

"I can," Lizzie said before Jeth could reply. "Even if they've changed the security lock, I built a back door into the code."

"Smart," Dax said, looking impressed. "Let's go."

"What about the others?" said Flynn.

"We've got to assume that whatever trouble they've run into might be coming this way. We best not be sitting here waiting to get caught."

Whatever trouble. A rushing sound filled Jeth's ears. He took a deep breath and pulled out his gun. He needed to stay focused. Celeste and Shady could handle themselves. Mostly.

Jeth followed Lizzie and the others out into the corridor. As Lizzie worked on overriding *Avalon*'s lock, Jeth kept his gaze focused on the west entrance. He thought he heard someone coming once or twice, but the corridor remained empty.

As soon as the door opened, Dax led the way inside.

At first Jeth thought the bay was empty, but then he saw the old man and the four guards lying on the ground around the container they'd been escorting. They were all dead. He was close enough to one guard to see he had been shot through the head.

"Oh." Lizzie covered her mouth and looked away from the gruesome sight.

"Did Sierra and Vince do this?" asked Dax, whispering.

Jeth shook his head. "I doubt it."

"Then who did?" asked Flynn.

"Let's find out." Dax glanced at Jeth. "You know this ship better than I do. What next?"

In answer, Jeth lifted his gun to the ready position and then walked cautiously toward the ladder leading up to the common deck. He could hear the sound of raised voices ahead of him. One of them belonged to Sierra. The others were male, although no one he recognized with any certainty. Jeth tried to make out what they were saying, but couldn't.

He motioned for the others to wait as he climbed the first few steps, then dropped to his belly as he neared the top. From that vantage point he could see into the common room. His pulse quickened as he took in the six people. One of them was Vince, lying on the ground in between the sofa and gaming table. Whether he was dead or not, Jeth couldn't tell, but he wasn't moving. Sierra stood not far from him, her hands above her head. Milton stood next to her in the same submissive position.

Across from them was Marcus Renford. He was accompanied by two men in plain clothes who Jeth figured were ITA soldiers, given their standard, ITA–issued guns.

Jeth eased back down the steps to the cargo bay, beads of sweat breaking out over his skin. He quickly explained the situation to the others in a low whisper.

"Liz and I can flank them from the other entrance," Flynn said. "No offense, but we're quieter. You and Dax can get the drop on them from here."

"It should work," Jeth said, nodding. "But you two stay

under cover until I give the signal. Especially *you*." He glared at Lizzie. She rolled her eyes but didn't argue.

"Let's go," said Dax.

Lizzie and Flynn slipped away, heading for the front ladder up to the common deck, while Jeth and Dax crawled up the back stairs. A minute or so later, Jeth heard a single click in his ear from the communicator patch—Lizzie, telling him she was in place. Flynn signaled next. Jeth glanced behind him at Dax, who gave him the go sign. Jeth stood up, ready to charge in.

The familiar sizzling crack of a stunner being fired echoed behind him, and Dax cried out. Jeth spun around in time to see him falling backward, arms flailing. Dax landed at the bottom of the stairs with a loud thump. The shooter stood just beyond the stairs, holding a stunner aimed at Jeth.

"Throw down the gun," the man said. Like the men with Renford, he was wearing civilian clothes. Then Jeth saw the silver badge on the man's belt, tucked underneath his coat, confirming his suspicions.

Jeth considered trying to get a shot off until six more ITA soldiers charged into the cargo bay. Celeste and Shady were with them, both held at gunpoint. But at least they appeared all right, unlike Sergei, who was slouched between the two soldiers holding him up. Blood ran down the front of one pant leg from a gunshot wound.

Jeth heard the sounds of a struggle behind him, but he didn't dare turn to see what was happening as he slowly bent down and placed his gun on one of the steps.

A moment later, someone prodded him from behind. "Head down the stairs." It was the familiar voice of Marcus Renford.

Jeth did as he was told, joining Shady and Celeste, who were kneeling in a line, hands behind their heads. The soldiers forced Lizzie, Flynn, and Milton into the same position. Jeth glanced at Milton, making sure his uncle was all right. Then his eyes found Sierra standing a couple of meters away, trapped between two soldiers holding her arms. Another soldier held an unconscious Cora. Jeth tensed at the sight of her. What had they done? Was she knocked out? Dead? Jeth forced his gaze away, guilt and fear making him dizzy.

Across from him, Renford stooped and rolled Dax onto his stomach, exposing the implant buried in his skull. He shook his head, making a disgusted sound. Then he glanced at Jeth. "So what happened to you? Last we spoke, you were supposed to be waiting for my men to pick you up."

"Yeah, well, Hammer got there first," Jeth said.

"So I gathered."

Jeth's mind was working fast as he tried to figure out his next move. "But I'm not so sure I understand this hostile reception. I thought we had an agreement."

"Ah." A hint of a smile danced across Renford's lips. "So you think to come here with Hammer's men, mount a failed assault, and then attempt to convince me that you still want to honor our deal?"

"I didn't know it was you in here, and I didn't have any choice about working with Hammer. Like I said, he got there first. And this is my ship. Of course I came for her."

Across from Jeth, Sergei was glaring so hard that his face had turned red. Jeth ignored him. His plan, if they got out of this, was to tell Sergei it had just been a ploy. Unless Renford actually did honor the deal.

"Yes, I understand." Renford's gaze moved from Jeth to Lizzie. "And you brought your sister. Excellent." He approached Lizzie, then bent down and lifted her chin, turning her face more fully into the light. Lizzie tried to pull away, but Renford held fast. "You look so much like your mother."

Outrage coursed through Jeth. Nobody touched his sister, not for any reason.

Renford addressed the soldier guarding Lizzie. "We'll take this one with us, too." The soldier immediately sheathed his gun, then stepped forward and pulled Lizzie to her feet.

"What are you doing?" In a panic, Jeth tried to stand, but the soldier behind him pushed him down, then pressed the barrel of a gun to the back of his skull mere millimeters above the implant architecture. Agony burst over Jeth's head.

"Stay put, or I'll blow a hole right through you," the soldier hissed in Jeth's ear.

Jeth went still, but he locked his gaze on Renford. "What do you want with my sister?"

Renford shook his head. "I'm afraid that's an explanation that would take more time than I can spare. But I am grateful you brought her to me. Of course, it would've been easier if I could've met you outside the Belgrave. I might even have decided you were worth bringing along with me, but not anymore. You're too much trouble and not enough value. Your sisters, on the other hand. They are most definitely worth it."

"What are you talking about?" Jeth said, convinced the man was insane. *Sisters? Value?*

"What's this?" Renford glanced at Sierra, his eyebrows raised. "You didn't tell him? About his mother? How very . . . *disciplined* of you." A smile that could only be described as proud rose to his face.

Sierra went pale, then red.

"What about my mother?" Jeth demanded, glancing between the two of them.

Renford chuckled. Then he crouched down, putting his face level with Jeth's, a delighted glint in his eyes. He was enjoying this, Jeth realized. Renford relished the power he held over him. He relished the cruelty of it. "I can't believe I'm the one to tell you this. Quite ironic, really. But your mother is still alive, Jeth." Renford paused, as if allowing time for his nonsensical words to sink in. "And Cora is her daughter."

ALIVE, ALIVE, ALIVE.

"That's impossible," Jeth said, breathless. The emotions churning inside him were so powerful, so confused, all he felt was numbing shock, as if his head had been plunged into a bucket of ice water.

"Oh, I'm afraid it isn't," said Renford. "Marian's execution was staged by the ITA. They needed her to appear dead— it was the only way to hold her and perform the experiments on her they intended. During that last trip your parents took into the Belgrave, something happened to them. Something that altered them biologically. And whatever it was, it affected the fetus your mother didn't know she was carrying at the time. *Cora.* She was born a mere seven months after they returned."

Jeth realized at once that it could have been possible. The timeline worked, at least. And if his mother had gotten pregnant during that trip, he wouldn't have known. All the information about it had been sealed. *And Cora's strange DNA. It all fits.*

Jeth risked a glance at Cora, still unconscious in the soldier's arms, his heart thundering in his ears. *Sister.* Was it true? And could his mother really be alive? *Experiments.* The ground seemed to shift beneath Jeth, his whole universe turning upside down at the possibility that everything he'd been told about his parents' fate was wrong.

He turned back to Renford, desperate for answers. "Why? Why would the ITA do it?"

"Oh, I'm afraid I can't tell you that," said Renford. He slid his hand into his pocket and withdrew a data cell. "That information is too valuable to share with just anyone."

Jeth stared at the cell. "What does my mother have to do with the Aether Project?"

"Jeth, your mother *is* the Aether Project. Along with Cora. And, soon, Lizzie, too." Renford motioned toward his men. "Bring those two with us. Kill the rest."

"No!" Sierra screamed, a crazed look on her face. She pulled hard against the men holding her. One of them lost his grip, and Sierra reacted at once. She yanked a small, round object off the soldier's belt and tossed it. The thing hit the ground with a metal clink. Smoke began to pour out from its top, flooding the room in seconds.

Jeth jumped up, turned, and wrestled the gun out of the hand of the soldier behind him. Then he spun around, trying to find Lizzie. *And Cora.* Smoke stung his eyes, and he covered his mouth and nose to keep from breathing it in as he ran forward.

Bodies pressed around Jeth. He felt panic clawing at him, trying to freeze him in place. He fought it off, desperate to save his sisters. A soldier appeared in front of him and threw a wild punch. Jeth ducked it easily and then struck the man in the back of the head with the butt of the gun. The soldier went down, and Jeth leaped over him, moving on.

"Get them out of here!" he heard Renford shouting.

Jeth ran toward the voice. He pushed and punched people out of his way but resisted the urge to start shooting. It was too risky.

"Lizzie!" Jeth screamed.

There was too much noise for him to make out an answer. Smoke burned his lungs, and a coughing fit racked his body.

Someone appeared in front of him. Jeth moved to strike, but held back when he realized it was Dax. He didn't understand how the man had recovered from the stunner already, but there he was.

"Come on." Dax pushed his way through the fighting, and Jeth stumbled after him. A moment later they broke free of the smoke. Jeth wiped his eyes. They were in the rear of the cargo bay, near the exit.

Lizzie.

A soldier was pulling her through the door.

Jeth lunged forward, but Dax grabbed his arm, stopping him.

"Wait," Dax said. Then he pointed a small, strange-looking gun and fired once. The shot made an odd whizzing noise as it left the chamber. Jeth turned, expecting to see the soldier fall. Dax's aim was legendary.

The man kept moving.

Dax had missed. Jeth couldn't believe it.

He pulled away from Dax. "Let go of me." Jeth broke into a run, but he made it only a few steps before a stunner bolt struck him in the side of the head and everything went black.

"Do you think it scrambled his brain?"

"Dunno. Guess we'll find out when he comes around."

"You mean *if* he comes around."

"Oh, he will. He's too stubborn to die. Besides, Milton said he'd be all right."

Jeth wished the voices would stop. Each word was like a pickax striking him between the eyes. But the speakers were Flynn and Shady, two people who rarely descended into silence by choice.

"Hey, I think his eyelids are moving. You awake, Jeth?" Shady shouted. Jeth groaned and then wished he hadn't as the pickax turned into a hot poker.

"He's awake," said Flynn.

Jeth opened his eyes and glared at the two faces staring down at him. "Shut up, already."

Both of them grinned.

"Welcome back, Boss." Shady held out a hand. Jeth took it and sat up. The world spun around him for a moment. *What the hell happened?* Then he remembered being shot in the head with a stunner. And before that . . .

Lizzie . . . and Cora.

Fighting back panic, Jeth focused his gaze on Flynn. "What happened?"

Flynn began to fidget with his shirt collar. "Um, Renford and his men got away. They took Lizzie and Cora with them. But everybody else is okay. Even Dax and Sergei. Well, everybody except for Vince. He got shot, but Milton's working on him right now."

Terror needled over Jeth's skin. Where had Renford taken the girls? With an effort, Jeth pushed himself to his feet. He swayed once he got there, but Shady and Flynn steadied him. He looked around, realizing they were still in the cargo bay. The dead bodies of the old man and four guards had been removed, but blood smears remained on the floor.

"Don't worry, Boss," Shady said. "Milton and Sierra are working on a plan to go after them."

"What?"

A wary expression crossed Shady's face. "Now don't go losing your crap about it. She's on our side."

Jeth shot him a glare.

"It's true," Flynn said. "Milton told us we should trust her. Says he knows everything about what's going on with your mom and your sisters and stuff."

The world has gone insane.

Ignoring them both, Jeth charged toward the ladder. He headed up to the passenger deck and then to sick bay, where he knew he'd find Sierra. If Vince was hurt, that was where she would be.

He froze in the doorway when he spotted her. She stood with her back to him, bent over Vince, who was lying unconscious on the operating table. Milton stood on the other side of the table, holding a jet injector against Vince's bare shoulder. He squeezed the trigger, and it made a loud pop as it shot whatever medicine it contained into Vince's bloodstream.

Jeth charged in, grabbed Sierra by one arm, and spun her around hard enough that she fell into the table. "This is all your fault." He grabbed her by the shoulders.

She twisted out from his grasp with remarkable ease and shoved him. "I had no choice! You were going to hand us over to Renford!"

"Stop it, both of you," Milton said, glaring at them. "We can assign blame for what happened later. There're more important things to do right now."

Jeth blinked, some of the anger going out of him at the command in Milton's voice. He caught a flash of movement out of the corner of his eye and saw Viggo walking across one of the counters, stepping in between medical equipment without a care in the world. Jeth lowered his hands. At least they'd taken care of Lizzie's stupid cat. That was something, he supposed.

"Fine," Jeth said. "But somebody better tell me what the hell is going on."

Sierra took a deep breath. "It all has to do with the Aether Project, just like Renford said."

Jeth swung his gaze back to her. "What—"

"Not now," Milton said, inclining his head toward the door.

Jeth turned and saw Dax coming down the corridor toward sick bay, Celeste following behind him.

"Good, you're awake," Dax said as he came in. He looked at Milton. "I just checked on Sergei. He's sleeping."

Milton nodded, then moved to the counter behind Dax and started reloading the jet injector with another dose of medicine.

Dax turned back to Jeth and patted him on the side of the head. "Good thing your skull is hard enough to handle a stunner."

"Sure doesn't feel like it," said Jeth. "How'd you recover so quickly, anyway?"

Dax grinned and raised a hand to his implant. "One of the advantages of the Brethren implant. This thing can—" Dax broke off at a loud popping sound. Jeth looked up to see Milton pressing the jet injector against Dax's neck. Dax let out a gurgled cry, then fell.

Milton set the injector down on the nearest counter. "That's better."

Jeth gaped. "What'd you do?" His sudden anger at Milton hurting Dax surprised Jeth. Then it occurred to him how much he'd grown used to Dax's presence, and he couldn't decide if that was a good thing or not. Not that it mattered. What did was that Hammer would be furious. He would blame Jeth for this, consider it another betrayal.

"It's just a sedative. He'll be fine."

Jeth shook his head. Milton didn't understand. He didn't *know*.

"It's all right, Jeth," Milton said, speaking more firmly now. "We can't let Hammer find out what's going on here. But the sedative won't last long. Not with that implant." Milton bent down and pulled the thing out. He set the implant on the table and motioned to Shady and Flynn, who were standing in the doorway. "You two take Dax down to the brig. Then get started on installing the metadrive."

Jeth glanced down at Dax—*too late to change it now*—and then back to Milton. "Metadrive?" he said.

"Yes," Sierra said. "It's down in the cargo bay. Got here just before you did. It might come as a surprise, but most of what I told you before was true."

"Oh, it's a surprise all right," said Jeth, realizing the metadrive must be in the crate the security guards had brought in. "What'd you do, lure the seller here and then shoot him?"

Sierra's face went red. "Renford's men killed him. Not me. I don't betray people who don't deserve it."

Jeth took a threatening step toward her. "Are you insinuating that I *deserved* having my ship stolen?"

"Stop it!" Milton slammed his fist on the table. "Lizzie and Cora are more important."

Jeth swallowed guiltily, then forced his gaze away from Sierra, trying to pretend he didn't see the tears standing in her eyes. He looked at Flynn. "Do you know how to install a metadrive?"

Flynn shrugged then grinned. "Guess I'll have to figure it out."

"It's not hard if you use the old one as a guide," said Sierra.

"Right. Okay then." Flynn punched Shady in the shoulder. "Let's go." They grabbed Dax by the arms and dragged him from the room.

"Celeste," Milton said, "go take out Sergei's implant and lock him in his cabin. Then see if you can help with the metadrive."

A look of disgust crossed Celeste's face. Jeth couldn't blame her. He wouldn't have wanted to pull out an implant either. But Milton's stern look kept her from arguing, and she turned and left.

Milton cut his eyes to Sierra. "I think we should head to the common room and bring Jeth up to speed. I just need a minute to fetch my copy of the Aether Project."

Sierra's eyes widened. "You made a copy?"

"Yes." Milton glanced at Jeth. "I thought it might come in handy sooner or later. And I'm glad I did, now that Renford has the other one."

Jeth's patience reached its limit. "What's going *on*?"

"What Renford told you is true," Milton said. "Your mother is still alive, and Cora is her daughter. Your sister."

Jeth swallowed. There was no denying it now, not with Milton confirming it with such certainty. "But what does that have to do with the Aether Project?"

"Everything," Sierra said. "The Aether Project isn't just information about metatech. It's about preserving our ability to travel through space. What you must understand is that the power source that makes metaspace travel possible isn't mechanical or man-made or even mineral. It's biological. A living organism. An alien life-form." She paused and took a deep breath. "And it's dying."

CHAPTER 26

A FEW MOMENTS LATER, JETH SAT DOWN IN AN ARMCHAIR in the common room and watched as Sierra slid the data cell Milton had given her into one of the ports on the gaming table. *Metatech . . . biological . . . dying . . .* The insanity of such a notion nearly made him dizzy, and yet, somehow, it made sense. Especially the idea that the failed drives looked the way they did because they were literally dying. He'd witnessed that for himself.

"They're called Pyreans," Sierra said, facing Jeth. "They're not quite animal and not quite plant, but something in the middle, something unlike any of the life-forms we know from First-Earth. They're also a superorganism, which means they're comprised of billions of tiny organisms that live together and are governed by a collective conscious- ness. The metatech hardware and computers that you are familiar with were invented centuries ago by the ITA— or, technically, by the various organizations that would become the ITA—to manipulate this consciousness so that it would allow ships to pass through metaspace. Since then, the ITA has refined this technology into the gates and drives that we have today, all the while harvesting the Pyreans like crops, using them to power the gates and drives. But in recent years the Pyreans have begun to die off, like they've been hit by a plague. The scientists who have been searching for a cure have named their search the Aether Project."

Jeth exhaled, trying to process this. He pictured the porous, colorful material that made up the power source for metatech. There was something fundamentally organic about it. He couldn't believe he hadn't realized it before. "Okay, so metatech is a living thing and not tech at all."

"No, only the power source is a living thing," said Sierra. "The tech is just tech, man-made."

"Got it. So where do these 'Pyreans' come from? And how has the ITA kept it secret all this time?"

Sierra took a step backward, resting against the edge of the gaming table. "I don't know everything. Only that the Pyreans were discovered about five hundred years ago by First-Earth biotechnicians, right around the time that Mars was being colonized. The Pyreans just appeared on Earth, right out of thin air. Out of metaspace, as the scientists would later discover. Back then, First-Earth wasn't governed by a single body, but rather several nations, who ruled the various parts of the planet. One nation in particular, America, I think it was called, was the first to discover the Pyreans, and they immediately took actions to keep them secret, for fear of the other nations claiming a piece of their power."

This, at least, was a concept Jeth understood perfectly. "So all the Pyreans originate on First-Earth?"

Sierra shook her head. "The Pyreans weren't unique to

First-Earth. They likely didn't originate there. But they are connected to other colonies of Pyreans through metaspace. Once the scientists discovered the existence of metaspace, this connection led them to new planets with more Pyreans for them to harvest."

"And keep secret, no doubt," said Jeth.

Sierra pursed her lips in agreement. "There was soon an abundance of Pyreans for them to access. And for centuries what they harvested would quickly grow back healthy, like when you prune branches from a tree. Only now the branches have stopped growing back, and the tree appears to be dying. The ITA has since been trying to locate the Pyreans' true origin, the root of the tree, if you will, in the hope of fixing whatever is making them sick."

Jeth tried to wrap his mind around such a concept, couldn't, and so moved on. "What does this have to do with my mother and Cora?" Jeth turned to Milton, who was sitting on the sofa across from him. "Is she really my sister? *Fully* my sister?"

"Yes," said Milton.

"But what about the DNA test you showed me?"

Milton shifted in his seat. "Well, it's like Renford said. During that last trip your parents took into the Belgrave, they were exposed to something that altered them on a genetic level. It caused the mutation I found on the results."

Mutation. The word felt nasty in Jeth's mind, like something diseased. "But what *is* the mutation?"

"The cure for the Pyrean sickness," Sierra said. "Or an

alternative solution, to be more precise. At least, as far as the ITA is concerned."

Milton frowned at her. "Let's not jump ahead. This will be hard enough for him to take in as it is. We should start at the beginning."

Sierra shrugged. "Whatever you say."

Jeth shifted his gaze between the two of them, wondering what had happened in the last few days. Then he glanced at the port where Sierra had inserted the data cell and figured he was about to find out.

Milton cleared his throat. "Your parents found the planet Empyria."

Jeth couldn't help his astonished smirk. "You're kidding, right?" His eyes flashed to the painting on the wall. "Empyria is a myth."

"It's not a myth, at least not anymore," Sierra said. "The Pyreans are where the legends about the planet come from. The scientists hypothesized that the Pyreans originated from an actual planet, one that, like them, exists both within the dimensions of our universe and the dimension of metaspace." Sierra paused, a frown curving her lips. "You do understand what metaspace is, right?"

"Uh, yeah. I'm not stupid."

Her frown deepened. "Okay, explain it to me then."

Jeth glared at the challenge in her voice. "I don't know all the technical crap about it, but I know what it is."

"Let me explain," Milton said, rubbing his eyes. "For the sake of argument, let's describe metaspace as the fifth dimension, never mind if that's not scientifically accurate. Humans can only perceive four dimensions." He raised his hand and began to tick off fingers. "Length, width, depth, and time, although the latter we can only perceive as a half dimension because we experience it in only one direction. That is, we can only move forward in time. Do you understand?"

Jeth nodded. He'd taken enough math and science classes to have a basic understanding of such concepts.

"Metaspace is a dimension that we cannot perceive or measure in any way," Milton continued. "We're not born with the correct biological equipment. We know about it only because of the Pyreans. But we can deduce that it is a dimension that exists around and through the other four. That is how we can travel so far across the universe in so short a time, because metaspace exists outside the dimensions of time and space. Understand?"

"Yeah, I think so."

Milton gestured to Sierra. "Going back to what she was saying about Empyria, this lack of the correct biological equipment is why we have never been able to find the planet before."

"That's right," Sierra said. "Most of Empyria exists within metaspace and therefore beyond our perception. But on their last expedition into the Belgrave Quadrant, your parents discovered that part of the planet *does* exist in our dimension. Or it might have emerged into it, perhaps."

Jeth blinked his confusion.

Milton stood up, walked over to the gaming table, and

opened a drawing program. He drew something on the screen and then switched on the overhead viewer, displaying the image for Jeth and Sierra to see.

"Think of it this way," said Milton. "The planet is like an underground tunnel with an entrance aboveground." He pointed to an area on the crude diagram he'd drawn. "The ground itself is the barrier between our four-dimensional space and metaspace. Everything above the ground we can perceive, everything below the ground we cannot. Yet we can still travel through the tunnel, through metaspace. Your parents found a part of Empyria that exists aboveground."

"Yes, they did," Sierra said as Milton sat down again. "The ITA scientists long suspected the planet might be located somewhere in the Belgrave. They believe Empyria is the cause of the energy field as well as the strange occurrences within the quadrant."

"You mean this invisible planet is what put those holes in *Avalon* and the *Donerail*?" asked Jeth, glancing at the holes in his favorite armchair, now sitting pushed against the far wall.

Sierra bit her lip. "Yes, the planet's disruption caused most of it. That disruption has been getting worse for years. The Aether Project scientists believe there's a connection between the Pyrean sickness and the Belgrave disturbance."

Jeth suddenly remembered how Lizzie had had to keep recalibrating *Avalon*'s nav when they were searching for the *Donerail*. *Almost as if there's some kind of massive gravity field out there that keeps pulling us toward it,* she had said. A gravity field like the kind created by a planet, he realized.

"So my parents found Empyria," Jeth said, accepting the fact at last.

"They certainly did," Sierra said, a note of awe in her voice.

He wondered if finding it had made his mother happy. Only the dream come true seemed to have turned into a nightmare.

"But when they returned," Sierra continued, "they refused to tell the ITA where it was located, and they destroyed all the ship's records about the discovery, making it impossible for the ITA to retrace their steps. That's where the treason charge comes into play."

"Yes, but they didn't execute them, right?" Jeth said.

Sierra folded her arms. "No. Your father, to my understanding, died during the arrest, an accidental shooting. And your mother, well—"

"They turned into a lab specimen," Milton said, his expression darkening.

Jeth stared at him, torn between disbelief and cold fury. His father murdered and his mother's death faked. And all for what? Because they'd destroyed a couple of records? He didn't understand why his parents had done it, but they must've had a reason. They were idealists, sure, but not stupid or reckless. Especially not his mother. What had happened to her out there?

"Tell me about this biological change," Jeth said.

Sierra shifted her weight from one foot to the other before answering. "Your mother's DNA, and Cora's, now resembles something like the Pyreans themselves. But the main measurable difference is increased cognitive abilities. The change seems to have activated a dormant region in their brains. Moreso in Cora than in your mother, but definitely true of both."

Jeth let out the breath he'd been holding. Increased brain power didn't seem so bad. He'd been expecting something far more drastic and scary. "So she's a lot smarter than she used to be. What does that matter to the ITA?"

"It matters," said Sierra, "because Marian and Cora are now able to perceive metaspace—and manipulate it. Both of them can move objects through it in the same way the Pyreans move spaceships across the galaxy."

Jeth's eyes widened. "My mother can move objects through metaspace?"

"Yes. We call it 'phasing' for lack of a better term."

"Right," Jeth said, deadpan.

Milton leaned forward. "It's true. I've seen it." He motioned at Sierra, his expression unaccountably stricken. "Show him file . . . file ten-dash-thirty."

She turned toward the gaming table and accessed the data cell. A 3D image appeared on the screen, depicting a large white room, austere and sterile looking, like a hospital. On one side of the room sat an empty table. On the other was a chair with a woman sitting in it, her arms, torso, and legs strapped down.

Not just any woman, though. *Mom.* Jeth's heart throbbed in his chest, and his mouth went dry as tears burned his eyes. He glanced at the time stamp on the bottom right-hand side of the screen and saw this video was made less than a year ago. *She's alive.*

But she was changed. Her face was still the young, vibrant one he'd seen in her video journal, but her hair was completely white, as if it had been dyed to match the room.

On the floor in front of her stood a table the same size and shape as the one on the other side of the room. On top of the nearest table sat a red rubber ball, like the kind schoolkids play with at recess.

A man stepped into view on the screen. He wore a white lab coat and was holding an electronic tablet in one hand.

"That's Dr. Albright," Sierra said, pointing at the man.

Albright gave Jeth's mother a cold stare. "Please phase the ball to the other table."

Marian shook her head. Jeth squinted at the screen, his eyes drawn to something attached to the back of his mother's head. With a terrible sinking feeling, he realized it was some kind of brain implant with white, spindly tentacles, nearly invisible against her hair.

Albright clucked his tongue "Come now. The more you help us learn about what's happened to you, the sooner this will all be over."

A horrible sneer twisted Marian's mouth, transforming her beautiful face into something ugly. "It will *never* be over."

The scientist sighed, then motioned to someone offscreen. The next moment, Jeth's mother began to scream as her body convulsed, limbs straining against the straps.

Jeth's fingers clenched around the sides of the armchair. "What are they doing?"

"Electro-persuasion therapy," said Sierra, shuddering.

"Your mother was never a willing participant in these experiments."

Jeth thought he might be sick. He realized that this wasn't any different from the way Hammer had ordered him beaten.

Marian's screams died a moment later. Jeth wanted to tear the self-satisfied look off Albright's face as he said, "Are you ready now?"

Marian didn't reply, but her eyes slipped closed. The next moment the red rubber ball disappeared from the table in front of her and reappeared across the room on the other one, the movement punctuated by bursts of bright light.

"Very good." Albright made several notes on his tablet, then motioned to someone offscreen again. A woman in a white lab coat stepped into view and placed a square metal object on the table. Jeth thought it might be a battery of some kind.

"And again," said Albright.

A second later the battery disappeared and reappeared. Next they had her phase a large rock so heavy it took three men to lift it onto the table. Then she phased a rat in a small cage. Then a rabbit and, finally, a monkey.

The monkey didn't make it. At least, not all of it. The phase cut through its head, feet, and tail, slicing them off in a roughly circular shape and leaving them behind.

Jeth covered his mouth, revolted by the sight.

He fixed his gaze on his mother, ignoring the mangled remains of the animal. Tears streamed from Marian's eyes, her body shaking with sobs. Like Lizzie, Marian was an animal lover. This was just another form of torture.

"Biological objects are harder to phase," Sierra explained.

"No kidding," said Jeth. "But why the implant?"

"It contains the same technology as the metaspace computers that communicate with the Pyreans."

Jeth nodded, losing the ability to speak as he imagined all the suffering his mother must've endured these last few years. She wasn't dead, but he didn't know if this was any better. He resisted the impulse to finger the implant architecture in the back of his skull.

Onscreen, Albright ordered another monkey be brought out.

"No, I won't do it," his mother hissed.

The scientist engaged the electro-persuasion therapy again. Marian convulsed in pain, the torture lasting longer this time. When it stopped, she slumped against the chair, eyes closed as if unconscious.

"Ready to change your mind again, Marian?" Albright asked, his tone smug.

Marian's eyes flashed open, and the look of hatred on her face made Jeth flinch. A bright flash of light burst across the screen, obscuring the view for a second. When it cleared, Jeth saw that one of the table legs had disappeared, only to reappear in the middle of Albright's chest. For one brief second the man looked down at the thing sticking out from inside him, blood oozing around its edges. Then he collapsed.

The other scientists in the room converged on Marian, knocking her unconscious with a couple of stunner blasts.

Slowly, Jeth realized that she had done it. That his mother

had phased the table leg right through the man's heart. He swallowed, bile burning his throat.

"Turn it off," Milton said.

Sierra did so, and nobody spoke for several long moments afterward, letting Jeth digest what he had seen. His mother was alive, but was she even still his mother?

Yes.

No. She killed someone with just her mind.

He deserved it. The ITA made her this way.

Jeth clenched his fists, his hatred so great that for a moment he thought he would go mad. He had to do something. They had to pay. Jeth took a long breath, wrestling his emotions under control. Anger would get him nowhere.

"So is my mother a Pyrean now?"

"She's the start of a new species," said Milton. "At least, she would be, except she has become infertile. Cora's birth was difficult for her, although they don't know for sure if that caused the infertility or not. Any number of things could be to blame."

Jeth wondered why his mother's fertility would be a topic of study for the scientists, but he was afraid to ask. For now, all he cared about was that she was alive. *If she's alive, she can be rescued.*

"Tell me the rest. Why did the ITA lie about her being executed? And what does this have to do with Lizzie?"

"They lied," Sierra said, "because they needed the Aether Project to be as secret as possible. From what I gather, your mother not only refused to disclose the planet's location, but she attempted to go public about the Pyreans. I don't know why. She's never spoken to me about anything that happened on Empyria. There are interviews on the data cell where the scientists try to get her to talk about it, but she sort of goes crazy at any mention of the subject."

"You've spoken to her?" Jeth said. It was so hard to believe, so terrible and so wonderful at the same time. *My mom's alive.*

"Yes," Sierra said. "She's the one who convinced me to steal the Aether Project and to rescue Cora. They never let your mom see Cora after she was born, but it was as if Marian could sense her. It's strange, but there's some kind of connection between the two of them. The scientists would sometimes run concurrent experiments on them, and Cora and Marian never failed to act in unison." Sierra took a deep breath. "I would've rescued Marian as well, but I could only manage one. Of the two of them, Cora was in more danger."

Jeth felt something shift inside of him, his anger toward Sierra easing just a little. "Why?"

"They were preparing her for AGT, Accelerated Growth Therapy. It's a form of gene therapy that can rapidly age a person both physically and mentally. Cora is much more powerful than your mother, you see, but she doesn't have the same control. Instead of sending just the object through metaspace, she'll sometimes send the entire table. She's unintentionally phased some of the scientists and techs. If she gets too excited or emotional, she can do even worse damage."

Jeth thought about all the destruction on the *Donerail* and wondered if Cora might've been responsible for some of it. But he held back asking about that now as Sierra went on.

"The problem is that the success rate of AGT is abysmal, especially in prepubescent subjects. Seventy-six percent of them die within the first year."

"But if Cora is so valuable, why would they risk it?" Jeth asked.

A sound almost like a growl issued from Sierra's throat. "Because they're desperate. The failing metatech is a massive problem, almost apocalyptic. There are hundreds of planets and spaceports with billions of people on them who won't live long without the gates to transport food and supplies. And since they haven't found a cure for the Pyrean sickness, they plan to replace the metatech with beings like Cora. They believe that once she is more mentally mature, she should be able to move entire ships through metaspace at will. To create those beings, they plan to harvest her eggs once she reaches sexual maturity through the AGT, and they also hope to successfully clone her."

Jeth gaped, disgust a bitter taste in his mouth. "But that's crazy. Aren't there supposed to be all kinds of problems with human clones? Like physical deformities and psychotic behavior? Wasn't that the reason cloning was outlawed?"

Sierra grimaced. "It was, and the problems you mentioned are definitely a factor. The ITA plans to deal with the mental issues by adding behavioral controls into the metatech implants, assuming any of the clones live past infancy. And that Cora survives the AGT."

"But how do they plan on getting away with it if it's illegal?"

"Because the clones aren't human beings, not technically. Not at the genetic level."

Jeth glared. "You can't be serious."

"Unfortunately, I am." Sierra tapped her foot. "Don't get me wrong. I agree with you, but that's the loophole the ITA plans on exploiting: that Cora isn't human and therefore not entitled to human rights."

"That's bullshit." Anybody who'd ever meet the kid could tell she was human. Mostly.

Milton grunted. "Yes, it is bullshit, but this is the ITA, the most powerful entity in the universe. If they say it's right, no one will question it. And whatever moral objection people might have, the need for interstellar travel will soon convince them otherwise."

Jeth tried to imagine what it would be like to have a clone, a person, on his ship doing all the work of a metadrive. It was outrageous, disgusting. He pictured Cora as a human battery, mindless, forever plugged into a metatech computer. Jeth wanted to hit something. Instead he took a deep breath, trying to focus that outrage into something useful. "So how does Lizzie play into this?"

Sierra scowled. "The ITA has been planning a way to abduct her for the last few months, now that she's thirteen and has reached sexual maturity. They want to harvest her eggs to try and alter them genetically to match Cora's. They're determined to produce a whole new species as quickly as possible."

Jeth clamped his mouth shut, too outraged to speak, to breathe.

"Apparently," Milton went on, "the ITA believes that

there's something unique in your mother's genetic makeup that made the change possible. They believe she passed this ability on to Lizzie and you. Of course, you, being male, are not quite as useful, as it's passed down the female line. Which is, no doubt, why Renford didn't bother trying to take you as well as Lizzie."

Jeth's resolve hardened inside him. "We have to get them back. The ITA can't get away with this."

Sierra sighed, her expression stricken. "That's the hitch. Renford isn't going to bring them back to the ITA. He stopped working for them a long time ago." She waved a hand at Jeth's shocked expression. "Oh, the ITA doesn't know it, or at least they didn't at the time that I stole the Aether Project. Renford is an Echo and head of a black ops division, which means that he works almost completely independently from ITA headquarters. He's been pursuing his own agenda for a while now. His endgame is to destroy the ITA by selling the secrets of metatech and making himself a wealthy man in the process. Now that he has a copy of the Aether Project as well as Cora and Lizzie, he has everything he needs to succeed."

Jeth swallowed hard as a wave of despair crashed over him. All the stuff about clones and space travel and AGT might not make sense to him, but Renford's motivation was something he understood well. This was Hammer's realm, one of con men and kingpins, where everything was a gamble, a game of cards.

And where Jeth had only ever held a losing hand.

JETH REMEMBERED THE DAY HIS PARENTS HAD BROUGHT Lizzie home from the hospital. It was one of his earliest memories, standing there beside the crib and looking down at this small, pink thing, hairless and squirmy. *Sister,* his parents had said. He hadn't yet understand what that meant, but in time he would. In time he would grow to love her, despite the fights and rivalries, despite how she drew his parents' attention away from him. Eventually he would accept the simple, steadfast truth—he would do anything for his sister.

Now I have two, Jeth thought, picturing Cora, the way she smiled and how easily she laughed. Of all the things he had learned in the past twenty-four hours, this was the easiest for him to accept. He wondered if he hadn't known it on some unconscious level right from the start, like the way so many of her mannerisms reminded him of Lizzie. *Two sisters.*

And I've failed them both.

Jeth stood up, unable to sit still any longer. "How do we find them?"

Milton and Sierra exchanged a look that Jeth didn't like.

"We're working on it," Sierra said.

Jeth put his hands on his hips. "What does that mean?"

He regretted it at once, watching her flinch. *She saved Cora,* he reminded himself. She risked everything for his baby sister.

But why didn't she tell me who Cora was back in the Belgrave? If he'd known, none of this would've happened. Jeth wanted to demand an explanation, but he held back. His mind was too full to handle anything else. Besides, he already had a pretty good idea why she hadn't. *My sister has a hard time trusting people,* Vince had said. And he was a thief in her eyes, a criminal only interested in the biggest payoff.

Jeth dropped his gaze, regret a painful wrench in his chest.

"I've reached out to some of the contacts I made when I first decided to steal the Aether Project," Sierra said. "They're the kind of people who have their own spy networks and the like."

"Wait." Jeth raised his hand. "You really *were* planning to sell the Aether Project? Even with all the stuff about Cora on it?"

"No, I was going to delete anything relating to her or your mother. Anything that would put them in danger. Even without it, the project is still incredibly valuable. There's enough in there to undermine the ITA's monopoly."

Jeth exhaled, feeling minutely better.

After a moment, Sierra went on, "I've asked these contacts to keep a lookout for Renford's ship. We'll hear something soon."

"That's it?" Jeth said. "We just wait around until we hear something?"

Sierra looked poised to argue, but Milton spoke up before she could say anything. "We'll find them, Jeth. It's just a matter of time and patience. And once we locate that ship, we'll steal them back. This crew can handle anything."

"Yeah, sure." Jeth turned toward the door.

"Where're you going?" Milton said.

"To check on Flynn's progress." It was a lie. Jeth didn't know where he was going except elsewhere. He needed time alone to think. Milton was right that the crew had a lot of skills necessary for a job like this. Except they didn't have Lizzie, and they didn't have access to all their usual tools. Not without Hammer.

Hammer. He's going to kill me when he finds out what happened here. That was the other thing Milton didn't know: how determined Hammer was to make Jeth one of his men. When he found out that Jeth and his crew had imprisoned Dax and Sergei, he'd send others after them.

And if Hammer learns about Cora and Lizzie . . .

You mean if he doesn't know already?

A shudder racked Jeth's body, and he almost stumbled as he took the first step up the ladder to the engineering deck. He righted himself, then froze at an odd, faint sound. It seemed to be coming from the deck below, someone shouting his name.

Jeth turned and headed downward, arriving moments later in the aft cargo bay. It was Dax, shouting from the brig. He stopped at Jeth's approach.

"What do you think you're doing?" Dax said, leaning

against the bars and glaring. *Avalon*'s small brig was nothing more than a metal cage with a heavy, old-fashioned lock on the door.

"What I've got to," Jeth said, screwing up his courage. "And that's find my sister, and then get her and my crew as far away from Hammer as possible."

Dax snorted. "Then I guess you really are as dumb as you look."

"You've got a lot of room to talk, considering that implant you like to wear."

Dax ran his hand over the base of his skull as if expecting the implant to be there. He grunted. "You might have a point. But *my* point is that if you want to find your sister, you need to let me out of this cage."

Jeth snorted. "Why? So you can report to Hammer what happened here? No thanks."

Dax rolled his eyes. "Not all of us live and breathe for Hammer."

"Oh yeah? Doesn't look that way to me. The big guy told me how those implants work."

A cruel smile stretched across Dax's face. "Oh yes, so I heard. He's got big plans for you."

Flinching, Jeth turned away. He was too tired and worried to be wasting time here. He would deal with Dax later.

"I can find her," Dax said. "I know exactly where your sister is."

Jeth stopped and swung around. "Yeah? And how's that?"

"I marked her just before the ITA got away."

"What do you mean, marked?"

"I shot her with a tracer. It's what I do, you know." Dax made a gun out of his forefinger and pretended to pull the trigger.

Jeth blinked, remembering how Dax had missed shooting that ITA soldier. It had seemed incredible that a man with his skills and reputation could miss at such close range. Now he understood. "Why did you do that? Why didn't you shoot the men abducting her?"

Dax shook his head. "My tracer gun was the only one I had, and I figured she'd make the most worthwhile target. Besides, there was no way we were going to overtake Renford's men. But what I want to know is why Renford wanted her in the first place."

Jeth went still. Dax didn't know Lizzie's value to the Aether Project. *And Hammer probably doesn't either,* Jeth realized. If he did, he would never have let her leave Peltraz. Hammer was too wise a businessman to make that kind of gamble. "I don't know why," Jeth said smoothly, "but tell me about the tracer."

Dax grunted. "I started the program to run the trace on her just before your uncle knocked me out. I'm sure it's located her by now. So long as she hasn't gotten too far out of range."

Jeth's stomach flipped over. If they could pinpoint her location now, they'd have a better chance of getting her and Cora back than if they waited for word from Sierra's contacts. "How does the program work?"

Dax laughed. "Nice try. You let me out of this cage, and I'll show you where she is. I'll even help you fetch her."

Jeth folded his arms across his chest. "Yeah? In return for what?"

"Your help in retrieving the Aether Project from Renford. I still have my job to do. I'm great at tracking, but I've little experience pulling off a heist."

Jeth supposed it made sense. Only . . . "How do you know Renford has it? You were unconscious."

Dax pointed to the back of his head, a glint in his eyes. "Nah, I only *looked* unconscious."

Jeth stepped nearer to the bars, watching Dax's reactions carefully. "So you're saying that if we get you the Aether Project, you'll let us go? All of us?"

Dax sighed. "It's not so simple as that, as you well know."

Jeth held his breath, braced for the worst.

"You'll never be able to outrun him. Hammer must want you bad to have had you prepared for an implant before you're even of age."

Jeth flinched and resisted the impulse to touch the architecture.

Dax flexed his fingers around the bars. "Hammer made it quite clear that there were two things I had to bring back from this mission: the Aether Project files and you. Anything less than that, and he'll kill me."

Jeth gulped, unsurprised by this threat and believing it completely. "What about my crew?" he said, trying to keep the tremor out of his voice and failing.

Dax shrugged. "He wasn't as specific about them. Not that he'll be happy if the rest of them don't come back with us, but he might get over it. You, though, well, that's a different story. And you're just a kid with no resources and nowhere to go."

Desperation made Jeth's voice strained and tinny. "Why? What does he want with me?"

A stricken look, so out of character, crossed Dax's face. He let go of the bars, then turned and sat on the bench in the rear of the cell. "What I'm about to tell you is something I've never willingly shared with anybody. And if you repeat any of it, I'll kill you, no matter if you are Hammer's latest golden boy."

Golden boy. The words bubbled and burned like acid in Jeth's mind.

"I was once the golden boy, too," said Dax. "Only I wasn't an orphan like you. I had a big family. Two sisters and three brothers. All younger. My parents were coal miners, if you can believe it. On Gallant Prime, a rathole, backwoods world if there ever was one." He chuckled, as if in fond memory. "When I turned eighteen, there wasn't anything I wanted more than to get the hell out of that place. Not because of my family, mind you. They were great. But because of the mining. Dirty, dangerous shit. So I decided I would join Gallant Prime's space fleet. Lucky me, I even scored so high on my entrance exam, I had my pick of jobs."

He took a deep breath, all the good humor vanishing from his face. "And then Hammer found out how well I scored, particularly in the area of cognitive reasoning under pressure, or some such thing, and he decided he wanted me as one of his Brethren. I turned him down, but he persisted, and then he got nasty. He threatened to hurt my family, but I didn't believe him. I mean, who takes the time to round up a bunch of harmless coal miners and torture them? I thought if I could outrun Hammer long enough, he'd give up." Dax paused, the silence pregnant with unspoken emotion. "I was wrong."

Even though Jeth could guess the answer already, he asked, "Did Hammer kill them?"

Dax nodded. "Except my youngest brother, who was only five at the time. Hammer spared him because I came back and let him implant one of these things." He touched the back of his skull again. "The only reason Hammer continues to spare him is because I stay and do what he wants me to do."

Jeth didn't say anything. He didn't trust his voice. In the back of his mind, he remembered how Dax had called him "test baby" when they'd first met. He understood the term all too well now.

Even worse, Jeth didn't have any trouble imagining Hammer doing the same to the people *he* loved. *I've never been afraid of doing what needed to be done,* he heard Hammer saying. Images flashed through Jeth's brain, of the starving man on Peltraz, the dead, hopeless look on his face, of Trent Danforth, unrecognizable, little more than a machine, and of himself, broken and beaten when they'd placed him on that operating table.

"So," Dax said, his voice far too casual for the topic of conversation, "I've been in your place before, and I learned the hard way that if you try to deny Hammer, your loved ones will pay for it in the end. But if you submit to him now, you've got a chance of saving them."

Jeth wanted to scream and rage and beat his fists against the wall. He hated being so helpless, hated being so trapped. So *owned*. But he would hate watching Lizzie die even more. He would do anything to spare her. *And the others, too. They're all my family.*

"And not that it should matter to you," Dax said, almost as an aside, "but if I fail to bring you and the Aether Project back, Hammer will kill my brother first and then me. It's that important to him."

Jeth forced his hands to his sides, keeping his voice calm. "I could just kill you now instead."

Dax nodded. "That you could. And Hammer might just leave my brother alone. But if you kill me, you lose your best chance of finding your sister." He tapped his wristwatch. "Better make your decision soon. It might already be too late as it is."

Jeth drew a breath and released it slowly. "So—I help you get the Aether Project while we're rescuing my sister. Then what?"

"Simple," Dax said, crossing his arms. "I turn a blind eye while she and your uncle and whoever else disappear into the unknown. We can tell Hammer they got killed or whatever you like. So long as you come back to Peltraz and so long as we can give Hammer the Aether Project, I don't believe he'll ever go hunting for the rest of them."

Jeth thought hard, his mind churning. Then he spotted a

new problem, one he should've realized earlier. He couldn't just hand the Aether Project over to Hammer, not with all the information it contained about Cora and Lizzie. No matter what Dax believed, Hammer would pursue Jeth's sisters to the end of the universe if he found out about their value.

Then he remembered that Milton already had a copy of it. A copy that Sierra could modify, deleting all the dangerous information off it like she had planned to do before selling the original to her buyer on Olympia Seven. If Jeth could get back Renford's copy of the Aether Project, it would be a simple thing to switch it out with the modified one before turning it over to Dax.

Satisfied by this part of the plan, Jeth turned to the other part, the one where he would willingly return to Hammer. Bleak and terrible as it was for him, it *would* be better for everyone else.

And that's okay, he decided, finally giving in to the urge to touch the hole of the implant architecture. It was starting to hurt less, his nerve endings adjusting to its presence. He'd known he was damned from the start.

"What about Sergei?" Jeth said.

Dax tilted his head. "Where is he now?"

"Unconscious and locked in a cabin."

"Good. We'll keep him right there until we're done. Then once we revive him, I'll smooth things over. I'm sure I can come up with a story that he'll swallow. And don't worry." Dax winked. "He may be the general, but he was never the golden boy."

Jeth didn't smile as unease settled into the pit of his stomach. He didn't want to trust Dax, despite believing his story. Dax was still Hammer's man. And yet he'd given up everything to save his little brother. *Not so different from me,* Jeth realized. *And he has a line on Lizzie.* For the moment, that was all that mattered.

Jeth stepped toward the cage. "Okay, it's a deal. But you're not getting your implant back."

Dax grimaced. "I'm afraid that's impossible. If I don't put the implant in, Hammer will know something's wrong. He won't wait long before sending someone to find out what happened."

"But won't he know what we're planning when he reads your thoughts?"

Dax shook his head. "It doesn't work that way. I'm Brethren, not Guard. I can turn the communication link on and off, and I control what information I send him."

Jeth thought about it, remembering what Hammer had said about wanting his Brethren to retain a measure of free will. "But how will I know what you're sending along and what you're not?"

Dax stared at him, unblinking. "You won't. But I gave you my word to help you. That'll have to be enough. And obviously Sergei won't be doing any communicating while he's unconscious. I'll tell Hammer we ran into a little bit of trouble at Moenia and that he got injured. Wouldn't be the first time."

Jeth gritted his teeth, hating the risk involved. But what

choice did he have? "All right," he said. "But just remember, this is my ship and my crew, at least for the time being. If you even think about betraying us, somebody will shoot you, I promise."

Dax grinned. "I hear you, Captain. Now let me the hell out of here so we can find your sisters."

IT TOOK LESS THAN AN HOUR.

"Are you sure that's where they are?" Jeth said.

"Yep. We can get there in a single jump," said Dax. "Assuming they don't go somewhere before we're ready."

Sierra leaned over Dax, examining the screen. "Can you tell anything about the environment off that trace?"

Dax nodded and entered a command. An image displayed on the screen. "It looks like a . . ."

"C-ninety-three Strata," Sierra said.

"Yeah, that's right. How'd you tell so quickly?"

"Because that's Renford's ship." She looked at Jeth. "She's called the *Northern Dancer*. She's black ops, with more than two hundred crew on board and enough firepower to blast a crater in a moon. It's not going to be easy getting in there."

Jeth winced at the doubt in her tone that suggested it wouldn't just be hard but a feat of miraculous proportions.

"I thought Stratas were luxury cruise ships?" Celeste said.

"Normally, yes," said Sierra. "That's one of the reasons why she's so effective for black ops. Most spaceports and passing patrols take one look at the *Northern Dancer* and deem her harmless."

Shady snorted. "Anybody who's ever been on a cruise ship should know they ain't harmless. All kinds of nasty rich people inside of them."

"What the heck do you know about being on a cruise ship?" said Flynn.

Shady grumbled something incoherent.

"Will you two shut up?" said Celeste.

Jeth cut them all off with a look. Then he turned his gaze on Sierra. "But you know the ship, right? I mean, well enough that you can help us plan how to get in and out without getting caught?"

"Sure, I can help," Sierra said. "But I have no idea how we'll get in there. They're sure to see us coming. And no offense to *Avalon*, but she's not big enough to take on the *Northern Dancer* in a firefight."

Jeth knew she was right. *Avalon*'s biggest assets were her speed and agility.

"We're not going to attack her outright," said Dax. "No reason to. All we need is a ship with a stealth drive."

Sierra scoffed. "And where're we supposed to get one of those?"

Jeth's spirits lifted and an eager smile rose to his lips. "Right here. In the spaceport."

"That's right," Dax said. "The *Citation* will be perfect for a job like this. We can pull right alongside, and they'll never know we're there."

"You came here on a ship with a stealth drive?" Sierra asked, raising her eyebrows.

"Sure did, sweetheart," said Dax.

"And it actually works?"

"Most of the time. Hammer's got a whole lot of really smart people trying to perfect the technology."

Sierra smirked. "I always heard Hammer was a force to be reckoned with."

"Oh, yes. He certainly is." There was a sharp edge to Dax's voice.

"Okay," Jeth said. "Let's start figuring out how we get onto the ship. We'll head out as soon as Flynn's got *Avalon*'s new metadrive working."

"Just a couple more hours," Flynn said with more bravado in his voice than his expression suggested should be present.

"Why wait?" Dax said. "Let's just take the *Citation*."

"No." Jeth said, casting him a significant look. According to their agreement, Lizzie and the rest were free to go once they finished this. They'd need a spaceworthy ship.

"Whatever you say," Dax said, clapping Jeth on the shoulder. "You're calling the shots."

For now.

Four hours later, Flynn declared *Avalon* flight ready. Jeth and Milton had spent the time filling in the rest of the crew about Cora and the reason why Lizzie had been taken. Jeth had decided the others needed to know, but they had to do it quietly, keeping Dax in the dark.

Jeth stared around at the compartment housing the metadrive, not certain he believed Flynn about them being ready. The engine room looked as if it had been ransacked by a group of feral monkeys. Loose wires dangled from the ceiling and stretched across the floor like snakes. The metadrive itself was an ominous shade of red, threaded with the minuscule streaks of white that Jeth now knew meant the thing was already dying. It was sad, really. He wondered if the entire species or super-organism or whatever the Pyreans were would soon be extinct.

"Good work, Flynn," Jeth said, despite his reservations. He imagined it wasn't easy messing around with that thing.

Sierra was ready, too. As Jeth and the others gathered in the common room, she gave him a look that told him she had successfully modified Milton's copy of the Aether Project, as he'd asked her to do shortly after making the deal with Dax.

Sierra began going over the plan for how they would approach the *Northern Dancer*. They would take both ships until just outside scanning range of the *Northern Dancer*'s position. Flynn and Milton would stay with *Avalon*. The rest of them would approach the *Northern Dancer* aboard the *Citation*, running in stealth mode.

From there, they would have to get creative on the fly for getting to Lizzie. It all depended on where she was being held, and with any luck, Cora would be with her. Once they had Lizzie to crack the *Northern Dancer*'s network, they would track down the Aether Project files. Jeth, Milton, and Sierra had agreed privately that they would have to get the original Aether Project data cell from Renford, instead of taking the easy route of pretending to find it and then handing over the fake to Dax. They couldn't leave the Aether Project in Renford's hands.

"Um," Celeste said when Sierra finished speaking, "I know Lizzie is brilliant and all, but how will she be able to track down the Aether Project files?"

"It'll take time and a little bit of luck," said Sierra, "but if Renford has put it on any computer on the *Northern Dancer*, she'll be able to find it."

Shady raised his hand. "What if he's using a computer on an isolated network?"

Everyone present turned and gaped at him in disbelief.

"What?" said Shady. "I know a thing or two about computers."

Celeste snorted. "Since when?"

"Since I watched this spy movie about—"

Jeth smacked him in the back of the head. "Shut. Up."

Shady rubbed the spot, grinning.

"It's a fair question," Sierra said, casting Shady a bemused look. "But unless Renford's had new hardware installed recently, he doesn't have the ability to set up an isolated network. He's never had a reason to. His men all hold top-secret clearances. Now—" Sierra swept her gaze over everyone present. "Are we all good with what's happening?"

When no one said anything to the contrary, Jeth stood and said, "Let's get ready to go. Those of us going to the *Citation*, get your gear. We head out in ten."

Everyone stood and moved for the door, except for Jeth, who lingered behind with Milton.

"Doesn't that include you?" Milton said when they were alone. "The *Citation*, I mean."

"Yeah, it does." Jeth tried not to think about how this might be the last time he was ever on board *Avalon*. The thought was so painful, he thought his heart might stop beating if he dwelled on it too long.

"What's on your mind?" Milton said.

Jeth swallowed, finding it hard to breathe. He knew what he had to say—he just wasn't sure he was ready. It wasn't that he expected Milton to be angry or to argue, it was knowing that he wouldn't. Milton would understand what Jeth was about to say better than anybody.

"When we get Cora and Lizzie back on *Avalon*, I want you to take the ship and get as far away from Hammer as possible. Find somewhere safe, maybe even something planetside. I hear Enoch is a good place to settle." He sucked in a breath, the words like acid in his mouth, the terrible taste of a dying dream. "Take the rest of the crew too, if you can convince them."

"Take them, but not you?" Milton asked, his voice a throaty whisper.

"I'm going back to Peltraz."

A muscle pulsed in Milton's jaw, and for a moment Jeth thought he'd been wrong, that his uncle *would* argue with him. But Milton only said, "Why?"

"I've got to go back. If I try to escape, Hammer will come after me and he'll never stop." Jeth took a deep breath and then told Milton about Hammer's promise that Jeth would wear one of the two implants.

Pity glistened in Milton's eyes as Jeth finished speaking.

"You don't seem surprised," Jeth said, running a hand over his shaved hair.

"I saw the implant architecture when I examined you earlier."

"Oh. Right."

Milton shook his head. "The architecture may not be permanent, Jeth. It's possible with the right equipment I might be able to remove it."

Jeth gulped, the idea of being free of it making him heartsick with longing. Only it wasn't an option. Not now. "No. Dax says that if I go back willingly with him, Hammer won't come looking for the rest of you. I've told him I will. At least this way I might have a chance at some kind of life. And it'll give Lizzie and the others a chance at something even better."

"You're going to take the word of one of the Brethren on that?" Milton said.

"I have reason to believe him."

Milton rubbed the scruff of gray beard on his chin. "Well, that might solve the threat from Hammer, but what about the ITA?"

"You'll have to rely on Sierra to help with that. She's already proven how far she'll go to keep Cora safe. But it'll be on you to protect all of them. It's the least you can do."

Milton flinched. "I'm sorry," he said, "for starting all this. I never should've gambled the ship, and I never should've stayed."

Jeth didn't say anything. There wasn't anything to say. If he told Milton it was all right, that he wasn't responsible, it would be a lie. Now didn't seem the time for lying. All of them were responsible, and none of this was all right.

"Do you know why your parents named her *Avalon*?" Milton asked, looking around at the common room.

Jeth nodded, his throat tightening with painful memories. "Because she was their paradise, their otherworld, like the *Avalon* in First-Earth mythology. The land of apples and eternal summer and youth."

"That's right." Milton exhaled. "And when they died—when I believed Marian was dead—I hated this ship. Hated her for what she was supposed to be and what she wasn't. But when I lost *Avalon* in that card game, and to a tyrant like Hammer, I couldn't just walk away. This was all I had left of your mother. She was more than my sister, you know. With our age difference, I practically raised her. She was like my daughter."

Jeth bit his lip. He'd known Milton cared for his mother, but he'd never realized it was like that. He never talked about her. "Well, *Avalon*'s yours again. Just take care of her and Lizzie and Cora." Jeth turned to leave, feeling the weight of despair press down upon him. He was leaving his ship. Maybe forever.

Milton grabbed his shoulder, stopping him. Jeth turned back and reluctantly met his uncle's gaze.

"You're not going back to Hammer just to keep him off our trail, are you?"

Jeth shook his head. Of course Milton would guess his secondary motive, the one so deep and secret inside him, he'd been afraid to give thought to it until now. "If I go back and have access to Hammer's resources, I might find a way to rescue Mom."

Milton swallowed, his Adam's apple bobbing in his throat. "But you have most of those resources here with this crew."

"No. Lizzie and Cora have to be safe. And I've already put everybody in enough danger as it is. As much as I want to rescue her, I know Mom would want me to take care of my sisters first."

Milton sighed. "You're right. That's exactly what Marian would want." He paused. "You're so much like her sometimes."

Sadness squeezed Jeth's chest even tighter. "I've got to go."

"I know," Milton said. "Be careful."

Jeth nodded and then strode for the door. He paused just outside and glanced back at Milton. "Make sure you keep an eye on Lizzie's cat. Until she gets back."

Milton smiled. "Of course."

Jeth turned and left the room, hoping the dread he felt was wrong, that this wouldn't be the last time he saw his uncle.

And as he walked down the corridor to his cabin, he trailed his hand along the walls of his ship, whispering good-bye, and hoping, praying, this wasn't the last time he saw his *Avalon* either.

CHAPTER 29

EVEN WITH THE STEALTH DRIVE ENGAGED, APPROACHING the *Northern Dancer* was risky. Celeste had to keep their speed low enough that the other ship's radar wouldn't pick up their movement. They crawled along, moving annoyingly, impossibly slowly.

Jeth had never seen Celeste so focused. She sat as rigid as a statue behind the *Citation*'s control column while he stood behind her, silently watching. Sierra sat copilot, using her knowledge of the *Northern Dancer* to help them. They couldn't rely on the autopilot for this, as Celeste had to keep making adjustments to their path to ensure they lined up successfully with the *Northern Dancer*. She could only make a change a fraction of a millimeter at a time. Several times, she pushed it a little too hard, and Jeth held his breath, certain they would be spotted.

More than an hour after starting their approach, they finally reached the *Northern Dancer*. The massive ship looked the same as any other luxury liner Jeth had seen, fat and cumbersome, as unthreatening as the manatee Hammer kept in his menagerie back on Peltraz. It was hard to believe she housed the kind of firepower Sierra claimed, and yet he didn't doubt her. He knew well enough from Hammer's enterprise that you shouldn't trust the outward appearance of any ship. Still, Jeth supposed the ITA had made a good choice in using her for black ops. If weaponized, a ship as large as a Strata would carry a devastating amount of firepower— enough to vaporize a ship as small as the *Citation*.

Once they were close enough to be out of range of the *Northern Dancer*'s radar, Jeth placed a hand on Celeste's shoulder. "Have I told you lately that you're amazing?"

She ignored him, her focus as rigid as ever.

"There." Sierra pointed out the window. "Get as close as you can beneath that wing, but don't break fifty meters. Even with a stealth drive, you'll set off the proximity alarm."

Celeste's answering nod was so slight, Jeth thought he might've imagined it.

"I've got a read on Lizzie's position," Dax said, looking up from the comm station monitor. "Looks like L Deck, stern."

Sierra rose from the copilot's chair and walked over. She examined the screen, then swore.

"What is it?" Vince asked, standing up from the nav station. He did it slowly, his face pale and pinched from the effort. He'd lost a lot of blood from the gunshot wound in his side. Sierra had wanted him to stay on *Avalon*, but Vince insisted on being near her. *Especially if you're going in there,* Jeth had overheard him saying during the argument.

"That's the brig," Sierra said, pointing at the screen. "Why would they put Lizzie in there? I was expecting her to be on one of the passenger decks. It's not like she's dangerous."

"She is with a computer," said Jeth, coming over to have a look.

"And she knows how to be a pain in the ass when she wants to," said Shady, standing just to the side of the comm station.

"Or maybe he's expecting us," Vince said, pressing a hand against his side as if each word hurt. "How detectable is this tracer you used?"

Dax looked up at him. "Not very, unless you've got the right equipment and know where to look for it."

"Then it is possible he knows we're coming," said Jeth, a bad feeling crawling across his skin. "That soldier might've noticed when you shot her with the tracer."

Vince touched Sierra's shoulder, his face drawn with worry. "This could be a trap."

She shrugged him off. "Maybe, but Renford can't know about the stealth drive, so he won't know we're here right now."

"Fair point," said Dax. He looked at Sierra "Did you include a plan for getting to the brig when you were mapping things out?"

She nodded. "I'll double-check it just to be safe."

"What about Cora?" Jeth asked. "Any idea where they're keeping her?"

"Nope," said Dax. "But her location might be listed if anybody knows how to do a remote hack."

Sierra grimaced. "I do, but it'd be risky. I'm not sure I can penetrate the security protocols, and the last thing we want to do is hack it poorly and let them know we're here."

"So what will you do?" asked Vince, a note of petulance

in his voice. Sierra might've given in to letting him come over to the *Citation*, but she refused to allow him to come with the rescue party. Jeth felt sorry for the guy, knowing full well what it was like to have your sister be in danger when you were not. He never would have stood for it. Then again, neither of his sisters was as fearsome as Sierra—at least not yet. Maybe in a couple of years . . .

Jeth stopped that thought before it could go any further. He couldn't bear the idea of what a couple of years might bring and what they might not.

"We stick to the plan," he said. "We find Lizzie and let her hack it from the inside."

"Right." Sierra pressed her hands together in a silent clap. "Let's go."

Jeth put on his space suit as quickly as he could, then headed for the *Citation*'s small top hatch. Sierra was the only one there so far. He stood across from her, a wave of anxiety washing over him at finding himself truly alone with her for the first time since she'd stolen his ship. His feelings about her were a jumbled mess inside him. He'd been doing his best to ignore them.

Still, Jeth couldn't help a quick glance at her face. He saw at once that she was more nervous than he was. She looked physically ill, although still as pretty as ever.

He frowned. "You all right?" She nodded, but Jeth wasn't convinced. He searched for something to say. "I, uh, suppose I ought to thank you for rescuing Cora like you did."

Sierra blinked in surprise. "You're . . . um . . . welcome."

She sighed. "And I suppose I ought to say I'm sorry for stealing *Avalon*."

Jeth gritted his teeth, the memory somehow more painful now that he was about to lose *Avalon* for good. "Yeah, you probably should."

Sierra said nothing.

Jeth folded his arms and leaned against the hatch wall, wanting to keep as much distance as possible between them. "So, why did you, anyway?"

"I thought you intended to betray us. I overheard you telling Milton you would call Renford instead of Hammer."

Jeth frowned. "I didn't say that exactly. I mean, there was more to it than that. And I didn't know who Cora was. Why didn't you just tell me?"

Sierra swallowed, her expression guilty. "I didn't trust you. Not at first. I had no reason to. You were just a thief hired to bring in the biggest bounty."

Face flushed, Jeth scowled. "Maybe so, but I'm her brother. Her *family*."

Sierra shook her head. "That doesn't mean anything. Not to me. Blood and family is a meaningless ideal. Only actions matter."

"You're wrong," Jeth said. "Family does matter. More than anything."

"I . . ." Sierra's voice trailed off, and she looked away from him. "I'd planned on telling you the truth about her. That same night, in fact. I thought I'd gotten to know you well enough that it would be safe for you to learn the truth. But then I overheard you and Milton. And later I saw you sneak over to the *Donerail*, and I knew you were searching for the data cell." Jeth started to protest, but Sierra cut him off. "I understand now what you were doing. Milton explained it to me, and Vince certainly thought I was being a little rash. But if you could have seen it from my point of view, you would understand my reaction."

"How so?" Jeth said.

"Because Renford . . . he's my guardian." She glared. "And I would rather die than be handed over to him again."

Shock froze Jeth in place. Renford was her guardian? The man who'd abused her so much that when she saw Cora being abused, she'd had to act? His gaze dropped automatically to her hands. He couldn't see her misshapen fingers through the space suit gloves she was wearing, but he remembered them well. He looked up. "That's how you know so much, isn't it? About Renford being a rogue agent and the *Northern Dancer*?"

Sierra's expression turned grim. "I lived on that ship for four years, until I took the Aether Project internship. Renford had a part in getting me recruited. He wanted me on the project so I could steal information for him. His home planet is Rosmoor, and he's been trying for years to bring down the ITA over what they did there with the embargo and the way his people have suffered."

"Wait," Jeth said, cutting her off. "Renford is from Rosmoor?"

"Yes," Sierra said, "although he's done a good job hiding that from the ITA. He joined long before the embargo, but even then you had to be from a Confederated planet, so he lied on his application."

"So does that make him some sort of freedom fighter?" Jeth asked, disliking the notion. It was far too noble a motivation for someone like Renford.

A glower darkened Sierra's face, and Jeth was glad to see it. "No, he's nothing but a mercenary. Oh, he acts like his intentions are good and justified, and they might have been at one point for all I know. But he only cares about the money he stands to gain through the Aether Project, and even more about the power."

"Yeah, I understand the type."

Sierra exhaled. "You have no idea. I went into the job on the Aether Project fully planning on handing it over to him. Obeying him was what I'd been raised to do, *conditioned* to do. But Cora and your mother changed all that. Watching them suffer forced me to break free of my own suffering. It was hard. Defying Renford was the toughest thing I've ever done. Then the moment I heard you say his name, I lost all sense. I hate him so much." She stopped speaking and drew a shaky breath.

Jeth stared at her, horrified by the confession and how close to tears she sounded. "If you don't want to go over there, I understand."

Sierra cleared her throat. "I have to. I can't let him win. I've come too far. And Cora needs me."

Jeth frowned. "She *needs* you?"

"It's like I said before: her ability to phase is extremely powerful, but she has a hard time keeping it under control, especially during times of high emotional stress. One of the reasons I was able to get so deeply involved in the project is because Cora trusts me. For whatever reason, I'm able to keep her calm. Most of the time."

Jeth remembered his earlier suspicions. "She caused some of the damage on the *Donerail*, didn't she?"

"Yes," Sierra said, her voice steadier with the new topic. "She's part of the reason we got so lost once we entered the Belgrave. She got frightened and phased the entire ship by accident. Or at least, I think she did. Milton believes there might be a connection between Cora and the Belgrave, or Empyria, to be more precise."

Jeth supposed it made as much sense as anything else he'd heard. "Is Cora a danger to herself? I mean could she phase herself?" The horrible image of the mutilated monkey flashed in his mind. How could he ever keep her safe from that?

Sierra pursued her lips. "The scientists doubt she would be able to harm herself directly with a phase, but harming herself indirectly is certainly possible based on what she can do to the environment around her. Like, what if she accidentally phased a hole in an exterior wall of the ship? She could get blown out into space."

Jeth cringed. "In that case, I'm glad you're coming with us."

A ghost of a smile slid across Sierra's lips. "I really am sorry. For stealing *Avalon* and for not being up front with you from the beginning."

Jeth didn't say anything, unsure how to respond. He did understand why she'd done what she had. But he didn't know if he was ready to forgive her. Not yet.

Fortunately, he was spared the trouble of an answer when Shady and Dax arrived. It was a tight squeeze with all four of them in the hatch, especially in space suits. They slipped on their helmets, trying to avoid elbows.

"Ready?" Sierra asked. She spoke softly, and yet her voice boomed inside Jeth's helmet over the comm system.

Everyone nodded, and Sierra deactivated the gravity drive inside the hatch and then lifted the latch, opening the door to the outside. The *Northern Dancer*'s hull loomed over their heads. This might be the most dangerous part of the job, the freefall upward to the *Northern Dancer*'s hatch.

Dax went first, pushing off from the *Citation* as hard as he could, arms stretched over his body as if he were diving into water. A moment later, he grabbed hold of the handrails outside the *Northern Dancer*'s hatch and pulled himself toward the ship. Shady went next, then Jeth, and finally Sierra.

Jeth held his breath as Sierra slid open the access panel on the *Northern Dancer*'s hatch and inserted a decryption card. He knew from Lizzie that such devices weren't to be trusted for this sort of thing, but Sierra had insisted that the code logic behind it was foolproof.

A moment later, the LED on the card flashed green, and the hatch slid open like a wide, welcoming mouth ready to swallow them whole.

One hurdle down, Jeth thought, giving a shiver.

And a million more to go.

CHAPTER 30

NO ONE SPOKE AS THEY CRAWLED THROUGH THE HATCH. To lessen the risk of detection, they would maintain comm silence unless absolutely necessary inside the ship.

The *Northern Dancer*'s hatch was a good deal larger than the *Citation*'s, and the four of them fitted inside more comfortably. Sierra activated the gravity drive, and they peeled out of their suits, which were far too cumbersome and noisy for crawling through the ventilation shafts.

Sierra retrieved the palm-sized tablet from her jacket pocket and switched it on. The tablet contained detailed schematics of the C-93. She examined them a moment, then motioned to Shady and pointed at an area low to the floor on the left side. Shady stepped forward, pulling out the plasinum cutter he'd carried over. The cutter was of the illegal variety, designed to penetrate the plasinum walls of most spaceships. Hammer kept one stocked on each of his ships.

Moments later, Sierra slipped through the hole Shady had made. Jeth followed behind her, with Dax coming after him and Shady in the rear. They emerged in a blower duct, the air moving past them hot enough to burn and reeking with that terrible chemical stench of treated spaceship air. Sierra led the way, scooting along on her belly with impressive speed. Sweat stung Jeth's eyes and dripped from his nose as he crawled after her. Behind him he could hear the others' labored breathing. *It'll be a miracle if no one hears us.*

They stopped twice while Sierra checked the tablet. She made several turns, some right, some left. As they went, they passed metal grates that looked down into various rooms. Whenever one of the rooms was occupied, Sierra would slow down to keep from drawing notice.

Eventually the duct opened into a main heating shaft that seemed to run the entire height of the ship. Jeth palmed sweat from his face as he stared at the opening, wishing they would be moving upward, away from the furnaces, instead of downward toward L Deck.

Sierra rolled onto her back, sliding her head out of the duct and into the shaft. She leaned to the right, grabbed the rails of the maintenance ladder, and hoisted herself out. Then she started downward. Jeth followed, trying not to pant as he descended.

Sierra continued on at the same relentless pace. A faint, eerie light from the furnaces below lit the shaft, casting orange shadows. Jeth counted the ducts they passed, knowing that each one represented a deck. He was up to five by the time Sierra finally moved into one of them.

After another long crawl through more ducts, Sierra at last came to a stop. She double-checked the tablet and then pointed at an area of the shaft between her and Jeth. Jeth took the cutter from Shady and started making another hole.

The machine itself was virtually silent, but what little noise there was seemed as loud as gunfire in the small space. Jeth half expected an entire brigade of ITA soldiers to be waiting below them as he pulled off the cover to the hole he'd made. The loud grind of machinery noise rose up to greet them.

Jeth moved aside, letting Sierra go first. She lowered herself through the hole and then swung outward, dropping down safely on a pile of discarded insulation. Jeth followed after her and stepped out of the way for Dax and Shady.

He looked around. They were in the recycling center where all the reusable shipboard waste was sent for reprocessing. It smelled like a combination of melted plasinum and rotting meat being cooked on a barbecue. More than a dozen giant bins filled the place, each one centered beneath a large chute.

"The brig is to the left of this door, one corridor over," Sierra said, pointing at the only exit. "There's no way to get into the brig through the ventilation system without triggering the alarms. They've got the place rigged with both electronic and bio sensors. There probably won't be any guards in the corridor, but there will be at the entrance to the brig around the corner. Two is standard, but I can't guarantee that's all there will be. Either way, we've got to take them out before they hit the alarm."

Tricky, Jeth thought. *But doable.* He was already running through scenarios, drawing on the many jobs he'd pulled with the Shades.

"We'll need to do it quiet like," Dax said, and he withdrew

a Luke 357 from his shoulder holster. It was outfitted with a silencer.

Jeth swallowed. He didn't like the idea of killing, ITA soldiers or not.

"No killing," Sierra said, her voice firm. "Enough people have died because of Renford."

Dax rolled his eyes. "They don't make silencers for stunners, sweetheart."

"I don't care," Sierra said.

"Oh, this is just great," said Shady. "You spent all that time planning how to get us in here, and nobody bothered to think about how we're gonna take out the bad guys?"

A flush blossomed in Sierra's cheeks.

"Normally," said Dax, his nostrils flaring, "it doesn't require any planning. You just take them out the old-fashioned way."

"I said no." Sierra's face was completely red now, but Jeth could tell she wasn't going to back down.

"I'm with her," Jeth said. "We shouldn't kill unless we have to."

"Okay, Captain," Dax said, his tone dry. "Then how do you suggest we get in to rescue your sister?"

Jeth looked around, searching for an answer. He spotted a row of safety suits hanging on the far wall behind Dax. They were the kind that a maintenance worker might put on when cleaning up something nasty or dangerous. An idea unfurled in his mind. Sierra wasn't going to like it, but he was pretty sure it would work.

"Let me see the schematics," Jeth said, holding out his hand to Sierra. She gave him the tablet. He studied it for a couple of moments, then handed it back. "Okay, here's what we're going to do."

Five minutes later, Jeth and Sierra stepped out of the room into the corridor beyond, both of them wearing safety suits. When Jeth saw the corridor was empty, he waved at Dax and Shady to come out. They emerged, both in suits too, but with guns drawn.

Sierra fingered the collar of her suit. "Are you sure this will work?"

Jeth smacked his lips. "Yep, we need them to think we belong on this ship just long enough to get the drop on them."

She frowned, still unconvinced.

Jeth smirked, the expression at odds with the nervous energy pulsing through him. "Celeste and I pull this con all the time. Trust me. It'll work."

He didn't wait for a response but headed left down the corridor toward an adjacent hallway. He stopped just before the turn into the brig corridor. He sensed Sierra standing behind him. If she was unhappy about the next part of the plan, she hadn't complained about it so far, which he was grateful for. Truth be told, he wasn't thrilled with what was coming next either, but it was the only way to take down the guards without killing them.

Dax and Shady got in position, one on each side of the corridor and as close to the edge as possible without being seen.

Jeth looked at Sierra. "Are you ready?"

She nodded, blinking nervously.

He squelched his own nervousness. "Make it look good."

"You too."

Jeth grinned with more bravado than he truly felt. "Always do."

He stepped toward her, cupping her face with both hands as he leaned down to kiss her. At the same time, he pushed her back into the other corridor, assuming the aggressive role that Celeste normally took. To his surprise, kissing her wasn't difficult. He hadn't forgotten the last time they'd done this. It had been pretty wonderful until she'd shot him.

Sierra resisted him a moment, her body as rigid as metal and her mouth like velvet-covered stone. Jeth's heartbeat doubled in alarm. *This isn't going to work.*

But a second later, she began to kiss him back. Her lips slid open against his, and he breathed her in, savoring the sweet scent and taste of her. Her body softened as she wrapped her arms around his waist. A sudden swell of desire, stronger than any he remembered, rose up in Jeth, muddling his thoughts. He dropped his hands from Sierra's face and gripped her hips, pulling her even closer. She leaned into him in response, head tilting farther back.

"What are you doing down there?" a voice shouted at them.

Jeth ignored it, unable to open his eyes, even to survey how many of them there were. For the moment, he didn't care. It was as if his body had risen up in mutiny against his brain.

Sierra whispered against his lips, "Two. Coming this way."

He recaptured her mouth in answer. He didn't have to worry about the ITA soldiers. They were someone else's concern. The soldiers were shouting at them, but Jeth couldn't make out what they were saying.

And it didn't matter. The moment the two soldiers reached them, Dax and Shady stepped around the corner and bashed them in the head with the butts of their guns.

Sierra pulled away from Jeth, and he almost forgot to let go. The moment there was distance between them, he came back to his senses.

"Go get us through the door," he said, risking a look at Sierra. Her face was flushed and her lips swollen. He looked away.

Sierra trotted past him down the short corridor to the security station in front of a sealed door. Jeth helped the other two drag the soldiers toward it, while Sierra worked on overriding the locks.

Pulling off the safety suit, Jeth stepped behind the security station and examined the control panel. Several monitors showed a live feed of the inside of the brig. All the cells were empty except for L-11. He saw Lizzie, sitting on the bench in the back, her knees drawn up to her chest. He couldn't see her face, which was buried in her arms, but he thought her body was shaking from sobs.

A fierce, protective anger surged through Jeth. *If they've hurt her . . .*

With an effort, he looked away from Lizzie's feed to the only other screen with activity.

"There's just the one guard," Jeth said, seeing the man in the top right monitor. He clearly had no idea what was going on outside the door he was guarding. Jeth guessed he should've been watching the monitor beside him instead of playing a video game on a handheld. If he had been, he would've noticed the absence of the other guards.

"I saw," Sierra said. "We take him out the same way." She yanked the decryption card out of the door's access panel as it clicked open.

Dax charged through the door first, dispensing with the guard on the other side in moments. He grabbed the man by the arms and dragged him into the nearest cell. Jeth and Shady pulled the other two soldiers through the door and into the cell as well.

"Somebody needs to stay out here, to let us out again," Sierra said. "The door might set off an alarm if it's open too long."

"Right," said Dax. "I'll stay here. You three go get Lizzie." Dax stepped back into the outer corridor without waiting for a reply and then shut the door behind him.

Sierra was already charging down the corridor toward L-11. Jeth turned and followed after her.

"Stay there, Shady, and back up Dax," Jeth called over his shoulder.

"Okay, but hurry up. I don't like just hanging around. Feel like a big fat target."

Jeth ignored him and hurried to catch up with Sierra. The corridor was narrow and brightly lit, like a hospital. None of the cells had windows or bars but were solid, barren little rooms, the kind of place that would drive a person mad if they were locked in it too long, Jeth thought.

Sierra halted outside L-11 and jammed the decryption card into the access panel. Jeth counted off the seconds, hoping it would work again. A click sounded a moment later, and the door slid open. Sierra stepped into the cell.

Lucky again, Jeth thought as he came in after her. He supposed Lizzie had either been wrong about decryption cards or the one Sierra was using was a top-of-the-line model worth as much as a starship.

This is too easy.

But Jeth dismissed the concern as he saw Lizzie's tearstained face looking up at him. Her mouth fell open in shock, and she leaped up. He heard the sound of the door sliding closed behind him, but he didn't panic. It was just a safety feature.

"Are you all right?" Jeth said.

"I'm fine. Just ready to get out of here."

"Let's go, then," said Sierra. She slid the decryption card into the access panel. A moment later the words ACCESS DENIED flashed on the panel's tiny screen.

"What the hell?" Jeth said.

Sierra pulled the card out, then jammed it in again. Another failure message appeared. "No," Sierra said through clenched teeth. "It can't be." She tried the card a third time, and the locks at last disengaged.

Jeth let out the breath he'd been holding and charged through the door, victory like a balloon swelling inside his chest.

He froze just beyond the doorway. More than a dozen

guards were waiting in the corridor, guns drawn and aimed at him.

"Put your weapons on the floor," the nearest one said.

Jeth's head spun. How did this happen? They'd been so careful, made no mistakes.

Then the explanation struck him full force. Dax stood among the soldiers, and not as a captive. He stepped forward as Jeth spotted him.

"You *betrayed* us," Jeth said. He couldn't believe it. Dax had seemed so genuine, his story so true and believable. *So much like my own.*

Dax nodded, his expression impossible to read. "Hammer just cut a deal with Renford. And it's like I said, Golden Boy: Nobody outruns Hammer. Not even you."

JETH STARED AT THE FOUR BLANK WHITE WALLS AROUND him. He'd been right. A person could go mad in here.

He'd been locked in the cell less than a day, but already the restlessness was eating away at him. *How long will they leave me in here? Forever?* Except he knew that wouldn't happen. Not with Hammer involved.

Jeth could only assume that was what Dax had meant about a deal—that Renford and Hammer had somehow decided to work together. At first he couldn't understand how it was possible, but then he remembered that Hammer had found Renford's calling card. After that, it was just a matter of logistics. Dax must've told Hammer what happened on Moenia and what they were planning. Once Hammer knew, he could easily have used that information to negotiate with Renford. The idea of them working together was so horrible, Jeth couldn't stomach speculating what their deal might entail.

At first his rage over Dax's betrayal blocked out all rational thought. He beat his fists against the door, screaming until his lungs trembled from the effort and his throat became a raw, quivering thing inside his neck. But the rage soon gave way to anguish. He had failed them—Lizzie, Cora, everyone. None of them were safe now. Not from Renford and not from Hammer.

Finally, Jeth forced his mind away from these thoughts, focusing instead on not giving up, on finding a way out of here. Only there didn't seem to be any hope of that. Nothing short of a plasinum cutter was getting through these walls, and he didn't have a clue how to hack into the security panel by the door. And no tools, either.

He supposed his best chance was to be ready when they came for him.

The minutes continued to tick by as long as days, the hours as long as years. Jeth caught himself drifting in between sleep and wakefulness. Telling the difference between the two grew harder and harder.

Finally he heard movement outside. He stood from the bench he'd been lying on and raced to the small space beside the door, taking cover. He held his breath, muscles tense in anticipation.

As the door slid open, Jeth charged through it, throwing a punch at the person standing just beyond. His fist collided with Sergei's jaw. Pain tore through his knuckles, but it didn't stop the pleasure he felt as Sergei's head snapped backward and blood burst from his lip.

Sergei wasn't alone, but the other guards with him, a mixture of Brethren and ITA, couldn't get to Jeth; Sergei was too big and the space in the corridor too small. Jeth kneed Sergei in the gut, grabbing the gun from his hand as he fell.

Jeth aimed it at the nearest guards, keenly aware of all the guns trained on him. "Go ahead and shoot, but I promise I'll take more than a few of you down with me."

"Oh, I wouldn't do that if I were you," a familiar voice said from Jeth's right.

He turned and saw Dax. He steadied his grip on the trigger. Killing Dax alone might be satisfaction enough. But he couldn't.

Sierra stood in front of Dax. Although she didn't block much of him, he had his gun pointed at her. For a second, Jeth didn't believe Dax would harm her, but he decided not to risk it. Dax had taken him by surprise once before. Jeth wasn't about to let it happen again.

He lowered the gun, and one of the ITA soldiers yanked it from his hands while two others grabbed him by the arms and shackled his wrists. He didn't bother trying to fight them off. There were too many of them and he had nowhere to go. No, he needed to be patient and wait for a better chance.

He took in Sierra's appearance, seeing nothing outwardly wrong with her other than the shackles on her wrists, too. Still, he asked, "Are you okay?"

She nodded, her expression grim. "Are you?"

Before Jeth could answer, a fist the size of a boulder collided with his stomach. He bent over, heaving in pain.

"Do anything like that again," Sergei said, leaning over Jeth, "and I'll cut off your feet with a dull saw." Then he spat on Jeth's face.

Struggling to catch his breath, Jeth wiped away the spit with his shoulder.

"Come on," Dax said. "Renford's waiting for them."

The soldiers herded Jeth and Sierra down the corridor after Dax. Jeth moved in close to Sierra as they walked and whispered, "Any word on the others?"

She shook her head.

He sighed. He'd expected as much, but still the disappointment stung. Where were Lizzie and Cora? What about Shady? Had Flynn and Milton managed to get away on *Avalon* or had they been captured, too? Dax had known their position, after all.

"Any idea what's coming next?" Jeth said, his dread increasing with every step.

"Nothing good." Sierra's voice trembled as she spoke, and any relief he'd felt at seeing her unharmed faded in an instant.

Dax led them into a large room not far from the brig. Strange devices filled the place, many of them outfitted with straps and shackles. Torture devices, Jeth realized. Some were simple items, like the row of vises in all different sizes hanging on the far wall or the large metal table in the center of the room. Others were more sophisticated, like a pair of large mechanized boots, the kind designed to shatter shinbones in small increments.

Jeth sucked air through his teeth. "Why do I get the feeling this room wasn't part of the original cruise ship design?"

"This is the interrogation room," Sierra said.

"No kidding." Jeth had a feeling she knew the place well.

He gulped, trying not to imagine what was coming next.

Renford stood near the middle of the room, not far from the table and in front of two identical metal chairs that resembled massive thrones. He waved at their entrance. "Good. Bring them over here and sit them down."

The soldiers pushed Jeth and Sierra forward and into the chairs. The chairs' surfaces were divided by thin, nearly invisible lines forming small squares that looked like tiny compartments. What those compartments contained—needles, knives, hot pokers—he was certain he didn't want to find out.

Sierra glared up at Renford. "You're wasting your time with this. Whatever it is you want from me, you're not going to get it."

He arched one eyebrow. "Why do you assume I want something? How do you know this isn't just punishment for your betrayal?"

Sierra swallowed. "You wouldn't bother doing it yourself if that was all there was."

Renford sighed. "True. You do know me so well, don't you?"

Jeth clutched the arms of his chair, resisting an overwhelming desire to hit the man. He'd never thought he would encounter someone he despised more than Hammer. Sure, Hammer tortured, manipulated, and killed people, but Jeth had never seen him do those things only for the pleasure of it. It always served a purpose. But there was pleasure in Renford's eyes now, perverse and twisted. Jeth couldn't imagine what life had been like for Sierra and

Vince, growing up under the care of this man. Even more, he couldn't imagine how she had turned out so *good*, so willing to sacrifice herself to save Cora. An ache blossomed in his chest at the thought.

Sierra didn't respond. She merely continued glaring at Renford, her body as rigid as the metal chair beneath her.

"It is true," Renford continued, "I do want something from you. I—" He broke off as someone entered the room.

Jeth craned his neck to see Hammer stride in. His stomach dropped, any childish hope he'd had that Dax had been lying about the deal vanishing in an instant.

"Sorry I'm late," Hammer said, eyeing Sierra and Jeth.

Renford waved him off. "No matter. Your presence isn't necessary for this."

Hammer grunted. The annoyed sound of it perked Jeth's ears. This was an unholy alliance, no doubt, but at least it didn't seem to be an easy one. "Oh, I think it's always necessary to protect an investment," said Hammer. "Especially one as big as this."

"What are you talking about?" Sierra asked, shifting her glare toward Hammer. Jeth felt a momentary wave of awe at her spunk.

Glancing at Renford, Hammer chuckled. "So this is one of yours, is it? I like her already."

Renford shot him a look sharp enough to cut glass.

Come on, Jeth thought, *why don't you two kill each other right now and save me the trouble?*

Hammer stared back at Renford, unfazed.

Renford dropped his gaze to Sierra. "Let me formally introduce you to my new business partner, Hammer Dafoe."

Sierra kept her eyes focused on Renford. "I know who he is. What I don't understand is what he's doing here."

"Yes, well, in the past few weeks I've come to realize that simply selling the Aether Project would be foolish," said Renford. "Why give up something so valuable for mere money? No. Rather than destroy the ITA, I've decided to take their place." He paused, then motioned at Hammer. "Excuse me. *We've* decided to take their place."

Jeth's mouth slid open. He closed it at once, teeth clacking. Hammer and Renford taking the place of the ITA? The idea of those two holding that much power was right up there with . . . no . . . he couldn't imagine anything quite as bad as that. The ITA was guilty of a lot of horrible things, but at least it wasn't a dictatorship. There was *some* measure of checks and balances and restraint, a public service that, however corrupt, still held the galaxy together. He couldn't imagine things holding together for long under Hammer's rule.

Sierra raised an eyebrow. "And how do you plan on doing that?"

Hammer folded his arms across his massive chest. "It's a simple principle of business. Their monopoly on space travel will soon be *our* monopoly."

"That's right," said Renford, keeping his attention focused on Sierra. "You know as well as I do that the ITA has failed to find an effective cure for the Pyrean sickness, and that it's just a matter of time before what remains of the Pyreans dies off. The only solution is to manufacture a new species for the job through Cora and, with any luck, Lizzie. Both of whom are under my control now. Add in Hammer's resources and infrastructure, and it's only a matter of time before we can offer the public an alternative to their failing ITA-issued metadrives. There'll be no saving the metagates, true, but with every ship equipped with its own metaspace navigator, no one will care much."

That image of Cora as a human battery strapped into a machine swam in Jeth's mind once again, all the muscles in his body clenching at the horror of it.

Beside him, Sierra visibly tensed. "Cora isn't technology. She's a little girl. A human being."

Hammer coughed. "I thought you said she was smart?"

"Oh, she is," said Renford. "When she doesn't let her emotions interfere with her reason."

"Don't talk about me as if I'm not here." Sierra glowered at both men in turn. "And I'm aware that Cora's DNA isn't strictly human, but that doesn't make her anything less."

"We're not here to debate Cora Seagrave's humanity or lack thereof," Renford said. "Instead we need to discuss her future."

Jeth scoffed, finding his voice at last. "What future? If you follow the ITA's agenda, she's going to die young."

"Oh, I wouldn't say that," said Hammer. "Not once my scientists have had a chance to refine the AGT process."

At first Jeth wanted to dismiss such an arrogant assertion,

but then he remembered how successful Hammer's scientists had been with stealth technology. Hammer employed people like himself—without scruples, willing to do whatever it took to succeed.

Jeth wanted to scream, wanted to do something rash, but he held back, willing himself to take deep, calming breaths. He knew right now he had to rely on that cool patience his father had taught him when he was learning to shoot. *The right moment will come. Wait for it.*

Sneering, Sierra said, "If you've already got such a fool-proof plan in place, then why am I here? Why don't you just kill me like you tried to do when you took Cora?"

Renford exhaled as if in regret."You're here because we've hit a snag with Cora. One only you can help smooth out."

"Oh yeah? And what is *that*?"

"The same task the Aether Project scientists needed. Help in keeping Cora under control. She was in such a state when we revived her initially that she destroyed half of the hospital wing. We've placed her in a coma for now, but I'm sure you're aware how dangerous it is to her health to be kept under for too long."

Jeth glanced at Sierra, seeing in her expression this was true. *Breathe, breathe.* The words became a chant in his head.

"Cora likes you," Renford went on. "She trusts you. If she were to wake up and see your face, no harm would befall anyone, including her."

Sierra bit her lip. "What will you do with her if I say no?"

Renford shrugged. "We'll try different medications or

keep her under as much as possible. Nothing good for her, I assure you. Nothing that will make her as happy as she would be having you around." Renford paused, and when he went on, it was with a persuasive tone that even Jeth had to admit was dangerously effective. "Think about it, Sierra. You'll be able to help her, teach her how to control her unique abilities. And, if you want, you can continue assisting with the scientific work as well. I might even give you a say in what happens to her—if you take strides to regain my trust in you, that is. But really, this is your *only* chance to help preserve Cora's so-called human rights."

"What about Lizzie?" Jeth said. "What do you plan on doing to her?"

"Oh, no need to worry about her, Jeth," said Hammer. "She'll be treated better than she would have been *otherwise*, given what's happened."

Jeth flinched, knowing perfectly well Hammer was referring to his plan to use her in one of his brothels if Jeth betrayed him one more time. Which he had. He didn't doubt for a second that Dax had told Hammer about his plan to get his crew and family away. Even if Dax hadn't, Sergei certainly would've told him about how Jeth had locked him up.

"Yes, no need to fret," said Renford. "She'll undergo some medical tests and a couple of surgeries, of course, to harvest her eggs."

Breathe, Jeth thought. *Just find a way out. Keep breathing . . .*

Sierra shook her head. "I won't help you. Cora and Lizzie

would be better off dead than under your control."

A sneer warped Renford's features, his persuasive persona of a moment before vanishing. "You of all people should understand the importance of what I'm trying to accomplish. You've seen the consequences of the meta technology failing completely. All the worlds will end up like Rosmoor, slowly starving to death, wallowing in disease. But that will never happen again with what I have planned. The ITA has held unchecked power for far too long."

And who will check you? Jeth wanted to say, but he didn't get a chance as Sierra said, "Exploiting Cora and Lizzie isn't the answer. Clones or test tube babies, it doesn't matter. They're all humans with human emotions. You're not creating a solution but an entire race of slaves."

"Better a few should live as slaves than billions die," said Renford.

"Don't do it, Sierra," Jeth said, glancing at the red implant in the back of Hammer's skull. She was right. Death was better. In the back of his mind he thought, *There has to be some other solution, some way to cure the Pyrean sickness.*

Hammer laughed, although anger smoldered in his eyes as he looked at Jeth. "I don't understand where such bravado is coming from. Do you think your friends will be coming to rescue you?" He laughed harder. "If so, I would give up the hope now. All of them have been captured. Why, *Avalon* herself is docked on the flight deck of this ship."

Jeth gritted his teeth, his calm breaking. Despair pressed down on him as hatred pumped through his veins. As always,

Hammer knew just the way to break him.

Sierra shook her head. "My answer is *no*," she said to Renford, her voice like ice. "I won't help you. And you can torture me all you want, but it won't matter. You know better than anybody how well I've been conditioned to withstand it."

A shiver slid over Jeth's body. He didn't want to know what she meant, although judging by the torture devices hanging around this place, he could guess. He wondered which machine was responsible for her deformed fingers.

Renford sighed. "Yes, I know. But that's why *he's* here." He pointed at Jeth.

"What?" Jeth's stomach twisted into a knot.

Sierra smirked. "Go ahead. I don't care what you do to him."

Jeth gaped at Renford and Sierra in turn, outrage and fear making his head pound.

"That's not what I saw on the brig security cameras," Renford said. "I've studied human interaction and body language enough to recognize genuine attraction when I see it. And I'm quite certain that you feel strongly about him."

"You're mistaken," Sierra said, but Jeth thought he heard a faint hitch in her voice. He *hoped* it was there. Was it possible Renford was right? Not that it mattered at the moment. Jeth fought to regain his calm but failed, his breath coming in quick, silent pants.

"We shall see." Renford motioned to the guards standing a short distance away. "Strip him down and put him on the table."

Jeth reacted at once, leaping up and swinging with both hands at the first person within reach. It was no good. The soldiers overpowered him in seconds. They unshackled his wrists, pulled off his shirt, pants, boots, and socks, leaving only his underwear. Then they forced him onto the metal table. He continued to struggle as they strapped him down on his back by his wrists and ankles. Finally, they tightened the straps until he couldn't move at all.

The cold metal bit at Jeth's naked flesh even as sweat broke out over his body.

"Don't forget, Renford," Hammer said as he stood watching nearby, "no permanent damage. This one belongs to me."

"No need to worry," Renford said, stepping into Jeth's view. He carried some kind of metal rod in his hand. "The effects won't be lingering. Not physically, anyways."

Jeth braced for pain as Renford lowered the rod toward him. The end of it buzzed and hissed with electricity. But nothing could've prepared him for the searing agony that shot through the left side of his body as the rod touched his shoulder. It was like being hit by a hundred stunners all at once.

He clamped his mouth shut, fighting with all his will not to scream.

The pain vanished as quickly as it had come, but Renford wasn't finished. He lowered the rod to Jeth's belly and this time held it there longer. Jeth jerked against the straps, his body desperate to curl into a fetal position, evading the pain. The straps cut into his skin, preventing him. Blood dampened his arms and legs.

On and on Renford went, prodding him everywhere, varying the length of time he let Jeth suffer so that his mind was in as much torment as his body.

"You can stop this, Sierra," Renford called out over the crackle. "Just say the word. I'm sure you can remember what it feels like to have this much electricity running through you."

Jeth wanted to shout at her that he was all right, but he couldn't open his mouth. If he did, he would cry out.

Renford lowered the rod again, but this time he touched the table itself. The sensation was like being burned alive. Every part of Jeth's body, every nerve and hair follicle, was on fire. He gritted his teeth, his mind frantic for some way to endure this, some way to escape. *It'll pass . . . it'll pass . . . it'll pass.*

Yet on and on it went. Tears leaked from Jeth's eyes as he squeezed them shut. All his hair stood on end. He felt on the verge of breaking, his entire body wrenching apart. Until at last he couldn't take it anymore.

The fight went out of him. His mouth opened, and the scream broke free.

It went on forever.

Until finally Sierra's frantic voice blended with his. "Stop it!"

Renford lowered the rod, and the last crackle of electricity vanished. But the pain lingered. Jeth's body hummed with it. His bones felt as fragile as needles. He stared at the ceiling above him, unable to move or think.

"What did you say, Sierra?" Renford asked, his tone smug.

"I'll help you. With Cora."

Through blurred vision, Jeth saw Renford beam down at him. "You see. I was right. She *does* care about you."

Jeth didn't reply. He hadn't the will for it. It had been sucked out of him. Summoning what little energy remained, he turned his head and spat blood from where he'd bitten his tongue and the sides of his cheeks.

"But only on one condition," Sierra said.

Renford turned away from Jeth to look at Sierra, a frown in his voice. "What condition?"

"Let Jeth and his crew go. Vince as well. Give them *Avalon* and let them leave unharmed."

Renford laughed. "This isn't a negotiation, Sierra."

"Oh, but it is. Sooner or later you will have to wake Cora up. She's no good to you unconscious or dead, and there's no drug she won't build a resistance to sooner or later. But give me what I ask, and I'll do everything you want me to do, no questions, no deception. If you don't, you'd better kill me now, because otherwise I'll do whatever I can to teach her how to use her power against you. She will tear this ship apart. And everyone in it."

From where he lay, Jeth saw a dark look cross Renford's face. Jeth watched him through the slits of his eyelids, fighting off the blackout now threatening to overtake him.

"What do you think, Hammer?" Renford said, shifting his gaze off Sierra. "Shall we let Jeth and the others go?"

Hammer took a long time to reply. "I suppose I'm willing

to part with the crew and the ship. *Avalon's* little more than a junk heap at this point. But not Jeth. I have plans for him."

"What plans?" Sierra said.

"That's not for you to worry about, little girl. But I promise that'll he be alive and in far less pain and stress than he is right now."

Jeth closed his eyes, understanding exactly what Hammer had in store. He heard Sierra exhale, the sound full of something like pity or maybe sorrow. He blocked it out as best he could, willing his mind to go as numb as his body.

"That's the best offer you're going to get," said Renford. "And you should consider yourself extremely lucky that I'm willing to let Vince leave here alive after what he's done to me. So do we have an agreement?"

Silence descended in the room as all of them waited for Sierra to answer.

"Yes," she finally said, the word ringing out like a gong.

Jeth pushed the air from his lungs then drew breath again. *At least the others will escape, if not Lizzie and Cora and me.* That was better than nothing.

"But I want to say good-bye to everyone," said Sierra. "Starting with him."

"As you wish," Renford said, sounding amused now.

Jeth heard Renford's heavy footsteps retreating and then lighter ones approach. Soft, gentle hands touched his face. He opened his eyes to see Sierra leaning over him. She stroked his cheek, her eyes glistening with unshed tears.

Then she leaned down to him, pressing her lips against

his. "I'm sorry," she whispered. "But don't give up hope. I'll find us a way out of this. Or I'll die trying." She kissed him, her mouth a balm against the hurt inside him.

Then she was gone.

Jeth managed to raise his head just enough to see her disappear through the doorway with Renford. Hammer moved into view, and Jeth recoiled from the sight of him, wanting to get away.

Only there was nowhere to go.

Hammer stooped over him and said, "Five more days, Jethro, and you'll be eighteen." He grabbed Jeth's chin and pushed his head to the side, exposing the back of his skull. Then he jammed a finger against the implant architecture hole. Pain arced over Jeth's head and down his spine, sparks flashing across his vision. He couldn't help the whimper that escaped his throat.

Hammer laughed. The terrible, triumphant sound crushed out the small flame of hope Sierra's parting words had given him.

CHAPTER 32

ONCE, WHEN JETH WAS SEVEN, HE SPENT THREE DAYS IN bed sick with the flu. It was the worst he'd ever felt in his life, as if his body had forgotten what it was and how it was supposed to behave. Food made his stomach clench. Any liquid at all set his throat to burning. His head felt like he was wearing it inside out.

Yet despite his misery during that time, his strongest memory was of the way his mother had cared for him. How she had stroked his face with a damp cloth whenever he finished vomiting or smiled down at him as she adjusted the pillows behind his head, pulling the covers over his body as he shivered with fever. He remembered the soft, lulling sound of her voice as she read aloud to him stories of other little boys having adventures, gallivanting around the universe in starships or exploring a jungle teeming with tigers and lions.

She had made those three days bearable. And it was only the memory of her that kept him sane now.

Five days I've been locked in here, Jeth thought, running his gaze over the empty, oppressive walls. *Maybe six.* He'd spent the last hour trying to figure it out for sure. They'd been feeding him at regular intervals, twice a day, as far as he could tell. It was so hard to be certain, though. After the torture, they'd brought him back here, where he'd slept for hours and hours, a bone-deep fatigue settling over him like an iron blanket. Only now was the tiredness finally starting to fade. His muscles still ached as if from strenuous exercise.

Five days, maybe six.

The knowledge of how much time had passed, how close he was to the end, made him want to stand up and pace the length of the cell, but he knew better. He would need all his energy when they came for him.

The waiting was even worse than the torture. He'd spent his waking moments the last few days hoping for some word from Sierra, some sound of tapping on the walls as she prepared to bust him out. He wanted it so badly, he'd even started imagining sounds.

Five days. Maybe six.

Had it been that long? It had to be. He was sure of it.

Which means I'm eighteen now.

And old enough for an implant.

He closed his eyes and leaned his head against the back of the cell, trying to figure out what to do, worry over when they would come driving him mad.

Click.

Jeth opened his eyes, and in a grip of panic he jumped up, his muscles screaming from the sudden movement.

For a moment he was sure he'd imagined it, but then the door slid open. Dax stood in the doorway, smiling in at him. In a second, all the tiredness and ache left Jeth's body, replaced by rage-fueled adrenaline. He leaped toward Dax, right fist clenched and arm swinging. He would bash the smile off his face.

Dax ducked at the last second and jammed his shoulder into Jeth's stomach, flipping him over. Jeth landed on his back, gasping for air.

Two pairs of hands grabbed him by the arms and hauled him to his feet. Jeth tried to pull away from them, but like all of Hammer's Brethren, these two were large and burly.

Dax faced Jeth, shaking his head. "You need to learn how to pick your battles, Golden Boy."

"No, I need to learn not to trust assholes like you." Jeth's voice came out rough from disuse.

Dax chuckled. "That too." He waved at the Brethren holding Jeth. "Bring him along. Hammer's waiting to see him."

The Brethren pushed Jeth down the corridor after Dax. Jeth expected to be taken back to the interrogation room, but Dax turned in the opposite direction. Questions darted through Jeth's mind. Where were Lizzie and Cora? Was Sierra still here? Did the others leave on *Avalon*?

He knew there was little point asking for information from a proven liar, but he couldn't help himself. "Where's my crew?"

Dax looked over his shoulder. "Gone. Except for Lizzie. They flew out of here almost a week ago, aboard *Avalon*."

Jeth wanted desperately to believe it. "Milton, Celeste, Shady, and Flynn?"

"Yep," said Dax, turning back around. "And Vince, too. Just like Renford promised Sierra. You, Sierra, Lizzie, and Cora are the only ones still here."

Despite his better instincts, Jeth believed him. Dax had no reason to lie, not about this, and not now. He tried to draw as much comfort as he could from knowing that some of them had made it out, but he had a feeling it wasn't going to be nearly enough to see him through what was coming.

As they walked, Jeth focused on his surroundings, trying to commit their path and how many people they passed to memory. The ship seemed as big as a city, populated with nothing but ITA soldiers and the Malleus Brethren and Guard. Each time Jeth's gaze fell on an implant—black or clear—a jolt of fear went through him.

They entered an elevator that must've been designed as a showpiece for the cruise line customers the Strata was originally intended for. It was made entirely of glass, edged with burnished gold. Although the front side of the elevator looked out onto only the elevator shaft, the back displayed a constantly shifting view of the ship. Jeth angled his head toward it, watching the decks slip by.

After a few moments, the view opened onto a massive flight deck filled with armored spaceships and short-range shuttles. Jeth scanned for any sign of *Avalon*, finding none. That was good. For a moment, his whole body ached with his desire to be back on his ship and far, far away from here.

They exited the elevator onto C Deck, making a left and navigating several corridors before finally coming to a stop outside a door marked C-19. Two more Brethren stood in front of it, and they bowed their heads in deference to Dax.

The door opened a moment later, and Dax entered. Jeth stayed put until the guards pushed him forward. He blinked as he stepped in, his eyes needing to adjust to the dim light that made the room seem as dark as a cave compared to the brightness of the corridor.

He was in what looked like the living room of a large, luxurious hotel suite. Then he realized that was exactly what it was, a stateroom designed for wealthy cruise ship patrons. The décor was completely to Hammer's taste, decadent to the point of gaudiness, with thick green carpeting and plush leather seats in between marble-topped tables.

Hammer was sitting on the nearest chair, leaning back with one tree-trunk-sized leg folded over the other. Standing over him, like the world's biggest servant boy, was Sergei.

"Ah, Jeth, welcome at last," Hammer said, waving at him. "And might I add congratulations as well. It's not every day you turn eighteen and officially become an adult."

Like I was ever a child, Jeth thought but didn't say. He didn't think he was capable of speech, for his gaze had just fallen on the two small cases sitting on the table in front of Hammer. He knew well what they contained.

"So I take it you and Renford haven't killed each other yet?" Jeth said, keeping his fear in check. "What a shame."

Hammer chuckled. "You'd be surprised how many differences can be set aside in order to achieve something as great as this venture."

Jeth rolled his eyes, sarcasm the only defense mechanism left to him. "You're not about to give me that crap about how the world will be so much better once you've brought down the ITA, are you?"

"Oh, but it *will* be," Hammer said, his piggy eyes gleaming. "Even someone as young and undereducated as you must have realized the kind of power the ITA holds. Did you know they refuse to sell metatech to certain planets based entirely on race? Whole groups of people have been locked down by the ITA to prevent them from spreading their culture anywhere else in the galaxy. To keep them from *infecting* others with their unacceptable ideals."

"As if you'll be any different. All you care about is wielding that same power yourself."

Hammer shrugged. "Perhaps. But at least I won't use it so indiscriminately. The only people who will suffer under my rule are those that deserve it."

Jeth almost laughed. It was so absurd. As if Hammer were fit to dole out justice and punishment. As if he would be any different from the ITA at all. No. He would be them all over again, only worse. Nobody should hold that much power. Those planets, those people, should be free to govern themselves, to come and go as they please.

And so should I.

"However," Hammer went on, "I didn't summon you here to talk business. At least not *that* business. But I'm sure you've guessed the reason already." His eyes flicked to the cases on the table, his expression daring Jeth to deny it.

Jeth didn't even consider playing dumb. If this was the end of the line, he would hold on to what remained of his pride and dignity. He had a feeling there wouldn't be much of it on the other side of what he was facing. "Oh, I know all right."

"Yes, I thought so." Hammer stood and bent toward the table, picking up both cases in his massive hands.

"Do I still get a choice then?" Jeth said, hoping that he didn't sound as desperate as he felt. If he was to be made a member of the Brethren instead of a Guard, there was still a chance he could save Lizzie and Cora, even his mother. And there was a chance some small part of who he was would remain intact.

Hammer stared at him for a long time. A trickle of sweat slipped between Jeth's shoulder blades and down his back, soaking the waistband of his pants.

Finally Hammer shook his head. "It pains me to say it, but no. The choice is gone. I gave you a chance to prove your loyalty once already, and you failed the test. You should never have believed that Dax would keep your plan from me. He knows the true meaning of loyalty. I also don't believe that you'll behave any differently in the future. And, well, you've become a liability to my new business venture."

Jeth's heart hammered in his ears like rapid missile fire. The two cases had been a show, a final act of humiliation designed to give Hammer the satisfaction of winning.

Again.

The sudden, sure realization that everything he knew and cared for was about to end hit Jeth, and he almost swayed beneath the rush of terror. He wanted to cling to every precious second left to him, which he could feel slipping away like sand through his fingers.

"What do you mean, a liability?" he managed to say at last.

"Your sisters, of course. I'm quite certain that, even if you did feel some genuine loyalty to me, it wouldn't remain in the face of what awaits them."

Jeth held his breath, fear turning to outrage.

"Normally," Hammer continued, "I would offer you a lifetime guarantee of their safety and well-being in exchange for your loyal service. It's an effective bargain, as I'm sure Daxton here can attest to. Isn't that right, Dax?"

Jeth risked a glance and saw Dax bristling beneath the outward mask of calm and compliance he wore. *So the story was true.* Not that it mattered.

Then again, maybe it *did* matter, just not in the way Jeth had thought. Hammer was right; he should've realized Dax would never show any disloyalty while his brother remained in danger. Even if Dax did sympathize with Jeth's plight, in the end he would always chose to protect his family over anyone else. Jeth couldn't blame him for that. He would've done the same.

But just because he understood what Dax had done didn't mean he was going to lie down and take this, either. *If I'm gonna die anyway . . .*

Jeth leaped sideways, going for the gun strapped in a

holster on Dax's hips. His fingers closed around the hilt, and he bent his knees, ready to roll and come up firing.

A foot struck him in the back. Jeth heard Sergei's laugh as he fell. But Jeth still had the gun. He clambered to his knees, struggling to release the safety in time to fire. His body was so tired from the torture, his fingers clumsy.

Hammer kicked the gun out of Jeth's hand with an almost lazy motion. A furious howl tore from Jeth's throat, and he flung himself after the gun, heedless of the stinging in his knuckles or the danger posed by the giant man looming above him.

"Get him," Hammer said.

Dax planted a knee in Jeth's back, pinning him as Sergei came over to help. Together they hoisted Jeth to his feet. Hammer opened one of the cases, revealing the clear-colored implant. He set the other case aside.

"Put him on his knees," Hammer said.

Sergei and Dax forced Jeth down, pulling his arms behind him so he had no choice but to lean forward.

Hammer took a step closer. "Bend his head."

Jeth fought the hands pushing his chin toward his chest. His neck muscles screamed as he strained against the inevitable force.

"Hold him still."

Jeth felt the point of the needle touch the back of his skull, probing for the architecture. His hair had grown enough to obscure the opening.

He closed his eyes, still refusing to give up the fight even as a voice whispered over and over in his mind: *This is it. The end, the end, the end. This is it.*

BOOM!

The room shook so hard, pictures fell from the walls and a decanter of liquor on a nearby table plummeted to the floor, shattering. The pressure on Jeth's arms loosened as Dax and Sergei were knocked off balance.

"Something hit us," said Hammer.

The ship rocked again with another fierce blast.

"We're under attack," Sergei said.

"That's impossible," said Hammer. Yet even before he finished speaking, they heard the unmistakable sound of distant gunfire.

Jeth pushed against the hands holding his head, and this time they gave way. He looked up at Hammer's annoyed expression.

"I can't get a straight answer from anyone," Hammer said, touching the back of his head where the red implant sat nestled against his neck. He motioned to Sergei. "Go find out what's happening. Take the others with you. Dax and I will finish here."

Sergei let go of Jeth's arm at once and trotted from the room, drawing the gun from his belt. Before Jeth had a chance to react, Dax grabbed him by his wrists and lifted his arms again, forcing him to bend forward.

"Hold him," Hammer said, stepping near.

Jeth struggled, but it was no good. Whatever was happening outside wasn't going to get here in time to save him.

Once the implant is inserted, it can never be removed.

Hammer finally found the hole in Jeth's skull. The touch of the implant's stem against the architecture sent a wave of pain cascading down his spine, the feeling intensified by his terror.

He closed his eyes and stopped struggling.

The end, the end, the end.

BOOM-BOOM-BOOM.

This time the sound wasn't from outside the ship but close, the loud eruption of gunfire. The door slid open and more bullets ripped through the air. The hands holding Jeth released him, and he fell forward, his face smacking the ground. He rolled over at once, his mind and body focusing instinctively.

Two people charged into the room—Sierra and Lizzie, both armed. No time for relief. Jeth jumped at Hammer, who'd been shot in the arm. He grabbed the gun from Hammer's holster, released the safety, and racked the slide in one smooth motion. Then he pressed the barrel to Hammer's temple.

Hammer froze, a big man reduced to cowering. He raised his hands in surrender. *Do it now!* a voice screamed in Jeth's mind. *Finish this. Once and for all.* It would be so easy, a slight increase in pressure and the bullet would eject from the barrel, tearing a death hole through the man's brain.

"Don't, Jeth," Sierra said, panic in her voice.

Jeth glanced over his shoulder, keeping his hand steady even as a shudder went through him at the sight awaiting him. Dax had somehow managed to capture Lizzie and was now holding her in front of him like a shield, a gun pressed against her neck.

Stalemate.

"Let go of Hammer," Dax said. His face was pale but his eyes hard and steady. He looked like he was having trouble standing. Jeth glanced down and saw blood pooling on the floor at Dax's feet. He must've taken a bullet in the leg.

Jeth froze, unable to move. Sierra had her gun aimed at Dax, but she had no angle to take him out. Not without hitting Lizzie too.

"I mean it, Jeth," Dax said. "I will kill her."

"Shoot him," Lizzie said, her terrified gaze fixed on Jeth.

But he couldn't risk it. Maybe if he already had his gun pointed the right direction. But if he wasn't fast enough, if his aim was off . . . *None of this will matter if Lizzie dies.*

"Why do you want to save him even after all he's done to you?" Jeth said.

Dax shook his head, the action oddly jerky, as if he'd developed some kind of nervous twitch.

"Don't deny it. I know the story you told me is true. Think about your brother. If we kill Hammer, he'll be free."

"No," Dax said. "Keeping Hammer safe is the only way to save him. The only way." Even Dax's voice had developed a kind of twitch.

Understanding clicked in Jeth's mind. He glanced at the red implant in Hammer's skull. It was the master implant, the one that controlled all the others. He reached for it, meaning to yank it out of Hammer's head.

The motion brought him in too close. Hammer lunged forward, snatching the gun from Jeth's hand and knocking him over.

Before Jeth could recover his feet, Hammer had the barrel pressed against his forehead.

"Get on your knees and put your hands on top of your head," Hammer said.

Jeth did so, turning his gaze toward Lizzie, who was still trapped in Dax's hold.

Hammer motioned to Sierra. "And you. Put the gun on the floor and get on your knees, too. We both know you're not going to let anything happen to Jeth."

Sierra hesitated, then did as Hammer ordered, kneeling down next to Jeth.

Hammer bent toward her, grabbed her ponytail, and twisted the blonde strands around his hand. He yanked her head back, forcing her gaze up to his. "If I wasn't so concerned about keeping things smooth with Renford, I would kill you." Then he let go of her hair and shoved her forward. He stepped on her back. "Stay down, why don't you?" Hammer waved at Dax. "Bring Lizzie over here and put her in front of her brother. I want her to have a front row seat for this."

Dax pushed Lizzie forward. He seemed to be using her as a crutch as he limped along.

"Don't do this, Dax," Jeth said. "Don't be like him. Help us."

Hammer chuckled. "Nice try, but Dax is Brethren. His loyalty belongs to me."

"His loyalty is *forced* by that implant," Jeth said. "Fight it, Dax. Do it for your brother. Help us."

In response, Dax pushed Lizzie down to her knees in front of Jeth, his actions in perfect obedience to Hammer's will.

"Now come around and hold Jeth still," Hammer said, stepping away from Sierra.

Dax shuffled over, leaving blood splatters on the floor. *If he would just pass out,* Jeth thought. They could easily overpower Hammer.

Outside in the hall, the noise of shouting and gunfire was growing louder, and every few minutes the ship shook as if struck by missile fire.

Dax holstered his gun and grabbed Jeth by the wrists again, pushing him forward. His grip wasn't as strong as last time but powerful enough to do the job. For the third time, Jeth felt the stem of the implant prod the hole of the architecture. The pressure against his skull grew stronger as Hammer began to force the thing in.

Then, without warning, Dax's grip on his wrists let go. Jeth fell forward as a wet, sucking noise sounded behind him. Jeth clambered to his feet and spun around to see that Dax had yanked the red implant out of Hammer's skull.

Hammer blinked dazedly, as if he couldn't understand what had happened. Jeth punched him in the face, throwing the full force of his body into it. The big man stumbled backward, blood bursting from his nose.

Dax caught Hammer before he could fall and held him there long enough to grab the clear-colored implant still hanging loose in Hammer's hand. Then Dax pushed Hammer down into a kneeling position.

Jeth stood there, transfixed by the scene unfolding before him as if in slow motion. Dax raised the clear-colored implant to Hammer's head, his body no longer shaking. Then he thrust it downward.

Hammer's eyes went wide with shock. It lasted only a moment and then his gaze turned hollow, his expression slackening into the dulled features of catatonia.

Dax let go, shoving Hammer forward onto his face, where he continued to lie, stupid and unmoving.

Jeth stared down at the back of Hammer's head, mere millimeters from his feet. The implant writhed a moment around Hammer's skull, as if adjusting to its new home.

It's over, Jeth realized. The big man was no more.

He tore his gaze away from the sight, certain he would be sick if he watched any longer. He stepped back for good measure and then turned to Lizzie, helping her to stand. He pulled her into a fierce hug.

"It's done," Dax said, a tremble in his voice. Jeth looked at him and saw Dax was holding the red implant, examining it with something like wonderment on his face. "Finally over."

Jeth let out the breath he'd been holding. "Thank you. For doing that."

Dax looked up, as if surprised to find he wasn't alone. He nodded. "You were right. Hammer always enforced my loyalty with this." He reached up with his other hand and removed his black Brethren implant, tossing it aside. "I'm sorry for handing you over to him, but I didn't have a choice. There was only ever one way to defeat Hammer. By taking this." Dax held up the red implant like a trophy. Then he lowered his hand toward the back of his head in a gesture Jeth knew well enough by now.

"What are you doing?" Jeth said, moving to stop him.

But it was too late. Dax thrust the red implant into his skull.

No one moved or spoke for several long seconds afterward. Dax simply stood there with his eyes closed. A muscle ticked in his jaw. Outside, the fighting had at last arrived at their door.

Finally, Dax opened his eyes and stared at the three of them. Jeth could tell he was a changed man. A hard, deadly glint shone in his eyes. He looked like an animal gone feral. Jeth swallowed, any relief he had felt at seeing the end of Hammer evaporating fast. He didn't know what exactly that implant did, but he knew for certain it wasn't anything good.

"Get out of here," Dax said to Jeth. "Find Cora and make your escape. I'll order my men to leave you alone."

My men. Dax was the new Hammer.

Jeth nodded. Then he, Lizzie, and Sierra each grabbed a gun and disappeared through the door, leaving Dax alone with whatever remained of Hammer Dafoe.

CHAPTER 33

FOUR BRETHREN STOOD OUTSIDE THE DOOR AS THEY emerged. Jeth froze at the sight of them, hauling Lizzie back behind him. They stared at Jeth, their gazes hostile and confused. But they didn't raise their guns. Jeth gaped, hardly daring to believe it. It seemed Dax's decree held true.

"This way," Sierra said, running past them without a second thought. She turned left down the nearest corridor.

Still dazed, Jeth followed after her, soon moving side by side with Lizzie. "Where're we going? What's happening?" he asked.

"We're rescuing you, of course," Lizzie said, grinning over at him. "Couldn't you tell?"

Jeth wanted to hug her. It felt so good to hear her joking. For a moment, he seemed to glide down the corridor, his entire being light with the relief of their escape.

Sierra said over her shoulder, "We've got to find the others. If we're lucky, they've reached Cora by now. We were headed there first when I realized Hammer had brought you up here."

"What do you mean the others?" Jeth asked, resisting the urge to haul her to a stop and kiss her. If she hadn't found out what was happening, he'd be like Hammer now, a prisoner in his own mind.

"Everybody's here," said Lizzie. "Well, Celeste and Milton were supposed to stay on *Avalon* so we've a way out, but the others are breaking in the same way we did before."

Nothing she said seemed to make any sense to Jeth. "What are you talking about?"

Lizzie rolled her eyes. "While you've been taking it easy these last few days, the rest of us have been busy."

"Ha-ha," Jeth said as they rounded a corner. The definite sounds of fighting echoed around them from other areas of the ship, but so far they remained in the clear.

Lizzie grinned. "It was all Sierra's idea. She managed to slip Vince instructions on what to do before he left. He was to get a hold of the ITA, the *real* ITA, I mean, and tell them everything he could about what Renford and Hammer were doing, and help them coordinate an attack. The one that's going down right now."

Jeth started to ask a question, but another missile struck the *Northern Dancer*, the impact hard enough to send him and Lizzie stumbling into one another. Lizzie's head collided with his mouth.

"Ouch," Lizzie said, grabbing the top of her head while Jeth spat blood.

"Hurry up," Sierra said. "We've got to get out of here before the ITA captures the ship."

Jeth understood at once. "They're still after Cora."

"Yes," Sierra said. "But bringing them here was the only way. We need this diversion."

Jeth nodded. If they could get Cora and get back to *Avalon*, the ship was fast enough for them to slip away in the chaos of the fighting. A good plan, even with all the risk involved. "But why did it take them so long to get here?" he asked.

"Because Renford's kept us on the move." Sierra said, slowing down as they approached an intersection. "I had to keep resending our new location to Vince, but usually by the time he received and translated it, we were gone again."

"How'd you manage sending it without anybody noticing?"

Sierra flashed him a quick smile. "When we were kids growing up here, we developed a method for sending each other secret messages. Used to be just a game, but it's come in handy for the real thing."

"I'm glad," Jeth said, stepping in behind her. "But what happens if the ITA gets to Cora before we do?"

"Don't be such a pessimist," Lizzie said, smacking his arm. Jeth thought the accusation a bit unfair. It seemed everything that could've possibly gone wrong the last few weeks *had*. A little pessimism was in order.

"We're going to get to her first," Sierra said with absolute certainty. She inched toward the turn into the other corridor.

Not entirely mollified, Jeth nevertheless decided not to argue. For the time being, he was content just to have someone else be in charge for once. The ache and fatigue, remnants of Renford's torture, were inching their way back over him. He did his best to ignore it, trying to stay focused on the task at hand.

Jeth moved to the opposite wall. They checked the turn together. Down his end, he saw half a dozen soldiers racing past from an adjacent corridor. He assumed they were Renford's, but he couldn't be certain.

"This way." Sierra charged into the hallway, moving away from where the soldiers had passed.

They reached an elevator a few minutes later, but when they called for it, there was no response.

Sierra swore under her breath.

"What now?" said Lizzie.

"No more elevators," said Jeth. "They might all be down."

"There's a maintenance shaft right through there." Sierra headed for an unmarked door a short distance away. The electrical power flitted in and out, the lights intermittent at best. The automatic release on the door wasn't working, but Jeth managed to pry it open with his fingers.

Just as he waved Sierra and Lizzie inside, more soldiers appeared in the hallway. Jeth stepped in and yanked the door closed, muffling the roar of their gunfire.

"Hurry!" he said, chasing after Lizzie and Sierra, who were already at the emergency ladder on the other side of the narrow room.

They climbed downward as fast as they could. Jeth kept glancing up, expecting to be pursued, but no threat came from above in the short time it took them to descend two decks.

Sierra climbed off the ladder into another maintenance room, this one larger than the first. She raced to the single computer station near the door and sat down.

"What're you doing?" Jeth said, stepping up behind her.

"I'm bringing the surveillance system back online. I took it down as soon as I knew Vince and the others were approaching so they could move about the ship undetected, but now I need it to find them. We also need to see what we're facing with Cora. Renford is bound to have increased the guard on her."

"Okay," Jeth said. "But how were you communicating with the others before?"

"Short-range comms, but the ITA started jamming everything as soon as they moved in for the attack. *Damn*." She slapped the top of the desk.

"What's wrong?" said Lizzie.

"It's not working."

"Let me." Lizzie pushed Sierra out of the chair and plopped down behind the computer. Then she started to work her magic. As always, Jeth found himself momentarily mesmerized by her abilities. Soon Lizzie had accessed the surveillance system and given them a look at how many men were guarding Cora. There were at least a dozen, all of them Renford's. Jeth wondered if there had been Brethren there too, before Dax had taken over. The truth of this still hadn't sunk in, that Hammer was gone from his life forever. *Now, if we can just get off this ship alive . . .*

"What is that place?" Jeth said, looking at the odd structures in the room where the soldiers stood.

"It's the kid center," said Sierra. "Where parents on a cruise send their kids when they want some free time. The area wasn't being used until now, so Renford never had a reason to take out the playground stuff. He's got Cora living in the caretaker suite attached to the place."

Before Jeth could ask anything more, Lizzie said, "Found them." She tapped a few buttons and the image flashed on the screen, showing Shady, Flynn, and Vince moving along cautiously.

"That's the old servants' corridor," Sierra said. "One deck below us, starboard."

"Let's go," said Lizzie, leading the way over to the maintenance ladder. They headed down.

Moments later, they emerged into an empty corridor.

"Are you sure this is the right place?" said Lizzie.

A loud commotion rose up from somewhere ahead of them. It was Shady, screaming obscenities at the top of his lungs in between bursts of gunfire.

"What's he doing?" Sierra said as they ducked into the nearest room, taking cover.

"Just being himself," said Lizzie. She giggled nervously. "Shady gets a little carried away sometimes."

Sierra scowled. "No kidding. But he's gonna get us killed."

"What do you mean, 'get us'?" said Jeth. "He'll be the one *doing* the killing." He poked his head around the corner and shouted as loud as he could. "Shady! Will you stop it already?"

"Is that you, Boss?" Shady hollered back.

"Yeah, it's me. I'm coming out now. So don't shoot me."

"Whatever you say, Boss."

Braced for disaster, Jeth stepped out. If Shady started

shooting again, he would dive for cover. Shady appeared around the corner, a massive grin on his face. Fortunately, he'd sheathed one of his guns and had the other propped against his shoulder, barrel pointed to the ceiling. Flynn and Vince followed behind him.

Jeth waved at Lizzie and Sierra, and they emerged. A brief, giddy reunion followed. Vince hugged Sierra hard enough to lift her off her feet. He kissed the top of her head as he set her down again. Shady did the same to Lizzie, only instead of kissing her head, he rubbed his knuckles in her hair.

"Ouch." Lizzie punched him in the belly.

"That's my girl," said Shady, grinning.

Lizzie ignored him and faced Jeth. "Let's go get *our* girl. Our little sis."

"Right." Jeth looked at Sierra. "You know the way."

She took off down the corridor, holding her gun in front of her, ready to fire. As the group moved along, Jeth described the situation waiting for them when they reached Cora.

"So how do we get past them?" Lizzie asked.

"We take 'em out," said Shady. He glanced at Sierra, who'd looked over her shoulder at his words. "And no arguments about it this time, neither."

"He's right," said Vince. "It's the only way."

"But they outnumber us," said Lizzie. "And I know Jeth and Shady are pretty good shots, but will that be enough?"

As they slowed down to navigate another turn, Shady pulled a grenade off the clip at his belt. "We'll use this."

Lizzie eyed the black, cylindrical thing. "You can't bomb them. You might hurt Cora."

"It's not that kind of bomb," said Vince.

Shady spat in agreement. "That's right. It's a stun grenade. Should distract them long enough for us to take most of them down."

"All right," Sierra said. Then she checked the corridor. A moment later, they were on the move again.

When they finally reached K Deck, after a climb down another maintenance ladder, the place was eerily still and silent. Even the missiles still hitting the ship seemed distant. Sierra led them out of the maintenance room into a corridor that ended at the kid center. She motioned to Shady.

He stepped forward, gripping the stun grenade tight in his hand. "On the count of three."

Jeth exhaled, focusing. *Aim and fire. Don't think. Aim and fire, don't think.*

Shady reached three, opened the door, and flung the grenade through it. The noise as it exploded made Jeth's eardrums quiver despite the distance and walls separating him.

Shady charged through the door a moment later and started firing. Vince came next, then Jeth. He stared around at the large playground full of playground equipment, a rock-climbing wall, and a merry-go-round. There were so many places to hide in here.

The next few seconds passed in a storm of chaos as screams intermixed with the explosion of gunfire. All the worry and fear disappeared from Jeth's mind as his body went into autopilot mode. Nothing else existed but the fight. The kickback of each bullet rocked his arm as he fired. A ceaseless ringing filled his ears, but it was far away, as if the sound belonged to someone else.

Jeth shot at anything that moved, diving for cover as Renford's soldiers returned fire. In moments the two groups had taken up position across from each other, Jeth and the others behind the playground and what remained of their opposition behind the rock wall.

"We need to get Cora before we run out of ammo," Vince shouted.

"I'll get her," Sierra said. "Just give me some cover."

Vince nodded. "Be careful."

"I'm going with you," Jeth said, following behind her.

Sierra looked like she might argue, but then she hurried on, racing from cover to cover. More than once, Jeth felt a bullet soar past him, but the closer they came to the door leading into the suite, the less danger the soldiers posed. They couldn't get a good angle on them over here, not without exposing themselves to gunfire.

Sierra reached the door and forced it open. Then she charged in, checking the corners as she entered with her gun poised in front of her. Doing the same, Jeth followed behind her.

"Be careful," Sierra said over her shoulder. "We don't want to startle her. There's no telling what kind of state she's in with all the fighting going on out—"

They both froze at the sound of heavy footsteps. Renford

was running down the hallway toward them, carrying Cora. She appeared to be asleep or knocked out, her head lolling against his shoulder. Renford slid to a stop, shifting Cora to one side as he pulled his gun from his holster.

Then he pressed the barrel against Cora's head.

CHAPTER 34

"GET OUT OF MY WAY, SIERRA." RENFORD GLARED AT HER, but there was panic in his voice. Jeth understood why. The ITA knew all about him now, and although they had come here for Cora, they weren't likely to let a rogue agent escape punishment. And they would be here any second. Jeth didn't dare move or blink, not with Cora in such a perilous position, clasped in the arms of a madman.

"No." Sierra held her gun steady.

"I mean it, Sierra. I'll kill her."

"No, you won't. She's too important, and she's the only leverage you have."

Renford swallowed.

Encouraged by Renford's hesitation, Jeth aimed his gun, forcing his breathing to slow and grow even. If he saw a clear shot, he would take it. Cora was small, too small for a grown man to use as an effective shield.

Only Renford knew what he was doing. He kept shifting his weight and bobbing his head around, his movements erratic. Even if Jeth saw a shot, he wouldn't be able to take it. One second too late, and he might hit Cora instead. And it had to be a kill shot: anything else and Renford might pull the trigger by accident.

"Then come with me," Renford said. "You're in danger, too. You've betrayed the ITA as much as I have. But I can get us out of here."

"No," Sierra said again.

Renford looked close to exploding. The veins on his neck were popping out, and sweat ran down his forehead. "You traitorous bitch."

"I am what you've made me," Sierra said. "Just like you."

"No, you're not," Jeth said, flashing a glare at her. He understood that Renford had the power to hurt her with his words, even now. "You're nothing like him."

"You stay out of it." Renford shifted his grip on Cora. "Then again, maybe you're just what I need." He turned the gun on Sierra but looked at Jeth. "I may not be able to harm Cora, but there's nothing keeping me from shooting her."

"You won't," Jeth said, fear expanding in his chest.

"Oh, yes, I will. And you've no hope of returning fire. Not unless you're willing to hit Cora."

"You raised her, like a daughter," Jeth said.

"She was only ever a project. A failed one at that."

Jeth risked a glance at Sierra, but she didn't react. She stood as still as if she were welded to the floor, same as the furniture surrounding them.

He turned back to Renford, hoping to catch him at a standstill, but Renford was still moving. Jeth struggled to keep his focus as frustration built inside him. He could feel the seconds passing. The ITA would be here soon. He reached for that calm place, the one that would let him see the shot and take it.

"Let me go, and I'll let her live." Renford took a step forward.

"No," Jeth said, feeling the calm stretch over him. He began to see the pattern in Renford's movements. He could almost track it. Predict it. Just a few more seconds.

Renford sneered. "You're so stubborn. Just like your idiot mother. Marian never knew when to back down either."

The calm Jeth had achieved shattered, and his hand began to tremble. Pain throbbed in his palm from holding the gun steady for so long. "What did you say?"

"Oh, that's right. You probably don't remember her well enough to know, do you? But trust me when I tell you it's true. Marian Seagrave never possessed a single iota of self-preservation. She's lucky she's even alive."

"Don't talk about my mother."

"Why not? It's only because of me that she didn't get herself killed by the ITA. You should be thanking me."

Jeth gritted his teeth so hard, a lightning strike of pain flashed across his vision. "What are you talking about?"

A hideous grin stretched across Renford's features, his eyes glinting with that perverse pleasure Jeth had seen there before. "She came to me for help, you know. When she and your father first returned from the Belgrave. We were friends once, both starting our careers with the ITA at the same time. We even went through the basic training class together. Of course that was before I became an Echo, back when I went by the name Charles."

A rushing sound filled Jeth's ears, making him dizzy as a vision of his mother flashed in his mind. *I tried to get a message* to Charles, he heard her saying. *Said he would help . . . he's not the person I thought he was.*

"My mother asked you for help," Jeth said, his hatred for the man writhing and snapping inside him like a live wire.

"Yes, that's right."

"You betrayed her."

"I did what was necessary."

Jeth's whole body shook. It was all he could do to keep from blasting Renford. Only the risk to Cora held him back.

"She *trusted* you."

"Be careful, Jeth," Sierra said. "He's baiting you."

Jeth knew it, too, but there was nothing he could do to stop it. He couldn't even dismiss it as a lie. He'd *heard* his mother say it.

"Yes, she trusted me," Renford said. "But not enough to give me the location of Empyria. If she had, things would've turned out differently for her." He paused. "But at least I have Cora now instead."

As if the sound of her name had called to her in her sleep, Cora began to stir. Renford tightened his grip on her, panic in his eyes again.

Sierra took a step forward. "Let her go."

"No!"

Cora's eyes slid open, and she began to struggle automatically.

"Stop moving," Renford hissed. He'd been holding her in one arm for too long, his grip weak. He jammed the barrel of his gun against Cora's cheek, and she cried out.

All the air escaped Jeth's lungs as he envisioned Renford's

hand slipping on the trigger. Cora pushed against him, her limbs wriggling.

Finally, impossibly, Jeth saw it. The clear shot. In his effort to still her, Renford had stopped moving.

Jeth inhaled, quick and shallow. The calm came at once, the patience his father had taught him, the surety and confidence of a well-honed aim.

Jeth slowly exhaled as he pulled the trigger.

THE BULLET BOOMED OUTWARD, STRIKING RENFORD between the eyes. Then it sailed onward, leaving a trail of blood and brain matter chasing after it.

Renford seemed to fall in slow motion, taking Cora with him. She landed on top of him, cushioned by his body. Cora rolled off him at once and began to wail.

Jeth stared in horror at the sight of his little sister soaked in the blood of the man he'd just murdered.

The noise of the door being wrenched open sounded behind Jeth. He spun as Vince, Lizzie, Flynn, and Shady came through it. In the brief moment before the door closed again, Jeth saw more than fifty soldiers in the kid center beyond. The real ITA had arrived.

They'd come for Cora.

Defeat pressed down on him. They'd come so far only to fail now.

Vince wrenched the control panel beside the door off the wall, sealing them in and the ITA out, at least for the moment.

"Is there any way out of here?" Shady shouted over Cora's sobs. Nobody answered.

Jeth just stood there, numb with shock. He kept seeing the

bullet hit Renford. Kept seeing him fall. Vince ran over to Sierra, who was kneeling beside Cora, trying to calm her as her distress worsened by the second.

"We've got to get out of here," Lizzie said. "Sierra, is there a way?"

"Shhhhh," Sierra said, stroking Cora's hair. She seemed to be in a daze, too.

"Sierra!" Lizzie said.

Sierra shook her head. "They sealed the emergency exit when they moved Cora in here."

Cora's cries turned into screams, the sound terribly familiar. Jeth drew a breath, remembering what had happened on the *Donerail*. The realization of what was coming snapped him out of his stupor. He took a step toward Cora, gaining control of himself. "Cora—"

She backed away from him, her wide, tear-reddened eyes fixed on his face. She was afraid of him. Of course she was. He'd just killed a man right in front of her. An ache far deeper than muscle flourished inside his chest.

"Step back, Jeth," Vince said. Jeth did so, reeling with guilt.

Sierra reached out and pulled Cora toward her, embracing her in a tight hug. "It's okay, Cora. It's okay. You've got to calm down. Remember what we talked about?"

Cora pulled away from Sierra, her expression confused.

The soldiers were banging on the door now, threatening to break through.

Cora's screams grew even louder, the terrible noise like something being rent alive.

"Calm down, Cora. Calm down," Sierra said.

Something like an electrical charge began to swell inside the room. Cora's shrieks seemed to pierce Jeth's skull. He dropped to his knees, the gun slipping from his fingers. He bent over, hands pressed against his ears, trying to block it out. Around him the others were doing the same. Except for Sierra, who was trying in vain to calm the now-hysterical Cora.

A sound like ripping metal mixed in with the screams. Jeth forced his head up, looking for the source of the new noise. A giant hole had appeared in the wall to his right, giving him a clear view of the kid center. Beyond it, he saw more holes appearing before his eyes, as if that first one had been a raindrop upon still water.

Anything in the path of those holes either vanished completely or was sliced in half. The rock wall came crashing down as a hole tore through its base. Jeth watched in horror as more than a dozen soldiers fell, their bodies in pieces.

Cora kept on screaming, the sound out of control now. The lights began to flicker and the floor to shake. Jeth looked left as another hole appeared on the opposite wall. This one was smaller than the first one, but it wasn't empty. Pieces of the soldiers cut down in the other room were inside it, their bodies phased into the wall itself.

"Stop it, Cora," Sierra was saying. "You've got to stop, sweetie."

Jeth looked back and saw that some of the remaining soldiers had worked up the courage to peer through the first hole. In a moment, they would be inside. Jeth closed his eyes, summoning the will to pick up the gun in front of him. It was so hard to move with Cora's screams inside his head. He grabbed hold of the hilt and managed to point it one-handed toward the soldiers.

A hot, searing pain went through his hand, and a scream tore from his throat. He looked down to see the gun had vanished.

So had his fingers. They'd been sliced off at the knuckles.

Jeth gripped his wrist with his uninjured hand, too shocked to scream again. There wasn't any blood, as if the phase had cauterized the cut, but there was plenty of pain. He was sick with it, his head spinning and his stomach gripped with nausea.

"Jeth!" Lizzie screamed. She crawled over to him and grabbed his shoulders. Jeth wanted to push her away but couldn't. His entire body was locked down by the agony rolling through him.

All the while, Cora kept screaming. Another hole appeared in the floor in front of Jeth, less than a meter from him and Lizzie.

Lizzie let go of him and turned toward Cora. She grabbed her hand. "Make it stop, Cora. He's our brother. Our *brother*! Don't you know what that is? Don't you understand?"

Cora's screams lessened a fraction in intensity. Jeth slumped forward, as if the strength of those screams alone had been holding him up.

"Please, Cora. Concentrate," Sierra said.

Cora's screams abruptly ceased.

Gathering what remained of his energy, Jeth turned his head to look at her. She stood encircled by Lizzie and Sierra, both of them kneeling in front of her, holding her hands.

"Send us away from here," Sierra said. "You can save us, Cora. Send us to the ship. All of us. You remember *Avalon*, right? And Milton? And Viggo? They're there, waiting for us. Come on, Cora. Come on."

"I'm sorry, Cora," Jeth said, somehow managing to speak through his delirium. His voice sounded no louder than a whisper, yet somehow she must've heard him as she shifted her gaze toward him. Her dark eyes glistened with tears. There was something so familiar about her, Jeth realized. Something comforting. He gasped. "You look just like her," he said, seeing the resemblance for the first time. "So much like Mom."

Then Jeth rolled onto his back as blackness began to slip over his eyes like ink pooling around the edges of his vision.

And just before he felt himself go under, a bright light filled his gaze.

And then there was nothing.

Nothing at all.

CHAPTER

JETH DREAMED HE WAS TRAVELING THROUGH METASPACE, only the gate he had used was faulty, the Pyreans afflicted with a nameless disease. Then he saw those Pyreans. They swarmed around him, no longer hard and stationary like he was used to, but fluid and moving like fish swimming in the ocean or leaves caught in the wind. They whirled about him, tickling his skin with their bodies, pushing him onward, guiding him through this never-ending sea of blackness. He heard them chattering, their thoughts connected to each other and to his.

Don't be afraid, they seem to say.

And he wasn't. There was something soothing about being here. It was like not having been born yet, but being wrapped in the warmth and darkness of a womb.

He thought he might stay here forever.

It seemed he already had.

Jeth woke in a daze. Black spots clouded his vision, and he blinked them away. He felt as if he'd been asleep a very long time.

"Where are we?" someone asked, the voice muffled and distant.

What happened? Jeth strained his eyes, trying to get his vision to focus. His head ached and his right hand felt strange, tingling and sore.

Then he remembered.

Jeth sat up, bracing himself with his left hand as he examined his right. The fingers were gone. A sick feeling gripped his stomach, and he lowered his hand again to keep from passing out.

He concentrated on his surroundings instead, his mind disbelieving the message his eyes were sending him. He was no longer in a suite on the *Northern Dancer* but in a cargo bay. Rusty water pipes and exposed wiring hung over his head. He would've known this place anywhere. It even smelled familiar.

This was *Avalon*.

"How'd we get here?" asked Shady from where he sat a short distance away. He stood up, his legs unsteady.

Jeth glanced around. The place looked as if it had been struck by a tornado. Debris covered the floor—crates and plastic bins, some of them blasted open, a table leg, the back of an armchair. The crates and bins had been here before, but the random pieces of furniture were new. Jeth squinted. Why were there furniture pieces in *Avalon*'s cargo bay?

Then he shuddered as his gaze fell upon a strip of clothing still wrapped around a severed arm.

Heart lurching into his mouth, he jumped to his feet. Where were the others? He spotted Lizzie at once, and then Flynn and Vince. "Where are Sierra and Cora?" he shouted.

Jeth stumbled through the mess. He came across Renford's body and recoiled from the sight. "Sierra! Cora!"

Vince and Lizzie were calling for them now, too. As he continued searching, Jeth slowly put together what must've happened. Somehow, someway, Cora had phased them onto *Avalon*, along with parts of the *Northern Dancer*. But where was she? Still on the other ship?

"Cora!"

"She's here," Sierra's voice called back to him. Jeth finally spotted them on the far side of the bay. He raced over. Cora was lying on her back, her eyes closed. A thin trail of blood ran out from one nostril.

"What's wrong with her?" Jeth said.

"I think she's just knocked out," Sierra said, standing up. "The phase must've taken a lot out of her. We should get her to—"

BOOM!

Jeth and Sierra fell into one another as the entire ship rocked sideways. The unmistakable sound of gunfire echoed a moment later.

"We must be caught in the ITA's firefight with the *Northern Dancer*," Lizzie shouted, and took off for the bridge.

"Why the hell haven't we jumped yet?" asked Shady.

"Because Celeste doesn't know we're on the ship. How could she?" Jeth glanced down at Cora, then up at Sierra, torn by what to do.

"I'll take care of her," Sierra said, taking the decision away from him. "Go. Get us out of here."

Jeth turned and headed for the ladder. The others raced ahead of him. He moved slower than usual, each footfall sending a stab of pain through his injured hand. He cradled it to his chest, covering it with his other hand.

He arrived on the bridge in time to hear Lizzie finish an explanation of how they'd gotten there. Milton looked as if he were on the verge of a heart attack. His bloodshot eyes flashed to Jeth, narrowing in on his injury at once.

"What happened?" Milton asked, striding over to him.

"Not now," Jeth said. "We need to get out of here." The pain wasn't as bad as it had been. He wasn't even sure the pain was entirely real. It seemed to be coming from the parts of his fingers that were no longer there.

Brushing Milton off, Jeth headed for the cockpit. Celeste sat in the pilot's chair, her hands gripping the control column. The view beyond the window showed a mass of ships engaged in combat, some the ITA's, some Hammer's. *Dax's now,* Jeth supposed. Celeste was flying *Avalon* through them, blasting anything they passed with the pilot guns. He moved to take the copilot guns, then froze as he realized he couldn't. Not with four missing fingers.

Ignoring the wave of despair at finding himself so useless, Jeth turned to Vince. "Take the copilot guns." Then he swept his gaze over the others. "Lizzie, you take the crow guns. Flynn take port; Milton, starboard. Shady, you head down to the chase guns. We've got to get clear of this so we can make a jump."

Everyone obeyed his commands at once. Shady and Flynn

took off at a run, while Vince sat down in the copilot's chair and immediately started firing at an incoming ITA Scout. Lizzie raced to the far wall and yanked the lever to lower the ladder to the crow guns.

Jeth sat down at the nav station. It wasn't where he wanted to be, but somebody had to prep the metadrive for the jump. He entered a command to calculate the farthest possible jump from their position. The nav computer complied in seconds, but the screen flashed red at him, indicating there were too many ships nearby for the jump to proceed. Jeth fixed his gaze out the window and waited.

Two ITA cruisers were bearing down on them from the left and right, gunfire lighting up the space in front of them. Celeste yanked the controls upward, sending *Avalon* into a roll. The force of it thrust Jeth back in his chair. He gripped the side of it with one hand, braced for pain and disaster.

Midway through, Celeste engaged the starboard thrusters. The engines roared from the strain as the ship looped sideways in a maneuver only a ship like *Avalon* could do. For a moment, she was a living, breathing thing, a bird of prey in flight. As the G force eased, he glanced at the nav station radar screen and watched the two cruisers collide into one another. They disappeared from view a moment later.

All the tension inside Jeth began to drain out of him. He patted the nav station dashboard with his good hand. There was no reason to worry, not with *Avalon*. His faith in her had always been certain. She wouldn't fail him now.

Celeste leveled out the ship, thrusting the control column forward and engaging all engines. *Avalon* charged forward, gaining speed. Jeth glanced at the radar. Four ITA ships chased after them, but in moments *Avalon* had pulled away.

Jeth now fixed his gaze on the metadrive computer. A second later the red light stopped flashing. "We're clear," he said to Celeste, triumph ringing in his voice.

She leaned forward and engaged the metadrive. Bright light enveloped *Avalon*, and then they were gone.

CHAPTER 37

into it a few hours later.

"It's the best place to hide for now," Jeth said, when the others questioned his decision. He didn't blame them for being afraid. But he knew as long as they didn't venture too far in, they should be safe. They needed time to regroup and figure out what to do next.

As soon as Jeth had given the order, Milton insisted he head down to sick bay for an examination. Jeth didn't argue. He'd known it was coming. He sat down on the exam table and watched as Milton prepped a jet injector with medicine.

"What's that?" he asked as Milton approached him with it moments later.

"Something for the pain."

Jeth shook his head. "I'm not in pain, at least not much." A dull throb like a toothache had settled over his hand, but it wasn't unbearable.

"Fine, it's something to help you sleep."

"I don't want to sleep."

"I know, Jeth. I know. But you should." Milton pressed the jet injector against his shoulder and pulled the trigger.

Jeth didn't protest, knowing deep down that Milton was right. The medicine worked quickly, taking him under in moments.

He woke some time later, alone. The lights in the sick bay brightened automatically as he sat up. Jeth blinked the spots out of his vision, then glanced down at his right hand. Milton had wrapped the entire thing in a thick bandage, obscuring the injury from view. The hand hurt less now, the pressure from the gauze easing the ache.

Jeth glimpsed movement out of the corner of his eye, and he turned to see Milton coming inside.

"Welcome back," Milton said. "How are you feeling?"

"Better."

Milton smiled, a knowing glint in his eye. He motioned at Jeth's bandaged hand. "It's not the end of the world. I'll be able to fit you with some kind of prosthesis or maybe even a cybernetic unit as soon as we can make the purchase. You won't even know the new fingers aren't real afterward, I promise."

"With what money?" Jeth said, bitterness making his voice uncertain. "Hammer took everything."

"Not everything," Milton said, still smiling. "All my money is in cash. And trust me, there's plenty of it to help us. I've got it stashed all over this ship, matter of fact." Milton turned to a nearby counter and stooped, opening the cabinet where he kept the bedpans and other medical items nobody ever wanted to touch. He pulled out a box and opened the lid, revealing several stacks of unis carefully bound in white tape.

Jeth gaped at the money, then looked up at his uncle, mouth still open.

"You didn't think I spent all my pension and what Hammer was paying me on booze, did you?"

Sensing the question was rhetorical, Jeth didn't answer. "So, a cybernetic hand. I guess that's better than nothing."

"A lot better."

Jeth nodded, his spirits rising. He desperately wanted to be whole. Only—he raised his left hand to the back of his skull and touched the implant architecture—he doubted he could ever be truly whole again.

"We'll do something about that, too," Milton said, picking up a vitals scanner from a nearby counter. "I still have a few old contacts who might know something about how to remove it safely." Milton turned on the scanner and pressed the end of it against Jeth's forehead.

"How's Cora?" Jeth said, wanting to move the subject elsewhere. There was too much uncertainty about the architecture. Too much uncertainty about the future in general.

"She's fine. Fully recovered, actually. You've been asleep nearly fifteen hours."

Jeth blinked. "Wow, that was some sedative."

Milton smirked. "The sedative wore off hours ago. Your body needed the rest. Sierra told me everything that happened, including the way Renford tortured you."

Jeth grimaced. "Did she also tell you that Renford used to go by the name Charles?"

"Yes, she did." A dark look crossed Milton's face. "I'm glad you killed him."

Jeth gulped, uncertain if he felt the same. He couldn't deny he was happy the man was gone, but he wasn't sure about having done the act himself. He'd never killed anyone before. True, he might've killed some of the soldiers they'd fought while rescuing Cora, but that wasn't the same. Renford's death had been so close, so intentional and *messy*.

"What happened to his body?" Jeth asked, remembering that Cora had phased it here as well.

"Vince saw to it. Pushed it out the garbage airlock, I believe." A grim smile passed Milton's lips as he turned off the scanner and returned it to the drawer. "Quite a fitting end."

Jeth didn't reply, his thoughts turning to his mother. What would she think when she learned how Renford had died? And she *would* learn of it. Sooner or later, he would go after her. He couldn't let her spend the rest of her life imprisoned by the ITA. Who knew what they might try next in their attempt to manufacture a slave race to replace the Pyreans? They had to be stopped.

"So," Milton said, breaking into Jeth's reverie. "Sierra tells me that Hammer is gone."

Jeth considered the idea, trying to determine if that was the proper term for what had happened. He remembered that blank stare on Hammer's face, the emptiness in his eyes. "I suppose you could call it that. Either way, he's as good as dead."

"Yes, which means you're as good as free."

Jeth shrugged. "I guess so." The knowledge didn't give him the relief he'd thought it would. He hadn't exactly improved his situation. "But I don't have the title on *Avalon*."

"If Dax is head of Hammer's organization, he might sign it over to you."

Jeth considered the idea. He hadn't liked the way Dax looked after inserting Hammer's implant. And he certainly didn't trust the man. He knew too well how valuable Cora was. "I'm not sure going back within his reach is a risk we can afford to take. Besides, just because he seemed to take control of Hammer's organization doesn't mean he'll succeed."

"True, but you still have a copy of the title, right?"

"So what? It's not signed and it's not electronic."

"Yes, but with the right equipment and Lizzie's exceptional skills, we might be able to make a good forgery. And we'll have to stick to Independent planets for now anyways, given our current troubles with the ITA." Milton nodded. "Yes, either way, we'll manage. We always do."

He stood and stretched his back, his joints popping like tiny guns. "It's almost dinnertime. Are you hungry? I can have someone bring you a plate. I'd like you to stay in bed for a little while longer. Your vitals aren't quite where I'd prefer them to be."

Jeth shook his head. "I'm not ready for food yet. Just some more sleep."

"Very well." Milton turned and headed for the exit. He paused in the doorway and said over his shoulder, "They'd be proud of you, you know. Both of them."

Jeth didn't speak, not even to ask Milton who he meant. He already knew.

Milton left, giving Jeth his privacy. He thought about his parents awhile and then about his sisters. He thought about the crew, too. They were all his family. Milton had been right; Jeth's parents *would've* been proud. And for the first time in years, that meant something to him.

Sometime later, Sierra came to visit him. She brought a tray of food. Even though Jeth had thought he wasn't hungry, his stomach growled in response.

She set the tray on the counter beside the bed and then stared down at him, hands on hips. "Milton said you didn't want anything to eat, but I decided to bring this up to you anyhow."

Jeth felt a smile threaten to break across his face. She was so stubborn, so hardheaded. He thought maybe that was what he liked about her most. And he did like her, far more than he was willing to think about at the moment.

"Do you want some?" Sierra said.

Jeth nodded.

She picked up the tray again and laid it across his lap. Then she turned and sat in the chair across from him. He picked up the fork with his left hand, the awkwardness of it making him hesitant. He was too aware of her eyes on him. He wished she would either say something or look away. When she didn't, he focused on getting the food onto the fork and then to his mouth. It was hard, but he managed.

When he finished, Sierra stood and returned the tray to the counter.

She sat down again, moving the chair close enough that she was within arm's reach of the bed. "I—" she began, her eyes lowered. "I just wanted to thank you."

Jeth cleared his throat, afraid to speak. "For what?"

She looked up at him. "For killing Renford. I don't think I could've done it. He always held a power over me, even up to the end. But it's gone now. He's gone." She took a deep, loud breath. "I know this sounds silly, but it's like I've been set free."

Jeth squirmed a little. This wasn't a conversation he felt like having. Ever. "You're . . . welcome, I guess."

She smiled at his stumbling. "And I really, truly am sorry for not trusting you from the beginning and for stealing *Avalon.* I'm glad she's yours again. She's a great ship. I mean, she doesn't look all that impressive at first, but she got us away from the *Northern Dancer,* and here we are safe and comfortable for once."

Jeth resisted the urge to beam at the compliment. "She's the best, all right," he said, managing a modest grin instead.

Sierra nodded, and the smile slipped from her face. "I'm not sure if you've thought about what you plan on doing with Vince and me, but I hope you know that Cora needs to be with me." She cast him a defiant look. "She doesn't know you very well, and after what happened . . ." Her voice trailed off, unpleasant memories of their last moments on the *Northern Dancer* filling the silence. "I can't promise that she won't lose control again."

Feeling nervous, Jeth said, "I understand, and you're right." He paused, his throat tight. "But what if . . . what if you just stayed here. On *Avalon*. With me . . . and the crew."

A shy smile rose to Sierra's lips. "I'd like that. Very much."

Bolstered by her admission, Jeth finally did what he'd wanted to do for a while. He reached out with his good hand and took one of hers in his. He stared down at her crooked, ruined fingers, ran his thumb over the misshapen knuckles. In that moment, he silently swore that no one would hurt Sierra again.

Finally he raised her hand to his lips and kissed each finger, one by one, the act like a sacred rite. Then he let go of her hand and cupped the back of her head, drawing her close.

He kissed her, and something moved between them, an unspoken bond pulling them together over what they had gone through and what they would face. But those memories and thoughts faded away until there was nothing but the sensation of his lips on hers, the exchange of breath and the soft harmony of hearts beating. For one blissful moment they were nothing but feelings and physical sensation.

The moment lasted a very long time.

° ° °

Afterward, Jeth climbed out of the hospital bed, ignoring Sierra's protests that he should stay put. Jeth felt made of air. He might be injured, but he knew his hand would be whole again. Milton would make sure of it. And for now, he wanted to see the others.

Lizzie shrieked with delight when Jeth stepped through the doorway into the common room. Everyone was there, burning off the sluggishness from the meal with games and conversation. Lizzie ran over and hugged him so fiercely, she almost knocked him over.

"I'm so glad you're up and about, Jethro." She kissed his cheek.

"Of course he's up and about," Milton said from his position on the couch. "Because that's exactly what I told him *not* to do." Milton winked. "Should've known better than to expect you would listen."

"That's right," said Shady. "You ought to take it easy on him, Liz. Seeing how he's a cripple and all."

Jeth rolled his eyes. "It's my hand, Shady. Not my leg."

"Oh, well, then I meant 'amputee.'"

Celeste slapped Shady in the back of the head. "That's not funny."

Shady grinned at her. "Sure it was."

"Who cares if he's an amputee," said Flynn. "He's the captain. All he's got to do is shout orders and sit around while we do all the work."

Jeth sighed as he plopped down on the nearest sofa. "That sounds like the best job ever. Not that it'll work with you bunch of lazy good-for-nothings."

"Does this mean we can call you Stumpy?" said Shady.

Jeth grunted. "I can still shoot you with my good hand."

The banter went on a short while longer, and when it died down, Jeth braced himself for the question he knew was coming next: *What do we do now?*

But to his surprise, nobody asked it.

Instead Shady said to Celeste, "So, do you want to see how bad I can kick your ass in matchmaking on Robot Revenge?"

Celeste smirked. "I could beat you one-handed." She flashed a grin at Jeth. "No offense, Stumpy."

Jeth scowled at her. "Next person who calls me 'Stumpy' is getting the boot."

A chorus of "Stumpys" answered him.

"I get no respect," Jeth grumbled. He tried to keep a straight face but failed.

"What's a stumpy?" asked Cora.

Jeth had been doing his best not to look at her as she sat next to Vince with Viggo asleep in her lap. He didn't know how she would react to seeing him again. He was afraid he would detect fear in her eyes.

"It's just a nickname," said Lizzie, going over to her. "And we're only calling Jeth that because it's funny."

"Why's it funny?" said Cora.

"Because he hurt his hand," said Sierra.

"Oh." Cora cast Jeth a furtive look, biting her lip. "But I hurt his hand, didn't I?"

"No," Jeth said, unable to keep from answering. "It wasn't your fault. You did everything right. You saved us all, Cora."

Cora looked uncertain for a moment, and then to Jeth's surprise, she smiled.

He smiled back.

"Go on," Lizzie said. "Give him a hug."

Jeth started to shake his head, but Cora was already pushing the cat aside and standing up. She dashed across the room and jumped into his lap. Jeth winced at the sudden pain in his hand, but he wrapped his arms around her automatically.

He didn't mind the pain, not with his baby sister hugging him like this, unafraid. He kissed the top of her head.

"Do I really look like our mom?" Cora said next to his ear.

Jeth blinked, remembering how he'd told her that right before she'd phased them off the *Northern Dancer*. "Yes, Cora. You really do. You're both beautiful."

Cora giggled and hugged him tighter. She stayed there a few moments longer, then got up and started chasing Viggo around the common room, filling the place with her laughter as the cat jumped and pawed at her, returning the play.

With the excitement of Jeth's arrival officially over, everyone settled into their favorite activities for relaxing. Lizzie turned on some music. Milton lit a pipe, while Flynn decided to make some after-dinner snacks. Vince joined Celeste and Shady at the gaming table.

Sierra sat next to Jeth, holding his left hand and resting her head on his shoulder. He leaned his head atop hers. Then he let out a sigh and closed his eyes.

I've been set free, he heard Sierra saying again in his mind.

So have I.

He didn't know if it was real, if freedom was something you could earn or win after a long, hard fight, or if it was just an illusion. But he decided it didn't matter. Only *this* mattered. This moment right here, surrounded by the people he cared about. And he realized this was the paradise his parents had meant when they named this ship.

There were other things he should be thinking about, decisions he should be making. Like where they went next. What they would do with the information they had. And most important, how he would save his mother.

But for now, he was content to leave those worries alone, to let them be silent and still inside him. For now, it seemed he'd found his *Avalon* at last.

ACKNOWLEDGMENTS

BOOKS ARE SURPRISINGLY LIKE SPACESHIPS—YOU NEED AN entire crew to navigate the storytelling universe, to go from an idea in the writer's mind to a physical object in a reader's hand. And just like Jeth would say, my crew is the best.

As always, thanks to God and his Son for all the good things.

A huge, galaxy-sized thank-you to my editor, Jordan Brown, for his enthusiasm, support, and especially his uncanny ability to see what I meant even when I didn't. Your insight and guidance are divine.

Thanks also to my rock-star agent, Suzie Townsend, for first giving this wacky story about spaceship thieves your blessing for me to write and then for helping me to make it better. You are my rock in this biz, a solid foundation in a crazy, up-and-down world.

To the entire Balzer + Bray team for giving my book a home and for making it readerworthy: Alessandra Balzer, Donna Bray, Alison Donalty, Ray Shappell, Renée Cafiero, Rebecca Springer, Caroline Sun, and Emilie Polster.

To the team at New Leaf Literary & Media—Joanna Volpe, Kathleen Ortiz, Pouya Shahbazian, Jaida Temperly, and Danielle Barthel—for giving me such a wonderful and cozy literary home.

To my amazing critique partners and beta readers: Lori M. Lee, Cat York, Sarah Goldberg, Kathy Bradey, Farrah

Penn, and Mallory Hayes. I am forever grateful for your support, insight, and friendship.

To my ultrasmart, sci-fi–loving brother-in-law, Jay Sharritt. Thanks for the long talks about deep things. Also for introducing me to *Halo*.

Much love and thanks to my parents, Betty and Phil Garybush—you make my life possible in more ways than you could know. Also love and thanks to my sci-fi loving dad, Jim Gaver, who took me to my first *Star Trek* movie and who never said no when I wanted to watch *Star Wars* for the tenth time in a single weekend.

To my husband, Adam, and my kids, Inara and Tanner— you are *my Avalon*.

To my sister, Amanda Sharritt. This book would not exist without you. Thank you for first wanting me to write a story like this one, and then for believing in it afterward.

And as always, thanks to you, dear reader. It would take all of time and space for me to express how much you matter.

418

TURN THE PAGE TO READ AN EXCERPT
FROM THE SEQUEL TO *AVALON*.

POLARIS

CHAPTER 01

THE SPACEPORT'S CASINO WAS THE PERFECT SPOT FOR THE deal to go down.

Jeth Seagrave knew it the moment he stepped inside. The place seemed to envelop him, the lights so bright they made it almost impossible to see and the noise a constant vibration, everything from the hum of the slot machines to the shouts of dealers calling for bets. Some kind of mild, hypnotic music played in the background, blending the sounds together in a reassuring soundtrack—*time does not exist here,* it seemed to intone. *Here you are safe. Here you belong.*

Jeth knew better. There was nothing safe here. Everything was suspect, and that was all right. His shady dealing would be one among dozens.

He made a casual scan of the room, getting his bearings in the maze of tables, gaming booths, and gamblers. Then he turned to the right and headed for the casino cage, which held more than a dozen cashier windows. Even though Jeth had seen his share of casinos, he couldn't help but be impressed by the size of this place. Of the few Independent spaceports in the galaxy, Nuvali was the biggest and the hardest to get to, which gave it the dubious honor of being the favored hub for drifters, criminals, and expatriates seeking refuge from the tyrannical reach of the Interstellar Transport Authority.

A sardonic smile crossed Jeth's face as he realized he could be described by all three. But any humor he might've felt at the notion dissolved at once. For the last eight months the ITA had been hunting him and his crew. Life on the run was wearisome and fraught with sacrifice. Even now his belly felt like a pinched, hollow ball. He hadn't eaten since yesterday, and that meal had hardly been enough to take the edge off his hunger, let alone assuage it.

The smells in this place weren't helping. The sweet, sharp aroma of steak frying in garlic butter, the salty tang of roasting peanuts, and half a dozen other scents, wafted out of the kitchen entrance a few meters down from the cage. Jeth sucked back salvia and fought off the almost overwhelming urge to forget the deal and just enjoy his first full meal in weeks.

Except he wouldn't. There were cheaper ways to eat, and despite his protesting stomach, he hadn't yet reached the limit of his endurance.

Jeth stopped in front of the first open cashier and pulled a roll of unis out of his left pocket. "Two-thousand, with a sixty-thirty-thirty split, hundred high," he said. This was the last of the reserve money. He didn't want to gamble with it, but he had to play the part until Wainwright arrived. He had a couple hundred in his boot, just in case, but that was it. *It won't matter if I lose some,* he reassured himself. *Just so long as the deal goes down the way it's supposed to.*

"There you are, luv," the woman behind the counter said as she finished loading the carrier with his requested breakdown of tokens. She smiled broadly at him, her teeth artificially bright in the lights overhead.

Jeth cracked the knuckles of his left hand and schooled his expression to something close to eager. Time to play the part. He picked up the carrier and turned back to the action on the floor. He did another sweep, this time searching for a game to join.

His gaze slowed when he spotted two of his crew standing side by side in front of one of the retro slot machines. Sierra and Celeste had arrived some ten minutes before, part of the backup plan in case the deal went sideways. Old habits died hard. Before they'd become fugitives, Jeth and the original members of his crew, the Malleus Shades, had been professional thieves for one of the most powerful crime lords in the galaxy. Tonight they would deal with another criminal organization, and Jeth wasn't leaving anything to chance.

Jeth's breath caught as he watched Sierra raise one slender, bare arm and pull the lever down, setting the digital reels to spinning. He'd never seen her dressed like this, in a glittery, fitted thing that made her look all curves and nakedness. There wasn't any reason for her to dress that way aboard *Avalon*. Spaceships made for cold homes.

Jeth knew that both she and a similarly dressed Celeste were armed, but he couldn't imagine how or where. Well, he *could* imagine it, but this wasn't the time or place for that sort of distraction. Especially when he was carrying two thousand unis worth of tokens around a roughneck space-port casino without a firearm of any sort. Wainwright's men would surely pat him down before they entered the final stage of negotiations.

As if she sensed him staring, Sierra glanced over her shoulder, her eyes meeting his at once. Celeste caught Sierra looking at him, and she stepped in close to whisper something in Sierra's ear that made a blush blossom over her fair skin and set her to grinning. To an outsider they were just two girls flirting with a stranger.

Grateful for Celeste's ruse, Jeth started to look away, but then he saw her gaze flick past him, her smirk deepening into her own grin. Jeth followed the direction of her eyes and spotted Vince sitting at the bar, his eyes fixed on the video screen overhead while he idly sipped a beer. The personal comm unit hanging from his belt was the backup for the backup plan.

More like the doomsday plan, Jeth thought, noting Vince's position. He doubted Celeste had meant to point Vince out to him. She just couldn't help herself. *No more than you can,* he mused, stealing another peek at Sierra.

Finally moving on, Jeth spotted an open seat at a poker table toward the back, not far from the private rooms where he would join Wainwright later. Exactly how much later, he wasn't sure. Wainwright had been sketchy on the details.

Jeth raised his right hand to his head and pretended to scratch behind his ear, activating the comm patch fixed to his skin. The touch of his cybernetic fingers always brought on a surreal feeling of detachment, as if the hand belonged to someone else. He'd had the prosthesis for more than six months now, but he didn't think he would ever get used to it.

Ignoring the feeling, and the shimmer of painful memories it brought to the surface, he said through the comm, "What's the buy-in three rows from the back, two over?"

"Hang on," Lizzie's voice answered a second later from her position a board *Avalon*. The ship was moored in one of the short-term docks several floors below, the closest spot they could get to the casino. Not that location mattered so much. Jeth's genius of a little sister could have hacked into the spaceport's security and surveillance systems from anywhere.

"Okay, looks like that table's . . . ouch, a thousand." She paused. "But two down is only five hundred and the guy with the blue hair is just leaving."

"Right," Jeth said, disguising the word as an exhale. He kept his voice low and hardly moved his lips at all. It was a trick he did well, from years of practice. "But give me some help with that omniscient vantage point of yours."

"That's cheating, you know."

"Consider it a tactical advantage, unless you like skipping meals." They might be preparing to make a goldmine of a deal, but they wouldn't be able to access the money right away. It would take time and caution, a transaction like that liable to draw attention. They would need every uni they could hold onto for food, supplies, and fuel.

"Good point." Lizzie fell silent again, but Jeth had heard the hint of something more in her voice and he braced for what was coming next. "Are you sure we want to go through with this?"

Jeth drew a deep breath and let it out slowly. Lizzie had sprung this argument on him yesterday, just moments after they'd finalized the deal to hand over the Mirage Cipher to Wainwright for a three million payoff. The amount wasn't the source of her protest, though it should've been: the cipher would give Wainwright the ability to decrypt all transmissions sent by the Mirage Corporation, including flight path information on shipments. Mirage was the leading weapons manufacturer in the galaxy, making the cipher the proverbial golden goose for a crime lord in the arms business. It was worth double what Wainwright was offering. But criminal beggars couldn't be choosers, and Wainwright's deal was the best they were going to get.

Lizzie's protest, however, was more sentimental.

"I'm sorry," she continued, "but it just doesn't feel right, not knowing what he'll use it for."

"You mean supplying criminals and terrorists with military-grade weapons?" Jeth said as he headed further into the casino toward the five hundred table.

"To put it *not* mildly—yes."

He sighed. "This is what we do. It never bothered you before, when we were working for Hammer."

"That was different. We didn't have a choice, and it felt less . . . personal."

Jeth didn't respond. He knew exactly what she meant. When they worked for Hammer it had been like a game. They never had to witness the consequences of their crimes, the impact it had on real lives—people caught in the crossfire of warring gangs, workers laid off when a targeted company chose to cut their losses from the bottom rather than the top. They had just been following Hammer's orders.

Now, the blood would be on *their* hands. Jeth swallowed, the memory of what they'd gone through to get the cipher threatening to upset his cool.

He pushed it away. Yes, the decision to steal the Mirage Cipher and then hand it over to a man like Wainwright hadn't sat well with him either. But there was nothing for it. *The story of my life.*

Wanting to end the argument once and for all, Jeth said, "Do you want to free Mom, or not?"

"I . . ." Lizzie's voice caught. "You know I do."

"Then drop this." He didn't mean to be cruel, but they had to make the deal. They needed a big score like this to buy a stealth drive for *Avalon*. It was the only way to complete their next—and last—job: rescuing their mother, held captive these past eight years by the ITA. Not only was the ITA the most powerful entity in the universe, but they were keeping her in a fortified lab on First-Earth, the most congested and heavily monitored planet in all the systems. Getting her out of there would be tougher than anything they'd ever faced with Hammer, damn near impossible.

Like trying to steal a piece of raw meat from a school of sharks.

He'd seen something like that when they had been working for Hammer, back in the aquarium at Peltraz Spaceport. A man who had crossed Jeth's old boss had been sliced open from nose to navel and dropped inside the tank.

With Lizzie silent once more, Jeth approached the table and set the token carrier on the empty space. "Mind if I join?"

The five players looked up in near unison. Their expressions as they assessed him were dubious, but Jeth knew what they saw: a young man, still a boy really, with plenty of tokens to burn. Even more, the prosthetic pieces he wore on his face to disguise his identity made him look faintly aristocratic. He appeared an easy mark.

He flashed an arrogant smile, encouraging the belief.

The dealer, a pretty brunette in a black tuxedo dress gestured for him to sit. Jeth did so and pulled out five hundred-worth of tokens, setting them in front of him. The dealer dealt the cards and, moments later, Jeth was down three hundred unis. Lizzie offered a few tips but he let them slide, afraid of drawing attention with too much good luck too soon. He had to blend in until Wainwright arrived.

With his thoughts on the meeting, Jeth slid his hand into the pocket of his flight jacket, his fingers closing around a false token. He waited to make sure no one was paying any attention, then slid it from his pocket and placed it on the table near the small pile he'd made with some of his real tokens. The new token looked exactly the same as the others except for a tiny deviation in the anchor emblem imprinted on the top. It was so small no one would notice unless they were looking for it.

"Remember not to bid with that," Lizzie said.

Jeth grunted at the reminder. He reached out and snagged one of the real tokens, a matching blue one. He waited a second, once again making sure no one was watching, and then slid the normal token into his pocket before returning his full attention to the game.

Sometime later, with his patience beginning to wane in direct correlation to the growing strength of his hunger pains, Jeth made another scan of the room. The arrival of four newcomers drew his eye. There was nothing conspic-uous about the men, stopped a few feet inside the doorway, other than their complete lack of conspicuousness. They wore plain suits of varying shades of drab. They were nei-ther large nor small, their expressions neither eager nor guarded.

"I think those are Wainwright's men," Lizzie spoke into his ear.

"I know," he whispered and turned back to the game.

The player directly across from Jeth, a man with dusty-colored hair and an indistinguishable accent, slid forward a tidy stack of black tokens, raising the bet. The man to the left shifted in his seat slightly, although his eyes did not move off the cards in his hand.

Jeth tapped his finger twice on the table, the sign Lizzie had given him to use when he decided he was finally ready to employ her tactical advantage.

"Call or raise," she said a few seconds later. "They got nothing."

Jeth called, keeping his gaze focused on the cards in front of him, even when he saw Wainwright's men moving toward the hall of private rooms out of the corner of his eye. He wondered if Wainwright was already inside. *Probably,* he decided.

"Incoming," Lizzie said, and a moment later, Jeth felt a tap on his shoulder. He looked up to see one of the men staring down at him. The man handed him a card that bore an invitation to a private game in the Ruby Room. Jeth pocketed it without a word and the man walked away.

Once all bets were in, Jeth showed his two pair, winning the hand just like Lizzie had predicted. This time his grin was genuine while he gathered the tokens in the pot.

"That's it for me. Seems I've got another engagement." He tapped his jacket pocket, then returned the tokens to the tray, making sure the false one was on top of the smallest stack, within easy reach.

He headed for the Ruby Room. Two of Wainwright's men stood guard just inside the door, but neither moved to stop him when he entered. The door slid shut behind him automatically, but he didn't hear the click of the lock. In a casino like this one, he doubted the doors could be locked by patrons.

It was darker in here, the air murky with pipe smoke. Jeth breathed in, managing not to cough thanks to years of living with his uncle Milton, who favored the same noxious pastime.

"Come in, Jeth, come in," Wainwright called from where he sat, at the single round table in the room. His wide, welcoming smile emphasized the narrowness of his face. The warmth in that smile did not extend to his eyes, which remained locked on Jeth as he stepped forward and set the token carrier on the table next to a tray of food. The sight of the food—fruit, cheese, vegetables—set his mouth to watering.

With an effort, he swallowed and forced his gaze away, making a quick scan of the room. It had earned its name. The walls were a uniform red, broken only by a couple of gold-trimmed paintings and the four vid screens hung in each corner. Red glass shaped like teardrop rubies decorated the chandelier centered over the table.

More noticeable than the decor were the two men standing behind the crime lord. Jeth couldn't see any weapons, but he knew they were armed. He cocked an eyebrow at Wainwright. "I thought this was supposed to be a private game? Looks more like an interrogation."

"I find life itself enough of a gamble." Wainwright waved to the man to his right. "Check him, Albert."

The man came around the table at once and began to pat Jeth down. As Jeth had hoped, Albert checked his pockets, soon pulling out the token. He tossed it onto the table.

Wainwright scooped it up with one small, feminine hand and examined it. "Is this what I think it is?"

Jeth adjusted his jacket and sat down. "We are here about the cipher, yeah?" He grabbed a grape off the tray and popped it into his mouth, doing his best to stifle a moan of pleasure as the taste burst over his tongue.

Wainwright cleared his throat. "I'd prefer to think of the cipher as just the opener."

Jeth's hand stilled mid reach for another grape.

"What does he mean?" Lizzie's voice whispered in his ear.

Jeth recovered quickly, but instead of a grape he picked up a die from beside the tray, its gold and silver surface glittering even in the murky light as he rolled it between his fingers. "I don't recall any talk about further business. The deal was for the cipher."

"It *was*." Wainwright picked up the pipe resting in the stand next to his elbow and took a long drag, filling his cheeks with smoke that he let out slowly a moment later. "But from what I hear you have something much more valuable to offer than the Mirage Cipher."

Jeth slid the die into his pocket for safekeeping then leaned back in his chair as if bored. Beneath his cool surface, his heartbeat began to quicken, sweat stinging his armpits. "Hate to contradict you, but you heard wrong."

Wainwright set the pipe down and brushed off ash from the sleeve of his pinstriped suit. "I have it from a reliable source that you possess something of great importance to the ITA, something to do with the failing metatech."

Jeth didn't move, didn't breathe, not until he managed to corral the thoughts stampeding through his mind. *He knows about the Aether Project.* Word was bound to get out sooner or later that Jeth possessed a data crystal that contained all of the ITA's secrets about space travel and the metatech that made it possible. But the timing couldn't have been worse.

He composed himself. How much did Wainwright know? If all he knew about was the data, things would be okay. But if he knew about Cora . . .

With a deep inhale Jeth let a slow, cocky smile stretch across his lips. "No offense, but if I had something that valuable, I wouldn't be wasting time on a deal as small as this one."

Wainwright rubbed his thumb and forefinger over his dark mustache, his expression inscrutable. "Perhaps. But my source was quite reliable. An undercover ITA special operative one of my captains found tracking an unknown target, one he later revealed to be you. He was a tough one, didn't want to tell me what he was after, but it's amazing how forthcoming a man can become when you start to remove his skin."

Jeth was too familiar with crime lords and their methods to react. He widened his grin, baring teeth. "Oh, I'm sure he talked a right storm, but you should know better than to believe he was telling the truth. ITA special ops don't break so easily. He fed you a story. An easy one to swallow, given my reputation, but that doesn't make it any more true."

Wainwright let out an exaggerated sigh. "I sincerely hope not. If you don't have the information I'm after, there's no point in our talking further."

Trying to ignore the flush spreading up his neck, Jeth shrugged. "If that's how you feel. I'm sure the cipher will be worth something to someone else."

Wainwright tented his fingers in front of him. "Wrong. The cipher *might* have been worth something if you hadn't left all those witnesses alive. Witnesses tend to talk, and it's only matter of time before word of the theft gets back to Mirage."

Jeth clenched his teeth. Not all of them were still alive. *Not that stupid woman. Why did she have to—* He stopped the thought and forced his jaw to relax. "Mirage won't be able to modify their encryption software overnight. There's plenty of time to gather flight intel and to intercept enough shipments to make it worthwhile."

Wainwright shook his head. "Mirage will double the security on all flights and give their pilots authority to fly unrecorded routes. No, the cipher is practically worthless already." He sat back in his chair, crossing one leg over the other. "This metatech information on the other hand, that would be worth a great deal. Rumor has it that the ITA has no idea why so many metadrives are failing. If things keep on the way they are, there won't be any shipments for my people to intercept at all. Travel in the universe will come to a complete halt. But if you have the key to changing that . . ."

Jeth racked his brain for a response. It was all true. The metatech was failing, and he did have the key to stopping it. But he wouldn't hand it over. Not for all the money in the worlds.

He opened his mouth to deny it once again, but before he could, the vid screens in the corners flickered to life, flashing a uniform red. For a second, he thought it was some part of the room's design, but then the star and eagle emblem of the ITA appeared across the screen. Gooseflesh broke out over his skin at the sight of it.

"What is this?" Wainwright said, turning.

No one answered as the banal background music cut off and a message began to play. For a second, Jeth couldn't make sense of it. This was an Independent spaceport; they had no obligation to broadcast ITA special bulletins. But then with a sickening wrench in his gut, understanding clicked. The bulletin was an announcement of a newly posted ten-million-uni reward for the capture of an ITA fugitive. Nuvali was Independent, but it knew its clientele well.

Too well, it seemed, as Jeth watched his own face and name flash across the screen.